My Greek Island Summer

Mandy Baggot

HEAD
of ZEUS

An Aria Book

This edition first published in the United Kingdom in 2020 by Aria,
an imprint of Head of Zeus Ltd

A CIP catalogue record for this book is available from
the British Library.

9 7 5 3 1 2 4 6 8

ISBN (PB): 9781838933432
ISBN (E): 9781838933425

Typeset by Siliconchips Services Ltd UK

Printed and bound in Great Britain by
CPI Group (UK) Ltd, Croydon CRO 4YY

MIX
Paper from
responsible sources
FSC® C020471

Aria
c/o Head of Zeus
First Floor East
5–8 Hardwick Street
London EC1R 4RG

www.ariafiction.com

This, my 20th book, is for YOU! To all my readers out there who have supported my books either from the very beginning or have joined in along the way and are playing catch up!

THANK YOU all so much from the bottom of my heart for allowing me to do this writing business as a full-time job so I can keep sharing my stories with you! Here's to the next 20 books!

One

'Soldiers!'

Twenty-five-year-old Becky Rose raised her head from bread and watched her sister Megan burst through the door of sandwich-making enterprise, It's A Wrap, looking less than her usually super-composed self. Megan's channelling-Amanda-Holden red trouser suit was crinkled like she'd been contorted into a magician's suitcase and locked in there for hours and her usually perfect sleek bob of blonde hair was now more comedian Milton Jones than it was Irina Shayk. Megan was also sweating, Becky noticed. Megan didn't ever sweat. She barely even glowed getting changed in the heady close-to-rainforest humidity of the leisure centre. Becky, on the other hand – shorter, not blonde, never really feeling confident in body-sculpting all-in-ones – always made a puddle on the floor big enough to give home to a couple of ducks…

Becky stopped spreading the multi-grain loaf and opened her mouth to answer her sister. Her colleague, sixty-three-year-old Hazel, beat her to it.

I

'Megan, dear, I know it's *your* business and I'm just staff, but we did *decide* at the crisis meeting last September that it wasn't economically viable, nor risk-assessment friendly, to start branching out into the breakfast arena.'

'What?' Megan asked, looking confused. She blew out a breath, moving through their lunch-making industrial kitchen, to the door of her office. She dumped files she was holding onto her desk before coming back in and facing her employees. 'I never called it a crisis meeting.'

She *had* called it a crisis meeting, Becky remembered. Another sandwich-making business had started up just a couple of miles away in Durrington and Megan had been insistent that all their customers were going to leave for the lure of new and exciting... and apparently a company with a budget that allowed them to advertise on local radio. Of course, bankruptcy hadn't happened, and Becky knew that was because It's A Wrap offered things their customers couldn't get anywhere else. The kind of personalised that took time, effort and a little bit of magic. And that was solely down to her.

'Boiled eggs and soldiers,' Hazel remarked, mixing up a bowl of their legendary cheese and spring onion filling. The cheese was sourced locally – from cows who all had names which apparently made them *exceedingly* happy and therefore the producers of award-winning flavoursome cheddar – and the spring onions were grown in the small garden at the back of their premises. 'I know we really, *really* considered breakfast baps, but we agreed no one likes a cold sausage and—'

'Who said anything about boiled eggs?' Megan asked. 'God, this radio is far too loud again. I've told you before, if it's up past five on the volume button the yoga people next door come round and complain.' Gone were the days when Becky and Megan used to make their parents mad with music cranked up to eleven and all the best Girls Aloud moves vibrating the floorboards. Becky couldn't actually remember the last time they had been to the leisure centre together either...

As soon as Jess Glynne was turned lower, mum-of-triplets, thirty-something Shelley looked up from her tortilla-rolling like she hadn't spiritually been in the room before, but had now had a deep, seismic awakening. 'Alright, Megan? How did the meeting go?'

'Finally!' Megan exclaimed, arms flailing out. 'At least *one* of you listened to me properly before I left.'

'*I* was listening to you,' Hazel said, frowning as she forked the mixture. 'You said you had to pick up something of Dean's from the dry cleaner.'

Becky grimaced a little. Dean always needed something dry cleaned. He was the messiest eater she had ever encountered. He could make a mess out of swallowing air. 'And you just said something about soldiers.'

'Yes!' Megan said, pressing buttons on the coffee machine and slipping a tiny espresso cup underneath the spout. 'But the ones dressed in khaki camouflage. Not the ones made out of toast.'

'Oh,' Hazel said like she had suddenly had her eyes opened to online shopping. 'Well, now I'm confused. Is Dean joining the army? I thought he was quite settled with the conservatory-building people.'

'The contract!' Becky exclaimed, suddenly. 'You got the contract!' She immediately realised what her sister meant. 'You got the contract at the army camp!'

'I got the contract at the camp!' Megan repeated, all high-pitched and excitable. She picked up the tiny cup and swigged the coffee back in one. 'I pitched for my absolute life. I'm sure there was a brigadier in the room – well, he looked like he could *be* a brigadier if he wasn't already – but they all seemed pretty unmoved at the beginning, even when I mentioned we grow our own vegetables and herbs...'

Becky smiled at her sister's excitement. It had been Becky's idea to grow their own vegetables and herbs. Megan hadn't been on board straightaway, as she was all about costs and bottom lines, until Becky convinced her that quality was more important these days. If customers had enough money to *buy* sandwiches instead of *making* them, they would certainly pay an extra few pence for something memorable. And that was where Becky excelled. She made her sandwiches memorable and kept the customers coming back. And it all went completely under Megan's radar. But, Becky supposed, you couldn't be all over everything when you were the boss. And Becky was, kind of – a lot – hiding it from her...

'So, what did you do?' Shelley asked, adjusting the hairnet they all had to wear over their heads because no one wanted a stray strand in their baguette...

'I...' Megan started, grinning from ear to ear.

'You got your tits out! Didn't you? You got your tits out!' Shelley announced at the volume of the roar of an Isle of Man TT motorbike.

'Shelley!' Hazel admonished. 'I thought we agreed on what was acceptable language in the workplace.'

'Well,' Shelley began, glove-covered hand pointing while holding a flapping-yet-to-be-filled tortilla. 'You said the word "bitch" the other day and I didn't say a thing about that. *And* you didn't contribute to the swear box.' She inhaled with authority. 'That's £1 you've cost the Women's Refuge. I hope you can sleep at night... in your king-size... with more springs than... than... those onions.' She pointed at the container Hazel was mixing up.

Hazel shook her head and sighed. 'I was talking about my neighbour's dog's puppies at the time.'

'Puppies! Baps! She definitely got her tits out, whatever you want to call 'em!'

Megan clapped her hands like she was a schoolteacher losing control of her children. 'Ladies, I'm telling a story here.'

'*I* want to hear, Megan,' Becky told her sister. The army camp contract was a big deal. And if it was as large as she was thinking, it could mean employing a new staff member – maybe even two – or starting earlier in the morning... Actually, that last idea didn't really appeal. Becky didn't function well unless she had had time for two mugs of coffee and a blast of feel-good on Spotify.

'I did their assault course,' Megan announced, pride shining in her eyes, underneath coming-off mascara and wayward liner. It sounded like she really had been put through it. No wonder she was still perspiring.

'What?' Hazel exclaimed, putting down her spoon and paying Megan her full attention.

'Fucking hell,' Shelley stated before slapping her hand over her mouth. Then she seemed to realise that she'd sworn *and* now needed another set of gloves. She quickly mouthed a sorry.

'I'm with Hazel here,' Becky said. 'What?'

'Well,' Megan began. 'I could just tell that whatever I said it wouldn't be enough. I knew we wouldn't be the cheapest option. I'd pushed all the quality, organic, locally sourced angles and they looked more bored than I look when Dean turns on the snooker. So, I had to think on my feet.'

'Don't tell me you did it in those heels!' Hazel said, eyes dropping to look at Megan's favourite pair of killer stilettos she always wore to meetings. Black patent leather, luminous yellow sole. They practically spoke 'this maker of bread-couture means business'.

'I did,' Megan squealed. 'And I had a rather nasty coming-together with the cargo net but, I was doing it for It's A Wrap. I was doing it for us, our roll-filling family.'

Becky felt immediately warm inside. She loved it when Megan was like this. It proved that there was a little part of her that was still a team player. It also showed that the business meant more to her than just turning a profit. Making money was obviously all-important, but Becky liked the notion that It's A Wrap was also about serving the community. And their community was heavily sprinkled with members of the armed forces, which made this particular win all the more special. Maybe, to celebrate, she could suggest they book a court for a game of badminton together some time. Tara never seemed interested in getting together now she had moved in with Jonathan and Becky had been close recently to watching *Dexter* in its entirety for the second time... from the very beginning.

'You're not covered in mud though,' Becky suddenly said. Her sister's outfit might be crumpled like a discarded McDonald's take-out bag, but it wasn't spattered with the brown stuff assault courses were renowned for.

'I put a coat on.'

'Megan!' Becky said, astounded. 'It's twenty-five degrees

outside.' No wonder her sister was sweltering.

'I'm aware,' Megan answered. 'I've upped the air-con in here a tad.' She sniffed. 'The coat's ruined. I don't know how I'm going to explain that to Dean, but I'm sure it was one of his old ones... I think.'

'Something else for the dry cleaning?' Hazel suggested.

'So, what obstacles did you do?' Shelley wanted to know as she pulled on another set of gloves.

'Well,' Megan said, adopting an expression Becky only usually saw when her sister was perusing the cocktail menu at the local bar, The Bank. 'First off was a balance beam.'

'Oh, even in those shoes I bet you nailed that one,' Becky said proudly. Her sister had always had excellent coordination. Megan had been the queen of gymnastics at school. Becky had been better at team games. Helping her class on the way to netballing victory in a cup game was a particular school career highlight. A lowlight had been losing ten-nil the only time Megan had come to watch.

'I did,' Megan agreed. 'All the soldiers were shouting and making a fuss about my shoes and I just ignored them and thundered on.'

'What was next?' Hazel inquired, her job of combining cheese and onion momentarily forgotten about.

'A trampette onto a low wall – the shoes weren't ideal for that either, but I only made the minutest of tears in the fabric. Then it was hopping quickly through two rows of tyres.' Megan smiled. 'That one was like trying to avoid too close a contact with the kitchen floor tiles in Dean's parent's house at Christmas.'

'Are they that cold?' Hazel asked.

'No, they have a very ancient dog who sometimes... you

know… can't make it through the night.'

Poor Nancy had to be twenty by now. Becky liked Nancy a lot more than she liked Dean's mother.

'I can't believe the shoes survived,' Becky said. It was impressive. Maybe *she* should invest in some killer heels. Except the 'killer' part on *her* feet would probably mean giving her murderous blisters. She was so much more a dressing for comfort kind of girl. Jeans and jumpers, not pencil-skirts and pashminas.

'I can't believe you did an assault course to get a sandwich-making contract,' Hazel said. 'Shouldn't they be testing you on your knowledge of fillings, or your spreading skills?'

'Oi oi!' Shelley erupted like she was a lairy hen about to line up the tequila. 'Deano will know all about her spreading skills.'

Hazel shook her head and rolled her eyes. 'Speaks the mother of triplets.'

'Anyway,' Megan said, waving her hands. 'I didn't do the clambering through the wet and frankly grimy-looking tunnel, or the bit where you have to get down and crawl under a net like someone out of *Strike Back*. But I did the cargo net, well, most of it. Until my shoe got stuck and I had to be rescued by Gunner Mitchison.' Megan breathed deeply. 'He was six foot three and almost as wide. You know, in a taut, muscular way.'

'I still don't know how the fate of their catering came down to you being able to bounce onto a wall and bunny-hop through some tyres,' Hazel remarked.

'Well,' Megan said, 'when I finished they all applauded and the man who might be a brigadier said he had never seen such effort put in to winning a bid before and he said, and I quote, "if your food is even half as tremendous as your determination, then my troops will be going into battle completely satisfied".'

'Was he taking the piss?' Shelley asked, one eyebrow raising.

'I... don't think so,' Megan answered, her sense of victory seeming to evaporate a little.

'Had your tits slipped out?' Shelley questioned. 'Were they all copping an eye full of your great British baps?'

'No!' Megan answered, pulling up the neckline of her outfit a little self-consciously. 'Of course not. It was all purely professional. I was just showing them all that I was prepared to go the extra mile to get It's A Wrap the gig. And, that being the case, they can therefore have complete faith in our lunch-preparing expertise.'

'It's amazing, Megan,' Becky told her sister. It was *really* good news. It was worth a lot of money to the business. It could be the growth they needed to push the enterprise to the next level. Maybe they should even submit an entry to the South Wiltshire Business of the Year awards. Becky made a mental note to suggest that to Megan later.

'My boys want to go into the army when they grow up,' Shelley announced with a sniff.

'But they're nine,' Hazel remarked. 'How can they possibly know what they want to do?'

'My Frank says they've got skills he never had when he was a boy. Like, we found out last weekend that they've been digging a tunnel at the bottom of the garden.'

'Oh, Shelley, that doesn't sound like a good thing,' Becky said. 'What if they burrowed all the way out and ended up... I don't know... *not* in your garden.'

Shelley's expression oozed pride. 'They said they wanted to dig until they'd reached the Chinese.'

'Oh dear,' Hazel said. 'Well, what are you going to do? Because you can't leave them unsupervised if they're going to try something like that. It's not safe like it was when I was a girl.'

'My Frank's gonna see if he can build them a zip wire,' Shelley announced. 'A distraction technique. But it should also help improve their other abilities, you know, balance and... hanging on.'

'That's lovely, Shelley,' Megan interrupted, looking at her watch. 'And, as much as I'd like to chat about the triplets' attempt at *The Great Escape*, I'm going to head home and have a shower. And you three need to crack on if we're going to get the deliveries out in time, yes?'

And there was Cool Corporate Megan back again. The roll-filling family vibe dissipated. But, Becky supposed, that was why her sister owned and ran the business and she just made the product...

'You've remembered you're going to the nursing home at eleven, Megan, haven't you?' Becky checked, recommencing her buttering.

'What?!' Megan exclaimed, eyes out on stalks. 'No. I'm booked in for a pedi at eleven. And I've literally just told you what my feet have been through this morning. No one needs the care and attention of Saffron more than me.'

'But you're pitching for their summer party,' Becky said. 'Sadie from the charity shop recommended us and the manager called me on Tuesday and I made the appointment. I put it in the computer diary *and* in the paper one.' She itched to get off her stool, go into Megan's office and hold the leather-bound book aloft. Times and dates were one of her fortes.

'Well, you'll have to cancel,' Megan stated, already halfway back to the door.

Cancel? Hadn't Megan just got all gleeful and excited about this new business she'd secured with the military? They couldn't afford to turn down potential work. They might currently be in a good position, but when the Great British high street was struggling, everything was always somehow balanced on a plastic catering knife edge.

'I'm not cancelling.'

Becky swallowed after she'd delivered the sentence. Where had that authority come from? Ordinarily she only used that tone when the prawn man was late...

'What?' Megan said, her hands going to her hips.

Becky could feel Hazel and Shelley looking between the two of them like they were opposing factions of a Nigel Farage talkRADIO show.

'You shouldn't cancel,' Becky said again. 'You can charge good money. They'll want scones and cake as well as sandwiches. We can even source some unique teas, there's a website I found—'

'Becky, we make sandwiches, rolls, wraps and paninis. We don't do cakes.' Megan spread her arms wide around the snug workspace. 'I'm not really one hundred per cent sure we have the capacity to butter all these baps for the army, but we'll have to make it work somehow.' She sighed. 'What we *don't* have time for is silly little teas at the nursing home. I mean, it's hardly bigtime, is it?'

Had her sister just said 'silly little teas'? Tears pricked Becky's eyes then, but she bit the inside of her lip and desperately tried to hold it together. She wasn't going to back down over this. This was important to her. And it should also be important to Megan.

'Well, *I'll* go then,' Becky stated. '*I'll* do the pitch.'

Megan let out a laugh. An actual, proper laugh. 'Don't be ridiculous.'

'What d'you mean?' Becky asked. 'I'll go to the nursing home and tell them what It's A Wrap can do for them and see what they were thinking of in terms of cake. If we can't do the cake then—'

'And pricing?' Megan asked. 'And working out exactly how many loaves of bread and rolls it all equates to? And how many more extra fillings we need to order in? Timescale, Becky? Stock control?'

Her sister was making it sound akin to organising that maybe-brigadier's military invasion, or booking a slot with Tesco for pre-Christmas Day delivery... It couldn't be *that* hard!

'Well,' Becky started, 'I can see what their requirements are first, how many people they expect to come and then—'

'No,' Megan said bluntly. 'No, you won't. Because I don't want the contract. And... you can't possibly do the meeting on your own.'

All Becky could do was watch as Megan flew from the kitchen like she was now powered by rocket fuel and her feet didn't hurt a bit. And, returning to her workstation, a little bit fragile, it felt like forever until Shelley reached a silent hand to the knob of the radio and turned the volume back up to six.

Two

'You know she didn't mean it, dear,' Hazel said softly.

From their seat in the window of the old pub, Becky was watching the gorgeous pink, purple and white flowers in the hanging baskets fluttering in the breeze. It was a breeze not quite cooling enough to bring down the summer temperature, hence sitting in the window for *any* breath of air that didn't feel like it was blowing out of the back of a vacuum cleaner.

'She *did* mean it,' Becky replied, turning back to her half a lager and lime. It was barely midday. She shouldn't be drinking. They shouldn't be in the pub at all, but Hazel had insisted after Becky had spent the rest of the morning virtually silent over the food prep. Usually, they would make jokes about the oddly shaped tomatoes or sing along to Spire FM, but after Megan's stand, Becky had nothing she wanted to share.

Shelley had gone out in the van for the deliveries, the clock had ticked around to ten-forty-five and Becky had made a decision. She was going to call the nursing home. But not to cancel. Only to delay. When she was properly composed, when she had figured out how many slices of thin-cut white it would take to feed a hundred octogenarians, she was going to take the meeting on her own. Why couldn't she? Apart from the fact that Megan didn't think she could manage it. But, then again, maybe her sister was right. Perhaps she *wasn't* capable. Except the thing that hurt almost as much as Megan not thinking she had meeting-taking abilities, was the fact her sister had apparently forgotten all about the care the nursing home had delivered to their late father.

'You know how she can be, dear,' Hazel continued, sipping at her Woo-Woo cocktail. 'Single-minded with tunnel vision.'

'Yes,' Becky answered. 'Yes, I do.' Megan was full-on, opinionated, boisterous, all-knowing, even when she really wasn't. In fact, the more Becky thought about it, the more her sister could almost be Katie Hopkins. No, that was a tad harsh. She took another sip of her drink and immediately felt guilty for even thinking that. They didn't spend as much time together as they used to, that was all. Yes, they might be at work alongside each other for a good portion of the day, but work wasn't a relaxing sauna or a few lengths of the local pool and a chat over a cool glass of wine after the exercise...

'What are you going to do?' Hazel asked, ducking her platinum-blonde curls towards the straw sticking out of her drink and sucking. 'About the nursing home?'

What *was* she going to do? She might have mentally just told herself she was going to go through with the pitch only a few seconds ago but... was she? That would mean asserting authority. And it was authority she didn't really have in the business. She was an employee, exactly like Hazel and Shelley. Being the sister of the owner didn't count for anything in contract law. *And* she would be going against Megan's express wishes.

'I've put them off for now,' Becky said, fingers in her shoulder-length caramel-coloured hair, trying to draw it away from her neck to feel a little less sticky in the heat. 'Until Friday. I'm hoping Megan might change her mind. You know, once her feet are feeling better and she's recovered from the cargo net.'

'If you want my opinion, dear, I think she's forgetting where she comes from,' Hazel said, ripping open a bag of salted nuts, some of which sprayed across the table between them.

'What d'you mean?' Becky asked.

'You hear about it, don't you? In the news and everything. These entrepreneurs who set up their own little companies then… boom!' Hazel made an explosion gesture with one hand, corralling peanuts with her other. 'The firm takes off and their humble beginnings are distant memories… or forgotten about completely.'

Becky really didn't want to believe that was what was happening with her sister. Megan had set up It's A Wrap with her share of the reasonably small inheritance she'd been left by their father. Megan had always had a will to succeed. It stood to reason that she would be the one to be her own boss and rise above her position as the daughter of a working-class family from Wiltshire who never really had much to rub together. When the idea was mooted, Becky had deliberated hard about leaving her straight-out-of-college job at the bank to assist her sister but, in the end, family loyalty had won out. And she enjoyed it, for the most part. All the parts that weren't today.

In complete contrast, Becky's small inheritance wasn't yet destined for anywhere. Hence why she'd been quite happy to lend most of it to Megan to buy the It's A Wrap van. And Megan had promised it was only a loan. Anyway, what did Becky need the money for really? She was perfectly happy renting her flat above the newsagent. It wasn't like the new estate home Tara and Jonathan had just bought, but the cost was reasonable because it wasn't double-glazed and didn't have a parking space. And when you didn't struggle with the cold and didn't have a car these things were of little importance. So, Megan had the business and a home with boyfriend Dean and their mother had used what *she'd* been given after probate to buy a mobile home in Blackpool. Margery Rose now spent her evenings and weekends quite happily playing 10p bingo and dancing at the Tower Ballroom with her sister, June.

'You were thinking about your dad, weren't you?' Hazel carried on.

'No,' Becky lied. She wasn't sure how much Hazel knew about the loss of her father. It's A Wrap had been established two years after his death and, still upset about the suddenness of his demise then, Becky hadn't really liked to talk about it too much. Even now, Megan liked to talk about it even less. For her sister, apart from the monetary foundations her life and enterprise were built on, it was like their parents had barely existed. Becky had been to Blackpool twice since her mum's move, Megan had simply made her excuses.

'Death is hard, dear,' Hazel told her. 'Especially when

you've got others wanting to brush it under the carpet.' She sucked at her cocktail. 'You're not a brusher-under-the-carpeter though, are you?'

'Apparently not,' Becky said again. And she didn't want to be. Not when she had so many wonderful memories of the times they had all been a happy family together when she was a child. Walks in the local woods, picnics at the park, watching motorbike racing at Thruxton... until the massive stroke had replaced the dad she knew with someone who had to learn to walk, talk and think all over again. But him being alive at all was much better than losing him completely. It might have been within the walls of the care home surrounding them, but Becky had still got to see him, to talk to him and to help him try to recover. There had been small shards of the man she'd looked up to still there, visible just under the surface. Until the second stroke took it all a year later.

'You know what you need, dear, don't you?' Hazel said, hand going into her handbag. It was one of those bags that turned into a backpack should leisure pursuits require it. 'A cruise!'

Spattering more peanuts, Hazel thumped down a wad of around six brochures Becky never would have believed able to fit in the handbag onto the pub table.

'That's what I'm going to be doing at the end of October. I've got two weeks booked off and I'm going to be wined and dined twenty-four hours a day,' Hazel informed her throwing open the first brochure that had a mammoth ship-to-rival-all-ships on the front cover, sitting like a cake-topper on a completely tranquil skein of azure-coloured icing.

Becky immediately caught sight of the prices. Wow! Cruises did not come cheap.

'And in the hours I'm *not* being wined and dined,' Hazel continued, 'I'm going to try my hand at shuffleboard, then acrobatics... and then more wining and dining.' Hazel inhaled. 'Look at that steak. Beautiful.'

Becky regarded the photo of an admittedly tempting piece of cooked-to-perfection steak, a string of watercress laying over its width. She did love meat. Probably a little too much. While Megan was all about sourcing her protein from shakes and pulses, Becky had always preferred animal. Tender beef loin or perfect pork medallions. Some boiled new potatoes with sprigs of mint plucked from the business garden or mash with garlic and rosemary the way her dad used to make it...

'It's missing a few more chips though, isn't it? Still,' Hazel said, 'it's eat-all-you-can on these ships. No one goes hungry. Even the fat ones. And my friend Hilary is a testament to that.'

'Is that who you're going with in October?' Becky asked, watching as Hazel turned the pages and more serene, gliding vessels were displayed, some docking near the waterways of Venice others underneath the famous blue domes of Santorini. It all looked perfect. Sun, sea, and *saucisson* was on offer for those boats docking in Cannes. Blackpool was the last break Becky had had. And watching her mum and Auntie June ride donkeys and purge their lunch after going on the Big One, hadn't exactly been the epitome of relaxation.

'Oh no, dear,' Hazel said screwing up her face in close-to disgust. 'No, I wouldn't wish holidaying with Hilary on anyone. She really would spend twenty-four hours at the all-you-can-eat buffet.'

'Then who are you going with?'

'Well,' Hazel said, 'I know I should be inviting Stanley from the bowls club, because I have been leading him on a little lately but... I quite fancy going on my own.'

'Really?' Becky said, taking a sip of her drink. It wasn't quite a cruise cocktail, but it was cooling her down and smoothing over her annoyance at Megan's rapid and angry departure earlier.

'Yes,' Hazel continued, flipping over another brochure page. 'Look at this, dear... Exhibit A you could say.' Hazel spread her fingers over the photos and inhaled again.

Becky took in the photo of three silver-haired gents in their smart beige trousers and jackets in varying hues of pastel, leaning altogether slightly too posed against the railing of the boat as it slipped past the Rock of Gibraltar.

'Maybe that's what you need too,' Hazel remarked. 'A holiday *and* a man. These cruises can deliver both, and even the lower-class rooms aren't exactly shabby.' Hazel sniffed like being a third-class passenger on the Titanic could have been bearable if they had been able to see Jane McDonald sing.

Becky pulled the brochure a little closer. These men Hazel was getting her to look at, actually make that *all* the people in the promotional photos, were Hazel's age. Not that there was anything wrong with being in your sixties, but Becky didn't want a sixty-year-old man-friend when she was only twenty-five. She didn't know if she even really wanted a man-friend at all after the disaster of her last date. Angus from the sausage shop.

Angus had the most gorgeous eyes – a piercing blue, the type you only really found in film stars wearing altering contacts. His eyes had been the first thing Becky had noticed when she'd decided to give in to her meat needs one evening. Tara had stood her up again, said that Jonathan had man flu and he couldn't cope alone. Unfortunately, it wasn't Angus's eyes that made the lasting impression, it was his constant indigestion. The poor guy couldn't seem to breathe without first ejecting the most horrendous belches. How she had managed to order sausages from him and agree to a drink without noticing this before, Becky didn't know. She had come to the conclusion that when he'd ducked down behind the counter to procure her chosen bangers he'd exhaled into a box or something so she couldn't hear. But you couldn't hide a condition like that over glasses of wine in a quiet beer garden for a whole evening. She felt sorry for him really, especially when he'd told her it was hereditary…

A holiday. It was a lovely idea. But it was just that. An idea. In reality, she had wraps to fold and buns to stuff to bursting for the rest of the summer and a care home summer party to coordinate if she could talk Megan round. And she did enjoy her job. On her van delivery days, she loved getting out and meeting the customers, hearing their 'oohs' and 'aahs' over her latest magic ingredients to expand their lunch repertoire.

'It looks nice,' Becky answered. It looked more than nice. It looked exotic and adventurous and all the things that secretly thrilled her, yet also terrified her. What would she do if she went away? Sunbathe on a ship eating steak and gateau? Visit the Pyramids? Swim with dolphins? How could she? It wasn't her style to do anything like that.

But then it hadn't been anything like her mum to decide to throw caution to the North Sea wind and take off for a new life on the coast either.

'I'll write down some of the websites Stanley recommended for me,' Hazel suggested. 'It doesn't do any harm to look, dear.'

Three

It's A Wrap, Amesbury, Wiltshire, UK

'Shelley's not coming in, dear. She texted me. Told me to let Megan know.'

Becky had got in early today to print off menu ideas for the nursing home summer party. She'd spent all night researching different types of tea – jasmine and hibiscus were her favourites – as well as looking up cake recipes with a D-Day feel. She should be able to knock up a Ration Chocolate Cake she'd gawped at on Pinterest. And there were plenty of bunting options for decorating the garden room of the care home. She was going to prove to Megan that she *was* capable of doing more than spreading margarine. She had even made more of a corporate effort with her clothes, hair and make-up today. She had swapped her favourite jeans for a pair of smart grey linen trousers she'd bought in Peacocks and teamed it with a cream-coloured short-sleeved blouse she usually reserved for weddings and funerals because it went with everything. She'd also pinned her hair up in a bun instead of simply winding it into a ponytail. No trainers on her feet, instead a pleather espadrille her mum had insisted she buy in Blackpool on her last visit. She felt a little bit different. Perhaps this was small scale power-dressing...

'Oh, is she ill?' Becky asked.

'Not her,' Hazel replied, hanging up her handbag and preparing to put on her working overall, hat and gloves. 'Remember she told us about the triplets digging for glory?'

'They didn't escape?!'

'Carter fell off the zip wire Frank made. Broke his arm.'

Becky didn't know whether to be shocked at how accident-prone Shelley's boys seemed to be, or astounded that Frank had constructed a zip wire in hours.

'She says she'll be back tomorrow once he's back at school.' Hazel began to fetch her ingredients for the beginnings of mixing. 'No Megan today?'

It wasn't lost on Becky that Megan wasn't in yet. Usually Becky was in first, then her sister came in about 6.30 a.m. to help with prep and remind them of any special events coming up that needed a change to their usual routine. Becky liked those couple of hours best. She and Megan on their own, not only information-sharing, but chatting like they used to pre-Dean. It wasn't high-brow conversation, more the 'have you binge-watched *The Witcher* yet' kind of talk, but it always reminded Becky of the relationship they had had when they lived at home together. The strain of their father's incapacity after his stroke had definitely affected their sisterhood. Then his death had impacted everything else too.

Shelley started at 8.30 a.m. when she'd dropped the triplets off at school. Perhaps today Megan had a business breakfast or a meeting that wasn't in the diary... or maybe she was simply avoiding Becky after their confrontation yesterday.

'No,' Becky answered. 'I expect Dean needs her to do something or maybe the army called her in... did she tell you when the contract for that starts?'

Hazel shook her head. 'No, dear. She didn't even say how many sandwiches and rolls they were going to want each day, but I'm thinking it's going to up our output at least three-fold, if not more.'

And they would definitely need another staff member if that was the case. Megan would have thought of that though. She was, after all, the one talking about costings and profit yesterday. The one in charge.

'And that's what I'll be going for on my cruise,' Hazel said, getting ingredients out of the fridge. 'Three of everything. Including potential suitors. I mean, if you fixate on one and he combusts before the first port, or he starts getting cosy with someone else at the captain's table you want a fall-back plan, don't you?'

'I... suppose so.' Becky hadn't had a fall-back plan after her date with Angus, apart from thinking about investment in Gaviscon and getting her sausages from somewhere else. Men she found attractive somehow didn't appear in droves – and she really didn't have high expectations. She just would have liked someone to share 'the looks' with. That simple first look that said: 'I see you and I like what I see'. The second look that said: 'I saw you, I wanted to look at you again'. And the third look that said: 'I am definitely coming over. I want to get to know you.' Everyone else in her world seemed to have found someone without needing a relationship road map or Rohypnol. They were booking couples' retreats or moving into new homes together. Becky felt it wouldn't be long before Tara swapped their monthly movie club nights for dinner parties with other couples and, without a partner, she wouldn't fit. No one liked a single at a couples' dinner party. It was like everyone was waiting for one of their partners to stray over the tiramisu.

'Did you look at the holiday websites last night?' Hazel asked her, closing the door of their large fridge room with her hip.

'A bit,' Becky admitted.

It was actually 'a lot'. Her whole evening had comprised the care home food research, in between lusting after impossibly beautiful mountain gorges around Austria, the Italian lakes and the tiny deserted aquamarine coves of Greek islands. It had given her shivers to even think about herself standing on those sandy shorelines or next to snow-capped peaks, a small person dropped into far-off lands she knew nothing about. But holidays didn't come cheap and she wasn't exactly flash with the cash. The little she had left had to be saved for a rainy day, didn't it? You never knew when double-glazing *might* be needed or if, one day, her landlord might decide to sell... or die... or put up her rent. All those scenarios were why, after she'd finished browsing the websites Hazel had suggested, she'd searched for something else. And that something else was... housesitting.

An article had popped up, while she was viewing self-catering apartments on the isle of Madeira, about how housesitting was a fantastic way to immerse yourself in another country's culture for *free*! All you had to pay was the cost of your flight, and there you were, paying *nothing* for accommodation in a gorgeous setting, looking after someone else's home while they were away. There had to be a catch. It almost sounded too easy…

The door burst open and Megan sashayed through it like she was a brand ambassador for ASOS. Wearing Jackie-O-style sunglasses, wide-leg plaid trousers and a simple black tunic top, she did look every inch the young entrepreneur, capable of making mincemeat out of Deborah Meaden.

'Good morning!' Megan greeted breezily, pulling her sunglasses away from her face and sitting them on top of her head. She sounded happy, Becky deduced. She didn't sound like someone who was holding a grudge after their disagreement of yesterday. That was good.

'Good morning, dear,' Hazel replied, starting to grate cheese. 'You sound bright today. Ooo, is that a new handbag?'

'Yes,' Megan said, slipping a rather nice-looking tan leather bag off her shoulder. It matched perfectly with the colour of the line in the plaid of her trousers. 'Do you like it?'

'It's lovely,' Hazel answered.

'It's a present from Dean,' Megan said, stroking the material with her beautifully manicured hands.

Becky couldn't help looking at her own hands. Nails cut to the quick to aid getting the gloves on faster and nothing sticky-out to pierce the latex. It simply wasn't practical to grow them. But maybe that was another reason she didn't fit in at the moment. Tara always found time for manicures. Perhaps Becky ought to make an effort and suggest going together…

'It was this gorgeous bag *and* another surprise,' Megan said, eyes glazing over like she was experiencing an intense daydream.

'If it's of the smutty kind that Shelley would appreciate,

you'll have to wait until tomorrow. She's not coming in,' Hazel said. 'Little Carter broke his arm pretending to be Spiderman or something.'

'I'm going on holiday!' Megan announced. 'In August! Can you believe it?! Dean's kept it secret for months!'

'Wow,' Becky said. 'That's great. Where are you going?' If it was a Greek island, she would feel a little bit jealous. She'd actually shivered when she'd looked at the photos of Kefalonia – the bright blue wooden chairs, checked tablecloths under a condensation-coated carafe of white wine and a feta-cheese-topped salad with purple olives almost the size of plums. A nice fantasy. Maybe soon to be her sister's reality. Thanks to Dean. She chewed her lip. She mustn't be bitter. And she didn't do sibling rivalry.

'Dean won't say where yet,' Megan continued. 'Isn't that romantic?'

'It might be Blackpool. To see your mum,' Hazel suggested.

Megan turned her nose up, as if Hazel had suggested her vacation might be to a one-star hotel near Auschwitz. 'Oh no, he's promised me we're going on a plane.'

'You can fly to Blackpool these days, you know,' Hazel told her.

'It's *not* going to be Blackpool,' Megan insisted.

'Blackpool's not bad. Mum loves it,' Becky added.

'That's because Mum's never been anywhere else,' Megan snapped. 'And she only likes it because Auntie June's there and because…'

Becky knew what her sister was going to say before she stopped. Megan had been about to say 'because Dad liked it'. But she couldn't bring herself to. *Erased. Forgotten about.*

'Anyway, as romantic as it is, it's left me with so much

to sort out,' Megan said. 'I'm trying to only think of the positives though. Like the sunshine and the white sand and the—'

'White-haired widows,' Hazel added with a sigh. She jerked suddenly, the grater taking off a strip of her gloves as she lost concentration.

'When does the army contract start?' Becky asked.

'Oh, that's not until the beginning of September. But it's wedding season coming up, isn't it? And we have five of those booked in already.'

'Shelley could ask her cousin to come in and help temporarily,' Hazel suggested. 'She's back from university.'

'I've already asked her,' Megan answered, taking a folio pad from her bag. 'I was talking about someone in a managerial capacity really. Someone I can hire in to hold the fort here while I hold margaritas for a few weeks.'

Becky was bristling before she ever realised it. Megan was going to employ someone to come in and manage the business while she went on holiday? Someone *not* already within their team. Someone who wasn't Becky. So much for her almost-power-dressing. She obviously did need Shellac to be noticed around here… She itched to say something. She wanted to ask Megan why she needed to bring in an outsider when *she* was perfectly capable of running the sandwich empire while Megan was away. But, after yesterday, after Megan's insistence that she couldn't count how many rolls were needed to feed the care home residents, her confidence was waning. And now she was beginning to feel stupid in these trousers… and the waistband was pinching a bit. Damn the slow-cooked meatloaf on a bed of mash she'd eaten last night.

'Oh... well... dear, I'm sure we'd be able to manage for two weeks, with Shelley back and her cousin helping out,' Hazel said. 'Wouldn't we, Becky?'

Now she had been put on the spot. Now she was going to have to say something and, the way she felt, she really wanted to be able to project her voice and make it sound like it came from inside someone with authority. Someone like... David Attenborough. She opened her mouth...

'I've got no doubt you'd manage the workload,' Megan forged on.

Becky closed her mouth again, clamping her teeth together as the chance was lost.

'But there's an endless list of things I do behind the scenes that really needs someone with a business brain to take on.'

Oh my God. Becky was gripping her butter-spreading knife like it had all the capabilities of turning into a lethal weapon at any second. Forget David Attenborough, if Megan kept this up, Becky might turn into Villanelle. Did her sister not even realise how rude and dismissive she was being?

'I mean, I need someone who's across contracts and the legal jargon that goes with that,' Megan continued.

She was still stroking that bloody new handbag like it was a guinea-pig at a petting zoo. If Dean had got that from his mate Terry, the chances were it was actually a knock-off. Becky should tell her. She should say, right now, that *she* could handle things in Megan's absence. She might not know every shortcut an Excel spreadsheet had to offer, but she knew enough. Definitely enough for the sandwich-business.

And she was *very* personable. Everyone said so. If there were new opportunities in those two weeks Megan was gone, Becky would be more than able to sell It's A Wrap's services and win bids…

'I thought the contracts were all the same,' Hazel piped up, recommencing the cheese grating. 'A template on the computer.'

'The basics might be,' Megan stated, sounding a bit annoyed. 'But every client is different. They all have little requests that need attention. And that always requires delicate tweaking of the wording, you know, additional clauses and sub-clauses… and sub-clauses of sub-clauses.'

How up-herself did Megan sound now? Becky's usual placid nature was disintegrating, morphing into bubbling acid that could melt platinum. If she didn't say something soon, her temper was going to lead to some sort of self-destruction, or ruination of their products. She stuck the knife in the butter tub like she was lancing a boil.

'Well,' Hazel continued, 'no one knows our customers' needs better than Becky.'

Hazel had said 'Becky' at a volume slightly higher than the rest of the sentence and Becky's internal furore was starting to make itself known on her cheeks. Now was her chance. *Make a stand.*

'Well, obviously I'll be counting on you all to keep things running at *ground* level,' Megan said, finally putting the handbag back on her shoulder. 'But, Hazel, if you do know anyone qualified to step into the breach and do management while I'm away, please let me know.'

That was it! That was absolutely it! Becky stood

up from her stool before she was tempted to hurl this morning's delivery of crab sticks at her sister. With as much composure as she had left, despite the trousers gnawing at her bellybutton, she swept out the door that led to the back garden, slamming it hard behind her.

Four

London, UK

'She's going to take everything, isn't she? Because that's what they do, isn't it? It's all whispered sexual promises and home-cooking at the beginning, and then it's commands about DIY and M&S meals you have to microwave yourself. And then... then it's bitter accusations that you've been ignoring their needs, when really you've been negotiating million-dollar contracts so they can carry on having spa weekends with their friends where they go all-in for facials and Watsu, but complain about how terrible their lives are and how their husbands are nothing but unreasonable bastards who haven't been able to find their erogenous zones since the honeymoon. Well, Elias, I challenge any man to find Kristina's erogenous zone when the hedges haven't been cut for a decade. Do you get what I'm saying? But, of course, it's all my fault, isn't it? Everything is always my fault.'

Solicitor Elias Mardas sat back in the hotel meeting room chair and regarded his client, Chad. Hair flecked with silver, wearing a navy suit from Moss London, this businessman would usually be the epitome of calm and controlled. Chad was used to negotiating hard with counterparts across the globe and here the man was, unravelling in a hotel in Central London. Not that Elias was surprised. This was what usually happened. Most of his clients became a shadow of their former selves, when it came to the topic of divorce. And that's where Elias came in. It was his job to control this whole process, legal *and* emotional, to ensure that his client dealt with the inevitable fall-out and arrived at Destination Decree Absolute in the best possible position. Matrimonial law might not have been his legal area of choice when he'd first qualified – originally he had intended to deal with property and real estate – but circumstances had changed and *he* had changed and this was his niche. His company, working alone, picking and choosing his clients. He excelled at it and it was lucrative. What more could you want from a career?

'Why aren't you saying anything?' Chad wanted to know. 'You haven't said *anything* in forty-five minutes.' He picked up his water glass and downed a mouthful. 'I'm not paying you an extortionate amount of money per hour to say nothing. I want strategy and planning. I want to wipe that triumphant look off Kristina's face when she realises that she isn't going to win this time.' He blew out a breath. 'She isn't going to *completely* win this time, is she?' He hesitated only for a beat. 'Fuck! Of course she is! They always do!' Chad stood up then, beginning to pace, along the carpet in front of the full-length window giving them a London summer skyline, all shafts of light gleaming off steel and glass.

'Sit down, Chad,' Elias told him, topping up both their water glasses.

'I can't sit down,' Chad replied. 'It's the stress! I've never been this stressed! It's playing havoc with my piles and she knows that. She *will* know that.' He aimed a designer shoe at the pot of a fake orchid plant in the corner, then yelped.

Elias figured that Chad was very nearly done. The anger *was* calming a little. When the meeting had started, Chad had exploded into a frenzied verbal tirade, his face turning a vibrant beetroot. He'd had to loosen his tie and undo the top button of his shirt, despite the air-conditioned atmosphere. He'd then patrolled the space like an over-zealous security guard, blaming mainly Kristina's signing up to a weekly book club as the reason their marriage had completely fallen apart. But Elias knew exactly why the marriage had fallen apart. He knew *exactly* how every marriage fell apart. *Communication*. Or, rather, the lack of it.

'Sit down, Chad,' Elias repeated. He adjusted his dark-framed glasses to make sure he was looking directly at his client when Chad decided to turn and face the table again. Unless he was going to go and put the boot in to every plant in the room, then re-joining the discussion was the only other option.

His client's shoulders lifted, up and almost to the top of his ears, then finally released. Chad turned around and hastened back to his seat. 'OK,' Chad said on an out breath, as he sat. 'OK. Tell me what I can do.'

Elias picked up his pen and toyed with it in between his fingers. 'You're not going to like what I have to say,' he began. 'But you have to trust me on it.' This was always his opening gambit in these initial meetings. It was tried and tested. It was a method he wished he'd been able to adopt during his *own* divorce. But he'd been wounded back then. *Naïve. Used.*

'I don't even like you saying I'm not going to like what you're going to say,' Chad admitted with a nervous laugh.

'But will you trust me on it?' Elias asked, blue-green eyes looking directly into Chad's brown ones. This approach only worked if his clients had complete confidence in his abilities. He knew the way he worked was contrary to most of his contemporaries, but his global recommendations among Chad's peers made his small firm one of the most sought-after divorce practices.

Chad gave a reticent nod. 'Yes.'

'Are you sure?' Elias asked. 'Because I am certain the other plants in this room do not want to feel your shoes.'

Chad took another deep breath, this time seeming to fully open his lungs, then slowly release a balloon's worth of stress-air. 'I trust you.'

Elias sat back a little and ran a hand through his dark hair, before adjusting his glasses for a second time. 'OK.' He took a breath, then leaned in, writing furiously on his notepad. 'Read this.' He pushed the paper towards Chad. 'Say it. Say it out loud. And let it settle on you. It's going to feel uncomfortable at first, but once it soaks into your subconscious, you'll start to feel better about it.'

Chad's eyes dropped to the piece of paper and Elias watched his body language immediately alter. *Discomfort. Denial.*

'Give in,' Chad read out through bitter lips. 'What?! No! No! Haven't you been listening to anything I've said the past half hour? Giving in is the absolutely last thing I want.'

Chad made to stand up again and this time, Elias reached a hand out and took a strong grip of his arm.

'Sit down, Chad,' he ordered. 'You promised you would trust me.'

'I know, but... but...' It seemed his client didn't have an answer.

'Say the words again,' Elias urged.

Chad shook his head, non-compliant.

'Fine,' Elias snapped. 'I will say it on your behalf.' He spoke, loud and strong. 'Give in.' He centred his core before speaking again. 'We are going to give in.'

Chad had closed his eyes now and was shaking his head as every bad moment from his marriage came back to him. Elias knew how it went. It would pass. Because, if it didn't pass, then Chad was not going to be successful in achieving the upper hand in his settlement.

'Kristina wants the house in Dorset,' Elias continued. 'I say we let her have it.' He waited a beat before continuing. '*Plus* the apartment in Kensington.'

'But... I like the house in Dorset,' Chad immediately complained. 'And the apartment in Kensington used to belong to my mother.' His eyes were open again now, but he had a childish, sentimental air about him. Why did people get like that over things that were essentially nothing more than status symbols or signposts to their wealth.

'What do you like more?' Elias inquired. 'The properties in the UK? Or the villa in Corfu?'

Elias already knew the answer to this question. He didn't take meetings with people he hadn't thoroughly researched. He had looked into Chad as a businessman, then Chad's personal life on social media. There were twice as many photos of the man in Greece than there were at the cottage on the Swanage coast and absolutely none of this family flat in a swanky area of London. Although Chad wasn't immediately answering. Maybe Elias had called this one wrong...

'Kristina hasn't asked for the apartment in Kensington,' Chad stated, folding his arms across his chest and sitting back in his chair.

'That is the whole point,' Elias stated. 'Giving in, remember? My job is to make sure you come out of this emotionally and financially intact, with the best share of your assets.' He sat forward, drawing pie-charts freehand on the paper in front of him. 'So, we propose Kristina takes the Dorset house and the flat in Kensington and then you get the property in Corfu and we suggest a three-quarter share of the main family home. Whether you buy her out of that place, or you sell and split the proceeds, we can battle that out later...'

'We raised our children in that house,' Chad whispered. 'We had so many family holidays in Swanage. Corfu was going to be something for Kristina and me in retirement.' His eyes were misting over and the reverie was starting to grate on Elias. He did hope that Chad wasn't going to be one of these clients who ended up unsure if he wanted to end the marriage at all.

'Your property in Corfu is on the expensive north-east coast. I believe you English call it Kensington-on-Sea. Ironic.' Elias shrugged. 'Weighing up the position of your Greek villa, the valuation provided by the estate agent, the British obsession with the Durrell family... and your own personal connection with the property...' He right away wished he hadn't mentioned the personal connection. He didn't want Chad to know he had cyber-stalked him. And he didn't want to make this about the heart... because it definitely wasn't, nor should it be.

'If we give her the house in Swanage and the flat in London, do you think she will let go of the Corfu house *and* go with me retaining three-quarters of the property in Kent?'

Elias smiled, knowing that Chad was now engaged and that they were both on the same page. He watched his client unfold his arms and change into far more switched-on businessman than wrecked shell of a defeated ex.

'I know she will,' Elias told him. 'Because I am going to make it happen.' He picked up his water glass and raised it a little as if it were the most expensive celebratory champagne and he was calling a toast. 'Step one. We give in, just a little. Step two. We take control.'

Five

It's A Wrap, Amesbury, Wiltshire, UK

Becky plucked at the herbs with much more force than was needed. This was anger management courtesy of horticulture. Plus, the longer she stayed out in the garden, the more chance there was that Megan would disappear to get on with the managerial stuff Becky couldn't possibly comprehend. Or maybe her sister would be swanning into Salisbury and mooching around the city centre looking at floaty kaftans and slinky bikinis for whatever dream destination *Dean* had booked that wasn't Blackpool. Wherever it was he'd probably got a dodgy discount somehow...

Pulling at the mint plant, Becky looked down into the basket she was holding. She'd harvested too many already. If she carried on furiously ripping the plants up, they'd end up with nothing left. And she shouldn't let her mini allotment suffer just because Megan had turned into a megalomaniac. But the way her sister had been, it was like time had rewound and they were aged ten and eight, sparring over who had done Barbie's hair better.

The sun at her back, Becky dropped down into the red and white striped deckchair that used to belong to her dad. He'd always sat back and relaxed in it at home after a hard afternoon's gardening. That's one of the reasons why Becky loved that she had created the vegetables and herbs here. All her father's knowledge on what grows best and how to tend young plants had been imparted so gently to a little girl keen to impress. And she had made sure none of it had gone to waste. Becky was only sad that her dad never got to see it. He would have loved this small corner of greenery she'd made. Even in the nursing home, when he was unable to speak, he had shown visual pleasure at the plants Becky had brought in to him. The doctors had said it was so important to keep all his senses stimulated to try and reawaken the parts of his brain that hadn't been permanently damaged. He'd smelled the herbs and touched their leaves and Becky had seen how much it had meant by the wobbly-lipped smile on his face.

Putting her fingers to her nose now, she inhaled the combined scents of mint, chive and basil. Scents of summer. Fresh, pure and simple, yet all incredible flavour-enhancers. And that was where the finesse lay. While their competitors offered the usual sandwich flavours – cheese and spring onion, ham and mustard, egg and cress, chicken and mayo – Becky experimented. Somehow, she inherently knew what herbs, spices and vegetables to pair with each filling to make the It's A Wrap flavours completely unique. When things had got tough with the bottom line, Becky had delivered their produce complete with a sample tray of her own creations, changing up ordinary lunch purchases and making each midday meal something to remember.

Jean Shering from the tyre factory's usual tuna mayo was pepped up with home-grown watercress. Adrian from the opticians liked pulled pork with asparagus. And Sally from the swimming pool ordered two cheese, pear and mustard bagels every single day. Often on Becky's delivery days, her customers would make culinary suggestions to her and she was always back with a mini sample for them to try on her next visit. Sometimes customer ideas worked – grated carrot, humous and chive – and sometimes they didn't – avocado, raisins and horseradish. So, she may not be management material, but she was top of the tree when it came to customer satisfaction. Not that she would ever get any praise from Megan for going the extra mile. Because Megan didn't know…

Becky slipped her phone out of the pocket of her trousers and flipped back on to the website she'd been looking at last night. Housesitting. What *would* that be like? Where would you get to go? The way Becky's luck was at the moment she'd probably type in Paris and end up in Texas. Not that she was thinking about France. Or even America. No, if she was going to go anywhere, she knew she would choose Greece. Nothing looked quite as beautiful on her web searches. Idyllic islands surrounded by turquoise water under heavenly blue skies… It wouldn't hurt to do a search, would it? She could pretend she was someone who could just drop everything and head off into the perfect sunset like Megan. Instead of being the backroom fixer everyone relied on to be reliable.

The Wiltshire sunshine in her eyes, Becky tapped at the screen of her phone, spurred on by a braver side of herself that appeared every now and then – possibly once every leap year – then waited for the results…

One result.

Corfu, Greece

Owner seeks housesitter for two weeks. Large villa with private infinity pool, steps away from the sea. A taverna within walking distance. Use of small car. Applicant needed asap.

One person only. Absolutely NO couples.

That was a little odd. Surely in this day and age you weren't allowed to be prejudiced towards people in a relationship. And ASAP spoke of being a little desperate. When had this advert been posted? A look at the date in the top left-hand corner said late last night. Becky swallowed. *Infinity pool. Steps away from the sea.* But who would really want to do that? Head off at short notice, somewhere unknown, completely and utterly on their own. But, for the first time in a long time she did fit the criteria. She *was* one person only.

'The coast is clear, dear. Megan's huffed off to some networking breakfast.'

It was Hazel, already by her side. Becky hadn't heard the door open and now she didn't have time to shove her phone out of sight. She tried to tilt the screen away, but it was too late…

'What are you looking at? Ooo, housesitting! How fabulous! My friend Hilary did housesitting once. Looked after a load of greyhounds in Norwich.' Hazel laughed. 'I've told you about Hilary, haven't I? Probably ate the dog food as well as everything the family had in the cupboards.' She sniffed. 'She enjoyed it though. Said they had a hot tub and it was worth getting coated in doggy dribble to get a dip in that.'

Becky went to put her phone away, but Hazel took hold of it, pulling it closer for inspection. 'This isn't Norwich. This is… ooo, Corfu. Ooo, look at that lovely villa! I do love a house with that thick, rustic stone. Makes me imagine all those brawny, olive-skinned builders putting it all together…'

Were there pictures of the property? She hadn't seen photos. It made sense there would be photos, if only to ensure the house you were sitting was actually there to be sat. Although, you could theoretically use iStock. Megan had done that for some of their food on the website, despite Becky's protests.

She stood up now, getting closer to Hazel in order to see the images on her phone screen.

'Oh, would you look at that sky! And those olive trees! And the urns full of blooms!' Hazel looked from the photos to Becky. 'That's what you'll be doing the whole time you're there. Watering. In the Greek heat in July, you're going to have your work cut out making sure they don't all die.'

But she liked gardening. Gazing back at the images in front of her, she took in the mismatched pots and the flowering beds lining the border of the house. It was all pink and purple petals, a bough of a lemon tree ripe with fruit and that divine-looking pool literally whispering an invitation…

'When are you going?' Hazel asked, letting go of the phone.

'Oh,' Becky said. 'I'm not going.' *She wasn't. She couldn't. It was a mad idea.*

'What?!' Hazel exclaimed. 'If I was twenty years younger, I'd have already booked my flight by now. What's stopping you, dear?'

What *was* stopping her really? The business? Well, it was Megan's business, not hers. The change in routine? Maybe it was time her world existed outside of Wiltshire. No one else seemed to worry about changing their routine at the drop of a hat. Becky sighed. Megan hadn't given a thought to her when she'd clamped her hands around the luxury bag and told Dean two weeks at a mystery location was fine by her.

'If you don't take the job,' Hazel said, 'I'd feel compelled to tell Hilary about it and her waistline really doesn't need the calorific pitfalls of moussaka.'

Could she do this? Really?

'Email the owner,' Hazel ordered. 'Then come and help me finish these orders. Bertram from the Co-op left a message on the answerphone. He said he's convinced by your sample of corned beef and blackcurrant jam.'

'OK,' Becky agreed. 'I'll be right there.' She hovered her thumb over the 'contact' icon on the display. There was no harm in registering and trying her luck. Besides, it was likely a luxury villa by the Greek sea had already been snapped up, wasn't it?

Six

A week later

Elias was going back to Corfu. Was he completely mad? No. He did have good reason. *Excellent* reason. He needed to meet with Kristina, away from her solicitor, and put forward Chad's proposal quickly. He would blindside her, choreograph 'bumping' into her at one of the local tavernas, make it a happy coincidence... before he followed it up with a visit to the villa and made a thorough inspection of the house. That was the way he worked. *Personal. Close.* No detail left unaccounted for.

It was just a shame he hadn't managed to secure a direct flight. Everything out of London was booked except this one flight to Athens. It was inconvenient to make a change in Greece's capital, but he only had a forty-minute connection time before the onward hop to Corfu that took less than an hour.

Sipping at his macchiato, Elias surveyed his fellow

travellers in the restaurant of the departure lounge. You could certainly tell the categories most of them fell into. There were the businessmen and women like him – all sleek suits and laptop bags looking harried, checking watches or reviewing paperwork. There were the families – mum, dad and children ranging in ages from buggy-board to just-plain-bored – equally as harried as the businessmen and women. And there were the stag parties. Matching T-shirts bearing the name of the groom – Steve's Rutting Crew was the chosen gang-brand in this case – all on a pint of Stella Artois, all loud with a complete lack of spatial awareness. Elias felt for Steve. This would be his last hurrah. As soon as he tied the knot he would be setting himself up for the three D's. *Disappointment. Disillusionment.* And ultimately, the biggest 'D' of all. *Divorce.* Perhaps he should slip the groom his business card.

He put down his coffee, about to check his phone, when something caught in his peripheral vision. He stood up.

Hazel's bloody cabin bag! Her colleague might have thought it said 'woman on the brink of adventure', but Becky had said from the outset it was too big and the straps were too long. As the bag crashed to the airport floor – for the third time since check-in – Becky was caught between making a grab for it or keeping control of her new four-wheel trolley case. And taking a second to make that decision meant the case rolled off like someone else was controlling it and the bag began to spill the contents of her summer. Newly acquired fast-tracked passport. Purse. Phone. Laptop and traditional paper notebook to both catalogue her holiday and prepare a sample menu for the nursing home...

'Lads! Look what we've got here! One of those dirty books!'

Face flaming as she gathered her belongings, Becky looked up to see a man with very gelled hair holding aloft a paperback she'd bought in WHSmith. It wasn't dirty... she didn't think. Granted, it *was* a romance. The blurb had said Greece and lemon groves and she'd been sold. After all, that was about to become her reality.

Ever since she had received the email acceptance from Ms O'Neill, the owner of Villa Selino in Kerasia, Corfu, with full details of the home that needed sitting, Becky's insides had been jumping like a kangaroo. Excitement and trepidation. She was *doing* this. Caution was being thrown to the sea breeze. All she'd had to do was maintain this braver, new-experience-seeking her when she told Megan. And she had. Until Megan had tried to deny her the break...

'It's too late notice. We don't know when Shelley is going to be back. It's a no.'

And then Megan turned her back on her, pretending to look through an A4 file that Becky knew was only full of food magazines. Her sister had always been good at trying to shut off conversations she found uncomfortable. Well, if Becky was going to be strong enough to get on a plane on her own and stay in a villa in Greece on her own, then she had to be able to make her sister listen and bag this time off. What was the alternative? She gave in her notice? Got fired? Lost her job? Megan wouldn't be that stupid, would she? Plus, Becky hadn't ever had any time off apart from the odd week here and there and her trips to Blackpool...

'Shelley's going to be back tomorrow,' Becky reminded her. 'I'm not going until next week. It's only for two weeks. I'll be back in plenty of time before you go away and the army contract begins.' Because even though it was late notice, her spur-of-the-moment decision still wouldn't impact too much on It's A Wrap. Megan didn't reply. She closed the magazine file and got down another one. This one Becky knew contained purchase invoices from 2018 – because it said so on the label.

'Megan,' Becky began again. 'I'm going. No matter what you say.' She put the holiday form on her sister's desk.

'You can't!' Megan said, whipping around and facing her finally. 'You can't go unless I sign that form. Because if I don't sign that form, and you go on holiday, then you're… in breach of your employment contract.'

'Megan!' Becky gasped. 'I've never asked for anything like this before.'

'Well,' Megan said, unable to meet Becky's eyes, her jaw rigid, 'if I start making allowances for you then I will have to make allowances for everyone else and that isn't the way to run a modern-day business.'

'Megan,' Becky said, trying to maintain calm, 'you do make allowances for everyone else. You let Hazel go at late notice to her country music week last year. And Shelley's always forgetting when the triplets school events are and dropping those in at the last minute.'

'Oh, so, now you're saying I've not been running this business right for a while?'

Becky shook her head. 'No, I was just saying—'

'I thought we'd had this conversation the other day,

Becky,' Megan said. 'About how I *run the business and* you *just make the sandwiches.'*

Just make the sandwiches. *There it was again. Proof that everything Becky put into the business was unappreciated. It was the reason Becky knew, this time she had to put her foot down.*

'I'm going away,' Becky said firmly. 'Next Wednesday. For two weeks. And I am going whether you sign that form or not.' There had been nothing left to say.

Thinking about that disappointment with Megan, Becky made a grab for her book but missed.

'Ooo,' another man cooed, snatching the paperback from his friend. 'Let's read a bit.' He began thumbing the pages. It was then Becky realised this group were all wearing matching clothes… like overgrown Scouts.

'Thank you for picking it up for me. Can I have that back now?' Becky asked the man now holding the novel.

'Smutty, is it?' he asked, running his tongue over his bottom lip and fixing eyes with dilated pupils on her.

Becky smiled, matching his gaze. She might be an inexperienced traveller, a woman on her own, but she wasn't about to let a half-drunk guy get the upper hand before she'd reached the boarding gate. She had signed up for being bold, independent and unafraid. Plus she'd re-watched one of her favourite chick-flicks at the weekend, *Bridesmaids*, and she was ready to channel Annie Walker.

'It's deeply, slightly darkly, erotic,' she answered, her expression set to serious. 'It's about a twenty-five-year-old woman caught at a crossroads in her life.'

'Oh, really,' the man answered, leaning in a little.

'Yes,' Becky continued. 'She's been waiting so long for a really big, *big* change. Because nothing so far in her life has come close to pushing any of her buttons.' She sighed. 'And that's what she wants more than anything. All her buttons pushed, in all the right ways.'

'Is that so?'

'Yes,' Becky carried on as the man leaned closer still. 'So, it's about one more-than-ready woman... a whole gang of gorgeous leading men...'

'Are you hearing this, lads?' the now-obvious-member of a stag party called. Becky hoped he wasn't going to dribble over her book... or her. She could almost grab it again now.

She waited a beat, then looked up at him. 'One long, *long*, unadulterated weekend...' She shook out her hair and sighed, a hand at her chest. 'With her TV... and Sky boxsets.'

She snatched the paperback out of his hands. 'Thank you!' Then turning her back on the group, she began hastily moving away, pushing her case in front of her. Her insides were wriggling like worms on the end of a fishing line. Where had that confidence come from? Was this because she had finally stood up to her sister? She should be congratulating herself. This was important. This little interaction with annoying passengers was a turning point en route to travelling outside of the country, not to mention outside of her comfort zone. She closed her eyes and exhaled... seconds before she caught her foot on one of the wheels of her case and crashed to the ground.

'Are you OK?'

Becky didn't want to look up. If this was one of the stag party, they were definitely going to get their fill of laughing at her expense. She got to her feet, pride dented but thankfully none of her bones. Whoever it was, she would act nonchalant. She could do nonchalant. It's what she did with the prawn man when he had a so-called *amazing* special offer she'd have to tell Megan about.

'I'm fine,' she breathed, picking up her bag and swinging it over her shoulder. Now she took in the concerned individual.

Wow. Forget the actors from the TV boxsets she'd just been talking about, this man was definitely worth pressing the pause button for. Tall, blue suit that looked made-to-measure, a pale blue shirt underneath, olive skin, clean-shaven, thick, dark hair – shorter at the sides than on top, where it waved casually backwards in a way only those with Mediterranean heritage seemed to be able to achieve. He had the brightest blue-green eyes – unusual for a man with such dark colouring, Becky thought – distinct under heavy black-framed glasses that were sitting on his not-unattractive Roman nose. God, she was doing way too much looking and not enough getting on with finding somewhere to sit down before her gate was called. Oh no, it *was* her *case* she'd got her foot caught up with, wasn't it? Or had she instead driven it into him? Her gaze went to his tan brogues looking for signs of scuffing. Thankfully, none.

'Do you need to sit down?' the stranger asked her. 'It was quite a fall.'

From three inches of pleather espadrille. Cursed Blackpool bargains. She should have worn her trainers.

'I'm fine,' Becky said again. Then: 'I didn't roll into you, did I?' *Clarify, Becky!* 'I mean, did my case hit you?'

The man shook his head. 'No.'

'Oh, good,' Becky answered. What else was there to say?

'I saw you drop your bag and you did not notice but... this fell out too.'

He held something out to her. *Oh God*! It was Hazel's book. The one she had gone on about! Hazel had mentioned it, Becky had ignored her, but then she'd found it when she was packing, tucked into the too-big travel bag. Why hadn't she taken it out and left it behind? She reached out and took it, stuffing it down into the bag quickly.

'*How to Find the Love of Your Life or Die Trying*,' the man said.

Becky inwardly cringed and sent a silent message to the weather gods to send Hazel stormy seas once she set sail on her cruise. How embarrassing was this? The gorgeous man speaking the book title out loud – with a bit of a European accent thrown in – made Becky's face flame faster than a child dropping their face into birthday candles.

'It's not mine,' she said fast. Not fast enough. He was already smiling. A self-satisfied kind of smile that said, looking like he did, he had either already found the love of his life or could, quite possibly, walk into any life scenario and snap her (or him) up quicker than you could allegedly catch the Coronavirus.

'Really,' Becky said again. 'It's not mine. It belongs to...'

'A friend,' the man said, nodding.

'Yes,' Becky answered.

'Have a safe flight,' the man told her, turning away.

'It really isn't mine,' Becky affirmed. Why was she affirming anything to a stranger? Why did she care? She might read the love guide once she had finished reading about lemon groves and romance on the beach. And why shouldn't she? She was single. It might contain something of interest… It couldn't only be about snagging a widower between backgammon and black forest gateaux. It might have vital chapters about finding a mate through an astrology app like Tara had…

She watched Mr Hotness navigate his way back to a table for two in the airport restaurant. Coffee. She definitely needed coffee, to stabilise her nerve and keep her awake after the early start. But she couldn't now order one here. Not with Mr Judgemental analysing her holiday reading material. She'd find another place. One that also didn't include stag parties.

Seven

Somehow, for some completely unknown reason, it had taken forty minutes to get from the start of the queue for the boarding gate to actually setting foot on the plane. Becky looked at her watch as she inched herself along the narrow aisle towards Seat 18D. Other passengers seemed to be making a real meal of getting their cabin bags into the overhead lockers. It was all elbows out and thick jackets being rolled into sausage-shapes. Giant bulging backpacks looking like they were holding an extra passenger inside, handbags stuffed with enough items to survive an apocalypse. Becky almost felt her one case and Hazel's bag wasn't enough. Her fellow fliers obviously packed for every eventuality and weather condition. Sun hats. Beanies. Sandals. Snow boots – yes, really. Capes, coats and one woman in *Scooby Doo* cosplay – Velma. And now they were already fifteen minutes past the time they were supposed to be taking off. That wasn't good. She only had forty minutes between the flight landing in Athens and her next flight taking off for

Corfu. She'd felt a little on edge about it when she'd booked it, but there had been no direct flights available unless she wanted to travel up to East Midlands. Forty minutes didn't seem like enough time to get off a plane, go through security, get to another gate and get on another plane. Before she'd purchased online, she'd phoned customer services and been told that forty minutes was the minimum time they allowed for a transit such as this and it was absolutely fine. Despite the reassurance, Becky was still ready to trot a little if she had to. There was no way she was going to miss the connection and be stranded in Athens with no pre-booked hotel room in the height of summer. Plus, she had promised Ms O'Neill that she would be arriving tonight. She was a bit sad that they wouldn't actually get to meet, but if Ms O'Neill had been at the property there would be no reason for her to need a housesitter, would there? Right now, Becky just needed to get to her seat, sit back, try to relax and spend the next four hours preparing a knockout menu for the care home party. If she still actually worked for It's A Wrap. If Megan hadn't sacked her for going on holiday without a signed holiday form…

The man in front of her finally slipped into his seat and her way was clear. Heaving her case up off the floor she carried it, Hazel's bag bouncing off arm rests as she moved, up to Row 18. Once there, she found her aisle seat, and lifted her case up into the overhead locker before plumping down and taking a big breath. She was onboard. She was doing this. She was heading to Greece.

'Excuse me.'

That voice. Becky turned her head and looked straight up into the face of the sexy specimen who had picked Hazel's book up in departures. What was he doing on her plane? Why was karma crucifying her?

'Yes?' Becky asked.

'It is you,' the man said, looking almost as surprised as she was. 'The girl with… your friend's book.'

'Can I help you?' Becky replied. He had taken his jacket off, she noticed, and undone a couple of buttons on his shirt. Was that the beginnings of a tattoo she could see at the edge of his clavicle?

'My seat,' he replied. 'It is there. By the window.'

No. No, this was not happening. What was next? Were the whole stag party who had taken the rise out of her other reading material going to conga down the aisle and take up residence in the rows ahead and behind?

'This window?' Becky asked pointlessly. Of course it was this window. That's why he was standing next to her pointing at the seat two along from where she was sitting.

'18F,' he said, waving a boarding pass.

And now she had to stand up again. Pushing Hazel's bag underneath the seat in front of her with her feet, Becky got up and shimmied out of her position, allowing Mr Handsome access to his seat. Except he didn't immediately slide down into the row; instead he began the task of putting his things into the locker above them. Becky could do nothing but watch and wait. Up went his suit jacket, rolled into the obligatory sausage shape, next was a leather portfolio bag that looked expensive, then finally his small black case. Each lift up and in provided Becky with a view of the movement of those obliques, defined under the slim-fit shirt tucked into his trousers. What was wrong with her? The first attractive man she'd encountered past the Wiltshire border and she was gawping like she'd never seen one before. Granted, when you were wrist-deep in tuna and lime-pickle chutney – yes, that really worked as a flavour – there weren't many attractive men to gawp at – make that *any* – but she shouldn't need to turn into a raging desperado before she'd even left the country. What star sign might he be though? Tara said most people were compatible with an Aquarius.

'Thank you,' the man said, finally shutting the locker door and making his way into the space and towards his seat.

Becky let him sit down before she got herself back into position. The middle seat was still vacant. She would probably be up and out, making way for their other travelling companion soon. So much for thinking an aisle seat would be better. She checked her watch. Another five minutes had gone by. She hoped the pilot would be able to make up some time in the air.

'So, you are heading to Athens,' her companion said.

Becky looked across at him. He was taking off his leather shoes! Taking off his shoes! What was going on? You surely didn't take off your shoes on an aircraft unless you needed to escape down the emergency slide! It was unhygienic. Never mind catching the Coronavirus! Who wanted to catch a verruca? Except hopefully he would leave his socks on…

'I…' Becky said. What had he asked her?

'Athens,' he repeated. 'You are on the right plane I take it?'

'Yes,' she replied. 'But I'm actually…' She stopped herself from saying any more. Both Hazel and Shelley had shot her a parting warning about imparting information to strangers.

'You're going to meet a lot of people you might only

want to share one conversation with,' Hazel had said. 'Don't give them everything. Save that for the ones who deserve it.'

'Have you watched "Don't F**k with Cats"?' That had been Shelley's offering.

'Have you been to Athens before?' she asked. There was no better way of avoiding talking about yourself. Get someone else to do the talking.

'Yes,' he answered. 'I visit practically every month.'

Or did he? Damn Hazel and Shelley. The beginnings of the first proper conversation she'd had and she was already questioning the truth of every single utterance.

'Wow,' Becky answered. 'You must like it a lot.'

'I do not always get to see the Acropolis,' he continued. 'Most of the time I am inside. It is for work.'

Or was it? And what kind of work did he do? What did she care? As long as his travelling aim wasn't to steal the identity of naïve single travellers…

'But that has its benefits in the summer,' he said. 'Great air-conditioning.'

He liked it cold. If that didn't smack of serial killer, she didn't know what did.

'Right,' Becky said. She weaved her foot around the straps of Hazel's bag and tried to pull it up onto her lap to save bending into the not-enough-space. It was time to get out her notebook and do something productive. Or look like she was doing something productive at least. Except the damn bag wouldn't move.

'How about you?' Mr Handsome/*Dexter* asked.

'Oh, I love the heat,' Becky answered. 'The hotter the better.' This wasn't quite true, so it ticked the vagueness box. She was more of a summer person than a winter one, but she preferred it mid-twenties rather than stifling thirties. Although she was hoping for great sunshine in Corfu to try out that private pool or the sea just steps away. She had a sudden thought. Did 'steps away' mean actual steps? How many steps? The photos she'd been sent hadn't really been plentiful. There had been six. Master bedroom. Guest bedrooms times two. The main bathroom. The kitchen. And the pool and outside space. But it had all looked glorious. Who cared about the potential of steps? Steps might do her good. Despite having had no one to go out with lately she hadn't focused her attention on her gym membership like she should have done. Instead, she had pledged her allegiance to rom-com films and a meat box delivered to her door.

'Athens will be hot,' the man answered her. 'Really, really hot.'

Becky stopped trying to hook her foot over the bag straps and looked at her companion. His voice saying 'hot' was oddly hypnotic in that accented English. It shouldn't be. He was a stranger who could be set to drug her drink the second her back was turned.

'Today it will be forty degrees,' he added.

'What?! Forty!' She hoped Corfu wasn't going to be quite that warm.

He nodded. 'You did not know this?'

'I...' She couldn't admit she didn't know the temperature of somewhere she was supposed to be staying. Because she wasn't staying. The only bit of Athens she was going to see was the airport floor as she went running to another gate. 'I... checked the weather last night and it was saying somewhere in the region of thirty-five, thirty-six.' Did that sound plausible?

'Sunscreen,' he told her with a nod. 'And definitely something to cover your head.'

Becky winced as her brain fed her images of him somehow suffocating her with a sick bag from the seat pocket. This was ridiculous. She needed to blot out everything Hazel and Shelley had told her before she left... except the bit about being carefully vague... or was it vaguely careful?

'Boarding complete,' a cabin crew member announced.

Finally. Becky fastened her seat belt and side-eyed the empty seat next to her. It looked like it was going to be just the two of them.

Eight

There was free wine on this flight. Hazel and Shelley hadn't mentioned that as a possibility when Becky had told them she'd booked the ticket. At first, she'd considered opting for something soft – tea or a Coke – but then she saw the free wine was in little bottles with a screw cap. A screw cap was much easier to reattach, do up tight and slip into her bag if she wanted to use the toilet. Not that she was thinking back to the mad warnings of drink-spiking from her crazy colleagues...

She cast an eye away from her notebook and glanced at her companion. He had put up the armrest between his seat and 18E as soon as they had received the all clear to undo their seatbelts an hour ago. And now he was spread. One leg crossed over the other – how in this confined area defied the space-time continuum – knee hanging over the spare seat, a laptop on the tray table. Yes, slightly before the spreading out, had come the asking her to get back up so he could retrieve the leather bag. Becky had almost broken her ankle because she'd finally managed to loop

Hazel's bag straps around her foot and had forgotten about it. Whatever he was working on he had been engrossed for almost the whole sixty minutes they had been in the air, apart from when the cabin crew had come round with the trolley service. He'd ordered a black coffee. No alcohol for him. Well, he had said he visited Athens for work…

Becky looked back to her notepad. She had written the word 'Spam' three times. As unconventional as it sounded, Spam was going to be at the centre of her menu pitch for the nursing home. And she meant the meat product, not the messages from Wayfair and Wish you got ten thousand times a day because you once clicked on a Facebook advert…

What would go with Spam in a light finger roll? Something not obvious. Something to signify VE celebrations. Bringing back memories had been all important in helping her dad try to recover from his stroke. She and her mum had used photos of family holidays and Christmases past, music he enjoyed, cricket commentary, anything to provoke a reaction that they had hoped would lead to more interaction. Except it wasn't to be and Megan had mostly stayed away. That was still something Becky failed to understand.

Was Spam and pickle too obvious? How about a mustard and chive mayonnaise? She had already decided she was going to do some kind of dessert featuring peaches, as Dolly, one of the more talkative residents, always spoke endlessly about the sweet tinned peaches the Americans had brought over with them in wartime. Here on the plane, with time to let her imagination and ideas flow, Becky didn't care that Megan didn't want the event. *She* wanted the job and she had already decided she was going to pitch for it whether it went through It's A Wrap or not.

'Are you OK?'

The question from her right startled her and Becky dropped her pen to the tiny table, quickly stopping it from rolling off onto the floor.

'Yes,' she answered. 'Why? Do you need me to get up again?'

'No,' the man replied. 'It is just... you have drawn a pig... I think... with another pig over the top and... you have put a hole in your paper.'

Becky looked at her pad. He was right. Why had she done that? How had she done it without even noticing? 'Well,' she said, flustered, 'you're... not wearing shoes.'

'You do not like to fly?' Elias asked her. He had been completely aware of her over the past hour for a couple of reasons. The first was that she was the complete opposite of relaxed, as well as not showing any of the hallmark signs of being excited for an upcoming holiday. The second thing was she had alternated between writing notes then staring into space drawing – or rather stabbing – random objects on the page. Usually he was seated next to a businessman like himself, with only the twin-tapping of their keyboards to accompany the roar of the Airbus. She was therefore a bit of a mystery and he couldn't help but be intrigued. Who was she? What exactly was she planning to do with a book entitled *How to Find the Love of Your Life or Die Trying*? Perhaps he ought to give her his business card as a way of warding off any cluelessness when it came to finding love for life...

'I don't fly very often,' she admitted. 'I've actually only flown three times. Once to Scotland because it was cheaper to fly there and onward to Blackpool than it was to go direct. Then I went to Germany to pick up some acai palm seeds I bought because it was cheaper to go there in person than it was to pay the postage. And the other time was a glider lesson my sister bought me as a present. I've no idea why. I've never wanted to be a pilot and I hated it. I mean, gliders have *no engines*.'

'I think that is why they are called "gliders",' he answered with a smile.

'I understand the concept of gliding,' she replied. 'I just didn't think, in this day, with all the health and safety rules they have now, that putting someone inexperienced in a vehicle with no engine when the only way is down, was going to be... you know... an actual thing. I really wished she'd just got me a gift card for Byron.'

She was cute. All large brown eyes and caramel-coloured hair that touched her shoulders. Had he just thought the word 'cute'? Perhaps he should have had something alcoholic from the in-flight service. Too much coffee wasn't good for him and he was about to be experiencing the deepest, darkest, strongest Greek coffee of all when he dropped in to see his parents while he was on Corfu.

'I didn't mean to sound rude,' he told her. 'About the gliders. I've never been in one myself.' He held out his hand. 'Elias Mardas.'

'Oh... Becky.' She picked up her notebook then put it down again and finally took his hand in hers. 'Just Becky.'

She had a firm shake for someone with hands that got a little lost in his. Neat fingernails. No fake tips or French polish. He cleared his throat and withdrew his hand, picking up his stylus and poking it at his laptop screen.

'What work do you do?' she asked him, turning a little in her seat.

'I am...' *You are a divorce lawyer. A highly regarded one. Tell her that and she will probably be both appalled and impressed.* 'Why don't you guess?' He turned in his seat now. 'What do you think I do for a job?'

'Not a gliding instructor,' Becky said quickly.

'Amusing.'

'Not something that involves getting your hands dirty.'

'Hmm.'

'Your suit says banker or... international playboy but...'

'Wow. I do not know whether I should be insulted or flattered.'

And her cheeks were flushed now. Like she wanted to retract her last sentence. She *was* cute. Too cute for him to try and give her his number and work for a casual hook-up some time. He didn't know why he had thought that. Casual hook-ups weren't that satisfying to him anymore.

'I'm a—'

'Doctor?' Becky interrupted.

He shook his head.

'Vet?'

'You think I look like I could fix people.' Well, she was kind of on the right lines.

'People or pets.'

'I don't cut things open.'

'Thank God... serial killer was my next guess.' A relieved breath left her and he wondered for a second if she was serious.

'I'm going to put you out of your misery,' he said, leaning a little into the seat space between them.

'I thought you said you *weren't* a serial killer.'

'I am an... estate agent.'

God. He had lied. Why had he lied? And why had he said he was an estate agent? Of all the occupations he could have picked! Estate agents weren't generally liked by anyone. But, then again, he didn't need to be liked. It was just a conversation on a plane. Something to while away the flight time and distract him from working on Chad's divorce for an hour or so.

'International, I'm guessing,' Becky answered. 'So, I suppose you get to walk around luxury villas all day long. Wow.'

'Well...' He was in a hole now and he had no idea how he was going to dig himself out. But... who cared? Not him. He could be an estate agent for an hour. It wasn't too far away from all that property law he had studied. And it might be refreshing. 'It's not always about the villas. I deal with all kinds of properties. From luxury penthouses to... tiny one-bedroom boltholes no one even knows are there.'

'It sounds exciting,' Becky said. 'Every day a new property to look at. It's very different to what I do.'

'And what do you do?' he asked her.

'I am...'

She wasn't immediately answering and that piqued his interest even more. She had secrets. But, then again, so did he.

'I'm... in the army.'

She had whispered the reply and looked over her shoulder. Except, given their location, the only thing her eyes connected with was the back of her own seat. He had not seen *that* occupation coming, which was perhaps a little judgemental of him. But seeing how she had handled her suitcase and a carry-on in departures he wasn't convinced she would be able to deal with swinging an automatic weapon. Then again, first impressions could definitely be misleading. He could vouch wholeheartedly for that.

'It's... not something I'm really supposed to talk about,' she whispered again. 'I've... you know... signed the Official Secrets Act.'

'And you're going to Athens on official business?' He had lowered his voice too now, moved his head a little closer. 'Greece has a military issue no one knows about?'

'Oh... no,' she said quickly, wetting her lips with her tongue. 'I'm going to Greece on holiday. Well, a working holiday.' She paused for a second. 'Sort of.'

'Where are you staying?' he asked. 'Or is that a secret too?'

She tapped her nose with her finger as if that was all the answer he needed.

'I was going to suggest some good restaurants for you to try, that is all.'

'Oh, well, that's very kind of you but...'

They were interrupted by an announcement that the pilot had turned on the fasten seatbelts sign. Now, his companion looked even more flustered.

'I hope there isn't going to be turbulence,' she said, a nervous laugh falling from her lips.

'Don't worry,' Elias told her. 'I have flown this route many, many times.'

With that said, the plane bumped violently upwards and the little bottle of wine on Becky's tray table fell down to the cabin floor.

Nine

It felt like hours before the rocking and swaying and up and downing came to an end. In reality, it was only around twenty minutes, but Becky stayed seated for another hour before she dared leave the apparent safety of her seat to use the on-board toilet. Lance Corporal Becky Rose and her unknown anxiety over turbulence... Why, oh why had she told Elias the estate agent that she was in the army? Actually, she knew exactly why. Because Hazel and Shelley's warnings about giving information about herself had come cheerleading into her mind – with pompoms and batons – and she knew she had already slipped up and told him her *real* name. Between trying to think of something a little like catering but *not* catering, Becky had thought about Megan's win with the army contract and there it was... her new fake occupation. One she knew exactly nothing about. Still, she had kept up the pretence that she was only going as far as Athens, so no harm done. It wasn't like the gorgeous Greek was going to follow her to her next gate...

There was a queue for the toilet, but it was good to stretch your legs on these planes, wasn't it? Hazel had tried to lend her some stockings to prevent a DVT. But Becky had been put off because Hazel had said she'd worn them in hospital when she'd had her gallbladder removed. When she pulled them out of her handbag Becky was quite convinced they hadn't been washed since…

'God! Hurry up, man in the checked shirt! He's been in there three whole minutes. You know what that means, don't you?'

The girl ahead of Becky in the queue turned around and faced her, as if expecting a response. She was possibly eighteen, maybe less and had her blonde hair in two neater-than-neat plaits, properly pleated from her very scalp and not a strand out of place. She was pretty and wearing skinny jeans and a T-shirt that said 'Nobody's Foo'.

'I…' Becky began.

'Number two,' the girl answered. 'Who even does that on a plane?'

Becky opened her mouth to reply but the girl carried on.

'The guy in the checked shirt. That's who.' She sighed and checked her watch. Becky noticed her arm was covered with multi-coloured wristbands. One said 'Bang Cock' and another 'Thighland'. Becky knew she hadn't had *that* much wine for her eyes to misinterpret the spellings.

'If this pilot doesn't put his foot down, I'm going to miss my onward flight.'

'Oh,' Becky said. 'Where are you going after Athens?'

'Corfu,' the girl replied. 'Supposed to be getting the flight with Olympic Air but unless they're going to hold the plane, there's a fat chance of that happening.' She sighed, smiled and stuck out a hand. 'I'm Petra, by the way.'

'Becky,' Becky answered, taking her hand and shaking it. Shit, she'd told someone else her real name! She steadied herself against a seat back as the plane dipped a little. 'Do you really think we're going to be that late? I'm meant to be getting that flight too.' It was OK to say that to this girl, wasn't it? She was in the same boat... or plane... whatever. Single girl camaraderie. Except she didn't know the girl was single. No one in Becky's orbit seemed to be single at the moment. Except Hazel. But she did have plans for debonair denture-wearers on her P&O break...

'Well, during my grand tour I've missed more planes than I've caught them so, going on that...'

'What do you do... you know... when you miss a plane and... it's not your fault?' Petra obviously had experience on this subject. It was always better to be forewarned about these things. If she really was going to miss the connection, Becky needed to find somewhere to stay before everyone else missing onward flights started thinking along the same lines. And she should email Ms O'Neill. Or phone her. Did she have her number? Whatever the form of communication, she should let her know about the delay. Except she couldn't do any of those things mid-flight.

'It very much depends on the airline and the length of the delay. Most of them will try and give you the bare minimum. The bare minimum in Indonesia seemed to be a bowl of beansprouts and a free T-shirt.' Petra took the top she was wearing between her forefingers and widened it out. 'But I quite like it. And I did quite like the food at Nobody's Foo. The beer was good too.'

Great. So, the chances were there was going to be a further cost to Becky if she missed the flight and wanted a bed that wasn't the airport floor. She had obviously brought some euros with her but that small nest-egg, having been sat there untouched for ages, was being pecked away at like a chick breaching its shell prior to birth. Too many cracks and Becky would have nothing for that rainy day she was always worrying about. Particularly if Megan decided to fire her…

'Oh, thank God. I thought I was going to have to fashion a makeshift Shewee.' Petra stepped forward as the man in the checked shirt appeared from the toilets. She smiled back at Becky. 'I won't be long. Just a number one. Unlike some.' She sent a glare to Mr Checked Shirt who seemed thankfully oblivious. Petra seemed completely unconcerned with revealing *her* name and travel plans as well as what she was going to do in the toilet. Perhaps Becky should be less Hazel and Shelley, and be a bit more Petra…

Elias put two fingers to the bridge of his nose and pressed hard. He was getting a headache and he knew it was over the email Chad had sent through last night that he had ignored in favour of another beer and writing his own strategy. Chad was concerned Kristina was still buying things with joint funds, frittering away money that should be his. If they couldn't be sensible about things it was going to make this case even harder. Elias sighed. This was what his life was – dealing with rich people who argued more over who kept the money than they did about who kept the children. He could of course bow out. Right now. Or at least tell Chad he was going to. Scare him a little. Except, he needed this case. Not for the money. But because it gave him an excuse to go back to Corfu.

Clicking on his laptop, he brought up the document he had prepared last night when he should have been emailing Chad back. It was a pro/con list in two sections. One section was headed '*Mitera ke Pateras*' (Mother and Father) and the other was headed 'Hestia'. Elias picked up his water bottle and took a swig as his eyes roved over the page. He sucked warm air from the bottle. *Empty!* He checked his watch. Were they going to come round with another drink before landing? They were still running behind schedule. If this kept up there was a chance he would miss his connecting flight. And now he had made the decision to return he just wanted to get there. Was that why he had suggested the option with the Corfu property to Chad? Because it fitted with his own agenda? Elias shook his head and focused on the screen. He couldn't let his home island and everything connected to it take over. Business first. *Of course* this was about Chad's divorce. The fact that it allowed him to check in was fortunate coincidence, nothing more.

Mother and Father

Pros
- *You can check on their health*
- *You can check on their wealth*
- *The next time you call they cannot say it is almost two years since you have seen them*

Cons
- *They will expect you to be re-married*
- *If you stay too long they will find you someone to marry*

- *They are still embarrassed by you despite what they say*
- *They will talk about Hestia*

Even writing his ex-wife's name had been painful. He'd almost turned the 'H' into a random animal like his row companion just so he could stab hard dots to make snout holes. Why was he still so angry about their ending? It had been two years. Recovery should have happened by now. Except what *actually* still happened was every time Elias thought about his ex-wife, he was faced with two images. The one with Hestia standing facing him surrounded by golden effigies of Christ in the Greek Orthodox church, her smile so perfectly beautiful he had struggled to draw breath. She had held his hands in hers and she had cried as they had exchanged vows. The second image was Hestia crying again, but this time she was throwing her belongings into suitcases and telling him it was all a mistake. She had told him that their whole relationship had been a mistake. Hestia was in love with someone else. She had always been in love with someone else. And that someone else was a woman. Thalia.

Elias *did* stab at her name then. In a pathetic attempt to make himself feel better, or maybe to remind himself that almost twenty-four months down the line he really ought to be moving on. Except being left like that, only six months after being married in front of everyone they knew, still kicked at him. And being left for a member of the opposite sex was the ultimate savaging of his Greek masculinity. He could imagine the raised eyes in the village, the whispers among the patrons of his mother and father's *cafeneon*, the not-so-whispered gossip of the village's president like a rally

73

bullhorn. Greek men didn't get left like that. Greek men absolutely never got left for a *woman*... if it didn't happen in mythology it didn't exist. Elias was hoping that Chad's case – his honest reason for being back on the island – was going to finally give him the strength to show his face in the village of Liakada again. Hestia was long gone. She and her new partner had left the island the second Hestia's suitcases were full and fastened. The divorce had been fought out by email. She had wanted an annulment. Elias had insisted on adultery. He got his way, but it hadn't made him feel any better. What *was* going to make him feel better? The short-term answer to that was simply 'winning'. The more men he could help settle complicated separations the better. With every small win – or rather multi-million-pound victory – he grew a little more in confidence. He just needed to find a way to work that confidence back into his personal life.

Hestia

Pros
- *She will not be there*

Cons
- *She will not be there*

Elias closed his laptop as his companion plumped back down into her seat, looking a little flustered. Immediately she picked up her notepad and pen and began writing... He strained his eyes to see. Egg? Watercress? Then her hand moved from forming letters to a shape. Another pig perhaps? What had any of that got to do with her job for the army?

'Is everything OK?' Elias asked her.

'Me?' Becky asked him. 'Am I OK? Yes. Yes, I'm fine. Perfectly fine.' She looked at her watch, a bead of perspiration above her top lip. 'Absolutely fine.'

'The plane is still late,' Elias said. 'It is lucky you do not have a connecting flight.'

For some reason, his comment prompted a laugh from the woman and more stabbing at the paper. The drawing seemed to be half-pig, half-chicken, with inky spots being bludgeoned into place.

'I do,' Elias continued.

'You do what?' Becky asked, her eyes flicking away from the paper and to him.

'I have a connecting flight.' He looked at his watch now. It was still an hour late. At this rate he really wasn't going to make his connection. 'I'm heading to Corfu.'

'Are you?' Becky asked, turning her body to him a little. 'With Olympic Air?'

'*Ne*,' he answered. 'Yes.'

'Oh, oh thank God,' Becky announced, relieved air rushing from her mouth. 'Because you said you travel all the time and I don't think you do the kind of travelling Petra does… with drinks served out of coconuts…'

'You have a connecting flight?' Elias asked her. 'I thought you were staying in Athens.' He lowered his voice. 'Exactly which part of Greece has a political problem the British army needs to assist with?'

'I… well…'

She seemed even more flustered now, her right hand still stabbing at the animal drawing. At any moment the nib of the pen might puncture the paper.

'Will they give us more than a bowl of beansprouts if we miss that plane?' Becky said, suddenly appearing half-terrified.

'You are heading to Corfu?' Elias asked her.

She nodded then inhaled rapidly before breathing out again, quick and hard.

'Do not worry,' Elias told her. 'I am sure they will hold the plane.' He wasn't sure. Usually they would delay it a little in these circumstances but an hour...?

'They will?' There was definite relief now and Becky finally stopped manically moving the pen like *she* was the crazy with murderous intentions in a horror movie. Perhaps she really did work for the military...

'Sure,' he said. 'There's nothing to worry about.' He smiled at her, watching her calm and settle back a little in her seat. She flipped down her tray table and began to write legibly again. Elias's attention went back to his laptop and he reopened the lid. There might be nothing to worry about here suspended peacefully in the skies, but he knew when he arrived back in the hamlet of Liakada nothing was likely to stay quiet for long.

Ten

Athens International Airport, Athens, Greece

'What do we do? Where do we go?' Becky was sweating. From the roots of her hair to in between her toes and she wasn't even out in stifling European air yet. But it seemed the more eagerly she leaned forward trying to encourage her fellow travellers to speed up their ridiculously slower-than-slug-speed overhead locker evacuation, the less actual movement occurred. 'Do we need to find someone? A stewardess? Someone at a desk when we get off the plane?' She looked over her shoulder at Elias who had only just started to put his computer into his bag. At least his shoes were back on now!

There was no sign of perspiration on him. She guessed it was his Greek acclimatisation. He looked just as cool and unfazed as he had done when he'd boarded. Meanwhile, even without looking, Becky knew she was one hot flush away from the appearance of past-its-eat-by-date ham left out of the fridge overnight.

'There should be an airline ambassador waiting for us on

the bridge,' Elias replied, slipping his bag over his shoulder, cool as a cucumber.

'Bridge? What bridge?' Becky asked him. 'Is there more than one bridge? How will we know which bridge?' If this woman in front didn't get her case out of the overhead bin and get on her way Becky was going to haul it down for her. Exactly how much faffing could one person be capable of?

'Relax,' Elias answered. 'The bridge is just the connecting tunnel from the plane to the end of the gate. Someone should be waiting for us there.'

'Should be?' Becky queried, dragging her case a few centimetres forward as the lady in front finally made a move. '"Should be" doesn't sound very concrete.'

'Most of the time there has been someone when I have made a connection here.'

'*Most* of the time,' Becky repeated. 'Like, most of the time, Tesco Finest steak is really good... or... black fly doesn't eat all the basil plants or...' *Sisters don't turn into complete bitches you barely recognise.* Becky closed her mouth and kept the internal monologue to herself. Besides, if she was going to keep this member of the armed forces ruse going, she needed to find better comparisons. 'Or most of the time twelve-gauge autoloaders don't jam up.' She sniffed, thanking her intimate knowledge of the script of *The Terminator*. 'I don't have time to be dealing with maybes today.'

'Then let's keep moving,' Elias instructed. He shifted out of their row, moving behind her, his body close as he swiftly and effortlessly retrieved his case. Still not any sign of even a sheen on his forehead. Dark hair perfect. Eyelashes obscenely long. Eyes an interesting whirl of blue-green... She hit her arm on a headrest and refocused. She needed to catch this flight. If she didn't, who knew, she might be in danger of losing this housesitting placement before she'd even set foot on the island. Could Ms O'Neill do that? Could she take the offer back if Becky didn't turn up on time?

Throwing a hurried 'thank you' at the crew standing at the doors of the aircraft – although she wasn't quite sure what she was thanking them for given the flight was late and the wine had been warm – Becky powered up the tunnel/bridge seeking someone who might resemble an ambassador. Ferrero Rocher anyone?

Despite her powerwalking that was almost akin to jogging, Elias was at her elbow, gliding along the incline with panache. Maybe the non-sweating, non-flustered appearance came with practice and years of varied travel arrangements. All it might take to derive pleasure from flight and everything it entailed was repetition. Although right now, with her next plane on the verge of departing without her on it, doing this all over again was about as appealing as resetting all her internet passwords. And if she was army-trained she really shouldn't be flagging at the first whiff of exertion. She stepped up the pace, almost expertly balancing Hazel's giant bag on her arm and giving guidance to her wheeled case now. But at the top of the slope she could already see a gathering and it was a gathering that seemed rather like a commotion. There were people in tabards – ambassadors? – and other passengers like her with bags and cases and seemingly no clue what was meant to happen next.

'Corfu! Do we have any other passengers for the Olympic Air flight to Corfu!'

'Yes!' Becky exclaimed, punching her arm up into the air. 'Yes, us! We are!'

'Come this way please and wait to the left-hand side.'

'What way?' Becky asked, looking to Elias.

Her companion spoke in Greek then, addressing one of the airline representatives. Becky looked from Elias to a woman with flowing curly Grecian-goddess hair and back again, trying to interpret what they were saying to one another. She didn't know any Greek.

And then suddenly Elias was taking hold of her hand and striding off with her.

'What's going on?' Becky asked. Was this the moment? Was it now when the mild-mannered estate agent turned abductor and all her fake background story and loose travelogue talk didn't matter a bit? She would never get to perfect effortless air travel. She would never get to ride Shelley's triplets' zip wire. She would never find out if she could perfect the catering pitch for the care home. She would never make up with Megan...

'We need to get to the gate,' Elias told her. 'I don't have a good feeling about this.' He still had her hand and was trying to guide them through the waiting splinter groups of people, to space, and hopefully the next part of the airport they needed to get to.

'Wait. Stop. What do you mean you don't have a good feeling about this?' Becky asked, grinding her espadrilles to the floor and trying to gain traction. He was still holding her hand and she remembered the last man who had held her hand. For eighteen months he had held her hand and then... he was holding someone else's instead. The less thinking about him the better. She let Elias go. 'You definitely said on the plane that everything would be fine.'

'I know,' he answered. 'But I think—'

'You think what?'

'I don't know,' Elias said with a sigh. 'Perhaps I am wrong. But I think they are going to make us wait until everyone meant to be connecting with the Corfu flight has departed the aircraft. And if they do that... if they make us all wait... I don't think they will hold the plane long enough for us all to make it to the gate.'

'Oh God,' Becky said, putting a hand to her perspiring forehead. 'Well, what do we do?'

'We could run for it,' Elias suggested. 'But we will have to go now. *Right* now.'

Petra. Where was Petra? She was meant to be getting this flight too. OK, so theoretically, Becky had no reason to feel any responsibility for a traveller she had shared one pre-toilet conversation with, but she hadn't seen her disembark yet, nor was she part of any of these slightly agitated groups.

'I don't know,' Becky said.

'You do not want to catch the flight?' Elias asked, brow furrowing. 'Before, you were behaving that your life might end if you do not make the flight.'

'Well,' Becky said, 'I don't think I was quite that dramatic. Besides, I am on very important... and secret... government business. It can be... stressful.' Who had she turned into? So many lies falling from her lips like she was an accomplished drug mule attached to a leading cartel... instead of someone who *just made sandwiches*. And she had actually told him she was on holiday from all the made-up 007 stuff.

'Everyone for the Corfu flight, you must wait here!' It was a tall, dark-haired man shouting this instruction. 'We wait until everyone has left the plane and then we go through the airport *together*.'

Becky looked to Elias then. 'This isn't good news, is it?'

'We are only going to be as fast as the slowest person,' Elias replied.

Becky turned around, sizing up who was left coming up the tunnel from their aircraft. A couple in their forties looked like they would be capable of putting a shift on to reach the gate. Two twenty-something lads might have giant backpacks that probably should have been checked luggage, but Becky reckoned they could motor if required – they were already in shorts and trainers. But then she watched them move to the ambassador who seemed to be collating passengers for the Santorini flight. And then it all went downhill. A family of six with two toddlers walking – barely – and two babes in arms, together with a pram and a buggy the male of the party was trying to put together while moving. Behind them were a man and woman possibly in their seventies, each with a walking stick. If either of those passengers were destined for Corfu, they were screwed in the hurrying stakes...

Becky watched Elias take his phone from the pocket of his jacket. Yes, *she* was sweating like a huskie in Dubai and the estate agent was still wearing a suit.

'What are you doing? We should definitely try to head to the gate.' Petra had come across as resourceful. She had survived Thailand – if those dodgy-spelt wristbands were genuine – and lived to get the T-shirt. She'd be fine. And it wasn't Becky's job to sister someone who wasn't her sister... Old habits apparently took longer than a week to get over.

'*Now* you want to go?' Elias asked, tapping at the screen.

'You basically said if we don't then we won't get the plane.' She let out a breath. 'I need to get the plane.' She didn't know quite what she did next if she didn't get the plane...

'OK,' Elias said, putting his phone away again. 'But you need to let me do the talking.'

'Hello!'

It was Petra, arriving at Becky's shoulder, her braids now immaculately pinned into a tight bun that looked like it had been wound into place by an Oribe style team.

'You're here,' Becky announced with a degree too much familiarity. 'I mean... I didn't see you get off the plane.'

'Well, I was doing my hair,' Petra said, pointing two fingers at her braids. 'No point rushing off when we're pretty much screwed for the next flight.'

'Do you think?' Becky asked, back to panicking again.

'Oh yeah,' Petra said with all the nonchalance of a seasoned backpacker. 'There's no way we're getting that plane.'

'Well,' Becky said, swallowing her fear, 'Elias is going to try and talk to the ambassador.'

'Whoa!' Petra said, slapping a hand down on Becky's sweaty forearm. 'Is *that* your plane hook-up?' She was gripping Becky tightly now, gaze trained on Elias's form. He seemed to be having an animated discussion with the airline representative that involved using his hands, arms and sunglasses for gesturing purposes.

'My what?' Becky asked.

'My plane hook-up was Marathon and he kissed like a

viper... you know... light, playful tongue at first but then desperate to poke the point home.' Petra sniffed. 'He's heading to Santorini. I'm going there, obvs, but in a few weeks, you know, after I'm completely done with Corfu.'

Becky swallowed. Petra made Corfu sound like a temporarily desirable dessert she intended to ingest until she felt sick. And as for Marathon... that couldn't have been his real name, could it?

'So, how does *your* guy kiss?' Petra asked, simultaneously pushing the straps of Hazel's bag further up Becky's arm then linking their arms together like they were about to commence skipping to the next gate.

'Oh... he's not... I don't know him... I mean... he's an estate agent.' Becky stopped talking before she said another word about her fake occupation. And although Hazel had mentioned single men on cruises, no one, not even Shelley, had mentioned 'plane hook-ups'. Perhaps there would be a chapter on it in *How to Find the Love of Your Life or Die Trying*.

'So, he's single and you're not interested?' Petra began fiddling with the bottom of her Nobody's Foo T-shirt.

'I... don't know that he's single.' She just knew that he was an estate agent, his name was Elias and he liked it cold. How pathetic must she seem? Almost four hours in a confined space and she only knew his name and occupation. Except everyone she had spoken to had warned her about sharing too much with strangers. 'I just sat next to him on the plane.'

'And you didn't even think about joining the Mile-High Club?!'

Becky looked at Petra's T-shirt. It was now tied in a knot

at her navel, the fabric tighter across her boobs and the weave of the material flush against her perfect figure.

'Well,' Petra said pulling a ChapStick out of the pocket of her skinny jeans, 'if you're not interested and he's on our next flight, I wouldn't mind a few minutes in the toilet with him.' She sighed, applying ChapStick to her eyebrows as well as her lips. 'I've nearly mastered wedging my arse between the tap and the hand towel dispenser. Although I'm sure the cubicles on Jetstar Asia are a few inches smaller than *any* other plane manufactured.'

Becky had no words. And then Elias returned, the expression on his face telling her all she needed to know.

'He is insisting we travel through the airport as a group,' Elias said with a sigh of frustration.

'Then we're fucked,' Petra announced. She stuck her hand out. 'Hi. I'm Petra. Are you single?'

And, just like that, Becky realised she had much more to learn about world exploration than what was written in any *Marco Polo* guide.

Eleven

'Does it say anything on your app?'

Becky was out of breath, but not too out of breath to ask Elias the same question she had been asking him intermittently since they had finally managed to get through passport control – snail-pace slow. Whenever a flight of stairs was encountered, the couple with walking sticks and the family with buggies all had to use lifts. This meant those not incapacitated rushed down the steps only to wait for the lift to deliver the remainder of their party an age afterwards. And no amount of trying to break ahead of the group seemed to be acceptable to their airline ambassador.

'Nothing,' Elias responded.

'He didn't look,' Petra announced. 'You didn't look.'

'There is no point in looking,' Elias insisted. 'We have to get through security first and then get to the gate.'

'There is a point. It might say they are holding the plane until a certain time and then we will have something to work to.' Petra readjusted her backpack. 'This one time, in Bangladesh, the pilot was actually sat on the tarmac eating *panta bhat* when we rocked up. We got on the plane and he finished his lunch before he got back on and flew us.'

'Could that happen here?' Becky asked, looking to Elias who still hadn't broken into any kind of a sweat. 'I mean... don't the Greeks like a siesta about now?'

'Siesta is in the early afternoon,' he answered. 'It is almost six now.'

'Is it? Bugger. They're not going to wait much longer. If it hasn't taken off already,' Petra continued. 'Maybe they're just pretending there's a chance we're going to get on it.'

'Why would they do that?' Becky asked. If she was soaking in her own bodily excretions for no reason she was not going to be amused.

Petra shrugged. 'Airlines do all sorts of shit. Like tell you they've run out of cheese and ham sandwiches because one of the cabin crew has earmarked the last one.'

'Your boarding pass is ready?' Elias asked.

'Yes, it's in my hand,' Becky replied. And that was sweaty too. She had been holding it carefully between thumb and forefinger for the last ten minutes in case the sweat started to make the ink on her name and seat number rub off. They were about to scan into a deserted security area. This had to be promising. If they zipped through here, they could be at the gate in mere minutes and on board and she wouldn't have to get in touch with Ms O'Neill at all. She might be slipping into her swimming costume and diving into that inviting pool in an hour or so... and right now, the thought of cool, refreshing water running over her shoulders and down her back was the best kind of daydream.

Elias scanned and was through the gate. Becky was next. Was this really happening? Was all her concern for nothing?

Bleep! She was through. She turned back to watch Petra scan her pass and then, no matter what the airline representative said, she was going to run for her life to the gate.

Just as Petra barrelled through the gate, rucksack almost getting caught up in the automation, a walkie-talkie crackled into life and their ambassador started talking into it.

'Let's go!' Petra exclaimed. 'While he's distracted!'

'Wait,' Elias said, holding his hand out as if he intended to stop anyone who tried to move. He seemed to be looking curiously at the airline man.

'We don't want to wait. We want to make this connection if there's a chance,' Petra said.

The talking into the two-way radio ceased and the man raised his arms in the air like he was about to conduct a philharmonic orchestra.

'Stop! Everybody stop!'

'Everybody stop?' Petra queried. 'What's he talking about? If those two with the walking sticks stop, they'll probably seize up and never be able to get going again.'

Elias said something in what Becky presumed was Greek. It sounded blunt and direct and was aimed at the guy in the tabard.

'What's happening?' Becky asked, shifting her espadrilles a little closer to Elias.

'Why do we have to go back to the desks?' It was Elias speaking English now. His question prompted others in the group to begin their own questioning of the man allegedly in charge. *Why weren't they scanning their boarding passes to head through security? Where had any sense of urgency gone? Why was no one moving at all?* Becky could feel this wasn't a good situation to be in. Something was afoot

– more than her sweaty toes in the pleather shoes.

'The plane has gone, hasn't it?' This was Elias too and as soon as the sentence was out into the airport air there was a collective gasp of despair from everyone in their group.

'We all need to keep calm and go back to the desks,' the man reiterated. He was whirling his arms now, like he was one of those crazy policemen directing traffic as if the road was on fire.

'Just tell us,' Elias ordered. 'Has the plane gone?!'

A general hubbub ensued, the largely previously mute party now all wanting answers and seemingly the representative was reluctant to give those answers. Until finally…

'I am afraid the plane has gone.'

Becky's heart sank. This was not a scenario she had envisaged when Hazel and Shelley were taking her through difficult eventualities that could occur while travelling. *Drink-spiking. Shark attack. Bumping into Lulu.* Apparently, Hazel had embarrassed herself at karaoke when Lulu was actually in the room. Becky had no real idea who Lulu was but the mortified look on Hazel's face even when she was retelling the story had been enough… But no one had seen a missed connection coming. What happened now?

Suddenly, amid a flurry of mobile phone gazing and backpack swinging, the two men in shorts and trainers were off, scanning back out of security and sprinting off to who knew where.

'Where are they going?' Petra asked out loud. Then her eyes seemed to come alive and she stepped backwards towards the scanners again. 'Is there *another* flight we can get on?'

'Please,' the man in airline livery began again. 'We all

need to return to the desks where we can help you further.'

'Is there another flight?' This time Petra was asking Elias.

Elias looked at his watch then nodded. 'Yes, but with Sky Express...'

'Well, what are we waiting for?!' Petra exclaimed, scanning her pass and looking to Becky as the gate slid away and allowed their exit back out of security. 'We can get on it.'

'And it is leaving in fifteen minutes,' Elias answered, still as cool as a cucumber. 'By the time you have made it to the desk and bought a ticket, you will not make it to the gate and onto the plane.'

'But those guys thought they could—'

'They won't,' Elias said with authority. 'And I suggest that we head back to the airline desk and hope they can book us onto the flight early tomorrow morning before the guys realise they are out of luck. Two less passengers to worry about.'

'Shit! You're right!' Petra exclaimed. 'Come on, Becks, get a shift on and scan out!'

'What happens when we get to the desk?' Becky asked Elias as they took it in turns to scan their boarding passes. 'We try to book on to another flight and then...'

'And then,' Elias began, 'you should call your superiors. Tell them that whatever mission you were supposed to arrive to settle in Corfu, that it will mostly likely have to wait twenty-four hours.'

Twelve

It was simply an inconvenience. That was all Elias should see it as. As annoying as it was not to arrive in Corfu tonight, it was the fault of the airline and not the universe trying to tell him something.

He hung his jacket up in the wardrobe and selected a pale pink short-sleeved shirt from his case. It was hot outside and currently he was cooling off thanks to the hotel air-conditioning. It was a standard room, but it was spacious enough and it was with the compliments of the airline. They were putting up the thirteen travellers (including the two who had tried to get a flight off the mainland with Sky Express) at the five-star hotel right opposite the airport. Tomorrow morning at 8.30 a.m. they would be on the next flight to Corfu. He slipped on the shirt and looked at his watch. Six-thirty and downstairs there was a complimentary meal waiting for him. Except he wasn't sure he wanted to stay in the hotel all evening. It had been a while since he had visited Athens for anything but business. It had been

91

even longer since he had walked through the Plaka district and taken in the Acropolis. The very last time had been with Hestia. Suddenly it was all he wanted to do. See the beauty of his nation's capital through fresh eyes. He began to fasten the buttons of his shirt with renewed vigour.

'What d'you mean you're not in fucking Corfu?'

'Shelley! Language!'

'Have I got to speak Greek because Becky's in Greece? I don't know any Greek!'

'I meant your swearing. Sorry, dear, say what you said again and I'll turn the radio down.'

Becky sighed. She had phoned the landline for It's A Wrap in the hope that Megan might answer. It was four-thirty in the UK, Hazel would be on the cusp of going home, Shelley shouldn't even be there. Now she was worried that something was wrong...

'Where's Megan?' She internally cursed herself for asking. One day away from the business and she was still unable to be the young, brave independent traveller she longed to be. She was still fretting about a sister who was perfectly able to do life without her and was forever saying as much...

'Oh, she headed off early, dear. Some double-glazing networking evening with Dean.'

Dean loved a good networking event. Becky had been to several with him and it always involved Dean telling his favourite jokes – ones everyone had heard before but were too polite to say.

'That's why I'm here,' Shelley blasted. It did sound as if they were on speakerphone. Either that or Shelley was snatching the receiver from Hazel and vice versa. Those two taking turns never worked very well, particularly with the sharper knives...

'Oh... well... I missed my connection so—'

'You missed your connection?!'

'Fuck!'

'It's OK,' Becky said before any more swears could leave Shelley's lips. 'Well, it was a bit daunting at first, but I'm not the only one. We all missed our connection because the plane was delayed. So, we're here in Athens... at a rather nice hotel.' She fanned her hand out over the crisp white linen on the queen-sized bed, enjoying the feel of the luxury thread count. 'And I'm booked onto the next flight to Corfu in the morning.'

'They gave you a hotel for *free*?' Shelley asked.

'Yes,' Becky replied. 'And it's actually five stars. There's a free dinner tonight and breakfast in the morning and there's a swimming pool with a view of the runway.'

'Five stars,' Hazel breathed. 'My favourite kind of constellation.'

'I've never seen a hotel with more than three and the last time I saw one of them was *that* weekend in Sussex. Frank's convinced those three stars was why we had triplets. Can you imagine if he'd paid for a Hilton?!'

'So, I'm OK,' Becky carried on, taking a breath of the cooling air. 'Just not in Corfu yet.'

'And have you called the owner of the villa to let her know you're delayed?' Hazel inquired.

'I don't have her number,' Becky admitted. 'Which I realise now is really, really stupid. But I didn't expect I'd need anything other than an email contact. And I've emailed her, of course, and I've given her my number, but I haven't heard anything yet.' She did feel a little uneasy about that, but she was trying to put it to the back of her mind. Ms O'Neill sounded like a very busy woman from her tone in their brief exchanges. It was likely she hadn't had a minute to check her email. And how much difference would twelve hours make to their arrangement? It wasn't as if housesitting was like babysitting. She wasn't leaving a small child unattended overnight... just a few pots of bougainvillea that might need watering.

'I wouldn't worry,' Shelley said loudly. 'I'd be making the most of that swimming pool and spa. Is it all inclusive? Because I'd be also making the most of the bar right now instead of talking to us.'

'Is everything OK there?' Becky winced at her own question. Of course everything was OK. She had only been gone a day.

'Well, Mrs Mount—' Shelley's sentence was cut short and there was a loud noise that sounded very much like someone had dropped a rolling pin against stainless steel. Either that or there was a problem with the phone line.

'Sorry, dear, the line went a bit funny then,' Hazel's voice took over.

'Is something wrong with Mrs Mount?' Becky asked. Mrs Mount was one of It's A Wrap's best customers. Not only did she order lunch for herself and all her employees at her Make Do and Mend sewing and alteration business every day, but she always made sure It's A Wrap catered for her personal parties and the functions undertaken by the local council, of which Mrs Mount was a huge part.

'No, no. Everything is tickety-boo,' Hazel insisted.

'We have to tell her.' It was Shelley again – in a rather audible attempt at a stage-whisper.

'Tell me what?' Becky exclaimed. 'Please! If something's wrong you need to let me know!'

'It's nothing, dear.'

'Hazel, Mrs Mount is a very important client. If she's unhappy then…' Becky began.

'Megan took the sesame, sunflower and poppy seed bread off the bakery order. She said not enough customers were ordering it so, it was coming off our range.'

This was insane. Mrs Mount had that particular bread every day. Mrs Mount brought in so much business. Megan must know that. OK, so it wasn't one of their biggest repeat orders, but it went wonderfully with thick slabs of strong, creamy cheddar with fresh chives and a generous smear of garlic and black pepper aioli.

'She phoned up to complain,' Hazel admitted. 'But I'm going to sort everything out, dear.'

'What did you give her instead?' Becky inquired. She was trying not to let the ball of stress lodged in her chest rattle around her ribcage. She was on holiday. This was not *her* drama to find a conclusion for.

'Rye,' Shelley admitted. 'That was my idea, but Mrs Mount said it was too thick and too dark and she—'

'Couldn't taste the chives,' Becky guessed.

'Yes,' Shelley said. 'That's exactly what she said.'

What should she do? The easiest thing would be to tell the women to get the sesame, sunflower and poppy seed back on the bakery's order so they had some fresh in the morning. But that would mean for them to override

Megan's instructions and she didn't want to get either of them into trouble.

'Use wholemeal for her sandwich tomorrow,' Becky said immediately. 'Exactly the same recipe she always has, but add just a little bit of fresh mint, the tiniest bit. Then, if Megan really won't get the bread back on the order, you need to get hold of some chia seeds. Try the wholefood shop first, but if you can't get them there, order them from Amazon.'

'Will that work?' Shelley asked.

'You need to be honest with Mrs Mount,' Becky said firmly. 'Tell her that the new bread you're using is the freshest yet, and say that chia seeds are full of protein and nutrients and they can help with tiredness. Say this new sandwich is going to make her able to stay awake during those long council meetings and increase her focus when she's working at the sewing machine.'

'But you just said be honest with her,' Shelley commented.

'I *am* being honest,' Becky said. 'That's what chia seeds can do.'

'Jesus! I might start eating them!'

'Just keep her happy,' Becky begged. 'She has a lot of influential friends. Sometimes putting yourself out a little to personalise the sandwich experience is worth it.' If only Megan knew that this personalisation was what was keeping the food empire going…

'Are you writing this down, Hazel?' Shelley asked. 'Mint and chia seeds.'

'Yes, dear,' Hazel said.

'Tell me, while I'm on the phone,' Becky said as she lay back on the comfy, cool covers. 'Did you see Milo at the hospital today?'

'Yes I did,' Shelley answered straightaway. 'He looked dreadful. Pale. No energy. I wanted to give him a spare muffin I had.'

'Tomorrow, try making his beef tongue focaccia with the lentil puree instead of butter and add some finely chopped red peppers and spinach. Tell him I've created it just for him.' Becky sighed. 'And don't tell Megan, obviously.'

'Obviously, boss,' Shelley replied.

Boss. She really wasn't. Becky sat back up and caught sight of herself in the mirror above the dressing table. There was no doubt she looked a little travel-weary but there was something else reflecting back at her now. Inner strength? Bravery? Perhaps a missed connection had awoken something inside her.

'I've got to go,' she told her friends. 'I'm not sure what time they serve dinner until and I'll need an early night before the flight tomorrow.'

'You will *not* have an early night,' Shelley ordered her. Becky could imagine the expression on her face. 'You will head to the luxurious bar with the expensive liqueurs and you will get royally five-star off your face on everything from the top shelf.'

'I don't think it's all-inclusive. Particularly for those of us who are getting the room for free.'

'Well then, get royally shitted on the cheapest, strongest booze they have.'

'But don't have too much *ouzo*. It can be quite potent if you're not used to it,' Hazel said.

'By not much, Hazel means not quite a whole bottle...'

Becky smiled as she said goodbye to them. They were excited for her trip and she needed to start getting properly excited too. Tomorrow she would be on the island of Corfu about to spend a few weeks in the sunshine being a home caretaker. The only thing to make it more perfect would be for the homeowner to respond to her emails. But there was nothing she could do to make that happen more quickly. At this stage she may as well indulge in that drink Shelley was so insistent on. After all, when on holiday…

Thirteen

Mesoghaia Restaurant, Sofitel Hotel, Athens

'I have to say,' Petra said through a mouthful of her third dessert, 'as good as the free noodles were in Thailand, this gig is even better.' She scooped another spoon full of berries and thick yoghurt into her mouth. 'I know the drinks aren't all-inclusive, but this free nosh makes up for it.'

The food *was* good, as you would expect from a five-star hotel. It wasn't completely Greek, but it *was* completely divine. From oversized white ceramic bowls of salad leaves mixed with croutons and seeds, quinoa and couscous, to thick sizzling medallions of meat in rich sauces, perfectly cooked pasta and roasted potatoes, there was something to tempt even the fussiest of eaters. Becky had opted for some beef in a rich red-coloured gravy with a few potatoes and a little salad on the side. She had indulged in a large glass of a sweet white wine though and it was slipping down extremely well.

'Are you having pudding, Elias?' Petra called across the table.

Becky sipped at her wine and watched Elias turn his head away from his phone. He was sitting a little way along from their table – no laptop this time – but seemed engrossed in his mobile phone. He had changed out of the corporate jacket and was wearing a pink-coloured shirt that went wonderfully with his olive skin tone…

'No,' he answered. 'I am heading out when I have finished this beer.' Instead of the sumptuous feast she – and particularly Petra – had devoured, Elias had picked at a *meze* of olives, cheese and what looked like cucumber.

'Heading out?' Petra queried. 'Out where? Because there doesn't seem to be much else but runway around here.' She winked. 'Or do you know some secret hotspots not on the traditional tourist trail?'

'I know Athens,' Elias replied nonchalantly.

'You're going in?' Petra gasped like he had announced he might be set to knock on the front door of Number 10 and run for Prime Minister.

'It is a while since I have seen the Acropolis or taken time to admire the view of the city.'

'He's going in!' Petra exclaimed, all excitement and swinging plaits now the bun had been unfurled. Becky's hair was still a little damp from her shower, but it did feel good to have washed the air travel – and sweat – from her skin. She wasn't sure she did travel glam quite as well as Petra did though. Petra seemed to look fresh and good-to-go in pretty much any scenario. She was wearing a different T-shirt now, neon pink with palm trees and the word 'Swingers' written in electric blue – presumably, or rather, hopefully, the name of an exotic bar. Becky had changed into one of the dresses she hadn't expected to be wearing quite this soon into her trip. It was pale lemon in colour with a scooped neckline and an A-line skirt that grazed her knees. The espadrilles had been swapped out for a pair of flat gladiator-style sandals Hazel had made her buy from Matalan.

'We're in!' Petra announced. 'I couldn't eat another thing anyway and I want to drink Greek beer in a Greek bar up a dirty alleyway no one but the locals know about.'

'What?' Becky had suddenly seemed to be included in this idea. An idea that was Elias's. A group outing he might not be up for. A group outing she wasn't sure *she* was up for. She had planned to head back to her room after the wine and get an early night seeing as they needed to be at the airport for 6 a.m. 'I… wasn't going to…'

'You weren't going to do what?' Petra asked, turning her body in her seat and scrutinising Becky. Petra did have a skill for putting people on the spot. Perhaps 'skill' was too complimentary.

'I was going to… go for a swim in the pool. Apparently it has views of the runway.' Now she sounded ridiculous. Who passed up the chance of going into the hub of Athens and seeing the might and beauty of one of the Wonders of the World? For sleep. Albeit in sheets with a super-high thread count. Embracing her inner explorer was what she needed to do. As she'd whispered to herself in the mirror earlier.

'Anyway,' Becky carried on, 'perhaps Elias would rather go alone. I'm sure he has friends in the city. He might want to…'

Petra turned herself and her body back towards Elias. 'Do you want to go alone? And are you single? Because you didn't answer earlier.'

Becky coughed at Petra's brazenness – in shock and slight

admiration – and covered her mouth with the rim of her wineglass. How did she just come out with things like that?

'You have not been to Athens before?' Again, Elias had made no answer to Petra's status inquisition.

'No, I haven't,' Petra immediately replied. 'But I always planned to. When I'm done with the islands. Right now, I'm all about the secret beaches and water so clear you can perfect your make-up in it. But tonight is a bonus, isn't it? A missed flight that's going to gift us a night in one of the most beautiful cities in the world.' She looked straight at Becky. 'If we can bear to tear ourselves away from runway vistas.'

'You are welcome to join me,' Elias told them. As if the poor guy had been given any real choice in the matter! 'But I will be taking the metro.'

'Ooo ace!' Petra exclaimed. 'I love a dirty train. And who wants to be cooped up in an extortionately priced taxi when you could be side-by-side with real Athenian life?' She sniffed. 'Is it true that one time there was a guy who actually took his horse on the metro?'

'It was not me,' Elias answered. Becky watched him finish his beer.

'Will you show us winding streets and white houses where people invite you in for whatever they've cooked for the evening?' Petra had got to her feet now and was shimmying into another backpack that was only slightly smaller than the one she was carting about earlier. And how could she even think about food when she had already eaten bigger portions than a hungry great white shark? Becky finished up her wine and picked up her handbag that was way smaller than Hazel's travel bag.

'He still hasn't said he's not single,' Petra whispered,

ducking her head into Becky's space. 'Did you hear?'

'I didn't hear him say he *was* single either,' Becky answered.

'I know, right? Totally a man of mystery. I love it!' Petra grinned. 'Come on, Becky, we're going into the city to see the sights with a hot guy. What's not to get excited about?' She linked their arms and giggled.

Bluntly direct or not, Becky couldn't deny that Petra was absolutely right.

Fourteen

Plaka District, Athens

'There was a man playing a violin with a cat! I actually can't believe it! I could die tomorrow and be completely happy now!'

Elias couldn't help but smile at Petra's enthusiasm. It had been random, seeing the instrument-playing old man on the train, his furry pet by his side, ears alert as if listening to every note. But it was typically Greek. Greece was the very epitome of crazy sometimes. There was life and then there was Greek life. The same but slightly madder.

He sucked in a breath as they arrived on the cobbled streets of the Plaka area. It was bustling, it was still humid and tourists congregated to take photos of the narrow lanes filled with shops and the ancient church plumped right in the middle of everything. This church –*Panagia Kapnikarea* – was one of the oldest churches in Athens and it never failed to impress Elias. With its three different cream brick sections, a domed tower at its centre topped with terracotta tiles, it was a reminder of the city's ancient past amid the taller, towering newer buildings around it.

'It doesn't look like part of a city.' This came from Becky. She was standing on the cobbles, taking everything in in a little more subdued way to Petra. 'It looks like a village that's been put inside it.'

Elias had never thought of it that way before, but she was right. Plaka was the most visited area of Athens for a reason and that reason wasn't just because here was the Acropolis, it was also because of the quaintness of its streets. It was like a throwback to simpler times. For all of Athens' business smarts and modern movement, visitors were always drawn to the ancient Greece and the old-fashioned Greece – the home of gods and *gyros*, where you still couldn't flush a piece of toilet paper down the pipes.

He could have come here alone. It would have been as easy to refute Petra's eagerness as it had been to go along with it. But what would coming here alone really have been like? No matter what he might have told himself, he would have moped. He would have gazed up at the proud monument glowing amid the skyline and he would have thought about Hestia and all the hurt he'd endured. Even now, all this time having gone by, he still thought back to the workings of his relationship with Hestia. Had there been signs he had missed? Were there critical moments he should have noticed, times maybe when Hestia had eluded to what was going on beneath her surface? More than the being left, what hurt Elias the most was his lack of realisation, the utter shock at what had transpired so quickly. He had been completely clueless to something his wife had no doubt been struggling with her whole adult life.

The day Hestia had told him she was leaving, she couldn't have sounded or looked more devastated. She had wept and apologised over and over, physically reeling from saying the words, while he had instantaneously solidified into stone. The complete bolt from the blue, the impact of her words sinking into him, had turned him cold. Cold and oh so angry. He'd had no capacity to feel anything else. He had simply never seen this coming.

Yes, being here with Petra and Becky tonight was giving him a purpose he only just realised he desperately needed.

'You think this is like a village,' Elias said to Becky. 'You wait until you see the houses along the walk to the Acropolis.'

'White-washed walls, Greek-blue shutters, hopefully more men playing violins with cats. Cats that dance to the violin would be amazing, I'm not gonna lie,' Petra told them both. She danced a jig on the spot.

Elias shook his head, a smile on his lips. Maybe this was exactly what he needed before he returned to Corfu. Reconnecting with his heritage first, creating a new Plaka experience by showing its charms to two people who had not been here before, then seeing his parents might not be as awkward as he felt it was going to be. 'Come,' he said. 'It is this way.'

Becky couldn't believe she was in Athens. The inside of the terminal had obviously always been the plan from the moment she found there were no direct flights out of London with space at this late notice, but she had never in a million years expected to be walking the streets of vibrant yet cosy, Plaka. It was amazing. It was exhilarating.

It was like nowhere she had been before. Restaurants full to bursting, their tables and chairs spilling out onto the street, glowing table lamps amid diners nibbling on crusty fresh bread or skewers thick with grilled chicken, purple red onion and green peppers, and waiters rushing back and forth perspiring in the humidity as they served. There was chatter, rising up from the cobbles, the music of an accordion, carefree smoking and a laid-back ambience that wafted from every eatery and bar. Becky wanted to imbed everything into her mind in case she never got to come here again. This could be a once-in-a-lifetime visit. That made it even more special.

'Come on!' Petra called from a few yards away. 'We're going to be walking the path that actual gods have trodden.'

Without any doubt this was so much better than a swim in the hotel pool with views of a landing strip. She stepped on to catch up her companions.

'Why are you going to Corfu?' Petra asked Elias. Becky stayed a step behind them, happy to admire everything they were passing. Leafy vines grew up crumbling buildings, mopeds whizzed up narrow lanes and alleyways and men tried to sell braided bracelets with the promise of late-night African music...

'I am on business,' Elias replied. 'And you?'

'I'm on business too,' Petra answered. 'The business of seeing the world. It's tough AF, but someone has to do it. What's your business?'

'Petra,' Becky said. 'Has anyone ever told you you ask quite a lot of questions?'

Petra went quiet for a minute and briefly Becky wondered if she had offended her. She hadn't meant to do that, but she wasn't used to sharing the miniature of life with anyone and she knew, after Elias, it was likely *she* would be investigated next. And what would she have to say? She was here because she had more or less lost her friend Tara to a Sagittarius who apparently cooked better and swore a lot less than Gordon Ramsay and she'd had a monumental falling-out with her only sibling to rival anything the Gallagher brothers could serve up in the angsty stakes?

'No, actually,' Petra responded. 'Although there was this one woman in Morocco who objected to me asking what her tattoo was meant to be. But, in fairness, you really couldn't tell what the fuck it was and I looked from literally every angle trying to work it out before I asked her.'

'What was it?' Elias asked.

'No clue,' Petra answered. 'She wouldn't tell me. I guess that will forever be one of life's great mysteries. So, do you have any tattoos?'

'Petra!' Becky exclaimed. She was cringing now. And she also knew the answer. Elias did have tattoos. Well, at least one, but in this change of shirt it wasn't as apparent as it had been on the plane. Actually, she wanted Elias to answer this question as tattoos had always intrigued her a little. What could mean so much that you wanted to have it inked on your body forever? Or perhaps some people – namely her – thought too deeply about it. Maybe people just liked a picture or a pattern and simply did it. For fun. Without it getting too deep and meaningful.

'Do *you* have a tattoo?' Elias had turned the question without providing his answer.

'Of course. Doesn't everyone?' Petra raised an eyebrow. 'Where do you think mine is?'

Oh God. Was this Petra flirting? No wonder she had hooked up with someone called Marathon. She really did have no filter.

'I think,' Elias replied, 'that wherever you have a tattoo, its location is personal to the owner unless they want to share it.'

Petra stuck out her wrist as they continued to walk upwards. 'Here. Here's mine.'

Elias looked to her arm and Becky stepped alongside too, reading the ink. 'Peter?'

'Yeah, I know,' Petra said with a laugh. 'I've heard all the jokes.'

'Is Peter your dad's name?' Becky inquired. Or perhaps it was a boyfriend or a hook-up she met over noodles…

'No such luck,' Petra answered. 'It's meant to say "Petra" but the tattooist was Indian and about eighty and he heard me wrong and, well, I was too drunk to notice until it was a done deal. Still,' she said, putting her thumbs into the loopholes of her jeans, 'what's life without a little bit of variety, right?'

The incline increased and suddenly the streets turned from streets into narrowing lanes. The higher they climbed the slimmer the walkways seemed to become. The buildings also began to change. Gone were the elaborate detailed architecture of below, instead they were replaced with tiny homes, most palely painted, large flagstones with white cement like crazy paving leading the way. It was as if this place was yet another village, dropped into the metropolis and unlike any of the other surroundings.

'Gosh,' Becky exclaimed. The walls were really closing in now. This path they were following wound between miniscule houses, some with their front doors wide open emanating food smells that quirked her entirely full stomach into wondering if in fact it did have extra capacity…

'It almost feels like we could just walk right inside someone's home,' Petra said, fair head almost creeping over thresholds in a bid to look into tiny kitchens. You could hear conversations and music from radios.

'This is Anafiotika,' Elias told them. 'A lot of people say that this area reminds them of the villages of the Greek islands.'

'The white cubed houses are a bit like Santorini,' Becky replied. The Santorini she had seen in Hazel's cruise brochures in any case.

'Yes,' Elias agreed. 'This is true.'

Suddenly Becky's foot skidded on the path and she had to put her hand out to the wall to steady herself. Luckily the walls were so close.

'You are OK?' Elias asked, stopping their ascent and looking at her as Petra powered on ahead like she knew exactly where she was going or didn't really care where she ended up.

'Yes,' Becky said with a nod. 'I'm fine. My foot slipped for a second, that's all.'

'The stones, they get worn,' Elias remarked as Becky stepped up to walk alongside him. 'When they get worn, they get shiny. It is the same in the Acropolis.'

'The path is so narrow,' Becky commented as they rounded a corner. And then she stopped, her body suddenly flush against Elias's as the path petered out into a walkway with only room for one person to pass. His skin against hers was a surprise and his body was warm. There were no aromas of food in the air now, simply the delicious scent of sandalwood, jasmine and manliness. Becky swallowed, caught between inching her arm back and disconnecting them or leaving it exactly where it was and taking a moment to appreciate all his handsome. He *was* handsome. And if she was Petra – or Hazel – she might have made a move. *What* move, she had no idea, and the fact they were literally gelled together with humidity in this tight space meant there weren't many moves she would actually be capable of making. It was almost difficult to breathe without clashing rib cages…

'I am sorry,' Elias said, finally shifting sideways a little then stepping up to disengage them. 'It is a while since I have taken this walk. I always forget exactly where the path does this.'

'That's OK,' Becky said with a laugh. She really *really* wished he hadn't seen the copy of Hazel's relationship book. He probably thought she was desperate now. Had maybe invented the foot-slipping situation… Still, Petra was here. If Elias *was* single and looking for a hook-up, Petra was a much more suitable candidate for him. She was adventurous and youthfully gorgeous and a little bit crazy. Becky didn't have half of Petra's confidence and she was still finding her feet with who she was in this new travelling scenario. Did she even *want* romance in her life? She hadn't actually thought further than that it might be nice to be included in couple's dinner parties if she had a partner, but she probably shouldn't make that the whole reason for wanting a relationship…

'Christ! I'm on top of the world!'

It was undoubtedly Petra's voice screaming from above them and Elias shared a smile with her.

'She is like a child,' Elias said shaking his head.

'Do you think she's found another violinist with a cat?' Becky asked.

'I hope not. I think she might scare them.'

'What is at the top of this path?' Becky wanted to know.

'Come and see,' Elias replied, smiling again.

Fifteen

Anafiotika, Athens

Becky couldn't believe her eyes. Standing in front of a rather unsubstantial fence surrounded by bushes and other curling green shrubs, Athens was laid out like a picnic blanket of muted Lego bricks before her, the sun starting to go down. Half the panorama was in shade, making it seem like the tops of the buildings were blue and grey. The other section was illuminated, creams and browns and stretching out so far and wide. She had never seen something so vast from a viewpoint anything like this before. And then there was a hump of greenery to the right, a hill in the middle of all the buildings looking so out of place.

'It's incredible,' Becky breathed. 'It's so vast and I feel so small. Like a tiny ant looking down on it all.' She almost *couldn't* breathe. She wanted to take a photo and a video, but she knew neither were going to do this vista justice. You had to be here. You had to stand in the midst of it letting it soak into your soul.

'Is that Mount Lycabettus?' Petra asked, already leaning

over way too much and now pointing with a fully stretched arm too.

'Yes,' Elias said. 'And it might look small from where we are here, but it stands three hundred metres above sea-level. Nine hundred and nine feet.' He pointed at the lump of green which Becky now noticed had a craggy peak to it. Even from here you could see it dwarfed the properties around it.

'You really are our tour guide,' Petra said. 'Is that what you do for a job?'

'No,' Elias replied but said nothing further. *He had told her he was an estate agent.* Why couldn't he tell Petra that and stop her endless questions?

'What do you do for a job?' Petra asked, skipping over to Becky and dragging her into a position for a selfie with the view as a background.

Oh shit. She should come clean about not being in the army. Right now. It was a lie she should never have trotted out in the first place.

'Becky cannot tell you what she does,' Elias said as he moved up next to them. 'It is confidential.'

'Ooo, now I really want to know!' Petra put a braid into her mouth and sucked. 'Are you a prostitute? You know, not one of those ones who stand on street corners wearing clothes that look like the 1980s threw up all over them. I mean one of the ones who suck off politicians and pop stars in classy hotels.'

'Petra!' Becky exclaimed in utter horror. 'Keep your voice down!'

'Oh my God! I guessed it right, didn't I?! Well, you're a dark horse. I didn't really have you pegged for that when you said you hadn't ever had sex in a plane toilet.'

'I'm in the army!' Becky shouted quickly. 'Not the sex trade!'

Her face felt like it was a member of the scotch bonnet family and she could only imagine what Elias must be thinking. Petra didn't seem to find *anything* inappropriate subject matter. And they were virtual strangers. Plane passengers who happened to miss the same flight and been given accommodation in the same hotel. Becky chanced a glance at Elias and saw he had an amused look on his face. *Great*.

'The army?' Petra said, screwing up her face as if 'the army' was gone-off chicken no longer fit for human consumption. 'To be honest the sex trade was more believable. What are you? A captain or something? Sitting behind a desk all day planning assaults?'

'I can't discuss it,' Becky insisted. 'No matter how many times you ask me.'

'Is that a challenge?' Petra asked, tilting her head a little.

'Come,' Elias said. 'Let us go and see the Acropolis.'

They didn't have to go far until they were in the perfect place to take in the view of Greece's most famous monument. Lit up in the last of the day's golden glow, the relic shone like the iconic star of Athens it was. Those crumbling columns constantly being maintained and restored to ensure none of the history was lost, stood proud above the city just as they had thousands of years ago. And the scenery hadn't changed in the slightest since Elias had last stood here... with Hestia.

Taking a breath of the still-humid night air, he remembered holding her hand at this very spot and believing that their love would endure anything that life threw at them, exactly like the monument above them. When that sentiment had struck he had been thinking about the everyday kind of rows about meal choices or what to watch on the television, hard monetary times or disciplining their children. He had not thought about someone arriving in Hestia's affections and destroying their marriage. Endurance was possibly a singular thing. Like with the Acropolis. It wasn't as if this mighty ruin had been partnered with anyone in its lifetime. It was strong and powerful all by itself. And that's where his focus should be. Building his business. Doing what he was good at. Avoiding what he obviously wasn't so skilled at. Like relationships.

'It's awesome. And when I stick an Insta filter on it it's going to look even better!' Petra announced.

Only this girl would think about putting a photo filter on something that was already completely perfect in his eyes.

'A filter!' Becky exclaimed. 'How can you put a filter on it? It's so beautiful just as it is right now.' As if to enhance her point, Becky began taking more photos, her fingers on the screen of her phone, zooming in and trying to get a close up, or maybe something a little more atmospheric.

'Everything looks better with a filter,' Petra said. 'I mean the sea in Thailand was obvs turquoise, but with a filter on it, it looked a touch *more* beautiful… plus, everyone does it.'

'I don't,' Becky answered. 'Otherwise people will be expecting something that looks like one thing when you've told them it looks like something else. My sister put a filter on a tuna and beetroot wrap once for our website and the beetroot looked like it could double for a bloody liver in *Holby City*.'

She had a sister. Who did things with beetroot and tuna. And had she said 'our' website. Elias suspected that Becky's job in the army might not be everything she had made it out to be. He sensed a nervousness from her – and obviously there was also the stabbing at pieces of paper and drawing animals without realising it – but what was it she was nervous about?

'And I expect you've seen your fair share of bloody livers on tour with your regiment,' Petra piped up. 'What does your sister do?'

'She...' Becky paused. 'She just makes sandwiches.'

Hadn't some of the words Becky had been bludgeoning with her pen onboard the flight related to food? *Drink.* Suddenly his throat felt dry and he longed for another beer. And here, in this district, there was only one place he wanted to go.

'Do you want to see somewhere else the Athenians love?' he asked his two companions.

'Is it where the locals hang out?' Petra asked, wide-eyed. 'Does it feature in *Lonely Planet*?'

'I think you'll both like it.'

Sixteen

'This place! It's absolutely lit!' Petra shouted, bottle of Fix beer poised for the next swig.

They were sitting on nothing more than cushions, coloured cushions – bright pink, green, blue – that had been sprinkled on top of steep steps that led from the road at the bottom that went back to Monastiraki Square and their metro station, to the start of the incline to the Acropolis. At each side of the cut through the rock were bars and tavernas, alive with customers eating, drinking and smoking beneath giant canopies, some framed by fairy lights. The whole ensemble resembled a chilled out yet buzzy party half-hidden from the rest of the city. It was like a secret exclusive hangout you felt lucky to have an invitation to.

'We can see if there is a table free inside if you would prefer a chair,' Elias said. He was looking like a cover model for perfectly chilled right now, again no perspiration apparent, feet resting on the step below them. Although the cushions weren't the most well-padded, Becky didn't want to go inside or find a table under an umbrella, she wanted to stay sitting right here, the absolute best place for people watching. The Greek world was all around – young, old, every age in between – every single one of the patrons seeming relaxed and content. The vibe was laidback, without stress, full of good humour.

'Are you kidding?' Petra said, beer dribbling down her chin. 'I'm literally sat in everybody's path here. I can see *everything* and *everyone*.'

For once Becky agreed wholeheartedly with her. She took a sip of her beer. This one was particularly nice, with a sweet undertone that complemented any harshness.

'Aww! Hello kitty! Aren't you cute?' Petra put down her beer bottle on the step next to her and picked up a tiny kitten. Its fur was mainly white with black splodges, and it relaxed into Petra's lap, immediately rubbing its head against her stomach then standing up and looking for more affection. It was sweet.

'Are you a cat lady, Becks?' Petra asked, rubbing the kitten under its chin.

What was that supposed to mean? The term 'cat lady' was always used in TV shows when talking about a desperate, single, left-on-the-shelf-forever woman with as much chance of getting a date as a Mother Superior. Was that how Petra saw her? Petra didn't even know about Hazel's book in her carry-on. But Elias did…

'I like cats,' Becky answered. 'But I wouldn't want to live with them… just them… on my own… for life… or anything.' That had answered the question and probably made her sound insane. She took a swig of her beer while her cheeks started to radiate enough heat to grill a kebab.

'Elias?' Petra asked, lifting the cat up and pressing her nose to its face. 'Cats or dogs?'

He shook his head. 'You English. Because I come from Corfu you think everyone is like the Durrell family? Remember, *they* were English like you.'

'And you haven't answered the question.' Becky hadn't meant to say that. Why had she said that? It was supposed to be an internal discussion only her brain could hear. But Elias did seem very good at not answering any questions posed to him. That was mysterious.

Petra laughed, coddling the cat like it was a newborn she had just birthed. 'Becks is right. You didn't answer. And you don't answer very much at all. What are you hiding? Because if you think you can avoid telling us anything about who you are because you think you're going to have your way with both of us when you get back to the hotel you can think again. I don't do threesomes.' Petra sniffed. 'Not that you're not attractive, Becky, but you know… sharing an aubergine, it's a step too far for even me.'

She wanted to be a cat lady. Kittens of the world unite and take Becky Rose to your leader right now! Becky was cringing so hard she didn't know where to look and no one was saying anything now. How had a conversation about pets turned into a talk about sexual preferences?

Suddenly there was a commotion. Three young men backed into their space on the steps, laughing and almost tripping on the stone stairs. Petra's feline friend took exception, miaowed, hissed and fled from her lap.

'Oi!' Petra exclaimed, getting to her feet, expression not amused. 'You frightened my cat!'

'*Signomi*. Sorry. My friend, he...' one of the men began to apologise.

Becky saw Petra's expression waver a little. Now she seemed to be transfixed, not angry, staring directly at this dark eyed, dark curly-haired twenty-something like he was right out of a *The Bachelor* episode she wanted to watch on repeat.

'Well,' Petra said, still a little indignant, her hands meeting her hips. 'You can help me get her back.'

'*Ti?*' the man asked, dark brow furrowing. 'What? The cat... is really yours?'

'For tonight it was. And you scared her half to death being all shouty and drunk and annoying!'

'You call me drunk?'

'Petra,' Becky said, getting to her feet and thinking that now might be a good time to calm the situation. Why did she feel responsible for Petra? Was it somehow inherently written through her that she was a caregiver? Someone who had to manage...

'Aren't you?' Petra asked the man.

'*Ochi*,' he answered, now as firm-faced as Petra was.

'Well, help me find the cat then,' Petra insisted. 'Now.'

'*Endaksi*. OK.'

And with that, Petra and the young man were off, together, beginning to look under tables and beside plants for the elusive stray Petra had claimed as her own.

'Well,' Becky said, sitting back down on her cushion. 'That was unexpected.'

'Petra being upfront with a stranger?' Elias asked. 'Really?'

Becky couldn't help but laugh. 'I meant Petra falling in love with a cat.'

'A cat without a violin to dance to.'

'The night is young,' Becky answered with a grin.

Elias got up then plumped back down on Petra's abandoned cushion right next to Becky. They were close again now, bodies almost touching as people passed by them, walking up the steps towards the road to the Acropolis or to bars and restaurants further up. It was completely at odds to a night spent in Amesbury, curled up on her sofa with a couple of grilled chicken thighs, watching *Come Dine with Me* on her own. She was in the centre of Athens sharing beer and conversation with two people she barely knew, one of whom was as attractive as men got. That thought made a bead of sweat appear on her top lip and she quickly drank a mouthful of beer to pass it off as some sort of condensation. Passing things off. She had been doing a little bit of that since she'd turned into *Dora the Explorer*. Maybe now was the time to come clean.

'So, you know how I said I was in the army,' Becky began. The words were almost choking her. She wasn't sure whether it was worse to have told the lie to begin with or to confess now. After all, Elias had been nothing but nice, letting them tag along here and showing them the main attractions Athens had to offer.

'I do remember that,' he answered, turning to look at her.

Incredible eyes. Total hotness. She could not ever tell Hazel or Shelley about him. They would both completely ruin her for not passing on her phone number. Unless...

She swallowed. 'Well, the thing is... I'm not.'

'You are not what?' Elias asked, one eyebrow raising up.

'I'm not actually in the army.'

'Not *actually* in the army?'

'I'm not quite in the army.'

'Not quite?'

Why was he making this so difficult for her? Or perhaps she was the one who was making it difficult for herself? She swigged from her bottle of Fix. 'I'm not in the army. At all.'

'Really,' Elias said, sitting back a little and cradling his beer bottle with his hands.

'I don't know why I told you that. Well, I do know really. I told you that because being in the army is about as far removed from what I really do for a job as I could think of. And I didn't want to tell you my real job because Hazel and Shelley both said that you don't go travelling and tell anyone you meet anything real about yourself. Because I'm a woman on my own,' Becky continued. 'And when you're a woman on your own, apparently every second person you meet is waiting to exploit you, or murder you or... exploit you and, well, I wasn't even meant to tell you my real name but I figured that actually my real name is Rebecca so if you were going to exploit me then telling you that my name is Becky wouldn't really get you into my credit cards.'

She needed a breath when she had finished. The air was still sticky and humid, despite the now dark sky, but having finally ended the elongated paragraph she would take any oxygen she could get.

'And you have decided now that I am not going to murder you or exploit you.' He raised his beer glass as if in a toast. 'I feel honoured.'

Oh dear. She had insulted him. And she knew from Marco Polo that Greeks – more so than any other nationality, it was professed – didn't take kindly to being insulted.

'I'm so sorry,' Becky said. 'But it was only a little white lie and being in the army is so much more interesting than what I really do. I just thought you would be someone who sat next to me on the plane. That it wouldn't matter if I told you something else. And then I said I was staying in Athens not Corfu and then we ended up *in* Athens and…'

'Rebecca,' Elias said, the timbre of his voice low, sultry, rippling up her backbone.

'Yes.' Her voice was stupidly breathy. Pathetic. Not the independent go-getter she really wanted to be on this break. Much more work was needed on that.

'I understand,' Elias replied.

'You do?'

'I do,' he answered. 'And it makes no difference to me. Conversation on a plane is simply conversation on a plane. You might be surprised to know that I was once seated next to a man who told me he was a builder.'

'I don't understand.'

'He passed me the inflight magazine because my seat pocket did not have one. This man had not one callus on his hands. In fact, his hands looked like they had been manicured.' Elias raised his beer bottle again. 'Now, I do not know why he lied to me. But I did not care. We had a brief conversation about the weather, the turbulence and the selection of in-flight snacks and that was it. We would never see each other again.'

'I know but… I don't tell lies.' Hiding what she did with sandwich personalisation from Megan wasn't anything like the same. 'I just said it for my own protection... or so I thought... and because of my stupid friends.'

Elias laughed then and it was a joyous sound. Deep, rumbling through his entire body, his mouth widening with an expression that rose up through his cheekbones right up to his beautiful eyes.

'I didn't realise it was quite that funny.'

'It is,' he answered, still laughing a little. 'Because I thought that maybe you were an artist with all the drawings of animals... but then there was the stabbing of them. I was worried that perhaps *you* were the murderer.'

'Oh,' Becky said. 'Well... I draw animals when I'm distracted. I was trying to put together a menu plan for a pitch I'm trying to win. It's a nursing home party and it's important to me and... it should be important to my sister but apparently it isn't... and I couldn't quite work it out on the plane. Hence the animals and the poking them with my pen.' This beer was making her share way too much information now. Maybe it didn't mix well with that white wine she had had earlier.

'You plan parties?' Elias asked her. His knee nudged hers as a couple meandered around them, coming down the steps. He edged a little closer.

'I... make sandwiches and wraps and rolls. It's my sister's catering company, but this pitch for the nursing home, well, she isn't keen on taking the job, but I really want to.' She sighed, frustration with Megan still bubbling under the surface. Why was her sister treating it like just any other job? It was much more than that. It was about doing something nice for the home that had looked after their dad. 'I just need to think up a menu that's going to be unbeatable by anyone else who pitches.' She really *really* wanted this.

'I get it,' Elias replied. 'You want to prove to your sister that you have this capability she thinks only she possesses.'

God. From the little information she had given him he had pretty much nailed that. 'Well… yes,' she answered and nodded. 'Do you have any brothers or sisters?'

'*Ochi*,' he answered. 'Sorry. No. I don't. Only me. My mother will tell you that as I was ten pounds in weight and it felt like she was evacuating a watermelon. There was no way she was going to repeat the experience.'

Becky couldn't help but laugh.

'You laugh at me? Being a child on my own growing up. No one to play with because my head was too large?'

Now she laughed even more. She was imagining him with a giant head. He didn't have a giant head. He had quite a beautiful head, if heads could be beautiful. His dark hair was shaped neatly, brushed back in that style that was popular now.

'You are now thinking of me with a watermelon for a head, are you not?'

'No.' But she didn't stop laughing. She put a hand over her mouth. 'OK… maybe.'

'You are cruel, Sergeant Rebecca.'

'Oh, I imagined myself a way higher ranking than a sergeant.'

'Is that so?'

She nodded and took a sip of her drink.

'So, how do you like Athens?' Elias asked her.

'I like Athens very much,' Becky replied, looking around her. The fairy-lights strung under the canopies casting a romantic glow over everything, the old stone with pots of bougainvillea spilling from urns and hanging baskets, the animated chatter from their fellow patrons. 'It's so beautiful. Not just the Acropolis which was the most magnificent thing I've ever seen. It's also the little shops, the incredible view over the city and here, sitting on cushions on the steps, underneath a thick dark sky, drinking beer I've not tasted before in the middle of... real Greek life.' She looked back at him. 'Thank you for showing it to me.' A sigh left her body then and the contentment loaded in it took her by surprise. She did feel content, as well as exhilarated. As those emotions floated over her she realised just how close Elias was to her and the fact that he appeared to be gazing into her eyes. *His eyes*. So in contrast to the olive skin and the dark hair, a flickering shimmer of blue meets green. Becky's heart was racing. This was attraction. There was no denying that. She was as attracted to this virtual stranger as she had ever been attracted to anyone. Even Mr Eighteen-Months. And what a big mistake that had been. Except she shouldn't judge every next man she met by the standards of someone else, should she? That wasn't fair. That wasn't giving herself or anyone else a chance. And she did want some of those feelings back again. Even if it was for one night with a stranger...

She moved, slightly, barely noticeable to even her, but enough to connect her thigh with Elias's. Would he react? Would he edge back? There were no people wandering up and down now, no reason to be so close. She was barely breathing. Did she move her face forward too? Did she really want to kiss him? What about Petra? Far more attractive. Younger. More vibrant and exciting. Nice. Petra was nice. And *she* fancied Elias too. But then again, she seemed to fancy most men. And she had run away with one a second ago in pursuit of a cat.

Nothing ventured. Nothing gained. Becky prepared to close her eyes…

'Would you like another beer?'

She felt the pressure of Elias's body leave her and suddenly she felt so stupid. Eyes fully open now, she looked up to see he had stood. He was looking down at her, so tall, fit and obviously totally disinterested in her as a romantic distraction. All she could do was nod and try not to sound like a moron when she spoke.

'Oh… yes… thank you.' She smiled. 'That would be nice.' Anything to numb the humiliation. Where *was* Petra? 'Let me get you some euros.'

'*Ochi*. It is OK. I will pay.' He stepped up onto the next stair and headed into the bar.

Moment gone. Moment not even there in the first place. She would definitely not be telling Hazel and Shelley about this. She would simply tell them she had met a nice guy on a plane and he had shown her all the best parts of Athens. She would *not* tell them she had briefly thought it might be a good idea to think about kissing him. Ridiculous.

She reached into her bag and pulled out her phone and it was then she saw she had three missed calls and a voicemail from an unknown number… It had to be Ms O'Neill. *Bugger*. For an unexpected evening in Greece's capital that had started so wonderfully, it now had the potential to turn the shape of a pear.

Seventeen

'I don't think I should have eaten the third piece of bread.' Petra let out a loud burp as they powered towards the gate they were boarding from, determined that nothing was going to make them miss it this time. 'Oh… that's better.'

Becky hadn't eaten anything at breakfast. Embarrassment and terror were filling her gut in equal measure. Terror because Ms O'Neill had seemed really quite annoyed that she wasn't yet at the house and had spent a long time ranting about security and solicitors and her husband being a control freak when they had eventually made phone contact. Then Ms O'Neill had carried on saying how Becky needed to get there to ensure no one tried to enter the house. For a second Becky wondered who exactly would be trying to enter the house because, as a woman on her own, looking for a quiet, idyllic Greek village, hearing someone might be trying to invade wasn't exactly heartening. But when the missed flight scenario had been fully explained, the English woman had calmed down a little. The embarrassment bit was still from her half-attempting to kiss Elias.

'Did you see Elias at breakfast?' Petra asked, her comment coinciding nicely with Becky's train of thought.

'No,' she answered. 'Not that I was looking.' She *had* been looking. She had been looking so she could avoid him. He was obviously going to be on this flight, but the less she saw of him now the better. She felt too awkward that she had misread things. Her signals weren't up to speed and reading *How to Find the Love of Your Life or Die Trying* when she got beneath the Egyptian cotton had basically told her the same. She had broken one of the golden rules. She hadn't waited the twenty seconds before moving in for the kiss. Apparently those twenty seconds were crucial. It gave both parties time to consider what happened next and the consequences of their actions. Except, Elias had no potential to be the love of her life. Perhaps she would have been better getting a copy of *How to Find Anyone of the Opposite Sex Even if it's Only for One Night or Die Trying*. If such a book existed. Maybe she should make notes on all her faux-pas and write it...

'He went a bit quiet when I brought Panos to join us on the steps last night. D'you think he was jealous? D'you think he really did think he could have us both later?'

'No... well... not both of us, I don't think. Maybe you. Maybe he thought he was in a chance with you until Panos came over.'

'Panos was so hot though,' Petra said, dragging her large backpack up her back. 'And sweet. I could have seen us getting a little place together with Plato and living on olives and sweet white wine for the rest of our days.'

They had called the cat Plato. But Becky had suggested it was better not to take the cat on the metro back to their hotel. Panos had come however and he and Petra had disappeared up to her room without even a side glance from the receptionist on the way in. Maybe Becky didn't need a relationship book at all. Perhaps she just needed to spend more time in Petra's company learning from the obvious Mistress of Seduction. Elias had excused himself pretty quickly when they'd got back to the Sofitel. And there Becky had been, alone, being internally crucified by her own shame. She hadn't even had the energy to look at the nursing home menu.

'No chance of us missing the plane this time, we're almost the first ones here,' Petra remarked. There was a small group of people sat on the seats waiting in front of the big screen displaying their flight number including the older couple with their sticks and the family with the young children who had all seemed to be covered in coco-flakes at breakfast.

And there was Elias. Sat furthest away from everyone, his laptop on his knee. Becky swallowed and hoped Petra wouldn't notice and suggest they went over to him.

Elias had seen them arrive at the gate but he had kept his head down. What had happened last night had literally scared him to death. That moment. A moment he thought he would never have again had ripped through him at a million miles an hour. Becky had laughed at the story of his birth and it had been so genuine. She had listened to him as if she was really interested. And such a carefree sound leaving her had suddenly and unexpectedly lightened everything inside of him. He had felt almost instantly weightless. Like the heavy worry he seemed to constantly carry around with him had been lifted for the first time in so long. He'd looked at her and an intense feeling had filled him up and he'd wanted nothing more than to cover her mouth with his and give in to the passion, the desire, the flush of a new connection. But when he looked at Becky again, thought about closing in, feeling her body against his, he had been flooded with memories of Hestia – the beautiful ones as well as the ugly. Disappointment, fear and regret had stalled him, broken into the perfect seconds and then the reverie had taken over. He'd backed off. He'd had to remove himself. And when he'd retreated, he'd been flooded with guilt as well. As nice and unexpected as it had been, he shouldn't want something else. Not with someone like Becky. Someone who was worried about giving too much in case she got exploited. Someone who carried around a relationship handbook…

He looked up from his laptop now, chancing a glance at the passengers around the gate. Petra had her plaits pinned to the top of her head making it look like she was balancing chopsticks on her crown. Becky was… looking as fresh-faced and naturally beautiful as he remembered last night.

It had been a little awkward on the metro back to the hotel. Petra and Panos's lips had been attached to each other like an aggressive vacuum cleaner suctioned to a rug. Neither he nor Becky knew where to look and he had actually prayed for another metro musician… He should have continued conversation. He should have made a vague attempt to normalise things. Because they should be normal. But they weren't. He found Becky attractive. And he couldn't switch that off. But when they arrived in Corfu, they wouldn't see each other again so... that would be that. He just needed to keep himself together until they arrived. It was an hour in the air.

'Where are you sat? What seat number?' Petra asked as they boarded a smaller jet than had got them over to Greece.

'6A,' Becky answered, checking the numbers on the seat backs.

'Aww bum! I'm in 12B. I guess they were fitting us all in around the paying passengers. Meet you at the toilets halfway into the flight?' Petra asked, moving down the plane. 'We can discuss more rom-com movies and the best barbecue we've ever eaten.'

Yes, over breakfast, in between the not-eating and the feeling embarrassed, she had discovered that Petra shared a love of romance movies as well as griddled meats. It seemed that Petra's go-to food was anything that had been expertly grilled and slathered in hot sauce. She had started a story about the Andes and a couple of guinea pigs, but Becky had stopped her short of the ending. She'd sensed it wasn't going to be a chick flick happy ever after for the furries...

'OK,' Becky answered. There was her seat. It was a little snugger with the legroom than it had been on the previous plane. She put her case in the overhead locker and shoved Hazel's huge bag under the seat in front of her. She slipped into the space and sat down, looking out of the window at the bright blue morning sky and the planes around taxiing into position or being loaded up with fuel and luggage. Athens had been more than she could ever have expected. Already she had ticked off a city she hadn't contemplated seeing.

'Good morning.'

She instantly recognised the low accented lilt and turned away from the window. *Elias*. He was standing in the aisle looking gloriously fresh but in relaxed attire: black cotton jeans and a white polo shirt skimming over his athletic frame. 'Morning.' What else was there to say? But now he was moving into the row, shifting into her space.

'6B,' he greeted. 'I guess because we checked in together when we arrived yesterday.'

'Oh,' Becky said. 'Well, I suppose that makes sense.'

'Maybe Petra is across the aisle,' Elias suggested as he made himself comfortable.

'She's not,' Becky replied. 'She's in row twelve.'

Elias nodded, unzipping his leather bag and removing his laptop. 'And Panos?'

Becky couldn't help a smile crossing her lips. 'No Panos,' she answered. 'But Plato's in her cabin bag.'

Elias turned to her then, his expression unsure whether she was being serious or not. She was about to confirm she was only joking when he cracked his own smile. 'You are joking with me.'

'I am,' Becky confirmed. 'But I did half-expect the cat to turn up at the entrance of the hotel as we were leaving.'

'There is still a chance it will come running up the plane steps and settle itself on her lap before we take off,' Elias suggested.

'Carrying a violin.'

They both laughed now and Becky felt herself relax. Perhaps she was worrying unnecessarily. Maybe she needed to put last night's mix-up down to experience. That's what a seasoned traveller would do. She mustn't dwell. She simply needed to forget it and move on. Elias opened his laptop.

'Properties you are exploring in Corfu?' Becky asked him.

'Just a spreadsheet,' he replied. 'If I cannot concentrate, I will draw animals and stab at them with my stylus.'

She shook her head wryly. 'Very funny.'

Eighteen

On board the flight from Athens to Corfu

The plane had been in the air for a while and they had been served a drink. No free wine this time, instead Becky had opted for a Coke. She had written a few notes for the nursing home pitch – more Spam (because apparently there was a great deal you could do with Spam) and perhaps making a cake in the design of a ration book. She was also thinking about really honouring her dad and having some of his favourite dishes in the mix. A hearty meat pie with fresh herbs from the It's A Wrap garden and maybe making those tinned peaches into a crumble… Elias's laptop had been on, but she hadn't noticed him typing much at all.

'So… in Corfu… where are the places I shouldn't miss? What should I try and see while I'm there?' Becky asked him.

He closed the lid of his laptop softly and gave her his full attention. 'For that I would need to know how long it is you are staying on the island.'

'Two weeks,' Becky replied. 'I'm looking after a house. If Ms O'Neill hasn't given up on me already.'

'Whereabouts do you stay?' Elias asked.

She swallowed. She wasn't about to give out her postcode. If they even had postcodes in Greece. 'In the north of the island.'

'You have a car from the airport?'

'I'm getting a taxi. But there is a car at the house I can use if I need to.'

'OK,' Elias replied. 'So, you need to go to the top of the mountain.'

'I do?'

He nodded. 'Mount Pantokrator is 906 metres and the view is incredible. On a clear day you can see for miles. It still amazes me.'

'Anything else?'

'Go out on the water... or *in* the water. You have not seen the best of Corfu if you have not seen it from the sea.'

'Do I hire someone to take me on a boat? Or book a trip or something?' It might not be one of Hazel's cruises but the idea of gently sailing down the coast underneath azure sky and sunshine appealed greatly.

'There are trips, but it is better to drive a boat with someone, or drive yourself. That way you can sail into some of the coves, drop the anchor and swim whenever you like. Do you have access to a boat?'

'No... I mean... I don't know.' Becky wasn't really sure what Ms O'Neill had at the house. She hadn't thought a lot further than the pool if she was truthful. She would have to get some groceries when she got there. How far away was it from a supermarket? And why hadn't she asked any of these questions in the emails she'd exchanged with the owner?

'There will be someone near you with a boat I am sure. There are a lot of boats on Corfu.'

'And I would... just ask someone to take me?' She hadn't wanted to divulge her name to her row companion, she wasn't about to ask a stranger to take her out for the day on the sea. Anything could happen, surely?

'Sure,' Elias replied with a shrug of his shoulders.

Suddenly the plane lurched upwards and Becky's seatbelt gripped her stomach like it was a too-tight gastric band. This wasn't good. Was this turbulence? She hoped so. What else could it be?

'You are OK?' Elias asked as the plane seemed to settle somehow. He was looking at her again, genuine concern seemed to be in his expression.

'Yes... I... what was that?'

'A little turbulence, I think,' he answered. 'I am sure it is nothing to worry about.'

The sound of the intercom connecting with the passengers disturbed them. 'Ladies and gentlemen, this is your captain speaking. I suspect you felt the turbulence we had for a while there. Unfortunately, this is set to continue all along our flight path and, for safety reasons we are having to divert. We will be landing in Kefalonia in thirty minutes. I am turning on the seatbelt sign. Please return to your seats and ensure your tray table is in an upright position and your arm rests are down. Cabin crew, prepare the cabin for landing.'

Becky chilled. It was like someone had put her whole body in a deep freeze. Had the captain just said Kefalonia. Another Greek island? Not Corfu. How could this be happening? An unexpected night in Athens and now somewhere else.

'I do not believe it,' Elias said, shaking his head and putting his laptop back into his bag. 'This is crazy. This has never happened to me before in all the years I have been flying.'

'I...' Becky didn't know what to say. 'How... what happens next? What happens when we get to Kefalonia? How will we get to Corfu?'

'I am assuming another flight.' Elias looked at his watch.

'But when? In a few hours? Today?'

'I do not know.'

'Well, who will know?' Becky asked. She was panicking. Her voice was sounding how it sounded when she stressed about an egg mayonnaise mix-up. She somehow needed to calm. But for crying out loud, she was already one day late! She couldn't be *any* later.

'Becky,' Elias said softly. He had put a hand on her arm now and it was only then that Becky realised she had been shaking, her whole body vibrating with the stress of this new news.

'You have to calm down,' he told her.

'I know,' she said, breathing rapidly. 'But I can't.' His hand was still on her arm and his fingers were very gently brushing her bare skin in some sort of rhythm she felt the need to count the beats to. It *was* distracting though. The breath wasn't catching quite as painfully in her chest any longer.

'We will be on the ground soon,' Elias told her.

'In Kefalonia!' Becky exclaimed. 'Not Corfu! I don't even know how far Kefalonia is from Corfu.'

'It is still in Greece,' Elias answered.

'Great. Thanks. Even *I* knew that.'

'Look at me,' he ordered.

She faced him. God, he was so beautiful. But taking that fact on board was not quelling her heartrate, it was actually making it worse.

'Just breathe,' he said, still brushing her skin with his fingers.

'What is that you're doing?' Becky asked, counting in her head the strokes his fingertips were making. Perhaps it wasn't any set 'thing' that he was performing. Maybe he was simply touching her because he wanted to touch her. Except he hadn't given her that impression last night. But perhaps after a night to think about it... Becky's mind shifted to Petra's talk of the Mile-High Club. Would Becky's arse fit over the sink?

'It is something my mother does to her chickens before she cuts off their heads,' Elias said. 'It relaxes them.'

Becky shifted her arm away from him and snapped down the armrest between them. 'I'm not a chicken.' She scowled. 'Not in the feathered sense anyway.'

'You are mad at me,' Elias replied. 'Good. That means you have the capacity to do more than panic now. You are cured.'

'I just want to know when we're going to get to Corfu,' Becky exclaimed. 'Can't someone ask the pilot?'

'I am guessing he is hard at work trying to keep this plane in the air.'

'Is he?' Becky said, eyes bulging. 'Is it really that bad?'

'The weather is too bad for us to land in Corfu. They do not divert flights for fun.'

'Great,' Becky said. 'Just great.'

Nineteen

Argostoli, Kefalonia, Greece

'Can you believe our luck? I mean you book one flight to one destination and you end up in two places before you even get to the place you're meant to be going!'

Of course Petra was treating it like one big adventure. Why wouldn't she? She was taking life as it came at her, travelling across the planet with one rucksack, hair that could do multiple things and an outlook more *hygge* than the creator of *hygge*. Becky was still mourning the lost hours in Corfu. She should be there now, getting into a taxi and heading to her *final* destination where she really hoped there weren't too many plants that needed daily watering attention. She sipped at her *ouzo* and Fanta lemon that Petra had ordered – but not yet paid for – and tried to loosen the muscles in her neck. All the passengers had been taken from the airport to Argostoli, where they were to wait for further instructions. Although the scenery here was much nicer than looking at an airport terminal, it didn't bode well for them leaving very soon. Elias had said this before they had boarded the coach that had taken them here. Apparently, if there was going to be a departure within the next few hours, they would have been given food vouchers to buy something to eat in the terminal, not been sent here with the taverna owner taking orders for free platters of food on the airline…

'I'm going to have steak and lobster!' Petra announced, downing the rest of her drink and waving a hand at a waiter. It was bustling here, yet still somehow relaxed.

'They said the budget for food was fifteen euros per person including a drink,' Becky reminded. Just looking at the skewers of meats coming to tables was making her hungry though. She had eaten far less than Petra at breakfast.

'Well, the woman sitting next to me on the plane this morning is allergic to seafood. She told me. So, she's probably going to order something cheaper, so I'll use what's left over of her fifteen euros and tag it on to my allowance.'

'I don't think it works like that.'

The comment came from Elias. His fingers had been thundering about on his laptop ever since they had got to this seaside taverna. It was scorching hot here, no sign of the clouds, thunder and torrential downpours reported in Corfu, but there were canopies to nestle under and cool in the shade. If it hadn't been an absolute inconvenience being here it would be almost idyllic. Peaceful. Quaint and charming. Like being sat in the midst of the set of *Captain Corelli's Mandolin*. Wooden tables with white cloths held carafes of wine and tiny porcelain bowls of slick purple olives, creamy white *tzatziki* and a bright pink paste Becky had learned from her guidebook was called *taramasalata*. She wasn't quite sure she was ever going to be able to say that with any great degree of confidence. Customers ate and drank and people-watched and the water rippled undisturbed apart from a few small boats, plus grander yachts further out, bobbing against their tethers with the tide.

'You're as grumpy as Becky, are you?' Petra said. 'Another two *ouzos* and Fanta lemon, please.' She had asked the last part to the waiter. 'Do you want another one, Elias?'

'Whose food allowance are these drinks coming from?' he asked her. 'Perhaps the rations for the two children over there who will only want fries and ketchup?'

'Ignore him. Just the two *ouzos* please,' Petra said to the waiter. 'What's your name?'

Elias said something in Greek to the man and the waiter laughed before leaving their table and going to the aid of other diners.

'What did you say to him?' Petra wanted to know.

'I said he should only bother to tell you his name if he owns a cat.'

'Rude!' Petra snapped.

'I hope the second *ouzo* wasn't for me,' Becky said. 'I haven't finished the first one yet.'

'Of course it was for you! *Yammas!*' Petra held her empty glass in the air. 'Here's to Jesse Metcalfe. He's my favourite Hallmark actor by the way. Who's yours?'

Becky didn't get to reply.

'*Skata!*' Elias erupted, slamming down the lid of his laptop.

He had had an email from Chad come in while they were in the air and had just read it. Chad had been *talking* with his wife. Communicating with the enemy! This was strictly forbidden under the terms of his contract with Elias. Negotiations were only supposed to be undertaken by Elias and Elias alone. Now it seemed Chad was wanting to soften their approach. But softening at the outset showed weakness. He really did need to get to Corfu and speak to the wife himself before Chad did any more damage to himself and his finances. His client would thank him in the long run. But he still wasn't in Corfu yet. And it was looking doubtful he was going to be there today, although it was only lunchtime now. Perhaps, once they were filled with free food, the weather would brighten and they would be able to get back to the airport, get on board and this time end up where they should be.

'Is *skata* a rude word?' Petra wanted to know.

'Yes,' Elias answered.

'Well, which one? Because I know how to swear in many, many languages.'

'But not Greek?'

'I can say "fuck you" in Greek so I know it isn't that.'

'Petra, sshh,' Becky urged. 'I'm getting a headache.'

Elias looked to Becky who had one elbow on the table, propping up her head, her fingers massaging her scalp. He swallowed, trying hard not to feel anything, but the memory of him trying to calm her when the turbulence had hit was right there. He shouldn't have touched her, but in the beginning, he had only thought about making her feel better. However, in the end, the sensation of her soft, creamy epidermis underneath his fingertips had set off a chain of events led by his libido. A week or so in Corfu surrounded by the affectionate but mostly unattractive old women of the village might be exactly what he required.

'That bubbling headache is all the stress you're creating,

worrying about not being where you thought you should be,' Petra said. 'Calm thoughts. Think Ryan Paevey. He's my second favourite BTW.'

'Well, it is a worry,' Becky reminded her. 'I haven't travelled quite as much as you before. I'm not used to getting on a mode of transport and ending up somewhere completely different… twice.'

'And Elias is stressed because of work, obvs. So, what was it you did again?' Petra asked.

He hadn't told Petra what he did. He had lied to Becky though. Repeating the lie would compound things. And telling the truth would let Becky know he had lied to her. But she had lied to him about her occupation… and that was when he should have confessed too.

'I didn't say what I did,' he replied.

'Cage-fighter,' Petra guessed as two more *ouzos* and Fanta lemon were delivered to the table.

'Only at the weekends,' Elias answered, deadpan.

'Male model?'

'Petra, for goodness sake. Do you think of anything else?' Becky queried.

'I haven't mentioned male models at all since we met each other,' Petra replied as if she was super-affronted.

And he remembered Becky had guessed 'international playboy' when they had played this guessing game. Elias watched Becky roll her eyes. This really was becoming a tense situation for her. He was guessing, from what he knew of her, that she liked organisation and order. She didn't seem to deal well with spur-of-the-moment or off-the-cuff. This situation with the flights was difficult for her. More difficult than it was for either Petra or himself.

'I am an estate agent,' Elias found himself saying.

'Well,' Petra said, 'I wouldn't have guessed that. You haven't tried to sell me anything yet.'

'You told me you were spending all your money on travelling the world.'

'So? Surely a good estate agent would try to convince me otherwise.'

'You would like a nice two-bedroom apartment in Corfu Town perhaps?'

'No,' Petra replied with a grin. 'I'm spending all my money on travelling the world.'

He watched Becky get up from the table quickly and walk towards the sea.

Twenty

Karavomilos, Kefalonia, Greece

'Are you hearing this, Haze? Becky still ain't in Corfu!'

Becky was standing at the very edge of the outside space of the taverna so as not to disturb the other diners. After a lunch in Argostoli they had been given the news that they were going to be staying the night on Kefalonia. Once they had checked in to the hotel and dropped off their luggage, it had been time to decide what to do next. Apparently, as was the case in Athens, you didn't stay in the immediate vicinity and wait the wait out, you embraced the new surprise location and picked somewhere else on the island to visit. After guidebook consultation, then Petra getting very vocal about a cave that was 'the most heavenly on Earth' – which Becky wasn't sure made any sense at all – the three of them had agreed on Sami and Karavomilos. The choice wasn't disappointing at all.

Hiring a taxi, they had dropped into the harbour at Sami where the evening waves lapped the grey stone walls and a cosmopolitan vibe rose from the cafés and tavernas surrounding the water's edge, then they had moved on to the white stone beach at Karavomilos. Here Petra had excelled at skimming the stones into the aquamarine sea until one had chinked off a larger rock, rebounded and hit her on the cheek. Much screaming had ensued, leading to a fisherman on the shoreline coming to ask if they needed help. Elias had explained in Greek what had happened and the old man had laughed so much his held-together-with-string-for-a-belt trousers had almost fallen down. Petra hadn't found it funny at all and now she had a slight bruise on her cheek that was 'going to be a bitch to cover up' with the sparse non-liquid make-up she'd brought with her.

And now they were here, at Karavomilos Taverna, about to order a dinner they were paying for themselves, so they didn't have to dine – albeit for free – with the other passengers at the hotel in Argostoli. Having shared some coffee with the family of six and the elderly couple earlier, it was apparent that being here with four small children was not an easy task – nowhere to settle, no promised Kellogg's products like the all-inclusive they were heading to – and that no matter how many times they were operated on, varicose veins never really went away properly and there was always *always* a chance you could bleed out if you 'gave one a little knock'.

'I'm in Kefalonia,' Becky informed. She wasn't so shocked at hearing those words now. Not after eating deep-fried cheese (*saganaki*), fresh sardines and a Greek salad with tomatoes that were so good she'd consider marrying them if they proposed.

'You're in Kefalonia!' It was Hazel's turn to sound shocked now. 'That's the wrong island, Becky. You're supposed to be in Corfu! C-or-fu. Not Kef-a-lo-nia. What happened, dear? How did you get on the wrong plane?'

'I didn't get on the wrong plane,' Becky answered. Did experienced vacationer Hazel think getting on the wrong plane was an easy thing to manage these days with digital boarding passes and enhanced security checks? Well, she supposed Hazel did cruise far more than fly... 'There was bad weather in Corfu so we couldn't land. We diverted to Kefalonia and we're having to stay the night.'

'Another freebie! You're on a fucking roll!' Shelley shouted, letting out a whoop afterwards. Then she laughed. 'And not the wholemeal kind you're fucking used to! Get it? On a roll?'

'Shelley! Language!'

Becky shook her head at their camaraderie. 'I just didn't want you to worry and... I wanted to tell you that I'm seeing another destination I never thought I'd see.'

'You're almost doing a cruise itinerary without the cruising bit,' Hazel said, sounding slightly miffed.

'Listen, I'd better go.' Becky looked over to their table right next to the sea view. Petra and Elias were in conversation and she wondered what they were talking about. Perhaps Petra was asking him if he was single again... 'Hopefully, the next time I call you I'll actually be where I'm supposed to be.' There was a degree of humour to the scenario now. Kind of.

'Megan asked about you today,' Shelley blurted out.

Becky's heart leapt. 'Did she? What did she say?'

'She asked us if—'

'She wanted to know if we had heard from you and whether you were having a lovely time,' Hazel interrupted.

'You go, dear. Go and find yourself a Captain Corelli. I would if I was there!'

Megan wouldn't have asked the team something like that. It wasn't her sister's style.

'Shelley,' Becky said. 'What did Megan really say?'

Becky heard Hazel give a tut of annoyance before Shelley continued.

'She asked if we knew if you had "stopped faffing around with ideas for the nursing home summer party". The manager had left a message on the answerphone apparently.'

Becky closed her eyes and held on to her resolve. She had planned to look at her notes – and drawings – later when she was tucked up in bed in the hotel that overlooked the harbour. Megan still didn't approve. Still didn't want any part of the party. And what had the answerphone message said? Had they brought the deadline for pitches forward? Was she going to miss out on the chance of the job anyway?

'She doesn't mean it, dear,' Hazel tried to console. 'You know how stubborn and single-minded she can be. I do think you going on your holidays was a shock to her.'

'Yeah,' Shelley agreed. 'I mean, you're always here, aren't you? Always the first one in and the last one to leave and the one who actually cares about the customers… well, you know, I care about them sort of. I care about them enough to wash my hands and that, so they don't get bacteria in their baps.'

Always there. Reliable. Dependable. Thinking of others. If ever there was a reminder that what she was doing by escaping was the right course of action, then this was it. Reliable was fine, commendable really, but being walked over was not.

'I have to go now. More not-sandwich-making to do.' Becky ended the call before anything else could infiltrate the slightly thicker skin she was desperately trying to grow with regard to her sister. That was it. When she eventually got to Corfu and got settled beside the pool that was waiting for her, she was going all out to make the best pitch she could for the nursing home party. And nothing was going to stop her.

'Becks! We've got to go!' Petra yelled.

Becky looked to their table. Petra had leapt up and it appeared Elias was gathering his phone, wallet and sunglasses together. Was there an earlier flight? Would they be heading back to the airport sooner than planned?

'If we want to see the cave, Agelos says we need to go now! And he's going to take us! We can eat when we get back! And there's gonna be Greek music later! Bonus!'

Who was Agelos? She had only been on the phone for a few minutes! Becky then saw that all the early evening diners were now focused on Petra like she'd shouted her plans through a megaphone. Which, to be fair, was how it had sounded. Becky adjusted the strap of her bag and walked back towards the table.

Twenty-One

Melissani Cave, Kefalonia

Elias had received another email from Chad. He had checked his phone on the slightly wild ride up the coast from the taverna, bumping along in the back of a flat-bed truck driven by waiter, Agelos. Somehow, Agelos seemed to have time to be Petra's tour guide despite the restaurant busying up substantially before they left. But, it was better news on the divorce front. Kristina had riled Chad on Messenger, talking about their boat and then the polo club membership. It was back to full steam ahead with Elias's plan and he couldn't help feeling a little more relaxed because of this turn of events. Relaxed enough to be looking forward to this detour from normal life.

'It echoes! Have you heard?' Petra called out, her voice rebounding around the cave surrounding them. 'Ooo, can you hear?'

'All anyone can hear is you shouting and the echo of you shouting,' Becky informed her in one of those whispers that seemed greater in volume than base-level talking.

They had descended through a tunnel into the bowels of the cave, taking in the stalactites – spiky shards of rock poking down from the roof, slick and shiny with moisture – and were now standing at the base of the steps they had descended down waiting for their transport. It was cool inside the cave, a subterranean world with colours and light virtually never seen above. Now here, at the edge of the underground lake of water, the rays of the evening sun poured through the large hole in the rock above them, creating an ethereal glow on the ragged rocks and lighting up the middle of the pool, changing the hue of the water to the most vivid of turquoise.

'Wow!' Petra breathed, eyes going to the sky.

It was how Elias imagined standing in the centre of a volcano would feel like – albeit an inactive and not white-hot one. One small person amid large-scale, intimidating walls of granite, sunshine spilling through a guardian of trees at the circumference of the ring of light above them.

'I can't believe this is real.'

The sentiment came from Becky who was gazing skywards, inching closer towards the edge of the lake. A guide was heading towards them, standing in a tiny blue-painted rowing boat. Agelos had called in a favour and they were going to receive their own private tour when really tours for the day should have been over. Elias had a feeling that if Agelos hadn't received a frantic call on his mobile phone from his uncle, he would have stayed for the tour too, but he was coming back to pick them up in an hour.

'It's so cool,' Petra agreed.

'I do not think "cool" is the right word to describe this,'

Elias told her as their guide encouraged them forward towards their craft.

'No,' Becky agreed. 'It's not... a Topshop must-have or...'

'Panos from Athens' hair,' Elias added. Petra gave him a glare and he immediately put his hands up as if in a show of surrender. 'You did say his hair was cool.'

'This... it's... striking and... spectacular,' Becky told them.

'Breathtaking,' Elias added.

'Alright!' Petra snapped. 'You don't need to verbalise the dictionary for me.'

'And if you put a filter on any of your photos of this,' Becky continued. 'Well... it would be sacrilege.'

'Are we allowed in the boat yet?' Petra asked, stepping nearer the edge and smiling at their fifty-something swarthy-looking guide. He had a sheaf of thick, salt-and-pepper curly hair and a beard to match. Agelos had told them he was called Kosmos.

Becky had seen a couple of photos of the cave on Google, when they were deciding where to visit, and as pretty as the images had been, they were nothing when compared to being here in person, breathing in the damp air, feeling the moisture dripping down the rocks, remembering exactly how old these walls of stone were and thinking of all the people – and creatures – that had been here before her, thousands of years ago. The pool was so still, translucent turquoise where the light trickled in, with darker shades of blue at its border. It was nature at its finest. Nothing manmade. Nothing artificial. Complete purity.

Petra leapt aboard and made the small rowboat, sway

back and forth with her motion. 'Whoops! Not my fault! It's a bit wonky!' She settled at the very front of the boat.

Elias was next and he stepped on, turning back to look at Becky.

'You are OK?' he asked, reaching out a hand to help her.

More touching. She wasn't sure she could deal with more touching. It was all getting too much for her. Hazel had told her that men still in the Eurozone were far more tactile than anyone she was going to find at Wetherspoons on a Friday night, and it was just their way. But it wasn't *her* way. And, it was equally stupid to have butterflies about it, being as he was the first male she had come into contact with on this trip – stag party excepting. He was nice. He happened to be attractive. She really *wasn't* thinking about what Tara would think if she turned up with someone like Elias at a dinner party. The last time she had ventured to one as a singleton, she had encountered 'dipping' foods and the couples had all fed each other. She mustn't wonder what it would be like to be fed by Elias…

'I'm fine,' she answered, taking care to step into the vessel with all the aplomb of a woman who didn't need her arm steadying. As her feet hit the wooden interior the boat wobbled and then Becky wobbled and it was all she could do to maintain her balance.

'Said it wasn't me!' Petra remarked with a laugh.

Bracing her core until the boat had stopped swaying, Becky finally sank down at the back of the wooden bench that circled the whole exterior and looked again at the lustre of the pool they were now floating on top of. She could see her reflection in the water, then, beyond that, pale rock, and next was shadow where it deepened.

'Are you ready to see the nymphs?' Kosmos let out a throaty laugh as he got among them, in the centre of the vessel, and picked up his oars.

'The what?' Petra asked.

'The nymphs in Greece are everywhere,' Elias replied.

'He is right,' Kosmos answered. 'But here, in Melissani Cave, their presence is felt even stronger.' He whispered but such was the cavernous nature of their surroundings it sounded much louder. 'This is because it is believed it is at this very place, in this *very* cave, that the nymph Melissani drowned after she was rejected by Pan, the god of the wild and the companion to the nymphs.'

'Oh, I see,' Petra said, folding her arms across her chest. 'Is this the story you make up for tourists? Are there keyrings of the drowned fairy at a gift shop on the way out?'

'Petra!' Becky exclaimed. 'This is the history of the cave. It did say about the nymphs in your Greece guidebook.' She really sometimes wanted Petra to put that filter she added to Insta onto her words before they made it out of her mouth. And this was coming from someone who believed in romantic comedies. Well, watched them anyway...

Kosmos put one hand on his heart, the oar almost slipping from his grip. 'I promise to you. This is the fact of legend.'

'Legend like a fairy story. Literally,' Petra answered with a roll of her eyes. She got her phone out of the pocket of her jeans and began to snap pictures. At least she was impressed enough by the cave, even if she wasn't into the myths. But this man was doing them a favour getting the boat out for them and all because *Petra* had wanted to come. The very least she could do was be respectful.

'I'm so sorry about our... friend,' Becky apologised.

'Everyone who comes here with a broken heart...' Kosmos continued, rowing a little, very slow, creeping from the rim of the lake towards the centre where the light was flowing in. 'They feel the sadness inside of them more than others.'

'What?' Petra asked, pausing in her photo-taking to stare at their guide.

'It is OK,' Kosmos said, looking directly at Petra now. 'The cave, it knows. And it will listen if you want it to.'

Becky watched Petra almost shrink back into herself. What was going on? Kosmos seemed to have hit a tender spot that had altered Petra's entire demeanour. She might have wanted the young woman to quieten down a bit – OK, substantially – but she hadn't wanted her to suck herself into a shell like a grumpy turtle. And that was a bit how she looked at the moment... but with great plaits.

As their guide continued his story, talking about the excavations of the cave in the 1960s that led to the discoveries of icons, plates and oil lamps, Becky felt herself relax into the moment. The sandwich-making enterprise was a million miles away. This relaxing, drifting into the centre of a cave-lake was hypnotically enchanting. The drip and gentle plopping of water spiralling from the stalactites into the cave was like soothing music. Time and reality were suspended.

'Can you hear the nymphs?'

Elias had whispered to her from across the other side of the boat and Becky smiled at him. 'No,' she whispered back. 'But I can't hear Petra either.' She felt instantly ashamed. It was wrong to make fun of anyone and Petra was uncommonly quiet at the moment. She already seemed to have developed a soft spot for her. Perhaps she was missing the interaction with Megan more than she had anticipated.

'Do you think she is OK?' Elias asked.

'I don't know,' Becky whispered back, leaning a little towards him. 'I don't know her very well, obviously, as I only met her yesterday.'

'Yes, but it is not always how long you know someone for,' Elias said. 'Sometimes the longer you know someone… the less you truly discover about who they really are.'

It sounded like he was speaking from experience and his eyes left hers to gaze into the grotto ahead of them.

'I don't think there's anything wrong with feel-good stories,' Becky broke the quiet. 'When have bare, blunt facts really made anyone happy?' She had got his attention back. 'I was always happier remembering Boris Johnson sliding down a zip wire waving little Union Jacks than I was hearing about what he may or may not have argued with his girlfriend about.'

'But the truth will always come out,' Elias replied. 'Always.'

Becky now had the intense feeling that neither of her companions' minds were on fairies from long ago. Maybe this cave did have magical powers. It seemed everyone was feeling *something*. Except her. Perhaps because she felt things *all* the time. *Responsible. Encumbered.* Here she felt the opposite of those things.

'This is the bright, light cave,' Kosmos carried on, pointing to the sky above them. Even sitting down, it made Becky feel a little dizzy.

'Next I will take you into the small dark cave,' their guide told them. 'So small that the oars will not fit outside the boat.'

'What do you mean?' Becky asked suddenly. She looked at Elias, feeling a little panicked. She wasn't the best in confined spaces. The tunnel coming down here had only been OK because she could see the bright blue of the water in the lake illuminating the way ahead. 'What does he mean?'

'I do not know,' Elias answered. 'I have not been in this cave before.'

'Do we have to go in the small cave? Can't we stay in this one?' Her heart was starting to flutter and not in a good way...

'You don't want to miss out on any nymphs, do you?' Petra said, turning her head and looking at Becky. 'I mean, especially the ghost of the dead one, complete with a hologram appearance. There's bound to be a hologram appearance.'

Was it Becky's imagination or had Kosmos's rowing sped up now? It seemed like the oars were going in deeper as well as quicker and it looked like they were heading to an eerie corner of the cave. This didn't bode well. The darkness was reminding her of the time she had got shut in the pantry at It's A Wrap and it was half an hour before she could get anyone to answer their mobile phones. If she hadn't had her phone with her, she could only imagine her anxiety at having to spend the whole night in there with nothing for company but chutney, mustard and Shelley's many *many* catering-sized jars of peanut butter she had bought through the firm's cash and carry account. Megan had come to the rescue, seeming slightly miffed at having to leave Dean at the poppadum stage of a curry evening, but when she had seen how distraught Becky had been she had instantly softened, wrapping her in the biggest of sisterly hugs and insisting on making them both hot chocolates exactly how their mum had made them when they were little – full-fat milk, cocoa powder, two sugars with cream and grated cinnamon on top.

'Are you OK?' Elias asked, as they drew further away from the circle of sky above them and moved into a cooler, darker atmosphere.

She nodded, holding her breath. She wasn't. But she had to be. And telling him she was close to being claustrophobic might bring on all kinds of sympathy. Or it would enlighten Elias to the realisation that she was a flake who shouldn't be holidaying alone. She could close her eyes. The 'small' had to be big enough for them to get the boat through. It was probably a lot bigger than she was imagining.

'Here,' Kosmos stated, his voice rebounding off the rocks. 'I bring the oars in so we can *squeeze* through. Very gently. Hold your breath as the walls appear to *close in* around us.'

Oh my God. Why was he talking like he was narrating a horror movie for the visually impaired? With her eyes closed, Becky was already imagining the cave clamping around the boat, splintering the wood first and then moving on to their internal organs before they met their death by crushing or drowning like the nymph!

'Here, where it is *very, very* narrow, I must pull the rope attached to the cave so we can make it to the next chamber. Do not worry. *Most* of the boats make it through.' Kosmos laughed, a throaty gurgle that with all the horror death imagery Becky's mind was conjuring up, sounded distinctly sinister. Perhaps it would be better if she opened her eyes after all. There were three other people in the boat. She wasn't on her own with the tight space…

She gasped at the scene that greeted her. Kosmos hadn't been lying. It *was* narrow. *So* narrow she was almost close enough to put her nose against the granite – not that she was going to move an inch nearer to it. On the other side of the boat were stalagmites – phallic-looking cylinders poking out of the stone. This much tinier cavern – with no hole in its roof – was lit by a golden light. Despite Petra's feeling about the legend and mystery attached to the place, there was certainly something ethereal about it. Becky tried to recapture the serenity and peace she had in the other chamber. She was safe.

'Listen,' Kosmos whispered.

'What is it?' Becky asked, eyes wide. If he said anything about bats she was going to grab the rope and pull them back into the other cave herself.

'Can we swim?' Petra interrupted.

'*Ochi*,' Kosmos said straightaway. 'No. It is too cold to swim. The water in here is only fifteen degrees.'

'But can we swim?' Petra asked again.

Becky furrowed her brow, trying to listen for the thing they were supposed to be listening for that hopefully wasn't part of the bat family... Hadn't Petra heard Kosmos's original reply?

'If you swim,' Kosmos began, steering their way in the near dark, 'you might drown like Melissani.'

'Really?' Petra said, standing up and making the boat sway. She was taking off her T-shirt now and Becky felt sick. Surely, she wasn't going to jump into the water their guide had said was perilously cold! *And* in the *dark small* cave, not the bright illuminated one! Becky held on to the side of the vessel and said a quick prayer to Pan.

'Well, I'm a much better swimmer than any nymph,' Petra informed. 'And I'm not scared of death anyway.' Her shoes were pulled from her feet and she started to wriggle out of her jeans. Was that a bikini or just underwear? Perhaps Petra was always prepared for anything. Becky, on the other hand, wasn't.

'Petra, please don't,' Becky said. 'The water isn't like it is in… Thailand.'

'I can see that,' Petra replied.

'Petra, sit down.' It was Elias talking now and he had a very stern look on his face. 'Jumping into that water puts us all at risk.'

'How do you figure that?' Petra asked, now wearing nothing but her underwear. Kosmos had put one hand over his eyes.

'If you dive into the water, that you have been told is too cold, one of us is going to have to come in after you and rescue you,' Elias stated.

'I don't need rescuing by anyone,' Petra answered, her expression set to defiant. She moved to the edge of the boat.

'Petra, please,' Becky begged. 'I know you want to embrace all the new experiences but… I need you to tell me all the things I should know about travelling and… I haven't told you my favourite Hallmark actor yet and… we need to talk about rib-eye versus T-bone before we go our separate ways tomorrow. Tomorrow, when we finally get to Corfu,' Becky continued. 'Not today in this… spooky cave.'

'If I don't resurface, just leave me for the nymphs and tell my aunt she can have whatever's left.'

With that sentence hanging in the damp air, Petra dived off the edge of the boat and into the black water below.

*

'Oh my God! Oh my God!' Despite the rocking and reeling caused by Petra's rapid disembarkation, Becky had got to her feet, her eyes scanning the half-light while trying to maintain her balance.

'She's fucking crazy,' Elias exclaimed, tearing at the shoes on his feet then shrugging off his jacket. This was not what he had signed up for tonight but what choice did he have? Too cold water and the exuberance of youth was all you needed to create disaster. Despite Petra's bravado, he couldn't just leave her to her own devices.

'I will put on my searchlight,' Kosmos said, reaching into the bottom of the boat.

'What are you doing?' Becky asked as Elias began to remove his shirt. He wasn't going to have time to lose his trousers. Once that cold water stabbed at Petra like a thousand of the sharpest of knives, she would start to struggle and here, in the dark cave, she could quickly become disorientated.

'I'm getting her out,' Elias replied. He didn't wait to say anything else. He dived into the water and hoped against hope he hadn't completely misjudged this situation.

Twenty-Two

Karavomilos Taverna, Karavomilos

Becky wasn't altogether certain what she was drinking, she just knew it was strong. And strong was good. Strong was excellent. Strong spirits would definitely help her recover from the shock of what had happened in Melissani Cave.

It was a humid evening and the chirruping of cicadas filled the air. Sitting on a green chair at a table for four on decking right next to the ocean, it was taking all the gentle sea noises and soft chatter from the other diners to quell the panic that was still lodged in Becky's chest. Her and Kosmos in the little boat, both searching the water with torches. One that looked like it had come from biblical times (Kosmos) and an iPhone (Becky). Until finally, heart-stoppingly ages after their initial entry, Elias had resurfaced, a very pale Petra in his arms.

Becky took another sip of the drink, letting the heat of the alcohol slip over her tonsils and beyond. She had somehow found the strength to pull Petra from the water and into the boat, at first shouting angrily at her in the hope it would be enough to bring her round, the next telling her that Jesse Metcalfe was actually there. Neither seemed to work. Petra hadn't quite been unconscious, but it was close; her eyes were rolling, she didn't seem really sure of her surroundings and she had violently shivered. Kosmos had passed over Petra's clothes and Becky had attempted to redress her, to warm her while Elias, out of breath and dripping wet too, had dressed himself, a furious expression on his face.

Thankfully, Agelos had come quickly after that. Once the call had been made and they had again experienced the waiter's terrible rally-driving, they had all arrived back at the taverna in double-quick time. Then the owners were on hand with towels and blankets and stiff drinks just like this one that Becky had almost finished. It had been quite the circus for a moment, onlookers wondering what had happened.

While Petra and Elias were spirited away to be offered a hot shower and dry clothes, Becky had come back down to the beachside tables and typed out a text to Megan, fingers shaking as she hit the letters. It was moments like these when you realised the frailty of life and what was really important. She had felt it for a time after their dad had died. Life hung by a fine thread. Each day was a gift. It shouldn't be wasted on grudges or arguments over catering contracts. Except Becky hadn't pressed send yet. She didn't know why. She should. What if she had done something crazy like jump into a cave-lake never to be seen again while she and Megan still weren't talking? Becky could be dead – nibbled by nymphs – and Megan would be living with the guilt. Or perhaps Megan wouldn't feel anything. Maybe she would sweep Becky's demise under cellophane sandwich wrap like she had with the death of their father.

'Agelos has been given the night off.'

Becky looked up to see Elias stood at the table. He was wearing a white shirt that was definitely a size too small for him. But the buttons straining, the material tight across his broad chest wasn't a bad look. In fact, it was a hot look that made Becky impulse-swallow. Black jeans covered the rest of him. She was back to imagining what it would be like for him to finger-hold steak dipped in pepper sauce, dangling the hot, juicy slither of sirloin over her more-than-eager lips...

'I've been given his clothes,' Elias replied, sitting down opposite her. His comment was enough to bring a smile to Becky's face. 'Someone called Adriana is washing and drying my shirt and trousers.' Despite removing his shirt before diving into the water, Petra had got it soaking when she'd landed back in the boat like a beached seal.

'Where's Petra?' Becky asked. She wanted to know the girl was alright, but equally she wanted to still be cross with her. She was irresponsible and careless and she had worried her. Not to mention she had put Elias at risk with her antics.

'With Agelos,' Elias answered with a raise of his eyebrows. '"Poor Petra being so cold. Poor Petra going through something so traumatic. Let me kiss it all better."' He had mimicked the waiter's voice perfectly and had now pursed his lips into a sarcastic kiss that Becky couldn't look away from. She had never really looked so closely at a man's lips before, but Elias had amazing lips. She blinked in a bid to stop herself staring.

'I don't know how she does it,' Becky breathed, cradling

her glass in her hands. It was idyllic here, next to the shore, under the shade of the boughs of a drooping ancient olive tree, pots of fragrant blossoming bougainvillea surrounding the tables, with subtle globes of light on posts casting a romantic glow. There was even a blue-painted waterwheel if the sea sounds weren't relaxing enough.

'Does what?' Elias asked, waving a hand to call a waiter.

'Exactly what she wants.'

Elias nodded with a sigh. 'Some people, they are just made that way.'

'But they shouldn't be! Should they?' Becky asked him. 'I mean it's completely selfish and stupid and... dangerous and she could have died and *you* could have died and—'

'Captain Rebecca,' Elias interrupted. 'What are you drinking?' The waiter had arrived and Becky realised she had been ranting and raving while he was stood there waiting to serve them.

'Oh, I'm OK at the moment,' she replied immediately.

'You are finished,' Elias remarked, indicating her empty glass. 'You should have another.'

She looked at him, feeling ridiculous. 'I don't know what it is.'

'It is fig liqueur,' the waiter told her. 'My mother makes.'

Was it? Now she felt awful for not fully appreciating it. It sounded like a local delicacy she should have been savouring.

Elias ordered in Greek and the waiter left them.

'What did you get?' Becky asked.

'Two fig liqueurs and a carafe of red wine... and I asked for the menu. I am hungry.'

Becky couldn't deny that she was hungry too. In fact,

being in Greece seemed to be making her hungrier than she had been in her life. Maybe it was the air. Maybe it was the aroma of all the delicious local meats.

'You are OK?' Elias asked her.

He was always asking her that. Perhaps what she thought was a resting face really looked like someone on the verge of mental breakdown. She'd have to check in the mirror later. That thought made her put a hand to her hair. She hadn't looked in a mirror even in the toilets earlier! She probably resembled a damp nymph, covered in sticking up seaweed. Definitely not worthy of anyone with nice lips...

'Try not to think about what might have happened,' Elias told her.

'But so many things *could* have happened. She could have drowned. You could have drowned. Kosmos could have—'

'Drowned?'

'I was going to say Kosmos could have had a heart attack. He did look quite pale at one point.'

'But, as I said, none of that happened,' Elias reminded. 'We are all here. All that occurred was we... and our clothes... got wet. That is it.'

Becky nodded. He was right, of course. But he didn't know how much of a worrywart she was on a day-to-day basis. And she was basically waiting for the message from Ms O'Neill to tell her she was sacked from the housesitting opportunity as she hadn't turned up yet. She wouldn't blame her.

'So much adventure in just a few days,' Elias teased.

'I'm perfectly happy for the rest of my time in Greece to simply involve sun, sea and...'

'Stabbing at animal drawings,' he replied.

'Quite.' She smiled at him, feeling a little of the tension drop from her shoulders. His positive attitude was a bit infectious, she had to admit. Plus, Petra had ruined what should have been a tranquil boat ride, Becky shouldn't let her spoil the rest of their one night in Kefalonia. As if sensing her need to tumble back into chill time, *bouzouki* music began to play.

'Your friend lives in Corfu all the time?' Elias asked her.

'My friend?'

'The one you are helping with looking after their house?' He took the menus from the waiter and passed one to her. 'I assumed she or he lives there and is taking a holiday?'

'Oh, yes... yes, they do... they are.' Becky took the menu and used it to cover her now burning-up face. Her stomach groaned as if in appreciation of all the traditional Greek fayre listed.

'Where have they gone? Somewhere else in Greece or...'

'Blackpool.' It was out before she could stop it. Of all the places she could have created for her fictional friend to have a fictional holiday and she chose the home of the Golden Mile and the Tower Ballroom where her mum and her aunt played fruit machines.

Elias hadn't replied. He was looking at her with those beautiful eyes, so intense...

'It's in Lancashire. The north of England. It has lovely... donkeys.' Where was more of that fig liqueur?

Elias nodded. 'It sounds... interesting.'

'Oh, it is,' Becky agreed with a heap too many nods. 'It really is but... I've been there and I haven't been to Corfu so... more interesting for my friend than for me.'

'Shall we order some food?' Elias suggested. 'Perhaps some seafood?'

'Well, I usually go for meat dishes but...'

'New experiences, Captain Rebecca,' Elias said.

'Yes,' Becky replied. And if she ordered a whole octopus, she could stuff it in her mouth to stop any more random lies escaping. 'New experiences.'

Twenty-Three

Elias watched Becky as she ate one of the giant prawns they had been served as part of their fish platter. Lobster, octopus, crab – she had tried it all – but the prawns seemed to affect her the most.

Eyes closed, a moan escaping her lips, he had to put his fingers to his wineglass to distract himself. The music, the lull of the sea and most definitely the wine, were all perfect partners in showing him exactly what relaxation was. And Becky's enjoyment of the Greek food was reminding him what he missed the most about his native country when he was in the UK. Thinking about Corfu he could almost smell his mother's special *stifado*…

'I can't even tell you how good this tastes,' Becky mouthed, finally opening her eyes but still eating. 'I source the best prawns I can get my hands on at home and I taste-tested *a lot*. But they don't taste like this.'

'Fresh from the sea today,' Elias told her. 'That is all it is. From the water to the plate in less than twenty-four hours.'

'But they must cook them a special way,' Becky insisted, finally swallowing, then washing it down with a drink of her wine.

'Simply,' Elias answered. 'Grilled, no seasoning, maybe a little lemon juice.'

'Really?' Becky said, looking a little shocked now. 'Do you really think that's it? Because if that's true it might just change my whole life.'

'I do not understand.'

'Well,' Becky said, leaning a little over the table towards him, 'that's what I do. For a job.'

'You cook prawns?' he asked. 'I thought you said you made sandwiches.'

She laughed and shook her head, hair bouncing. 'I make sandwiches *memorable*. And that means all-natural ingredients, but always something added. Combinations you wouldn't expect to go together.' She took a breath. 'That's what I'm good at. I combine foods to allow the sandwich or wrap to give a whole sensory experience – taste, texture, aroma, a vitamin someone might be lacking they don't know about… if I get to know them really well, like Milo.' She took another breath, her words coming out faster. 'And if you're telling me that the best tastes are one thing, cooked simply, with nothing added, completely on its own then…'

'Then?' Elias asked, intrigued to hear the answer.

'Then perhaps what I've been doing counts for nothing.' She stopped suddenly, completely still in her seat, like she had just told herself the Tooth Fairy wasn't real.

'Nothing counts for nothing,' Elias said quickly. He wanted to change that expression on her face. 'What you do must work or it… wouldn't work.'

'But maybe it *would* work. Maybe I overcomplicate things.' She drank more of her wine. 'Maybe I offer everyone too much choice. Perhaps they would be just as happy with plain prawns.'

'These are Greek prawns,' Elias reminded. 'The freshest there is.' He poured some more wine into her glass. 'Prawns in the UK…'

'Nowhere near as good,' Becky replied. 'I'm already thinking about how I can get the prawn man to source them from here. But I think Megan would have a fit about the shipping.'

'And they would not be as fresh,' Elias said.

Becky smiled. 'Is that how you sell your houses? This one has an unrivalled view of the spooky cave-lake, whereas this one's view is slightly interrupted by fisherman seeking the best of the day's catch?'

He had almost forgotten he was supposed to be an estate agent. Why was he yet to come clean? He swallowed. He didn't want to spoil what was left of the evening. They both deserved to unwind after the earlier events and he knew finding out his real occupation would unsettle her.

'Something like that,' he answered.

'Do you live in the UK or do you live in Corfu?' Becky asked. 'Are you going to Corfu to sell a particular house?'

'I live in London,' he replied. Something he could at least be honest about. 'I am going to Corfu to see one house, yes. It is a house belonging to one of my long-term clients and he wishes to put this onto the market.' Half-truths but not too far from the mark.

'Gosh,' Becky replied. 'You must be good at what you do to pop over to Greece to sell one house.'

'Well…' He *was* good at his job. And he had made being good at his job his entire life's work, particularly after Hestia. If he hadn't found professional success in the divorce arena he didn't know where he would be now. Where *would* he be? Would he have floundered, sunk into the deepest, darkest depression or would he have found the bravery to stay on the island, face up to the humiliation? Might he have stepped away from law completely? Settled for helping to run the family business? That was a whole world away from where he was now. One room above a *cafeneon* was not his penthouse apartment with river views…

'Is it a big house?' Becky asked. 'Or with views to die for? Or both? Is it near the sea?'

He smiled at her enthusiasm. The wine was helping her relax. She seemed less buttoned-up now – literally – her top sliding off one shoulder, her hair just touching the skin…

'It is near the sea,' he answered. 'With the most incredible view.' He paused to take a drink himself. 'It is not too big. There are three bedrooms and it is done in a style that is sympathetic to its surroundings. Thick stone walls, paved outside space with a few borders for plants and colour, a large pool…'

'It sounds heavenly,' Becky breathed. 'I hope my friend's house is as nice as that one sounds.'

'You have not seen it?' Elias asked her.

'Well, no, I mean, yes. You know, photos.' Becky shrugged. 'It looks lovely. But, even if it wasn't quite as lovely as it looks, it would still be… what I want right now.'

He didn't say anything else. She had dropped her eyes to her wineglass now, looking thoughtful. What was it she wanted or needed right now? Did it have anything to do with that self-help book she was carrying around? He shouldn't want to know...

'I had a row with my sister before I left. It was stupid really. It was *really* petty when you consider what happened with Petra earlier.'

'What was the argument about?' Elias asked her.

'On the surface it was about a job I wanted to cater for but really... I think it was about everything.'

'You have not spoken to her since?'

Becky shook her head. 'I was going to... earlier... at least, I think I would have. But she wasn't there.'

'And the longer the not-speaking continues, the worse it makes you feel.'

She nodded and he watched her eyes tear up. Immediately he was reaching for a serviette, passing it across the table to her. 'Here.'

She took the napkin and dabbed at her eyes. 'Sorry, I don't know why I'm getting like this. Megan probably isn't thinking about me at all. She has Dean... and the business to run... and apart from my skills in buttering the bread, she doesn't really need me.'

He raised an eyebrow as he looked over at her. 'I think she needs you to make the sandwiches memorable, does she not?' She had talked with such passion about that. He almost wanted to taste something she had made so carefully, with so much thought and attention to detail.

Becky sniffed, dabbing at her nose with the serviette. 'Well, that's the other thing,' she said. 'Megan doesn't know I do any of that.'

Before Elias could make a reply, someone was touching his arm and trying to encourage him from his seat. It was a female dancer, one of the professionals, in traditional costume. He shook his head. '*Ochi.*'

'Those dresses are so beautiful,' Becky said, eyes a little glazed as she looked at the woman close to their table. There were other dancers amid the dining tables now, who seemed to be creating a ring of people on the dusty ground as the *bouzouki* and mandolin continued to play.

'You would like to dance?' Elias asked her. What was he saying? He hadn't danced since the last village festival in Liakada. Things had been so different then. For one, he had been married.

Becky waved a hand in the air like she was swatting away a mosquito. 'I don't know how to dance like a Greek.' She spoke again. 'Is it hard?'

His mind went to inappropriate for a second. 'No,' he answered. 'It is very simple.' He held his hand out to her. '*Ela.* Come.'

Twenty-Four

'This isn't *my* idea of simple,' Becky said, her breath catching in her throat. It was taxing and it was tiring. The frenetic pace matched with the sticky air was causing perspiration she was praying wouldn't show through her clothes. She hoped Ms O'Neill's home had a washing machine because if she kept going through outfits the way she currently was, she'd be buying local or smelling like a stray dog.

Elias laughed. He had a gorgeous laugh too. Deep but light and uplifting somehow. Was there anything that wasn't nice about him? 'You do not have to get every step perfect.'

'Everyone else is!' Becky moaned. They were still in a circle, their arms around each others' shoulders, moving left and right, putting one leg forward them moving left and right again.

'The man with the walking cane is not,' Elias told her.

'That's mean. He can't help it.'

'I am just pointing out that not everyone is perfectly in time and no one cares about this.' He paused, dropping his mouth to her ear. 'Getting each step perfect... that is not what Greek dancing is about.'

'No?' Becky asked.

'No,' he insisted. 'It is about expression. These dances, they tell a story, not just of the traditions of the country or here, of this island of Kefalonia... they are a story from the heart of each and every dancer.'

'So... OK,' Becky said, swaying left and lifting up her leg, hanging onto Elias's shoulder as the tempo increased again. 'What story is the woman in the yellow dress trying to tell?'

'I don't know!' Elias exclaimed with another laugh. 'That story will be personal to her.'

'Come on!' Becky said. 'The chances are she's simply a holidaymaker enjoying the wine and the Greek customs and she's probably feeling just as challenged as me in the footwork department.'

'Perhaps,' Elias said with a shrug. 'But all I know is that in the village where I am from, when we dance, we dance to show an emotion.'

The sincerity in his words fizzed over her skin and she shivered like a cool breeze had tickled the fine hairs on her arms. 'What kind of emotion?'

'All of them,' Elias said as the line broke apart and everyone clapped for the ending of the song. 'Greeks, they dance when they are happy. Then they dance when they are sad, or in mourning, or when they are angry. There is a lot of stamping when we are mad.'

The mandolin player struck up a new song, a soft tune, his fingers strumming quickly over the strings to produce that atmospheric sound everyone who had seen Nicolas Cage as *that* Italian soldier on this very island was familiar with. It made Becky get goose bumps all over. Here she was, gently perspiring in the middle of a makeshift dancefloor, standing under a full moon with the warmth of a Greek night surrounding her, listening to the most beautiful music, on an island she wasn't meant to be visiting. Suddenly she felt so lucky. She looked at Elias and smiled. 'So, what you're saying is that there's a dance for every occasion.'

'I'm saying there is an expression of emotion for every occasion. Not always organised steps.' He clapped his hands and moved his feet, holding out his hand out to her.

'What are you doing?' Becky asked.

'We should dance some more,' Elias encouraged, taking her hand and leading her into the middle of the space.

'But no one else is dancing anymore,' she gasped. 'The circle has gone. We need the circle.'

'We don't need the circle,' Elias reassured her. 'In the UK do you need a circle to express your emotions?'

'Well… I… don't ever usually express my emotions in public… or ordinarily through the medium of dance.'

Elias laughed. 'What are you afraid of, Captain Rebecca?'

What was she afraid of? He was holding her hand. Wasn't this something she had told herself she would be open to on this trip? *New experiences.* They'd practically toasted to it. Being sensibly cautious, but not so cautious that she could be cast in a TV show entitled *Diary of an Introvert.*

'OK,' she said to him. 'What emotion are we expressing?' The look she gave him was bold.

The fire and determination in her eyes took him by surprise. He liked it. He was finding there was quite a lot more to his aeroplane companion than first impressions would suggest. And it seemed she was keen to accept this dancing challenge now. Which was good, because the minute his feet had hit the olive tree leaf-spattered dust, he knew he needed to dance to rid himself of the memories of the last time. The last time had not been just an ordinary festival in Liakada, it had been the night after he had married Hestia. So many feelings had come to the fore that night, and so many of them, on reflection, had perhaps meant something entirely different. His parents had been so proud of him back then. *A solicitor.* A job he had got himself qualified for through hard mental work. The opposite to the hard, physical work his parents had both done to make money. *A husband.* Married to someone they knew, someone they loved like a daughter, someone who would provide them with grandchildren. And then it had fallen apart. He strengthened his core. He was on a new path now, no matter what anyone else's opinion was on it.

'How do you feel right now?' Elias asked Becky, now holding both her hands in his. Her skin was warm, her face was a little flushed from the dancing.

'Ridiculous,' Becky replied. 'But not giving in. I feel… free,' she admitted. 'I'm going to dance like I am free.' She let go of his hands and twirled around ever so slowly in time to the lilt of the mandolin.

Elias watched her, caressing the dusty earth with her shoes, sliding a foot back and forth like she might be making a pattern with her soles. She drew her arms up, swirling them around, in rhythm with the music, circling her wrists, fingers moving like she was tickling the night air. He couldn't take his eyes off her. And now she was encouraging him forward, beckoning him to join her. He stepped closer.

'You have done this before,' he whispered, shadowing her movements.

'I haven't,' Becky laughed. 'I promise you I haven't. Maybe,' she mused, 'I have Greek ancestry no one knows about. Perhaps my mum or dad's lineage involves some of your gods and goddesses. Maybe I'm not Captain Rebecca Rose, the English rose. Maybe I'm part Greek, the goddess Aphrodite's great-great-great-great-all-the-rest-of-the-greats niece or something.'

'Your dancing would suggest this could absolutely be the case,' he answered.

'I think it's the wine,' she whispered, stepping closer to him. 'Or the fig liqueur. But don't tell anyone. Let them think my skills – if they are skills and not just fortunate swaying – come from my fictional heritage. Bring on Ancestry.co.uk.' She laughed and he felt his insides clench.

God, he liked her. He didn't just find her attractive. He actually liked her, wanted to get to *know* her. How did that happen after less than forty-eight hours and a couple of plane rides? He had barriers in place. He didn't *feel* like that anymore. He didn't need it and he did not want it. Except the rest of him, the meant-to-be-broken emotional side of him was fully awake and demanding more interaction. He put one hand on her waist and drew her towards him. Maybe for one brief moment he could let himself feel again. After all, after tonight they would never see each other again...

Becky gasped involuntarily as they connected in their dance, their bodies close, the musicians providing all the lento. This was Becky Rose out from behind her wrap-filling station, soaking up all the Greek ambience and being (virtually) unafraid about doing it. This absolutely gorgeous man – seemingly gorgeous inside and out from what she had discovered in the short time she had known him – was holding her hand in his, stunning eyes locked on hers. He smelt so good – something pine woodland mixed with citrus – and this was beginning to turn into a dance like no other. She needed to take this moment. Own it. He was no longer a stranger. She didn't need to hold back or worry he was going to murder her or defraud her... Was he moving closer still? Those beautiful full lips! What would they taste like? She shut her eyes, shaking with anticipation...

And then the heat disappeared. Sharply. Suddenly his hand left hers and she snapped open her eyes to see Elias departing rapidly from the dance space. What had happened? What did she do? How embarrassing was this? All alone on the dancefloor now, feeling the weight of eyes on her, she moved from foot to foot with a lot less enthusiasm than she had felt before. She would end the song and then she would beat a hasty retreat back to the table.

She tracked Elias's movements with her eyes. It looked like he was heading to the bar. Waiters were still delivering platters of steaming delicacies, carafes of wine. And suddenly there was Petra, coming into view, bouncing out of the taverna, wearing a bright white dress that barely covered any of her. Smiling, glowing even, looking completely in opposition to the half-dead individual who had to be hauled from the lake earlier. A miraculous recovery, and why did she look so effortlessly good in obviously borrowed clothes?

It was then Becky wished she had looked away, focused on the talented musicians, or stopped dancing and gone back to the table to finish the wine. Because the next thing that happened seemed to occur in slow motion and it wasn't the good kind of slow motion like running back a scene of a chick flick you wanted to relive in all its detailed glory. No, this was the slow motion of disaster waiting to occur that you had absolutely no control over and definitely did not want to see. Becky still couldn't look away, even when her gut realised exactly what was going to happen. Her breath tight in her throat, her newly found self-confidence nosediving down to her espadrilles, she watched Petra connect with Elias. Lips to lips. Mouth to mouth. Meeting in a kiss.

Twenty-Five

On board the flight from Kefalonia to Corfu

Becky now knew that figs made into a liqueur were definitely not as good for you as figs ingested in other ways. OK, it was probably the fault of the alcohol content of the liqueur and not the fruit, but she had never known a hangover like this one and she remembered a New Year's Eve party where she had happily scooped up homemade punch out of a bucket with a cracked *The Simpsons* mug. That was one of the things she still blamed Dean for.

She had avoided everyone in Argostoli this morning and last night, when Agelos had sped them back to their hotel, she had pretended to be asleep in the back of his truck, so she didn't have to look/talk/interact with Petra or Elias. It had turned out to be quite hard to feign sleep when every time Agelos hit a pothole – of which there were many – her head had slammed against the window. And it was even harder to pretend she had nodded off when Petra was running her hands through Agelos's hair as he drove, telling him they should swap numbers and meet up again on her travels, maybe in Corfu. Becky had gritted her teeth hard, the image of Petra and Elias locked together in an embrace still in high definition in her memory bank. Was no man safe with Petra around? Why didn't Agelos seem bothered Petra was loose with her lips? Or was everyone a lot more unconcerned with everything than she was?

This morning Becky's thoughts had felt a little clearer, if not the whole of her head thanks to the fug of her hangover. Clarity said that Petra did what Petra wanted. And Becky hadn't ever voiced that she quite liked Elias herself. Perhaps, because until last night, until they had talked and drank and danced together, she hadn't *really* known that she might want to kiss him, dinner party meat daydreams aside. And with that taken into account, she only had herself to blame. She should have acted more quickly. Sod the so-called kiss waiting time as suggested by Hazel's book! If she had taken charge and kissed Elias herself, he would have been with *her* on the dancefloor and not near Petra. But, in turn, if Elias *had* felt anything for her, if he had wanted to kiss her, he wouldn't have run away in the first place. However, even if second thoughts had made him flee, it wasn't exactly great etiquette to end up locking lips with someone else within seconds. Still, at least Becky had now discovered that there *was* something not nice about Elias after all. So much for being Mr Flawless!

As the passengers filed onto the aeroplane Becky took a swig from her bottle of water and prayed both of her original travelling companions would be seated elsewhere on the plane. A few dozen rows back would be ideal. She had hidden at the very rear of the coach from the harbour to the airport and waited for them both to depart before she got off outside departures. Strangely, given their closeness last night, Elias and Petra hadn't sat next to each other on the transfer. Petra, sitting alone, had loudly told the tale of her cave rescue – with an added man-eating jellyfish as an enhancement – to the two lads with the giant backpacks. Elias had sat at the very front of the coach, eyes glued to his phone.

'Good morning.'

Oh no! This could not be happening again. Becky had read several articles about how difficult it was to get seats together on a plane if you were travelling with a family, or even as a couple, that prior booking was the only sure way, but it seemed through some twist of fate she and Elias were destined to be paired together on every plane they stepped onto.

'Hello,' she answered with a sigh, undoing her seat belt and moving out into the aisle so he could shift in.

'I did not see you at breakfast,' he said, popping his case in the overhead locker then moving to his seat.

'No,' Becky answered.

She needed to sound less mad. Sounding mad would give the impression that she cared. She needed not to care. Or at least project to Elias that she didn't care. In her drunken haze last night she had read a few pages of *How to Find the Love of Your Life or Die Trying*. Confidence was key. No one fell in love with someone who thought little of themselves. Not that falling in love or finding that elusive 'the one' was going to be a thing on this housesitting holiday. But she was going to be open to a romantic connection… just not with someone who led her on then snogged someone else. Had Elias actually led her on? Or was that simply her own mind filling in pieces that weren't really there?

'No,' she said again, forcing her mouth into a smile. 'I took a walk to the harbour to see if I could see the turtles everyone says live here.'

'Oh,' Elias said, settling into his seat. 'I would have liked to have seen them too.'

If he wanted to be asked, he should have not kissed Petra. Grr! She was taking this too seriously again. She did not need someone to couple up with her, nor wear matching tracksuits or cuddle up and gorge on foods covered in humus! *Confidence! Love you!*

'There weren't any there,' Becky responded. It was true. She had broken two bread rolls into pieces and tossed them into the sea, the early morning sun warming her shoulders. But no turtles arrived and the bread was happily eaten by a shoal of fish.

'That is unfortunate,' Elias answered, putting his bag under the seat in front of him.

'Well, being on this island at all was really already an unexpected treat,' Becky said.

'Like our visit to Athens,' Elias told her.

Out of the corner of her eye she could see he was looking at her. She must not engage with those beautiful eyes. She did not need to be thrown back to thoughts of a lonely mandolin solo and her swaying like a less lithe, less dark-haired version of Penelope Cruz. As for those perfect lips… not so perfect anymore.

'I cannot wait to finally get to Corfu,' Becky breathed. No whiff of having enjoyed the memories they had made. It was time to move on to what she had come on this trip to do – housesit, indulge in sunbathing and sea-swimming, luxuriating in more space than she had in her flat in Wiltshire. She whipped the safety procedures card from her seat pocket and tried to look engrossed.

Elias watched Becky reading instructions on how to vacate the plane should an emergency occur and knew she was doing this to avoid talking to him any further. It was entirely his fault. He had felt such a pull towards her it had terrified him. He should not have suggested they danced. It hadn't exorcised any ghosts, it had just made him yearn for a feeling he had told himself he could live without. He did not want to admit the possibility that it might not be true. Instead of telling Becky some kind of truth – maybe without the finer details – he had fled. And then there'd been Petra. That young, silly, fickle girl who had no real life experience. She had pounced on him, a full-on kiss he hadn't been able to avoid, but just for a millisecond he had responded. A millisecond where he acted out the emotions that *Becky* had pulled from him. And now conversation was stilted between them. He had done that. He had hurt her. And that was what feeling something did. It hurt people.

'Becky...' he began. He wanted to say something. But 'sorry' wasn't the right word. How could he explain that he had wanted to kiss her and that had scared him so he had run away and lingered a very brief moment too long on the lips of someone he had absolutely no care for? Perhaps it was better to say nothing. Nothing had really happened on that dancefloor, nothing other than the reactions inside of him.

'The weather is nice over Corfu right now,' he told her. 'There should be no turbulence and... we should arrive on time.'

'Good,' Becky replied quickly. And, just as quickly, the conversation was over.

Twenty-Six

Ioannis Kapodistrias Airport, Corfu

All the members of the original flight from London Heathrow cheered when the plane touched down on the tarmac of Corfu. It seemed to unnerve some of the other travellers until Petra took it upon herself to make an announcement that it had taken them almost three days to get here. With no elaboration on the tale, it didn't really seem to help.

Becky was planning to get through passport control and jump at the first taxi-driver she found. Hazel had suggested she got verbal quotes before she settled on one driver, but Becky wanted 'away' and now she knew the Greek word for 'no', she was sure she could manage not to be ripped off. Besides, surely not everyone was out to fleece her.

'So,' Petra said, sheening her cheekbones with ChapStick. 'Where are we headed?'

The girl had somehow ended up right next to her on the super-short-almost-unnecessary bus jaunt from the plane to the arrivals hall and hadn't really stopped talking since. *Agelos is probably going to ask me to marry him the next time we meet. Who's hotter? Agelos, Elias, Panos or Marathon. You didn't see Marathon, did you?* Elias had got himself on Petra's list. Marvellous work. Becky had hidden her annoyance, but instead taken it out on Hazel's giant bag instead, zipping and unzipping the too-stiff zip. Really, she'd wanted to take a pair of scissors to the too-long handles. Perhaps she would, later, maybe turn them into a voodoo doll of the whole world.

'Well,' Becky said, 'I'm getting a taxi to where I'm going to be staying.'

'And where is that?' Petra asked, kicking her case along as the queue to have their passports checked moved a little.

'In the north,' Becky said, giving nothing away.

'Cool,' Petra replied. 'I want to see the north too.'

'But where are you staying?' Becky asked her. An uneasy feeling was suddenly hugging her shoulders.

'Wherever I end up,' Petra answered with a grin.

'But haven't you booked somewhere?' Becky inquired. Who went away without booking any accommodation?! It was July! There were no direct flights to Corfu left, it stood to reason that accommodation was likely hard to come by too. Wasn't the holiday industry still reeling from the demise of Thomas Cook? *Petra didn't have a room.* And as Becky processed that thought she realised what was going to come next.

'I could stay with you, couldn't I?'

'Petra…'

'I mean you told me you were housesitting a big house with three bedrooms and no one's there but you, is there? Three bedrooms for one person doesn't really make any sense at all. Three bedrooms is basically a guest house and I'm a guest. I could… buy all the *ouzo* and the *gyros* when we go out and I could help you clean… get leaves out of the pool and stuff. I'm good at getting stuff out of the pool. This one time, in Bali, I fished out a gold chain, a pair of Vans *and* a blow-up doll. A female one if you want to know.'

Becky tried to interrupt. This was *her* adventure. Hers. She wanted solitude and being at one with Greek nature and all the customs, drinking in all the differences between the two cultures with maybe a little more of that *sirtaki* dancing she had performed last night. Definitely with a different partner…

'I can be really quiet if I need to be. Honestly, I can,' Petra continued. 'Once, when I was seven, I did a twenty-four-hour silence and then after that twenty-four hours I wrote a sign that told everyone if they doubled their sponsorship money I was going to do a second twenty-four hours concurrently. I made shitloads. For charity obvs.'

'Petra, it isn't my house. I don't make the rules.' And Ms O'Neill had said 'no couples'. That meant she wanted *one* person, not two, didn't it?

'But you do, don't you?' Petra asked, kicking her case again, the two Greek men in the light blue shirts of the police uniform ever closer. 'Because no one else is going to be there, are they?' Then Petra gasped and put her hands to her cheeks. 'Unless… someone else *is* going to be there. Unless you've invited Elias.'

'I'm housesitting,' Becky said, checking the passport in her hand still contained a photo of her. Another one of Hazel's scare stories had involved arriving at the terminal and finding out she had turned into Malcolm Greengage. 'I haven't and *won't* be inviting anyone because I am there to do a job.'

'An unpaid job,' Petra reminded.

'Well, I'm getting to stay in a luxury villa with a pool that's only steps away from the beach. Who wouldn't want to do that for free?'

'Well,' Petra started again. 'I could be your... security. This one time, in Japan, I absolutely floored this supposed expert in karate with one decisive move.'

That *did* sound impressive. 'Do you know karate?' Becky asked her.

'No,' Petra replied. 'I headbutted him.'

'Petra,' Becky said with a sigh. It was almost their turn to be checked. 'I really don't think—'

'Please,' Petra begged.

There was a change in her voice now, a real cutting emotion to it and when Becky focused on her properly, she could see there were tears forming in the girl's light blue eyes.

'Petra...'

'Please, Becky,' Petra said again, more emotion evident. 'I really like you. I do. And I... I've been completely on my own for so long I just feel like... I don't know... I feel like company... maybe.' She cleared her throat suddenly, as if she wanted to clear the emotion she had just let seep out. 'And we haven't even talked about the greatest chick flick of all time yet... *Legally Blonde.*'

Becky took in the young girl anew. She was so young. Eighteen? Not much older surely. And despite all the bravado, outlandish remarks and acting-out behaviour there was something vulnerable about her right now.

'I promise I won't bring anyone back. I will be completely on my best behaviour. Guide's honour. I wasn't in the guides, but I've heard they are honourable girls like... Little Mix. I'll be like Little Mix. But quieter. No singing or dance routines.'

This was when Becky should have said a final and definite '*ochi*'. Except she was thinking about this too-good-looking girl who would be using her feminine wiles to get herself a room in Corfu. If Becky said no to her staying at the house in Kerasia, then where would she end up? And if where she ended up wasn't safe how would Becky feel then?

'Pool duty,' Petra continued. 'Every day. Twice a day if there's a nearby tree dropping leaves in it. All the *ouzo* on me.'

'Petra...'

'The poo bin!' Petra interrupted. 'I'll do the bin the bog roll goes into. Every day.'

Becky was a decent human being who had been brought up well. She cared. It was a good trait, but also her ultimate downfall. There was only one thing she could say.

'A few days,' Becky told her. 'Only a few days and there will be rules. Strict rules that you will have to promise to abide by and—'

She was unable to get the rest of the sentence out because Petra had slammed into her, body hitting hard, long arms wrapping around her and crushing hard like an over-zealous boa constrictor. She could feel the girl trembling and breathing softly in and out.

'Thank you so much!' Petra exclaimed. 'I mean it. Thank you!'

Becky was still being fiercely hugged and it was only

a command in Greek she had no understanding of that prompted her to disengage from Petra's grip. Then Becky saw who had shouted the instruction. One of the policemen. They were next in line to have their passports inspected and unless they wanted an irate queue of people behind them they needed to step forward.

'So,' Petra began, grabbing Becky's arm before she could move towards the desk. 'What *are* these rules I need to abide by?'

He was back. Back on the island he was born on. Here at the place he vowed he would visit only when absolutely necessary. Elias took a breath as he waited in the queue to rent a hire car. It was necessary. Or, instead, had he *made* it necessary? It was too late for second thoughts now though. He was here and he was going to make the most of it. He was going to collect all the evidence he needed to ensure Chad came out of his divorce on top and he was going to assure his parents that his life without Corfu – without Hestia – was good. It *was* good. He had an expensive apartment. He had a health club membership. When he wasn't working he had friends he vaguely socialised with. It was enough. It had to be. What was the alternative? Open himself up to being let down again?

He swallowed, seeing Becky and Petra emerge from the arrivals hall. Whatever 'good' was, it wasn't 'great' and those feelings on the dancefloor in Kefalonia had reminded him of what it felt like to be part of something else. To be in tune with *someone* else. But he wasn't ready for it, was he? He should just let them walk out of the airport. They were travelling companions, people he had shared a couple of evenings with simply because they were in the same sticky situation.

Petra was taking Becky's bag off her and looking like she was going to try and tie a knot in the too long straps. Perhaps they were sharing a taxi together. He didn't even know where they were heading. Becky had said 'the north' but that didn't narrow it down enough. Enough for what? What was the matter with him? Mere minutes back on Corfu and he was weakening…

They were still there. If he wanted to get a number or say goodbye there was still time. Except if he moved now he might lose his place in the queue. *Damn it*. His feet were already moving of their own accord and he found himself heading over towards the women.

'Where did you buy this bag? It's not practical at all, it's practically useless,' Elias heard Petra say, one of the bag straps between her teeth.

'It's not mine so please don't bite anything off it!'

'Hi,' Elias greeted. He felt like a teenager, not knowing what to do with his hands, feeling the need to put one of them through his hair and the other onto the handle of his case.

'Oh, hello!' Petra greeted. 'You got a knife at all?'

'A knife?'

'Ignore her,' Becky ordered. 'She's trying to help me with my bag but I've just told her it isn't mine so she can't maim it.'

'Are you getting a taxi?' Petra asked, tying a tight knot in the bag straps then shoving it back at Becky. 'You could share with us.'

'I am getting a car,' he replied. What did he want to say? That he could take them wherever they were going? That it was nice to meet them and goodbye?

'We could share with you!' Petra announced. 'Well, by share I mean you could give us a lift. What's the name of the village you're going to live in, Becks?'

'It's fine, thank you,' Becky replied. 'We're getting a taxi. We don't want to impose. I'm sure you're very busy with your estate agency work.'

Why had he expected anything else? He had blown it. He had run away. He had engaged with Petra for a meaningless millisecond. He was a *malaka*.

'It was so nice to meet you!' Petra said, throwing her arms around him. There was nothing he could do to avoid it but he platonically patted her back and kept his face well away from any contact whatsoever. It was a shame he hadn't done that the night before.

'You too,' Elias replied. 'Both of you.'

Becky wasn't even looking at him. Her gaze was inside the giant bag, as if searching for something... or nothing at all.

'Maybe we can meet up,' Petra suggested. 'You know! Have a reunion of the travellers who got stuck together in Athens and Kefalonia. I've got the numbers of Greg and Mark.'

Elias had no idea who Greg and Mark were. 'I don't...'

'The lads with the biggest backpacks in the world. Seriously, Mark's was the size of a small house. You could fit a family of refugees in there. This one time, in Algeria—'

'We ought to go and get a taxi arranged,' Becky broke in. She obviously wasn't struck on the idea of a reunion meet-up. It didn't sound like she wanted to see him again, ever.

'Sure,' Petra answered. 'Rule Number One, you're the boss.'

'Bye, Elias,' Becky said. She was looking at him now, with the faintest of smiles. He had ruined things. They had shared a closeness that his bad experience with Hestia had put paid to. And there was nothing he could do about it now. But perhaps it was for the best…

'Bye, Elias!' Petra said. 'Thanks for one of the best travelling stories ever. It's not every day you get saved from a cave-lake by a real-life Adonis!'

Becky had already turned away and Petra scuttled off after her. There was nothing left to say.

'*Yassas*, Captain Rebecca,' he said to thin air.

Twenty-Seven

Kerasia

'Aww! This place is *all* the cute!' Petra gabbled as the taxi drove them down a rather winding and steep descent Becky wasn't sure any vehicle should attempt unless it was a tractor. The landscape on their journey from the airport had changed from town to port, then to cypress trees and roadside tavernas, to real rural, the edges of the roads now lined with vegetation, restaurants in shaded nooks, trailing vines over their pergola-rooftops.

'How far is it?' Petra asked Becky.

'I don't know,' she answered. She only knew the vague directions she had been given, on a printed-out email she was holding, but the driver seemed to be confidently heading around sharp bends and tight turns towards somewhere.

'It is not far,' the taxi driver replied.

'Five minutes?' Petra asked. 'Ten? Do I have time to sing "Ten Mythos Bottles Hanging On A Wall"?'

'Petra,' Becky said. Why did Petra have to talk to

everyone? Sometimes it was a bit much. And this was the person she had invited to stay with her...

'We are here,' the taxi driver informed. 'No time for singing.'

Becky gazed out of the window. Through green-painted iron gates, she was looking at the most beautiful rustic stone property. It appeared to be everything Becky had hoped for. It seemed warm and cosy and traditional. There were cream-coloured urns spilling bright blooms in red and violet either side of a large wooden front door and pieces of driftwood art hanging from the eaves. She wanted to race out of the vehicle and dash in, dump her case in the hall – if there was a hall – and head out to explore the back garden and that promised pool.

There was a thumping on the window from outside the car. 'Are you getting out?'

Petra, it seemed, had already left the vehicle. No money offered towards the cab fare. Becky got her purse out of her bag. 'The fee we agreed?' she asked, selecting a note.

'*Ne. Fisika*,' the driver replied.

'What does that word mean? Fishy car,' Becky repeated.

'*Fisika*,' he repeated. 'It means "of course".'

'*Fisika*,' Becky said again, trying to commit it to memory. She was determined to pick up a few words of Greek while she was here. It said in her guidebook that the Greeks really appreciated efforts to converse in their native tongue. She handed him the money. '*Efharisto*.' That meant 'thank you'.

'*Parakalo*.'

And that meant 'please' or 'you're welcome'. That was a handful of words already. She felt ridiculously pleased with herself.

She got out and took her case. Petra had already popped the boot and hauled out her backpack and the girl was at the front of the building peering in through one of the windows.

'It's got a nice view!' Petra yelled. 'I can see bi-fold doors!'

No quiet discovery like Becky had imagined it. Softly padding into each room, waiting to see what came next. Petra was going to shout a description for her.

'Have you got the keys?' Petra called again.

'No, they're going to be left in a plant pot.' She had remembered thinking that was pretty lax in the security department but maybe that's what they did in Greece. And would it have been any safer if Ms O'Neill had posted them to her?

'Which one?' Petra asked, scurrying about. 'There are at least three hundred pots.'

There weren't, were there? She obviously *was* on watering duty like Hazel had suggested.

'Shall I start picking them up and looking for the key?' Petra asked, her hands either side of a very chunky-looking urn she surely had no chance of lifting. Or if she managed to get it up it was most likely going to drop down and break...

'No!' Becky said quickly. 'It will be one of the ones by the door.' She hoped so. She put both hands on the pot and rocked it back and forth until it did reveal a set of keys underneath. Bingo! She snatched them up and went to the lock. She was resolute she was going to be the first person over the threshold.

She put the key in the lock and turned. She could imagine it already. It was going to be all light linens and gauze curtains, sunshine streaming in and dappling cool tiled floors... Instead, the first thing that hit her when she opened the door was a foul stench. It was awful! It was sick-inducing. It was worse than bad eggs or bad prawns or a past its eat-by date egg and prawn panini. Becky coughed, almost choking. She put a hand over her nose and mouth and desperately tried not to inhale.

'Fucking hell! What's that stink?! Ugh! I'm gagging! I'm gagging! I'm going to puke!' Petra yelled.

'No, you're not!' Becky shouted back. Despite wanting to retreat back into the fragrant courtyard, she needed to find out what it was. Perhaps it was a blocked toilet or a leaking pipe. She took steps forward. There was wood flooring here, dark and distinguished, possibly reclaimed. The smell got worse as she moved past the door to the kitchen and into the main living area of the house. Natural stone walls, a few paintings, gaps on the wall where perhaps more paintings used to be, mirrors, a lot of mirrors...

Then she stopped dead in her tracks, hearing movement. There was someone in the house! Had Ms O'Neill's warnings about people trying to get in not just been a case of being over cautious? Was there someone *already* in? Was she about to walk in on an attempted robbery? Maybe that's why there were absent paintings. But a robbery didn't explain the smell...

What did she do? What was the telephone number for the police here in Corfu? Why hadn't Hazel or Shelley told her information like that?! That was much more vital intel than what someone who potentially carried a credit card reading device could look like.

'Is there someone in here?' Petra whispered *really* loudly. The noises coming from the next room stopped. There was no doubt whoever was in there had heard.

'We should confront them,' Petra said, slightly more quietly. 'Look around for a weapon.' She picked up an expensive-looking mantle clock. Petra couldn't use that. It was probably an heirloom. The very last thing Becky wanted to do was break an antique in her first few minutes at housesitting.

'I'm going in,' Becky announced. 'Put that clock down.'

Scared to death, but knowing she had to be the one in charge of the situation, Becky marched around the corner ready to give the intruder a piece of her mind, or her fists if needs be. But the sight that greeted her had her gasping in shock. She let out a scream and the cawing, growling and spitting of a menagerie of animals came back at her.

'Becks! Are you OK... what the... holy shit! It's a zoo.' Petra was next to her now and, getting over the initial shock at animals being inside the property, Becky now started to take in exactly what they were.

'Three cats,' she counted, her voice shaking. 'Are there three?'

'Definitely three,' Petra concurred.

'And an owl.' Becky screwed up her face. 'Why haven't the cats eaten the owl?' And didn't owls only come out at night?

'I don't know what that brown and white bear thing is, but I don't like the way it's looking at us,' Petra said.

Becky then took in the carnage surrounding the animals. There were faeces all over the floor. The cats were licking themselves and each other on a whiter than white sofa that had tinges of absolutely not white all over it. The owl was spinning its head looking like it wanted to take flight and the evil bear thing was growling as if it would take great delight in murdering all of them!

Becky's eyes went from the animals to the mess and back again, unable to compute any of it. And then she noticed the bi-fold doors, slightly open, paw marks distinctive in the bright sunlight. An azure sky was visible and the greenery of trees. She longed to forget this carnage ahead of her and seek the pool and those promised views…

'Why are there pink feathers everywhere?'

Petra interrupted Becky's thoughts of relaxation. And then there was shouting in Greek. Perhaps an intruder after all…

'*Oh! Kakos! Kakos! Skata! Skata pantou!*'

Petra had put her hands up like she was about to attempt a karate move and in bustled a Greek woman who could have been anything between the ages of forty-five and sixty-five. She was of medium height, wearing a grey A-line dress, but with the widest bush of black curly hair on top of her head. Should Becky attempt a few words of Greek? Except 'please', 'thank you' and 'of course' probably wasn't going to get her very far in this scenario.

'*Fyge! Fyge makria mou!*' the woman said.

Suddenly the woman clapped loudly, like thunder banging clouds together, then opened her arms like she had the wingspan of a condor and began flapping as if she was preparing for lift-off. The cats immediately scattered, squeezing out of the gap in the doors and next the owl began to fly around the room making a terrible racket. Becky ducked, Petra screamed and the evil bear-thing bared its teeth at the Greek lady.

'*Exo! Exo tora!*' she ordered, getting closer to it. Becky watched through one eye as the owl swooped over her head.

She had to admit she didn't know who she was more afraid of. The bear or the woman. And Becky really should be doing something... Taking a deep breath she made steps across the room towards the bi-fold doors and pulled them open wider. This seemed to please both owl and bear-thing and the bird flew through the opening, the bear-thing scuttering out after it.

And then there were three women left in the living room, the awful smell still lingering, the droppings and mess still all over the floor like it was an enclosure at an animal sanctuary. Becky didn't know what to say but someone had to say something. The Greek woman seemed to be sizing them up, looking them up and down and down and up, a grim expression on her face.

'I only know Greek swear words,' Petra whispered, standing close to Becky. 'This one place, in Thessaloniki, it was full of sailors and...'

'You are the English girl. Come to look after the house.' The Greek woman had spoken and she had a deep commanding voice that said that Becky definitely *wasn't* the one in charge here.

'Yes, we are,' Petra answered. 'And obviously someone has left the door open and let animals in here.'

The Greek woman raised an eyebrow and her abundance of hair seemed to move too. 'Ms O'Neill told me one girl. One. Which *one* is the *one*?'

Becky cleared her throat. 'That's me. I'm Becky.' She put out her hand in an attempt to smooth relations. The woman made no move to shake it or suggest she was going to offer the obligatory two kisses they had started to become accustomed to in this country. This wasn't a good start.

The woman was looking very stony-faced now and Becky wondered if she was going to say anything else or whether it would be up to Becky to try and speak again…

'I am Eleni. My business has been waiting for you to finally arrive.' She turned her attention from Becky to Petra. 'I lock all the doors yesterday and I do not like to be made of accusations.'

'Oh… no, Petra wasn't… isn't…' Becky started. Where were her newly learnt Greek words now, when she needed them most? What was it the taxi driver had said…? She had it. She looked as remorseful as she could then said: '*Fisika*.'

The woman immediately brightened, the scornful look lightening considerably, her stance less warrior. 'You know Greek?'

'A very small amount,' Becky answered with a hopeful smile.

'I know all the…' Petra began.

Before her companion could get the sentence out Becky stood on Petra's toe making her yelp.

'Petra, why don't you go and have a look upstairs?' She lowered her voice to a whisper she hoped only Petra could hear. 'I'll let you have first choice of bedroom if you go away now.'

Petra didn't need to be asked twice. She was picking up her backpack in youthful excitement and bounding towards the gorgeous natural stone staircase neither of them had had a chance to marvel at when faced with a clutch of wildlife…

Becky smiled at the Greek woman who had finally taken her hands off her hips. 'Ms O'Neill didn't say there would be someone to greet me. It's lovely to meet you.'

'Ms O'Neill said one person,' Eleni said. She stubbed her

foot at some of the droppings and the smell in the room seemed to ripen. '*Ena.*'

'I know,' Becky replied quickly. 'Petra, isn't staying very long.'

'How long?'

'She isn't staying here at all. I mean, when I said "staying", I really meant she's only here to see that I am... settled in.'

'Settled in?' Eleni asked. She came a little closer to Becky, droppings on the toe of her shoes now and then she sniffed as if she had lie-detector nasal skills.

'Oh, you know, making sure I've... found the local supermarket and that... I know how to lock all the doors. Maybe a couple of nights.'

'The local supermarket,' Eleni repeated. '*Ochi.*'

Becky knew what *ochi* meant. It meant 'no'. Was this woman going to run her out of the local village. Where even was this local village? They seemed to be pretty much in the middle of nowhere here. And she hadn't noticed the promised car for her use outside of the property. If she wasn't allowed to shop locally how was she going to get to a shop she *was* permitted to go in? All these scenarios and more were dropping down into her mind like... droppings from the bottom of a bear-thing.

'You will shop in my *cafeneon*,' the woman told her. It was definitely an order and not a request. 'I have everything you need. It is a short walk down the hill, to the left from the gate.'

'OK,' Becky replied, actually too scared to say anything else.

'And you will clean this mess. There are products in the kitchen. And if you run out...' Eleni began, seemingly heading for the hallway and the door out.

'You have some at your shop?' Becky asked, feeling the need to follow in the woman's footsteps.

'*Cafeneon*,' she corrected, looking over her shoulder. 'It has supplies and a bar and a post office. For *local* people.'

Becky swallowed. Was she meant to use the facility or not? Now she wasn't quite sure.

'But we do not turn down the money from foreigners.' She grinned then and continued down the hallway.

'Becky!' Petra yelled from upstairs. It sounded slightly manic and Becky's heart skipped a beat as the Greek woman stopped her retreat and they both looked up. 'I know why there are pink feathers down there! There's a fucking flamingo standing in the bath!'

Twenty-Eight

Liakada Village

Elias was sweating and it had nothing to do with the heat of the day. Being back here, on the outskirts of his home village, was the only thing creating the perspiration. And why he had decided to park the car here and walk the rest of the way he wasn't really sure. Perhaps a part of him was still not completely committed to the idea of being back. Maybe quietly arriving on foot was going to be easier than driving in, parking at his parents' place and having the neighbours peeking out from behind their shutters to see who the unrecognised vehicle belonged to. That was what had always happened. Tourists having taken a wrong turn because of their sat-nav could be literally terrified by the looks from the locals as they tried to find a space to turn around and leave...

Liakada was a typical Greek village full of tiny little houses all quirky in their own way. Varying degrees of pastels, some painted smartly, others with parts peeling off, small dogs yapping in the courtyards, half a broken tractor on a scrub of land (this one belonged to Makis and hadn't been moved since before he was born, his mother had told him), flowering vines, lemon trees and bushes bearing figs and kumquats, empty giant cans of feta cheese now used to collect rain water... It was so at odds with the life he had made for himself in London.

'Elia!'

He froze, standing completely still. The voice was coming from above him and he didn't know whether to run away or look.

'Elia Mardas!' His name was shouted even louder and unless he wanted the whole village opening their doors and joining in, he needed to respond.

Turning, he looked up onto a balcony above, a washing line spanning the length of its concrete overhang. He waved a hand. It was Areti. One of his mother's closest friends. It wasn't her house. He couldn't have expected to run into her here.

'*Yassas, Areti*,' he responded with a small smile. '*Kalispera*.'

'It *is* you!' she clapped her hands together, pushing apart the sheets she was hanging and sticking her whole body out, standing up against the railings. 'Oh, look at you. You have lost weight. You are too thin. I will need to make you much of my *moussaka*. How long you stay? You move back? Your case is very small.'

So many questions. Already. He should have remembered talking to the people in his village was always like getting an inquisition from a government agency.

'I am here for work,' Elias answered. That told Areti nothing much... and he knew exactly how much *moussaka* she intended to give him! It would be enough to feed the whole village, if not the whole of Greece.

Areti whisked away another sheet, as if all the linen was getting in her way from seeing him properly. 'How long you stay? My cousin has a house for sale. No parking but...'

'I do not want a house.'

He had said that rather abruptly and immediately regretted it. It was because he remembered the house he had lived in with Hestia. It was his grandmother's old home that had needed complete renovation. He had stripped the wood, taking it back to its original state, hours spent on his hands and knees getting calluses and splinters, then sealing the restored natural pine. Hestia had decorated, made it a home, until it wasn't anymore. Now it was lying empty because, for the time being, he didn't have the heart to sell it out of the family. It didn't make any commercial sense to hold on to it but, for the moment, what could he do? His failed marriage had already broken his mother's heart...

'I am sorry, Areti. I have had a long flight. But it is very good to see you. Are my parents at home right now?' He checked his watch again. Usually they would be there, in the shop, preparing bags of bread or making coffee...

'I... well... I should get this washing finished. It maybe rain later.' Areti began bustling about on the balcony. It was almost like she now wanted to be hidden by the sheets.

'It is July,' Elias reminded her. 'It never rains in Liakada in July.' There was no response. 'Areti!' he called. Areti was the gossip of the village. There was nothing she liked more than to talk. Something was definitely wrong here, and unlike his previous decision to quietly slip into Liakada, he quickened his pace.

*

'Elia Mardas!'

'Yassou, Elia!'

'Elia, ti kanis?'

Elias waved a hand or had a brief passing of the time with the people of Liakada who all seemed to appear from pathways or allotments or from behind shutters greeting his every step, but he did not stop moving. He held his resolve, kept the smile on his face like he had not a care in the world. The fragrant scent of jasmine and wild lilies filled his nose, but he bit back the memories until he arrived in the centre of the village, the hub of Liakada, the small *plaka* stone covered square with the gnarly ancient olive tree providing shade. There was one restaurant, Panos's Taverna, its inside dark against the bright sunlight of the day, its tables outside underneath a canopy of lush green vines, white cloths floating on the slight breeze, two couples who had likely hiked down from the hills enjoying a meal and drinks. And then there was his parents' place. It was like time had stood still. The yellow sign indicating it was a place to collect and send post, his mother's long oblong planters around the windows blooming light pink and white. There was the usual clutch of locals drinking outside, their glasses full of *ouzo*, their plates holding a *meze* of black olives, feta cheese and *dolmades* (stuffed vine leaves). The door was open and Elias's gaze went to the dark, smoky cross burned into the lintel above the threshold. A tradition from Easter to bring luck to houses for the coming year. Life here was exactly the same... or was it?

He removed his sunglasses and looked a little closer at the patrons drinking *ouzo* and playing backgammon. One of them was very familiar. One of them should not be drinking *ouzo* when he was supposed to be in charge of the business.

'Papa,' he called, pulling his suitcase to a halt and stopping outside the steps to the terrace.

The grey-haired man turned his head towards him and Elias could clearly see there were far more lines etched into his father's face than he remembered. His father's eyes were glazed and he seemed to have to concentrate hard to focus. Perhaps he needed glasses? It would be just like him to stubbornly deny the aging process.

'Spiros, it is Elia.' It was his father's friend, Petros, acting like some sort of visual aid for the blind. Maybe his eyesight really *was* failing…

The instant his name hit the air there was an audible intake of breath from the other customers. Elias took the steps noisily, clattering his case, uncaring about the disturbance. Something was not the same with his father and he needed to prioritise that before he dealt with the curious looks and whisperings. He had always known he was going to be the centrepiece of village gossip whenever he showed up. Time may have gone by, but the villagers didn't ever forget a good scandal. And his separation had given them one of the very best.

'Papa,' Elias said, standing right at the table, looking at his father now, ignoring the gazes from Petros, Dimitri and Spiros Beach. There were so many Spiros's on the island – some also with the same last name – you sometimes needed to distinguish them by the job they did. Spiros Beach worked renting sun loungers. His father was Spiros Post.

'What are you doing here?' his father asked. Now his father was looking directly at him and it wasn't quite the expression he had hoped to see. There was something like hostility there. Not even a flicker of I'm-pleased-to-see-you.

'He said "what are you doing here",' Petros said, looking up at Elias like he needed the translation.

'I am not deaf,' Elias retorted. Then he addressed Petros. 'What is wrong with him?'

'Well,' Petros began. 'It is almost time for siesta…'

'That is not an answer.' He looked to his father again. 'Why are you not in the shop? Why are you eating and drinking with your friends?'

'Why are you here?' his father asked again. 'You tell me there is nothing for you here.'

Elias bit the inside of his cheek. There was no doubt his father was halfway to drunk, if not completely there already. But sometimes when you were intoxicated your real feelings escaped from that tight lid that was usually fitted to your heart when sober. He could vouch for that.

There was more whispering from the drinkers at the other tables, even one of the stray dogs – this one black and white and missing an ear – had quietened its yapping and was gazing intently at Elias, its head through the metal railings.

He took a deep breath dampening down the desire to snap back at his father. Now was not the time – he had just set foot in Liakada after an exhausting few days – and here in public was definitely not the place. 'Where is my mother?'

'Pfft!' his father spat. He picked up his *ouzo* glass and drank back the whole contents in one go. 'Why do you ask me?'

Why was his father being so infuriating? OK, so Elias hadn't expected to be hugged and kissed like he was returning alive from a long drawn-out, bloody war, but he had expected to be able to hold a civil conversation.

'Elia…' Petros began, taking a rolled-up cigarette from

behind his ear and putting it between his lips.

'Do not answer for him!' Elias was raising his voice now. Something he didn't want to do. It showed a lack of control. And he was all about control now. He lightened his tone a notch. 'Is my mother inside?'

'How do I know?' Spiros retorted like a child. 'Why should I care?' He took hold of another glass of *ouzo* and downed that drink too.

Now Elias really was at a loss to know what was going on. His parents had always lived in each other's pockets. One would not be able to sneeze at the other end of the village without the other one knowing about it instantaneously.

'You are not making any sense,' Elias told his father. 'You have drunk too much.'

'Oh, you think I have drunk too much.' Spiros picked up a third glass and waved it under his nose as if breathing in the aroma like it was a fine wine he was trying to distinguish. 'I only just begin.' He downed the third glass and there was another audible inhale from the villagers who seemed to have increased in number. There was also another dog – cream-coloured with ringlets of fluffy fur – staring at Elias as if waiting for his reaction. And the truth was, he didn't know *how* to react. He looked at his father anew. His shirt was badly creased. There was a stain on the fabric of his trousers. His hair wasn't greased into place like usual. His father was always well-turned out. His mother always made sure of that...

'Petros,' Elias said. 'Where is my mother?' Perhaps the only logic he was going to get would come from his father's friend after all.

'She is checking on one of the villas she cleans,' Petros answered.

His mother cleaned villas now? Before, she would always be busy with the shop and café. Had business taken a downturn? Was this why his father had turned to drink?

'She will be with Leandros.' This came from his father as he leaned over and snatched another *ouzo* from in front of his friend, Babis. 'Or Constantine. Or perhaps,' he continued, proffering his glass to emphasise his point, 'perhaps she will be like your wife and start to fall in love with women. Maybe she is in the arms of Areti.'

The crowd didn't even try to contain their sighs and gasps and there was even a hand clap and a little laughter. Elias's temper was rising fast and he wanted to grab hold of his father, pull him from the chair, drag him inside the building and shut away the nosy residents in order to get to the root of his behaviour.

'Enough!' Elias roared. He had directed the word at his father, but he had made his voice loud enough so that everyone could hear. He was not about to be made a laughing stock here for a second time. 'Tell me, what is going on?'

It was at that moment his father crumpled. Gone was the ouzo-shotting bravado and in its place was a man falling apart, tears slipping from his eyes, shoulders rolling forward and shaking with emotion. Spiros opened his mouth like he was going to say something, but the words didn't appear to be able to come out.

'Your father does not live here anymore,' Petros spoke up. 'Your mother threw him out six months ago.'

And now it was Elias who needed the *ouzo*.

Twenty-Nine

Villa Selino, Kerasia

Becky dipped her head back into the cool, refreshing water of the most relaxing, tranquil pool she had ever had the pleasure of swimming in. To be fair, the only pool she had really spent any time in was at the local leisure centre. And her fear of seeing a damp, used plaster on the floor was always at the back of her mind when she used that facility, so not fully as relaxing as it might be. Megan had been the real swimming enthusiast. Her sister had read that it was the best form of exercise for an all-over workout and as most of Megan's friends didn't seem to like getting their hair wet, it had been Becky who had accompanied her. It had been fun. They'd done lengths, occasionally they'd turned up on an inflatable session and braved the enormous floatie taking up most of the pool and they'd chatted about the latest drama in the life of Henry the Bachelor who lived next door to the family home. That was pre-It's A Wrap when Becky worked at the bank and Megan was toying with the idea of a business course at college. It was before their dad had died. Before either of them knew how much life was going to change…

But here was a world away from everything in Wiltshire. Here it was like she had slipped into someone else's life for a second. Someone else who was rich and powerful and had other people to butter their bread for them…

Suddenly there was water in her eyes and mouth and she was struggling to maintain her head above the surface. Spluttering, and grabbing onto the wall of the pool, Becky saw that Petra had jumped in, creating the kind of wake a powerboat would have been proud of. It seemed that half-drowning in a cave-lake hadn't put her off water.

'This is worth all the scrubbing, isn't it?' Petra remarked, arriving at Becky's side, hair still beautifully in place.

'Have you finished?' Becky asked. She had made Petra shoo out the flamingo – goodness knew where it was going to end up, but a quick Google search had told her that flamingos did hang out in Corfu, but usually on the lake at the south of the island and not up here in the north. But no amount of internet searching could tell Becky exactly how far flamingos could walk, or fly. Then, once the villa was free of animals – as far as they could see without opening every cupboard door or wardrobe – they had started a clean-up with every product the large modern kitchen possessed. There was even a literal miracle product called Koh that Becky was going to look into buying when she got back to It's A Wrap. But, after an hour of scrubbing until her fingers were numb, Petra insisted Becky leave her to finish things while she got in the pool. And Becky hadn't argued. The pool was what she had been looking forward to the most and it was even better than she could have imagined.

'All finished,' Petra said, putting her arms on the stone surround and lying her head on one of them. 'Shit scrubbed, sanitised and now spotless.'

'Are you sure?' Becky asked. 'Because this place seems to be very high-end. I don't want any kind of leakage ruining wood imported from Africa or something.'

'The grumpy Greek woman didn't mention expensive imports,' Petra said with a sniff. 'And if that flooring was imported from Tanzania or somewhere, I'll... eat my plaits.'

Becky took a breath and leaned a little like Petra was leaning. It wasn't just the water trickling over her shoulders that was incredible, it was the view too. You could see the sea from the pool and not just the smallest of glimpses over rooftops or through the branches of olive trees, a wide, shimmering blue expanse was stretching out into the distance. Simply watching its movement was making Becky feel a little less tightly wound.

'Relax,' Petra told her. 'We made it to Corfu. We fought strange wildlife and an even stranger Greek lady.'

Becky let out a breath, kicking her legs beneath her. 'We haven't found the car yet. If she won't let us get supplies in her shop, we might be barbequing the local wildlife to survive.'

Petra looked lost in the conversation. 'She has a shop?'

'Yes, she told me, when you were... finding the flamingo.'

'But she won't let us use it?' Now Petra seemed even more confused.

'She said it was for local people and she said the word "local" with a lot more emphasis than was needed. But she didn't want us going to the supermarket either.'

'So, she wants us to starve?' Petra queried, splashing

away a wasp that had landed in the water. 'That's not very hospitable and Greece is meant to be one of the most hospitable nations there is. Julia Bradbury didn't seem to have any problems getting doors opened for her.'

'Now you've said the word "starving" I'm really quite hungry,' Becky admitted. She had had nothing since the divine meal on Kefalonia the previous night. Becky had put her need to avoid Elias and Petra above a spread of cheeses and hams at breakfast... and look where that had got her. With one of them as a new housemate!

'There's bottled water in the fridge and a platter of fruit. I ate some grapes,' Petra admitted. 'OK, I ate *all* the grapes but there's other stuff left... peaches, nectarines and cherries.'

Now Becky's stomach was really waking up to the fact it was empty. Her new approach to life had to be not to be bullied by anyone with a larger personality than her. She may not talk the loudest or have the most interesting stories for parties like Petra, but that didn't mean her thoughts and feelings didn't matter. And she wasn't going to be told where she could or couldn't shop.

'Right,' Becky said, taking one hand off the wall and kicking her legs a little harder. 'Once we've finished our swim we're going to have a good look around the grounds and we're going to find the car and we're going to drive to the nearest supermarket and buy our provisions.'

'Ooo, *provisions*,' Petra said with a laugh. 'How old are you again?'

Was that a real question or was Petra taking the rise out of her use of the English language? She hadn't quite got the complete tell of Petra yet... but there would be no real need to, would there? Because Petra was only staying *very* short-term. She needed to continue to make that clear. No amount of shovelling of bear-thing shit and cat pee was going to make Becky give in to Petra staying for the whole duration of her working break.

'Shall I guess?' Petra carried on, letting go of the wall and treading water as she seemed to survey Becky in a bid to work out her age.

'Oh, you were serious,' Becky replied, copying Petra's move and swimming her way into the centre of the pool.

'Thirty…' Petra began.

'Whoa, whoa, whoa. We won't be having any more guessing now!' Becky exclaimed. Did she really look thirty-something? OK, she didn't have the whole skincare cleansing routine that seemed to be on fleek at the moment, but she washed her face morning and night and generally ate healthily. She might do well from a bit more exercise but wouldn't anyone?

'I'm twenty-five,' Becky informed her.

'Really?' Petra said, looking a lot like she didn't believe her.

'Yes, really,' Becky answered. 'How about you? Thirty…'

'Very funny,' Petra said, poking her tongue out and swimming away from Becky. She chased her companion, trying to keep up with Petra's strokes. Perhaps that exercise was more needed than she thought.

'I'm twenty,' Petra said, turning around and resting her back against the other end of the pool, arms outstretched across the length of the wall.

'Wow,' Becky replied. 'And you've done all this travelling already.'

Petra shrugged her shoulders. 'Life's too short to waste it being someone's workplace bitch.'

'I... guess it is,' Becky agreed. But wasn't she Megan's sandwich-making workplace bitch? She was sure Petra would have an opinion on her sister's outburst about her having a holiday. But she wasn't sure she was quite ready to hear it.

'And I never really had any plans for my life before... before I started travelling.' Petra smiled. 'So, I've made travelling my life. And no regrets so far.' She sniffed. 'No pension pot for my retirement, but I'm hopeful of a rich sheikh or oligarch one day, you know, when I'm done toying with the Greek gods.'

It was a simplistic view. Some might say it was a ridiculous, frivolous idea for her future, but it was Petra's life to live and she was definitely living it. Perhaps Becky could take a small lesson from her. Not the kissing lots of random men with only the briefest of introductions, but perhaps the living in the moment and not caring less what anyone else thinks part. Being true to herself. She sighed. The first thing she needed to do was stop feeling guilty about this argument with Megan and stop checking her messages for some sort of apology or at least a checking in, how-are-you-doing text. Becky didn't regret anything she had said to her sister, therefore she shouldn't be constantly going over it in her head thinking she might have said something different simply to keep the peace. Sometimes it was good to be confrontational, especially if you were confronting people with the truth from your heart. Who could ever go wrong with the truth?

'Right, Petra,' Becky said, confidently pushing away from the stone surround of the pool, arms and legs working the water around her body in nice smooth and fluid movements.

'We are going to find this car. We are going to drive to the nearest place with a proper supermarket and we are going to buy lots and lots of...' She stopped herself before she said the word 'provisions' again. 'What should I be saying instead of "provisions" that doesn't make me sound like the thirty-something I'm not? Shopping? Food?'

'*Ouzo* and shit,' Petra said with a laugh. 'We're going to go out and buy lots and lots of *ouzo* and shit.'

'*Ouzo* and shit,' Becky said, relaxing her shoulders into the water and preparing to push her stomach up into a float on the surface. 'Great.'

Petra swam up close to her again, one of her plaits in her mouth, sucking it like a baby might suck a pacifier. 'Are you really only twenty-five? Like, for reals?'

Thirty

Liakada Village

The sun was setting, turning the bright blue sky of the hot day into a fiesta of pink and purple. Elias watched it from the table he had chosen inside the *cafeneon*. He had drunk a half bottle of *ouzo* with his father that afternoon and now he was determined to drink his way through a carafe of his mother's homemade white wine and get to the bottom of what was going on with his parents. His father was no longer at home. His father had made a place to live out of the storage shed they owned lower down in the village, next to the goats and the chickens. His parents were separated. And as he spoke that sentence in his head it still made him shudder. His parents, he had thought, were unbreakable. Together since school, so completely in tune with one another, so vital in each other's lives... If a relationship like theirs crashed against the rocks what hope was there for anyone else? He swigged at his wine, not really tasting it. Except he didn't believe there *was* hope for anyone else, did he? Surely this underlining of the mantra he lived by shouldn't be coming as any sort of surprise. But sometimes, being right about something when you had thought there was *one* exception to the rule, didn't feel so nice.

'Why are you sitting there?' his mother asked, bustling over with a terracotta clay pot in her oven-gloved hands. 'You are in the centre of everything. Move to a table in the corner.'

Elias slugged at his wine. 'No.'

'What did you say?' his mother asked him, the clay pot still in her hands. Elias could smell its contents on the steam rising from the small hole in the centre of its lid. *Stifado*. Beautifully tender pieces of beef that had been simmering slowly for hours – possibly days – together with baby onions all swimming in the thickest tomato and herb sauce. His mother's *stifado* was almost legendary among the locals. It was a recipe that had been handed down through generations.

'I said,' he began, trying not to lick his lips and make his mother realise just how much he needed the food she was holding. If he wasn't careful, she could just as easily put it down in front of the locals outside, still sitting around their backgammon games. 'I am happy with my choice of table… and this wine is… better. A good year for the apples this year?'

Something seemed to shift in his mother's eyes then, a dulling of her furore perhaps. She put the pot down in front of him and he reached for the lid. Immediately she slapped him away with one of her gloved hands. 'What are you doing? It is hot like fire! It has come straight from the oven! Do you want to burn your hands off?' She picked up the lid, her hands protected from the heat, and carefully put it down on the table opposite him. 'And there is nothing different about the wine. The wine is always good.'

'The wine is not always good,' Elias told her. 'The wine is usually terrible. But no one complains, either because they are locals and have been drinking it for thirty years and have got accustomed to the terrible wine, or they are tourists and they think it is meant to taste like that because the grapes have been crushed by hand – or foot – or by goats.'

His mother sat down in the seat opposite him, hands still gloved.

'Mama,' Elias said softly. 'What is going on?'

'Nothing is going on. Eat your *stifado* before it goes cold.'

There was not going to be anything cold about this dish for at least an hour judging by the amount of steam that was coming off it and misting his eyeballs. It was good he wasn't wearing his glasses.

'My father is living in a storage shed,' Elias said boldly.

'Did he take you there?' his mother asked, tutting and shaking her heavy head of hair, the style unchanged in all the time he had known her. 'He has a luxury mattress, a fridge-freezer and a poster of Nana Mouskouri on the wall.'

'Mama,' Elias said again. 'Why is he living there? Why is he not here with you?'

'I expect he told you a grand story about how he is completely innocent in all of this. I am guaranteeing that he said I am going crazy and it is my hormones, or inherited from my mother or... both of these things.'

'He said very little,' Elias answered, picking up a fork. 'He said I should ask you.'

'See!' his mother exclaimed, raising both gloved hands

in the air then, seeming to suddenly realise she was still wearing them, she shook them off onto the table where they knocked over the pepper pot. 'He blames this all on me, like always.'

And Elias still had no idea what had transpired to cause a solid marriage to be on such unstable ground... in his father's case, ground that was covered in ants marching to and fro with some of the dregs of the smaller contents of his fridge-freezer. If this separation had happened, why wasn't his father staying in Elias's house? His late grandmother's house. The one he had been given as a wedding present. The one he wasn't sure he could ever go in again. He opened his mouth to speak.

'Why are you here?' his mother asked him. 'Did someone from the village contact you? Was it Areti? Because I told her if she contacted you, I would make her drink a tea made from the juices of the cooking of lamb lungs.' She sucked in a breath. 'I should have known she likes this! She must drink this all the time!'

'No one contacted me,' Elias replied. 'I am here for business.' And he was. He needed to stay in Liakada because it was near Chad's villa. The 'happy' coincidence was seeing his parents and setting foot back in the village that had all but ostracised him. It was a challenge and a challenge he was accepting. Except he hadn't bargained on coming up against this separation issue.

'You have a property you are helping to sell?' Now his mother was fully turning the attention away from her marital problems. And here was the other white lie he had laid down when he had set up his own business in London. His mother didn't think he was an estate agent, but she did think he was still in conveyancing. He knew if he told her his speciality was now divorce, that she would make something of that. And there was nothing to make of it…

Before he knew it, he was saying: 'Yes.' He physically cringed at himself and had to adjust his position in the chair and top up his wineglass as the humidity of the night seemed to increase ten-fold. There was no air-conditioning in this snug of a shop-cum-bar just a couple of fans that had seen better days whirring slowly. Even the mosquitos were able to evade the barely moving blades, almost dancing around in the air between them, mocking. Elias cleared his throat. 'It is a house not far from here. One of the villas near the sea. An English woman lives there. Mrs Carmichael. I really need to meet with her. Has she been here at all?' He reached into the pocket of his trousers to retrieve his phone. He had a photo he had plucked from Chad's Instagram ready to show.

'Why do you not go to the house?' his mother asked. 'If she is living there, waiting for you to come to help with the sale of her house?'

His mother was as astute as ever and was now looking at him like he was ten years old and still the naïve boy who had had his hand slapped for taking still-warm *baklava* from the oven.

'It is… a difficult case,' he answered coolly. 'There is more than one owner involved and I want to… get a feel for… how she is.'

'How she is?'

Elias fanned the neck of his shirt, needing some movement of air. 'Yes.' He thumbed icons on his phone, calling up the photo.

'You are expecting her to bark at you like a stray dog?' his mother asked. 'Or snap at you with venom like a viper?' She chuckled then, seeming to find his show of uncomfortable amusing. 'Such a fuss over bricks and stone!'

'Have you seen her?' he asked. He held out his phone with Kristina Carmichael's photo on it. His mother grabbed it, holding it close to her eyes, closer than she had held things to her face before. He couldn't deny that both his parents had aged since he'd been gone.

'I know this woman,' his mother announced almost immediately. 'But you are calling her the wrong name.' She handed the phone back to Elias. 'Her name is not this Car-Michelle you keep saying. Her name is Ms O'Neill.'

Elias nodded. So, Kristina must have already started using another name before the divorce was even halfway to being finalised. It made perfect sense with everything that Chad had been telling him about her distancing herself for the longest time.

'And she is not here,' his mother continued. 'She has not been here for the past two weeks and she is not coming back for at least the next two more.'

This was terrible news! How was he going to sweettalk her over the distribution of marital assets if she wasn't here in person to be charmed? Although, perhaps it wasn't all bad. If the house was empty that meant easier access for him to assess exactly what assets were there. He had long suspected, with Kristina's passion for high-end shopping, that maybe Chad was right and there could well be items in that villa her husband knew nothing about – expensive items his client was due a share of. He would take a walk there tomorrow.

'Now, eat your *stifado*,' his mother ordered. 'I have a bar to run.'

And just like that, his mother stood up and left the table. Now there was no chance for him to ask any more questions about what had happened between her and his father. Elias had learned all his avoidance techniques from his mother, but she was still the master.

He put a fork to his food and hungrily guided it to his mouth. Closing his eyes, he let all the richness coat his taste buds, before chewing and enjoying the light texture of the meat and the gentle pop of the baby onions. There really wasn't anything like his mother's *stifado*.

Something was bothering him about Kristina not being at the property, though. What was she up to? And there was something familiar about the name Ms O'Neill. It was niggling at him that he had heard that name before. But, right now, he couldn't think where.

Thirty-One

Taverna Kerasia, Kerasia Beach

Becky was the kind of fuzzy drunk that made you feel like a luxuriating cat who had been so well-fed that all it could do was lay out, belly upwards, eyes closed and doze under a warm sky. Perhaps Petra's cat Plato was doing that right now back in Athens... Becky had all those feels, however she wasn't laying outstretched on the white pebble beach, nor was her belly out, but she was mellow, humming inside from the delicious white wine she and Petra were sharing and the sound of the waves tumbling gently on the shoreline.

They had found the car. Or rather the car had found them. It had been half-hidden by vines and Petra had walked into it, her slight form rebounding off the bodywork and crumpling onto the patio. It was kind-of-red, kind-of-green-with-mould and looked like it hadn't been driven in at least a decade. Neither of them had had the energy to start peeling off foliage to even see if it was moveable, so instead of heading to any shop or supermarket, they had taken steps down to the beach and had arrived at this picturesque shoreline. They had gazed out over the water, drinking in the serenity – Petra skimmed some stones again but without getting maimed – and then the heavenly aromas coming from the taverna had pulled them in. They were now sitting at a table closest to the water, under softly glowing lights, feeling all of the holiday contentment. At least Becky was. It had been at least twenty minutes and a whole slab of feta cheese since she had thought about It's A Wrap and her pending pitch to the nursing home that she really needed to get on with. Perhaps now she had the stability of a house to work in instead of an aircraft, inspiration would strike.

'I've gone from famished to fat in like ten minutes,' Petra announced, putting her hands on her flat-as-a-Portobello-mushroom stomach and exhaling.

'We've been here an hour,' Becky said, finally taking a look at her watch. Back home in the UK she was forever looking at her watch. It was almost a compulsive tick. How long did she have to finish buttering the rolls? What time was Megan back from her meeting? How much time to kill before she could reasonably go to bed with a book and not feel guilty about not being a twenty-five-year-old party animal?

'Have we? Shit. Time flies when you're eating and drinking yourself stupid.' Petra grinned and filled her wineglass up with more.

'And we still don't have… *ouzo* and shit for the house.'

Petra laughed. 'Living together is going to be so much fun now you're all loosened up.'

Living together. She only had two weeks. As fun as Petra was, they were very different people. And did Petra really see her as someone who was more tightly wound than a Coleen Rooney tweet? Was that the vibe she gave off to everyone? Maybe that's what had made Elias run away and sucker his lips to someone who was free and easy and didn't think through every scenario possible before making a decision? And *why* was she still thinking about Elias? He was someone she had met for a couple of days. Free and easy. Time to get back to *How to Find the Love of Your Life or Die Trying*. One of the crucial steps, the book said, was knowing when to cut your losses...

'Where are you from, Petra?' Becky asked her, sipping at her wine. 'I mean, when you aren't travelling the globe. Where's home?'

'I... don't really have a place of my own right now,' Petra admitted. Her mouth went back to her wineglass and she took a swig before giving Becky a small smile. 'I bet you have a place of your own though. You seem like someone who would be solid in the sorted stakes.'

Sorted in some ways but completely floundering in others. 'I've got a tiny flat. And when I say tiny I mean tiny. My bed touches both walls and there's no room for a wardrobe so I have to fold and roll all my clothes into a chest of drawers.' Becky smiled. 'But it's mine. So, do you live at home in-between voyages of discovery?'

Petra shook her head, her expression tightening a little. A heavy silence seemed to descend and Becky waited for her to say something. It appeared nothing was forthcoming and the young girl was now picking at breadcrumbs on the tablecloth.

'Well,' Becky started, 'I moved out of home because my mum was moving away and because... my dad died.'

Petra looked up then, her eyes wide, her body language giving off that she was reengaged. 'Oh… that's sad.'

'Yes,' Becky replied with a sigh. 'It was sad. It was very sad. But, he had been… not himself for quite a while and although we did everything we could to give him the best quality of life we could after his initial stroke… I don't know.' She took a breath. 'Sometimes I think he was carrying on for us. That maybe the enjoyment he showed in trying to improve was for our benefit not his. He couldn't do any of the things he loved anymore.'

Becky suddenly felt Petra's skinny fingers in hers and the girl squeezed her hand tightly, reassuringly, as emotion threatened to get the better of her.

'It's alright,' Petra said softly. 'I lost my dad too.' She blinked damp eyes before continuing. 'And when I was little, he told me that… everyone we lose turns into part of the moon.' She paused. 'You probably think that sounds like something cheesy from a chick-flick, but that's the reason he gave for the moon changing size and shape. I know it's not a scientific fact – I'm not *that* stupid – but I like it.' She smiled, eyes going skyward. 'And when I look up at the moon, I imagine everyone up there having a big party and looking down at us waiting for us to come and join in.'

Becky's heart was fracturing little piece by little piece. It was a beautiful thought that her dad and Petra's dad and everyone else's loved ones were part of something bigger, something they could all see every single night.

'Any-hoo, enough nostalgia. I don't do the past,' Petra said, withdrawing her hand. She banged on the table then raised a hand in the air. 'Waiter!' She looked back to Becky. 'I know I said I was feeling fat but let's have some more little plates. How about some mussels or something? They don't make you feel bloated.'

'Petra, I couldn't eat another thing,' Becky told her.

'Ice cream!' Petra continued. 'How do you say "excuse me" again? Everyone always has room for ice cream. Why isn't "waiter" an international word?'

Petra was suddenly all frenetic energy, waving spaghetti-like arms, as she tried to attract the attention of one of the servers. Gone was the soft, emotional Petra as quickly as that side of her had arrived.

'You need to say *signomi*,' Becky told her. She had been reading the little vocab section at the back of her guidebook. Now the waiter was approaching, another good-looking Greek that Petra had flirted with when he'd taken their order earlier.

'Hello, yes, we would like some *signomi* please,' Petra ordered, seeming a little less than her confident self.

'*Ti?*' the waiter asked, looking confused.

'No,' Petra said. 'Not tea. *Signomi*.' She turned to Becky and pulled a face. 'Are you sure you got the word for "ice cream" right?'

Suddenly, Becky understood. '*Signomi* isn't the word for "ice cream". It's the word for "excuse me" or "sorry". For you to call the waiter over.'

'You would like some ice cream?' the waiter asked.

'Yes please,' Petra purred in response. 'We're not picky about the flavour. Whatever you recommend.' She smiled with her eyes as well as her lips. 'Make it a couple of big, round balls each.'

Becky almost choked on her mouthful of wine as Petra delivered Smut 101. And then her phone began to ring. She checked her watch – habit again – before picking her phone up and seeing it was It's A Wrap's number. It would be six o'clock in the UK right now, no one should be in the premises unless they were running behind schedule for pre-prep for the next day, or they had an evening event to prepare for. Or perhaps it was Megan. Maybe this was the phone call from her sister she had been waiting for. Megan would apologise, Becky would apologise – even though she didn't think she needed to – and all would be well.

'Hello,' she greeted.

'Thank fuck! I don't know what I would have done if you didn't pick up! Probably called the emergency services and hoped police, fire or ambulance knew something about pairing honey roasted ham with… marmalade.'

It wasn't Megan. It was Shelley and she did sound hyped up. More hyped up than Shelley usually sounded.

'Shelley, what's wrong?' Becky asked, standing up from the table and moving to the steps that led down to the beach below. She always hated it when people took phone calls in restaurants. Hopefully when she returned to the table Petra would have eaten all the ice cream…

'Megan's getting all hands-on with sandwich-making,' Shelley hissed. 'She came in when Hazel was creating Barry's half-vegan, half-mystical bagel this morning. She asked Hazel what she was doing and Hazel had to say she hadn't managed to have breakfast and it was for her. So, then Megan goes off on one saying Hazel's eating her profits and what was this mysterious mixture anyway, and I had to tell Megan it wasn't made from It's A Wrap ingredients, it was something the triplets had made at school. To be fair, that shit Barry likes does look like something the triplets would mash up and make a bird feeder out of.'

Becky closed her eyes. This was what she had feared if she went away. Without her there to coordinate the tight ship, hide the detailed contents of some of food orders – or get the suppliers she knew best to call everything 'cheese' on their invoices – Megan was going to realise that they were selling far more elaborate products than she knew. And this was entirely Becky's fault. Not just the not being there now, but the not having the courage to tell her sister that her basic business model and use of traditional sandwich fillings hadn't been cutting it in the catering arena for a long time and that Becky's secret ingenuity was what had been tiding the firm over. She had always planned to tell her – maybe – and she was definitely not going to interfere with the army contract. Well, not unless sales slid a bit…

'Oh, Shelley, I'm so sorry,' Becky said, looking out to sea. What had she been thinking assuming Shelley and Hazel would be able to keep what they did every day under wraps – literally – while she was away? It wasn't fair to make them as complicit in deceiving her sister as she was. They didn't get paid enough to put up with dealing with the stress of it. It was different for Becky, she needed Megan's business to succeed for so many reasons…

'It's OK,' Shelley breathed. 'Well, it's not OK because she's coming in at 6 a.m. to help with prep, so that's why I'm still here now. Hazel's coming back in in a minute, after she's had her corns done. We're going to do as much as the preparation for the "other" rolls as we can tonight, but neither of us can find the list for tomorrow and I know you sent them all to me on my phone, but I can't find it on there either. I'm low on storage and one of the triplets probably deleted it and replaced it with sixty-five selfies of them with their fingers up their nose.'

'Shelley, it's fine,' Becky responded. 'Right, so, we can do two things here.' She took a breath. If she was in England right now, she would be melting down over the prospect of Megan finding out what she had been doing this past year. But here in Greece she felt strangely powerful. Yes, she should have told Megan but equally, Megan had always made it very clear Megan was not the bread-butterer. Megan was the business-planner, the networker and face of the company. Becky was at grassroots – well, the roots of a garden of herbs anyway. Becky had taken the decision and she was going to own it. 'You can both go home now and I will phone Megan and tell her everything about the secret sandwiches which I should have done a long time ago…'

'What's the second thing? Because if she finds out – even if you tell her really *really* nicely like you're Claudia Winkleman cuddling a crying celebrity because they've fucked up the rumba – she's gonna explode and we're here and you're in Corfu.'

'The second thing is—'

'Hang on, Hazel's here and I'm putting you on speakerphone,' Shelley interrupted.

Becky held her breath. The second thing had been to tell their customers that the bespoke orders were now off the menu. She could easily draft an apologetic flyer and email it to Shelley and Hazel to hand out with one last batch of the good stuff. She could blame Brexit for the lack of availability of certain ingredients or something. It would test the loyalty of their fan base but, the traditional fayre was good too, it just didn't wow quite like the other fillings. They might lose a few customers to their rivals but was there really a choice? Megan simply wouldn't get the concept and wouldn't even try because Becky had pulled the wool over her eyes. The only certainty now, with both courses of proposed action, was Becky's skill at knowing exactly what their customers liked, needed and craved, would no longer be required. She would just be the girl who buttered bread again...

'I told Shelley *not* to call you.' It was Hazel talking now and Becky could imagine her hanging up her bag and tying an apron around her waist. 'I have found the list for tomorrow and a packet of Trebor mints I thought were gone forever so there's no need to panic, dear.'

'*I'm* panicking,' Shelley said. 'Because I'm shit-scared of Megan.'

'Language, Shelley.'

'She's like one of those silent but deadly types. Quiet and controlled on the surface but underneath I reckon there's a raging psycho ready for go-time. And... and she has all the tools in this kitchen to do unspeakable fucking things to every body part I own.'

'Shelley, Hazel...' Becky tried to talk.

'Becky, dear, please ignore Shelley. She's like this because she's left Frank with the remote controller as well as the triplets and she thinks one of them is going to delete her series link for *Hollyoaks*. Now, you listen to me. We are both here tonight to get the specials orders ready for tomorrow if Megan really *does* make an appearance at 6 a.m. However, I saw Dean in the Co-op earlier and happened to mention how tired I thought Megan was looking lately and I wondered if perhaps a few later alarm calls this week might be in order. I said we had everything covered here and we were worried about her.'

Becky smiled and shook her head. Her colleagues were nothing short of geniuses at subterfuge. Should she feel pride? This was not like her. She was straight-down-the-line Becky except when it came to this. And this hadn't ever really been about her. It had always been about her sister.

'We are going to take care of everything, dear,' Hazel continued. 'And you are not to think about it for another minute. You are to continue exploring everything Greek – the weather, the food, the men.'

Immediately Becky's mind was back to Elias and their ruined near-kiss in Kefalonia. He had felt so good in her arms, he had smelled so good...

'Yeah, the men especially,' Shelley broke in.

'But keep safe, dear,' Hazel added.

'I gave her every flavour of condom I own,' Shelley reminded. 'But check the expiry, won't you? Because some of them were freebies from the pub we booked our Sharon's hen do in.'

The complete familiarity of her friends' chatter rippled over Becky like the warm Corfu breeze blowing up her fringe. She let Hazel and Shelley carry on among themselves as she looked out at the water. There were boats a little way from the shore, some with tall, pointed masts that sails would appear on tomorrow morning, others luxurious bowriders with cabin space underneath. Were there people aboard? Couples cosying up together and steaming up the portholes? What would that feel like?

'Becks! Come and help me eat the *signomi*!' Petra shouted from the taverna above.

Somehow her housemate had still not realised *signomi* was not the word for 'ice cream'.

'I've got to go now,' Becky told them both. 'But thank you. Thank you both for what you're doing. Even though Megan doesn't know it, we are all helping save her business.' *Maybe even save her.* She kept that thought to herself.

'You're an excellent sister, dear,' Hazel told her. 'One day she will realise that.'

'But not tomorrow,' Shelley said. 'Because I don't want to be having to hide the garlic crusher or the apple cutter if she turns all *Friday the 13th*.'

'Bye,' Becky said, a smile on her face.

'Bye, dear.'

'Bye! And, you know, don't forget what I said about the condoms.'

Thirty-Two

Villa Selino, Kerasia

'You won't believe it,' Petra called. 'I've found two more sets of car keys and another set labelled with the word "garage".' She bounced up and down on the spot like she was attached to a pogo-stick. 'That thing covered in weeds might not be our only ride!'

It was the following mid-morning and Becky had been up early to take in the beginnings of a Corfu day with one of the last spoonsful of coffee and a scraping of dried milk powder. They really did need to get some groceries today. There had been signs of a little shop on the beach, but it hadn't been open last night and Becky suspected it was more for inflatable doughnuts and snorkel masks than it was for bread and milk. After her coffee she had taken up residence at one of the rattan-style tables and started proper work on her catering pitch for the nursing home. So far it was going well. It had structure and order and was peppered with all the *good* memories of war times and VE Day celebrations. Bunting, beef dripping and eggless cakes to tie in the rationing aspect, without missing out on any of the flavour. She simply needed to hone the pricing more accurately, making sure she had accounted for every ingredient, then mark it up enough so It's A Wrap made an excellent profit, but also ensure the client wasn't put off by the end price. Becky might not have professionally pitched for the company before, but she knew all about costings and was an avid watcher of *The Apprentice*. There was no way her task of securing this party was going to melt like artisan ice lollies or sink like Tommy the Talking Turtle…

'Where are you going?' Becky called as Petra – dressed in one of those one-piece swimsuits that showed *all* your hips – danced past her, keys jingling between her fingers.

'I'm going to look for the other cars,' Petra announced. 'Can you imagine what they might be? I mean, this place *is* high-end now the critters have gone. Did you know there's a TV that pops up out of the breakfast bar? I had to press the button a few times but then it rose up like… like…'

Becky braced herself and closed her eyes hoping Petra wasn't going to mention anyone's erection.

'Like the moon last night,' Petra finished with a gentle smile. 'Or the sun this morning.'

Becky opened her eyes and looked to her housemate. 'You were awake when the sun rose this morning?' It seemed unlikely that Petra was an early riser. It had been after one a.m. before they had gone to bed and Petra had been reluctant to go then, declaring it *way way* too early.

'I ran 4k this morning at 6 a.m. I found the little village. It's sweet. In a little village kind of way. It had nice flowers and houses all on top of each other with washing hanging out and rusty sunbeds on front porches. Oh, and there were a couple of cute dogs I almost brought back with me.'

'Petra, no,' Becky said. 'We can't have animals in here.'

'I know! Keep your knickers on!'

Had Petra really gone out at 6 a.m.? And why hadn't Becky heard her leave? She was supposed to be in charge of the home's security. How was that working if she didn't even know when someone had left the property?

'Ooo! I've found a garage!'

Now Becky was on her feet. Perhaps the wreck of a car wasn't the one they were supposed to be using. It did seem at odds with the rest of the house being bright and elegant. But surely if she was meant to find a car in the garage, Ms O'Neill might have said something. Perhaps she wasn't meant to go in the garage at all. 'Petra! Wait!'

'What for? We need transport, don't we?' Petra called.

Becky could already see Petra had inserted a key into a lock and was jiggling it about to see if it would fit. If it didn't, it seemed likely the forcing motion was going to end up snapping the key in half. 'Petra, just stop a minute.' She caught up to her, one of her flip-flops – with watermelons on the inside that Hazel had insisted were a must-have – slipping off her toes. 'We shouldn't really be poking about in places that are locked up.' It didn't appear that Petra was listening. She was still manipulating the key when it seemed quite obvious it wasn't going to unlock anything.

'Weren't you promised a car you could actually use?' Petra asked her, finally taking the key out and jabbing another one in in its place.

'Well, it did say "use of a car", I think.'

'So, what are you going to be able to use that heap of

junk under the weeds for? Apart from recycling?' Suddenly the door gave way and sprung open under Petra's pressure. 'And... we're in!'

'Petra...' Somehow this felt wrong. But she had to follow her housemate, didn't she?

'Wow, it's not like a garage at all! It's as clean as the house! Well, the house *after* I cleaned up from the animals.'

Petra was right. There were no cobwebs, no signs of lawnmowers with their innards out on workbenches or scattered seed packets like there had been in her dad's shed. All at once Becky was hit with a thump of nostalgia. Time spent with her dad repairing bicycles or bringing on saplings of plants he had been given from the neighbours because of his legendary green thumb...

'Dustsheets, Becky!' Petra announced, prowling into the centre of this pristine office of a garage where if you took a hammer or shovel from the wall its outline would be visible like chalk marks around a body in a crime scene. 'You don't put dustsheets over cars that are falling apart. You put dustsheets over cars that are valuable... or collectible... or valuable *and* collectible.' Petra was now standing in between two indistinct mounds in the centre of the room covered in what looked like grey-silver cloths. Even the coverings seemed to suggest expensive...

'We really shouldn't be uncovering anything that's covered.' Although, apart from the not-letting-anyone-into-the-property insistence – which theoretically Becky had broken already with Petra staying – Ms O'Neill hadn't said uncovering wasn't...

'Oh my God! Look at these beauties!'

With a hand on each cloth, Petra had made light work

of stripping them off and two vehicles were revealed. Even with her limited knowledge of cars, Becky could tell these were not your average middle-class ride.

'This! This is a Ferrari! From the Sixties! My dad lost out on one of these in an auction! This is proper, proper vintage and worth an absolute fortune.'

Becky cringed as Petra ran her hands all down one side of the wing of the bright red vehicle, immediately getting finger marks all over the shining paintwork. 'Petra, perhaps we shouldn't touch them.'

There was another inhalation of breath as her housemate moved to the second car. 'Oh! This one! This one!' Petra put her hand to her chest. 'This is an Aston Martin. Oh my God! I think I might faint.'

Despite Becky's worry that they shouldn't be in here doing this, Petra's excitement over the cars was really interesting. This was something else to 'know' about Petra… and she had mentioned her dad again. Perhaps Becky should ask her about her love of cars and more about her family over dinner tonight. In the meantime, although it would burst her friend's enthusiastic bubble, she needed to ensure the cars stayed exactly where they were. If these were worth a mint, there was no way Ms O'Neill would be offering them to the housesitter to drive. It would be back to trying to shift the mouldy car or… what was that in the corner of the garage? Was that a bicycle?

Both girls jumped as a chiming sound ensued.

'God!' Petra exclaimed, hand at her chest again. 'I thought that was some sort of alarm I triggered by touching the Ferrari.'

'Is it the doorbell?' Becky asked.

'No idea,' Petra said, opening the door of the Aston Martin and preparing to get in.

'I'm going to check,' Becky said, heading towards the way out. 'Do not start up either of the cars or...' She had been going to say not to get the upholstery dirty, but as Petra had already slipped into the driver's seat with more flesh than swimsuit touching the leather interior it was probably a little too late.

Becky headed back into the house and hurried – as fast as the flip-flops would allow – down the hall towards the front door. Once there, she paused, hand on the door, remembering the insistence from her owner that she wasn't allowed to let anyone in. Well, she wouldn't let anyone in. She would just see who it was. Perhaps it was the pool man. Although, in the notes in a folder that had been left for her on the kitchen island, she thought the pool guy was supposed to come on a Friday. Maybe it was the postman. Did they have postmen in Greece? Taking a breath, Becky opened the front door to... no one. She looked out, past the hanging bougainvillea and potted begonias, up the driveway to the road where the arching branches of olive trees gently fluttered in the light breeze. Nothing. No one. *Was* the ringing in the garage something to do with the security of the place and not the doorbell? Becky stepped outside, onto the stone porch step and pressed the button herself. It chimed. Definitely, what they had heard on the receiver in the garage. Had whoever had rung the bell gone already? Like an Amazon delivery driver – unable to wait thirty seconds for someone to come to the door. Was there a parcel lying somewhere? Possibly broken...

'Becks!' she heard Petra scream. 'You won't believe it! Elias is here!'

Thirty-Three

Elias couldn't believe it. It was the worst thing. Or, possibly the best thing. He hadn't decided yet. His mind was still catching up to this whole new situation he should have envisaged the second he realised the name 'Ms O'Neill' was familiar to him. But it was all too much of a coincidence, wasn't it? The very villa he needed to get inside was being looked after by two girls he had met and befriended on the plane here...

Right now, as Petra waved her hands around the garden, pointing out the pool and the hammock between two palms and a car she said was 'minging', like it was her own personal residence, Elias was glad he had decided to ring the bell. He had taken a chance that a key would be under a plant pot when he walked here from Liakada, but then a quick text to Chad had confirmed it and told him exactly which one. Except the key hadn't been there and then he had heard voices. Ready to turn on the charm and be Elias Mardas, estate agent again, he had expected to encounter a stranger. Instead, when someone didn't immediately come, he had decided to head into the garden and see if any of the doors or windows were open. And now, this. Petra wearing barely anything and Becky…

He felt that strange sense of desire mixed with affinity the moment she appeared on the patio. She seemed to be wearing swimwear too, but only the merest sight of it was visible underneath a sheer white cotton sundress. Her hair was loose, caramel waves just touching her shoulders. He hadn't thought he would ever see her again. Had he wanted to? His body was trying to tell him the answer to that one and he wasn't sure he liked it.

'Here she is!' Petra exclaimed. 'Look, Becky, it's Elias!'

'So I see,' Becky replied.

She was looking a little stern now. Like she might quite like to skewer him into a *souvlaki* and grill him on the barbecue. He had to remember what it was he was here for.

'I had no idea you would be here,' he apologised. Why was he apologising? Was that the right tack?

'What are *you* doing here?' Becky asked him. 'Did you ring the doorbell?' She had folded her arms across her chest, as if defensive. She was right to be. She didn't know the man he was, or the job he had to do.

'Yes,' he replied, nodding. 'I have business here.'

'Here?' Becky asked, still killing him with those eyes dialled in on him like they were a sight on a sniper rifle. 'At this house?'

'Yes,' he answered.

'Ooo,' Petra said. 'What kind of business? Has Becky accepted a job housesitting for a celebrity? Is "Ms O'Neill" really Rylan *Clark*-Neal? I would *love* that!'

'And how would that work out being Elias's reason for

being here?' Becky asked her. 'He's an estate agent.'

'Oh,' Petra said, sitting down on the edge of the pool and shielding her eyes from the sun with her hand. 'Is this lovely house for sale? It won't go through before two weeks, will it? Because we're here and...'

'And *you* won't be staying here two weeks,' Becky told Petra. 'We said a few days.'

'How much is it going on the market for?' Petra asked, swirling a long limb into the water.

'Just a second,' Becky said, coming down from the top patio area to join them nearer the pool. 'No one has said anything to me about the house being for sale.'

'They haven't?' Elias said. 'Well, it was a decision made only a short time ago. Only a little before I got on the flight from the UK.'

'I would have thought that Ms O'Neill would have mentioned it to me if it was for sale. I *am* in charge of the house while she's away. If I was to meet an estate agent then I would have expected her to warn me about it and, the only thing she did warn me about was—'

'The mosquitos?' Petra jumped in. 'Because if she did you could have warned me too. Despite all my best Australian-grade repellent, last night one absolutely feasted on my arse. Look!'

Elias made a point of *not* looking as Petra leaned sideways and pulled away a section of her swimsuit. And it was abundantly clear that Becky was already suspicious of his being here. He needed to get her back on side. With his parents' marriage up in the air he had to be able to normalise *something* and that meant getting back on track with this divorce case.

'You didn't say your parents live in Kerasia,' Becky said, standing close to him now. He was right in the direct sunlight and beginning to perspire.

'You did not say you were coming to housesit in Kerasia.'

'So, where do your parents live?' Becky continued with the questions.

'Not in Kerasia,' he answered. He needed to be less cagey. 'But not far from here. Liakada.'

'Great!' Petra said. 'Do you have your car? We need to get shopping.'

'I walked,' Elias replied.

'Well, talking of cars—'

'Thank you, Petra,' Becky interrupted. 'Why don't you go and get Elias a drink? He looks a little warm.'

'You could cool off in the pool,' Petra suggested. 'If you've got trunks... or, if not.'

Elias shook himself, wiping his hand over the back of his neck. 'I am OK.'

'Then what do you need to do here?' Becky asked him. 'Put a sign at the front? Take some measurements?'

He nodded. 'Yes. That exactly.' He paused briefly before continuing. 'It is a great property. Made from local stone.' He walked up to the nearest wall and laid his hand on it. 'So much care and attention has gone in to getting the aesthetic just right. Don't you think?'

'Why are you looking in through the window?' Becky asked him.

'I'll make some *ouzo* cocktails,' Petra announced, clapping her hands together and heading into the house. 'It's about all we have in the cupboard and we can celebrate our reunion.'

*

Something wasn't quite right about this. Becky could sense it. 'What's the name of your company again?' she asked Elias.

'My company,' Elias answered, stepping away from the property and looking back at Becky.

'Yes, the company you work for, as an estate agent. What's the name of it?'

'You are worried because you have not been told about the sale?' Elias asked her. 'Well, I can tell you that this property is owned by two people, and I am working on behalf of the party that is not your Ms O'Neill.'

Becky frowned. What did that mean? Was this why her instructions had been firm about not letting anyone into the house? Had Ms O'Neill been *expecting* someone to come here? Expecting Elias to come here with his tape-measure and 'for sale' signs? Was the matter of the sale somehow contentious? Now she was wondering just how much she really knew of this man she had met on the plane. The man she had nearly kissed...

'It's a beautiful home,' Elias said, stepping forward and seeming to admire the view over trees to the glistening sea only a few metres away. 'One of only a few prime beachfront properties along here.'

'One that I'm in charge of for a few weeks and... I don't think I believe what you're telling me.'

That was bold. That was so bold. And so not like the Becky Rose from Wiltshire. She also didn't really have any evidence that Elias was lying to her. Except this feeling in her gut that this man stood beside her now, was not the person she had got to know amid their aeroplane escapades. His behaviour now didn't feel genuine.

'Which parts?' Elias asked. He looked away from the scene to her, and Becky felt the weight of his gaze. Was that a flicker of what they had shared in Athens and Kefalonia she could see in those beautiful blue/green irises?

She took a deep breath, stood a little taller. 'I don't... think you're an estate agent.'

He said nothing. He simply carried on looking at her. And as the milliseconds turned into seconds and the seconds started moving from one second to three, Becky wondered if she had actually spoken at all. Should she say something else? Clarify her accusation? Or perhaps retract it?

And then Elias nodded, slowly and deliberately. 'OK,' he said simply.

OK? What did that mean? It told her precisely nothing. Was he confirming she was right? Was he angry she had all but accused him of lying? And what response did she make?

'I mean... if you *are* an estate agent then you would... look like one. They wear... tweed or... pink trousers.' Or was that just the British ones? She had no idea the 'uniform' for Greek estate agents. But she continued none the less. 'And you would be... already talking about the outside space... and the infinity pool and, I don't know, maybe pacing out the square-footage.'

'It is OK,' Elias said, finally moving away from her. Where was he going? Was he leaving? Without giving her *any* answers. 'I understand you are concerned about your responsibilities here.'

*

She *knew*. Becky knew he was a fraud and Elias hated that for several reasons. Firstly, because it meant he was not getting into the property to make that much-needed inventory for Chad and secondly, because he loathed having lied to her in the first place. He *was* being underhand by being here, he knew that. But he *had* initially wanted to meet with Kristina, attempt to be reasonable and offer her the deal he had fleshed out. However, finding out she wasn't here, coupled with snippets of conversations Chad had shared, he had reason to believe the woman was hiding something. But now Becky and Petra were here, and it didn't feel at all fortuitous. It felt even harder. This wasn't a situation he was in control of anymore. Becky had deep suspicions of him. He doubted she would even let him inside to use the toilet…

'Are you leaving?' Becky asked, following him across the *plaka* stone towards the gate he had entered through.

'I am leaving,' he responded. He swallowed, suddenly feeling ridiculously sad. This was someone he thought he would never see again. And now he *had* seen her again it had proved those feelings he had experienced in Kefalonia were not isolated. She looked even more beautiful here in Corfu, that soft spirit she didn't seem to appreciate, gently shining out of her. Why did she have to be at this house? If she really was in reach, here in Kerasia, why could they not have met again under different circumstances? He needed to go, and fast.

'But…'

Elias stopped at the gate, beneath the clematis that wound its way around the ironwork and tumbled like a lilac-coloured waterfall. 'You are right,' he said with more conviction than he currently felt. 'You do not know me. You cannot let someone you do not know into a house you are looking after for somebody else. It would not be right.'

'I know that I'm being cautious but...'

He could make her back-track. He could turn on the boardroom charm and fix this right now. But he didn't want to do that. With Becky it was... well, it just didn't feel right.

'No,' Elias said. 'You are doing the right thing.' And he meant that sentiment absolutely – as crazy as it felt that he cared.

'Well, I will call Ms O'Neill about it,' Becky said as Elias pushed through the gate to the driveway, his shoes crunching on the loose stones.

'There is no need,' Elias said, waving a hand. 'I will call my client. I will tell him that his co-owner is away and we will delay things until she returns.'

'Are you sure?' Becky asked. 'If I was wrong... if I am going to get you in trouble or something then...'

'I am sure,' Elias replied. But as he crunched up the gravel to the road he was certain of only two things. One, if he was going to succeed in getting into the house, he would have to do it when Becky and Petra were out. And, two, if he wanted to maintain his sanity, he was definitely going to need to avoid Becky completely, unless he wanted to walk around in a permanent state of arousal.

Thirty-Four

Imerolia Fish Taverna, Imerolia

Becky and Petra had visited the supermarket. They had filled the back seats of the car with bags full of essentials – plus *Petra's* idea of essentials that included some sort of bronzing fluid she couldn't read any of the details of because it was written in Greek, plus a flagon of unknown liquid that could-be-wine-could-be-cooking-oil-or-could-be-something-to-polish-the-Aston-Martin-with. Becky had driven the Aston Martin. The cream-coloured Aston Martin Petra kept Googling the price of even now as they sat outside at this beautifully peaceful taverna, close to the water's edge that Becky knew she really shouldn't have driven the classic car down to considering the state of the road.

'This website says five million! Five million!' Petra announced, picking a meatball from the meat and fish platter they were sharing and popping it into her mouth.

'Petra, this isn't making me feel any better about it. I didn't even want to take the car out,' Becky reminded. 'I can't think about it being that expensive if you want me to drive us back to the house again.' She was already worrying that Ms O' Neill probably had photos of the mileage on the dashboard and was going to instantly know someone – namely Becky – had used it. But there was no way that wreck under the vines was ever moving again without the aid of a tow-truck.

'That's OK,' Petra answered. '*I'll* drive it back to the house again. I haven't had a turn yet.'

'You told me you don't have a licence,' Becky reminded. She sipped at her water. She was not-so-secretly coveting the sweet-smelling rose wine that Petra had ordered, but being in charge of a luxury vehicle she was scared stiff of even brushing close to a bush with, it was much better to stick to water.

'I bet, if we did a survey, half the people driving on Corfu wouldn't have a licence.'

'But not any of them would be driving a car worth five million pounds,' Becky said. She dipped a piece of soft fresh bread into a bowl of *tzatziki* and put it in her mouth. Five million pounds. It was a crazy amount of money for a car...

'*This* website says 7.5 million!' Petra announced, waving her phone in the air.

Becky looked out over the sea. She knew why she had given in to Petra's whining about the car. It wasn't really to do with getting shopping – they could have walked to the nearest mini-market in the little village Petra had found while running if they had to – it was what had happened at the house with Elias. What had that all been about? And why had she accused him of not being an estate agent? For all of Hazel and Shelley's pearls of wisdom about travelling, their tips seemed to be starting to make her deeply paranoid.

'What do you think about Elias?' Becky asked Petra suddenly. Had she *really* asked that? What was she expecting Petra to say? Possibly all she would tell her would be what the inside of his mouth felt like… Becky picked up a sardine and sucked the salty, juicy flesh from its bones. It might taste a little bit like this. Tantalisingly fresh and tender but hopefully less fishy…

'It was mad the way he turned up then disappeared before I could make cocktails,' Petra answered with a frown. 'Not that I had anything to mix with the *ouzo*… only water… and some sort of white and red beans I found at the back of the cupboard. Hope they weren't slug pellets or rat poison or something.' Petra put her hand around her throat and feigned near-death.

'Do *you* think he's an estate agent?' She had to know if it was only *her* who thought Elias's behaviour at the Villa Selino had been off. Petra had known him just as long – or rather as little – as her.

'Don't you?' Petra asked.

'I… don't know,' Becky admitted.

'Did he *tell* you he was an estate agent?'

'Yes.'

'Or did you assume from something he said?' Petra asked again, leaning forward across the table. 'Maybe he said something about buying and selling houses and you made an estate agent assumption?'

'I… don't know.' Had she? Becky tried hard to remember the whole conversation from the plane to Athens. It all felt so long ago. All she really recalled was her telling Elias she was in the armed forces…

'Do you think he's stalking me?' Petra asked, now all

wide eyes and cheekbones yet somehow showing deep vulnerability. Becky was starting to feel differently about Petra since the revelation that she too had lost her father.

'No… I… no.' She shook her head. That wasn't the vibe she was getting. But she *was* second-guessing her every thought at the moment.

'Because it wouldn't be my first stalker rodeo,' Petra said, inhaling a mouthful of wine. 'This one holiday in Nicaragua there was this nature reserve guide who started turning up everywhere I went… and I mean *everywhere*. The final straw was when I went for a pee, behind a tree, on a hike in the middle of nowhere and there he was! I mean, WTF!'

'I don't know,' Becky said with a sigh. 'I don't know what it is. I just, have this feeling about him.'

'He *is* hot,' Petra said, running her tongue over her top lip. 'If I was older maybe…'

What? If she was older? Hadn't she already been there in Kefalonia?

'Or, you know,' Petra began again, 'if I was looking for something serious. He comes across as a bit serious, don't you think?'

He did. Sometimes. Other times he came across as light and fun and full of some sort of unique energy Becky was drawn to. And then there was his eyes and the tattoo she was intrigued by…

'We could Google him,' Petra announced.

'No!' Becky said at once. Why had she responded so vehemently? It would give her every answer she required. Or it could tell her nothing at all.

'Ooo, let's do it!' Petra said, thumb already working all over the screen of her phone. 'He was super cagey when

I asked him what he did for a job. Why wouldn't you be honest unless you had something to hide! This is a great idea of yours.'

'Stop!' Becky ordered. Her heart was racing now. The last time she felt this panicked it had been when Megan had been admitted to hospital with suspected appendicitis. It hadn't been. It had been severe constipation put down to a weekend of too much prosecco and not enough fibre ironically at a food and beverage expo. But the initial fear that her sister might have to have an operation, and the fact she was the next-of-kin on hand had been terrifying. That had been after their mum's move to Blackpool, when their relationship became more about the business than it did about them being sisters… 'Petra, please don't.'

'Why not?' Petra asked, fingers poised.

'Because…'

'Because?'

'Because… perhaps…'

'Perhaps?' Petra shook her head. 'Are you sure you're only twenty-five because sometimes you talk like my auntie and she's sixty.'

Becky knew why she didn't want Petra to use Google. Because the parts about Elias she wanted to recount when she got back from her travels were all the *good* parts, the bits where she had felt free and strong and alluring in his arms. That's what she wanted to keep as a sweet Greek holiday memory. If they used Google to find out more about him, she was confident she was going to be faced with a different reality. Perhaps it was a case of the less she knew the better. Although, as far as the security of Villa Selino went, maybe it was better to be forewarned. She had already tried to call

Ms O'Neill but there had been no answer. She would try again before she emailed. As much as she wanted to know if the villa really was going on the market, she also didn't want her employer to think she couldn't deal with day-to-day tasks. That *was* what she was supposed to be here for.

'I don't know,' Becky responded with a sigh. She should be feeling relaxed, gazing out over the bright water, the headland of nearby Kassiopi jutting into the ocean, sunshine sprinkling the water with flashes of silvery light, boats tied off to day-glow buoys... but something was amiss. She either had to try and find out what it was, or she had to let it go. There was definitely nothing in the opening chapters of *How to Find the Love of Your Life or Die Trying* about how to deal with potential suitors pretending to be estate agents. If he *was* pretending...

'Googling now,' Petra announced, as if Becky hadn't offered any warnings at all.

'Petra, no! Please!'

'Well, well, well,' Petra said, eyes out on stalks as she gazed at her screen, picking up another meatball and biting into it.

'What?' Becky asked, taking another slice of bread from the basket and tearing a section off. She had to have something to occupy her while Petra went all erotomaniac.

'There is absolutely nothing on the internet about him. *Nada. Nicht. Rien. Mῑmῑ xarῑ.*'

Becky didn't have a clue what language the last words had been spoken in, but her heart was beating softer now. If there was nothing on the internet, then perhaps she had misjudged him entirely. What had she been expecting to find? That he was that axe murderer they had joked about in-flight? Maybe she even owed him an apology. What was the name of the village he said his parents lived in? Lia-something. Was that the village Petra had run to? The one with the burgeoning boxes of blooms and the cute stray dogs? They should find it. Find *him*. She would hopefully have heard from Ms O'Neill before tonight...

'Of course,' Petra began. 'It's very suspicious that there isn't *anything*. I mean, if he's an estate agent that has flown from England to sell a house, he must be good at what he does. And if he's good at what he does there should be *something* on the web.' Petra scoffed. 'Even *I* get a mention for winning a thumb-wrestling competition in Amritsar.'

Becky sighed. If she Googled Rebecca Rose what would come up about her? A big, fat blank? Or maybe something about It's A Wrap? Perhaps her father's obituary? Loving husband and father taken too soon – a life half-lived, half-of-the-life lived in a garden shed and the rest in a nursing home. But loved and very much missed...

'I say we walk to the village for some drinks tonight,' Petra stated, crushing a sardine head between her fingers. 'It must be that village that Elias is from. We can check out the locals and get the lowdown on him from the villagers. These Greek villages are a hot bed for gossip. If there's something amiss with him they are going to know about it. What d'you think?'

'I think we shouldn't have taken the Aston Martin out,' Becky told her. 'I think I probably shouldn't have come to Greece at all.' Did she really mean that?

'What?!' Petra exclaimed. 'But if you hadn't done that, you'd never have met me!'

Becky made no reply but smiled at her newfound friend.

'Come on, you can't help but like me. I *am* the party,' Petra said, pouting then thrashing her head around, her plaits whipping at the air then slapping her cheeks as they descended.

Becky couldn't help but grin at Petra's nonchalance towards pretty much everything. But until her softly spoken reminiscence about her dad last night, she was almost as secretive as Elias. There wasn't much she could tell anyone about who Petra was. If the girl turned into a grifter and the prized cars went missing the police would be laughing into their Greek coffee if all she knew was her first name and the fact she had 'Peter' tattooed on her arm.

'Where are you from, Petra?' Becky asked her for the second time, sipping at her water. 'You never said.'

'Where are *you* from?' the girl countered.

'Wiltshire,' Becky replied. 'A village really close to Stonehenge that's nowhere near as impressive as the ancient circle people come from all over the world to see.'

Petra gave a small sigh. 'Kent. But I haven't been back there for ages. Home is wherever I lay my hat now… or my Nobody's Foo T-shirt,' Petra answered with a grin. 'Or my Thai-Kwondo T-shirt. You haven't seen that one yet!'

'Does your mum live in Kent?'

Petra's wineglass suddenly tipped and she leapt up from the table, her short denim shorts now covered in rose wine. 'Shit! I'll have to go and clean this off quick. Do you reckon that Australian cleaning stuff will work on stains like this?'

But Petra didn't wait for Becky to reply. She skipped off into the taverna.

Thirty-Five

Liakada Village

Elias had been drenched in sweat when he arrived back at his parents' home above the *cafeneon* and he knew it wasn't simply the thirty-degree temperature, it was the damned situation with Becky and Petra being at the villa and it was... Hestia. Still it always seemed to come back to Hestia. Every stumbling block he hit in his career, every seemingly inconsequential rut in the road, all brought him back to that moment his marriage had ended and the utter humiliation that had come with that. He needed to succeed. He needed to win. But he wasn't feeling like a winner at the moment. He was feeling like a man who had planned a whole future for himself, based on the actions of someone else, and now he didn't know where his centre was or what happened next.

His shirt off his body and tied around a rickety fence post, his non-designer jeans hugging the rest of him, Elias hit the hard earth with the largest pick he had found in his father's temporary home. Amid the mattress, empty coffee cups and remnants of loaves of bread and unwashed clothes, there were still tools in the shed. And, to work out some of his frustrations, he had decided to dig over his father's allotment. He knew it was completely the wrong time for any kind of planting, but the earth could be turned over, made fresher, prepared. That was what he was telling himself. In truth, he either slammed the pick into the ground or he found a brick wall to demolish. The chickens were squawking at his movement and three of the goats were looking over the fence like gardening was a spectator-sport.

Elias drove the pick into the rock-hard soil and enjoyed the slight pain rolling through his muscles. He drew it up again and then smashed it back down.

'What are you doing?'

It was his father. He didn't need to look up to know that. And, as his father hadn't wanted to talk about anything that was going on with his mother, Elias didn't see why he should talk about how *he* was feeling right now.

'Have you even planted anything this year?' Elias responded, not stopping in his work.

'What is the point? Your mother has made other arrangements with vegetables.'

Elias looked up then. 'What other arrangements?'

'You will need to ask her,' Spiros answered.

Elias stopped then, wiping his forehead with his forearm and fixing his dad with a stare. 'What is wrong with the two of you? I speak to one and they say I should ask the other. I speak to the other and they say the same. No one is telling me anything.' He was shouting now and he had already seen Areti pottering around in her garden, hanging yet more washing on a line. 'And why, why are you living in a shed when there is an empty home in the village?'

Spiros had rolled a cigarette and it was hanging out of his lips while he patted down his body – white vest with no pockets, black trousers. He worked his way down to his ankles then pulled out a Zippo from inside his sock. Elias watched his father light the cigarette then blow a thick plume of smoke into the air. 'Do not tell your mother I am smoking.'

'You have been smoking every day since you were eleven years old,' Elias reminded him. 'You told me – when *I* was eleven – when you offered me my first cigarette like it was going to somehow make me a man.'

'I am not meant to be smoking. Since the heart attack…'

Elias froze, had to lean on the worn wooden handle of the garden tool for support. 'Since the what?' He had to wet his lips. 'Did you say "heart attack"?'

Spiros waved a hand in the air, taking another drag on the cigarette before flicking ash onto the soil Elias was cultivating. 'Last year,' he answered. 'Another lifetime ago. When your mother and I were still talking.'

Elias couldn't believe this was the first he was hearing of this. He was angry and concerned all at once. 'You had a heart attack and you never told me?!'

'I was in the hospital for three days. I had to leave in the end because Areti kept sending in parcels of her *moussaka*,' Spiros replied. 'She has started substituting aubergine for turnip. I do not know why. It does not work.'

'Papa, come on, I was a phone call away. You should have

let me know. I could have come back. I could have helped with the *cafeneon* or… brought you food without turnip.'

'You would have come?' Spiros asked, kicking at a bump of soil. 'With Hestia in the village?'

Elias swallowed. It was the first time either of his parents had mentioned his ex-wife's name since he had been back. 'Hestia was in the village?' *Was.* He was clinging on to that past tense. Had she stayed in their house? No, it was not hers. It had been a gift from *his* family. She would not do something like that. Despite everything, despite the anger he felt, Hestia wasn't a bad person.

Spiros nodded, drawing on his roll-up. 'She was here for a while. She rented a house with the woman for maybe three months. Until, I think, she decided making a stand was more difficult than she had thought.'

The woman. The woman's name was Thalia. Still the village was unchanged in its views about what was right and what was not. As much as he had been hurt by what had happened, it was the reaction of the village that had made everything so much worse. People and their opinions…

'I would have come,' Elias replied, taking a breath and lifting the pick again. 'Of course, I would have come.'

'I do not believe you,' Spiros said. 'And, your mother and I, we decided we did not want to put you in that position. You were settling in the UK. You were putting the past behind you.'

Elias dropped the pick again. 'I am not ashamed of being in Liakada again. Are you?' he asked. 'Are you somehow ashamed to have me here? Are you both still governed by what the village president thinks and feels about things?'

'Elia,' Spiros stated. 'No one was ashamed of you. The situation was difficult, that is all.'

'Why?' Elias asked. 'Because Hestia fell in love with a woman instead of another man? Would it have been less of a drama if she had slipped into an affair with Panos from the taverna?' His temper was rising again, a prickly heat developing across his bare shoulders.

'Elia, Panos is eighty this year.'

'That is not the point I am making!'

'Then what point *are* you making?' Spiros demanded to know. 'Your mother and I might not behave as if we love each other at the moment, but we always have and we always will love you.'

There was a depth of emotion in his father's voice that cut Elias to the quick. He lifted the pick quickly and smashed it into the ground once more with the loudest of grunts. The chickens leapt up into the air, flapping their wings and washing swayed a little on Areti's line. Was she behind a double sheet listening? Why did he care? He didn't live his life by the laws of gossip like this village did. He looked at his father, swallowing a lump in his throat. He should have come back sooner. What good had hiding done?

'So,' Spiros continued, waving the cigarette in the air as he gesticulated. 'While we are on the subject of not knowing things and relieving the stresses of life with the help of soil and tobacco, when are you going to tell us about your real job?'

'I... don't know what you mean,' Elias replied.

'Elia,' Spiros said, stroking a hand through his thinning hair, slightly better tamed today. 'Your mother had to find out from the pages of a glossy magazine belonging to one of the villas she cleans for.'

His mother knew what he really did? When he had lied to her about conveyancing? Could this day get any worse?

'Lawyer Elias Mardas on modern-day matrimony and going for broke when it comes to divorce and dissolution.' Spiros sniffed. 'I memorised it.'

He cringed at his father citing word-for-word an article that had singlehandedly caused his business's rapid growth. He had been sad and humiliated and oh-so angry when the reporter had caught up with him, but he had also been completely focused on making a success of the worst moments of his life.

'I did not recognise the man in the photographs,' Spiros carried on. 'Sitting confidently on white leather sofas wearing suits that look a size too small. He was handsome and, without a doubt that is something he has inherited from his father. But there was a fierceness about him. He was not the person who smiled and laughed and danced around a lamb on a spit with honey in his hair.'

All the reverie from his childhood hit Elias then. Running through the olive groves, bright wildflowers licking his shins, sunshine all around, crunching over Avlaki beach and diving into the waves…

'She hurt me.' It took Elias a second to realise it was him who was speaking. He should stop. He should withdraw. There was safety in withdrawing. But his words came again: 'She hurt me so much.'

And then there were tears. Tears he thought he had spent long ago at the very beginning of this break-up, pouring out of him in front of his father. He ached to stop, but his emotions simply weren't complying.

He felt a hand on his back then, a solid and comforting pat from the man who had raised him. The man who had had a heart attack and not told him. The man who was living in a shed...

'I do not live in your house, Elia, because it is *your* house. Marriage or no marriage, it was always going to be your house. It is yours to do with what you wish,' Spiros said, continuing to pat as Elias attempted to recover. 'And, in life, there is nothing that cannot be reversed. If that is what you want.'

Reversing. No, he did not want a backward step. He only wanted to move forward. Except he still wasn't exactly sure what that looked like now. It definitely wasn't going to involve his house in Liakada, but it was quite possible it was going to involve Villa Selino.

'I suggested reversing to your mother,' Spiros told him, throwing the cigarette down into the dirt and stomping on it with his shoe. 'I said it was time for us to change up through the gears and start again. Begin a new journey and add miles to our map of marriage.' He sighed. 'After three months of watching her dance with Constantine every chance she got and admiring the produce of Leandros, I told her I thought we should try living together again. And do you know what she said?'

Elias shook his head, sniffing as he looked through damp eyelashes.

'She said, "Spiro, until you realise the difference between the handbrake and the accelerator then we have no hope of even getting to the nearest petrol station to refuel",' Spiros stated, hopelessly. 'I have no clue what she meant. And *I* started off with using the car terminology!'

Elias put a hand on his father's shoulder. 'Papa, you need to tell me what's happened since I've been gone,' he ordered. 'All of it.' He held Spiros's shoulder firmly, shaking a little. 'OK?'

'OK,' Spiros agreed with a nod of his head. Then his father turned to face the fluttering double sheet at the end of the garden. 'Did you get all that, Areti?' he shouted. 'My son, Elias is back to see his parents and he does not care what any of the village thinks about that. I love my wife and I do not care who knows that either! And we are now going to drink *ouzo* in the middle of the day!'

There was no sound until the interruption of the lone cockerel, crowing loudly from the enclosure at the bottom of the plot and then Areti's voice called:

'Good! *Yammas* to you, Spiro!'

Spiros nudged Elias with the point of his elbow and raised his eyes.

'And,' Areti continued loudly, 'just so that you know, there is nothing wrong with turnip in a *moussaka*!'

Thirty-Six

'People are staring. Why are they staring? Did I get more than the twenty mosquito bites I've found on the walk here? Is my body covered in welts I can't see that have already started weeping?' Petra alternated between looking at the backs of her thighs in the short red playsuit she was wearing and meeting the gaze of villagers sitting at tables outside an establishment that looked like neither taverna nor bar. There was a yellow sign attached to the railings that showed an emblem of a Greek-looking warrior and the words 'Hellenic Post'. It was a post office? Where people could drink while they sent letters? How civilised! Past the tables outside, through the front door were signs of groceries. Was this the shop Eleni owned? What had she called it? A café-something...

Petra had been right about the boxes of blooms and houses clustered together, clean washing swaying in the humid air. It was as chaotically charming as it was peaceful, locals going about their business – on mopeds, 4x4s, a donkey – ramblers with their walking poles and backpacks strolling along or stopping at the square to guzzle water, cats sitting outside the one taverna in groups of three, waiting for the slightest indication that a tit-bit might arrive.

'Are *you* getting bitten?' Petra asked Becky. 'I considered putting that cleaning fluid on me instead of my bug spray, seeing as it seems to successfully eradicate everything. I think it's saved my cut-offs BTW.'

'I read before I came here that everyone gets bitten by mosquitos, but that some people simply react worse to them.'

'What a heartening, slightly middle-aged fact that is,' Petra responded, rubbing her calf. 'Why have we stopped here? Aren't we going into the bar-shop place and trying to get some juice on Elias from Scary Eleni? She seemed like a woman to know everybody.'

'Maybe we should have something to eat in the taverna instead,' Becky suggested. She had agreed coming to the village tonight to either find Elias or to find *out* about him was a good idea, but it was bothering her she hadn't managed to make contact with Ms O'Neill yet. It would have been handy to touch base before they arrived here. She was still half-hoping the owner would say that, yes, the house was about to be put on the market and she hadn't told her because her partner was organising it and she hadn't realised it was all happening so soon.

'You can't be hungry,' Petra exclaimed. 'That lunch we had was mammoth.'

She didn't want to tell Petra that actually *she* had eaten most of her share of sardines and meatballs and Becky had mainly had bread and *tzatziki*. But, despite that, she wasn't really hungry, just a little bit unsure about drinking in a locals' bar when the woman who had met them at Villa Selino hadn't been the most welcoming kind. Becky toyed with the brown leather belt around her navy-blue dress, playing for time and pretending to be highly interested in a curly-haired dog with its head stuck through the railings.

'Come on,' Petra said, grabbing her arm and pulling her towards the entrance. 'We need deets. As in details, not as in what's supposed to be in that repellent. And wine. We definitely need more wine.'

'We had wine before we walked here,' Becky reminded.

'One glass each,' Petra said, powering up the short run of steps.

'Petra, it was a pint glass.'

'Was it?'

The eyes all followed them, chess games – or whatever it was the men were playing – paused, conversations hushed. They were met, before they could even get into the building, by Eleni.

Becky swallowed as the woman stepped in front of them, arms folded across her chest. She was wearing a black dress this time, an apron over it, flecks of something that looked like flour in her cumulus of dark hair. There were shades of Governor Joan Ferguson from *Wentworth Prison* about her.

'You come to eat,' Eleni said, blocking their path.

'No,' Petra answered. 'No, thank you. But we would like some drinks. Please.'

'*Parakalo*,' Becky added. She remembered the woman liked her attempt at talking the language.

'No,' Eleni responded. 'You will eat.' She moved through her customers sitting outside, taking a table with plastic game pieces on it and pulling it free from one group and dragging it to a vacant space at the end of the terrace. Then she swept the pieces off into her cupped hand and deposited them back into the middle of the group's game. No one said a word. There was no protestation about the upheaval or the ruination of the draughts, or whatever it was, simply silence, all eyes on them as newcomers.

'We can eat,' Becky said quickly. 'I am slightly peckish.'

Petra made a face at her – either because of her alleged old age language or because she couldn't ingest another meal – as Becky headed over to the table while Eleni stole two chairs from next to a woman who appeared to be doing crochet.

'You must be very hungry,' Eleni told them. 'To have not had food or drink since you arrive in Corfu.'

'Oh no, we…' Petra started.

Becky slapped Petra's arm as hard as she could, making the girl yelp and hold onto the sore spot. Her friend didn't seem to get it that they shouldn't mention shopping elsewhere.

'Ow!'

'Sorry,' Becky apologised. 'Mosquito. A really big one just feeding on your arm.'

'Really?' Petra said, studying her flesh and looking for the mark.

'I have made *stifado*. Sit.' It was definitely an order and Becky plumped down onto one of the wooden chairs, her bum taking up the whole of the had-to-be-tiny seat.

'You will have wine,' Eleni continued, producing placemats and knives and forks from about her person. 'I make.'

'Lovely,' Becky replied.

'And you will buy food for the villa before you leave.'

'But we…' Petra began. She was sitting opposite Becky

now and Becky struck out a foot, connecting with her shin. 'Ow! That can't have been because of a mosquito!'

'What is *stifado*?' Becky asked Eleni. Anything to deter the woman from Petra who was about to reveal they had bought groceries from another mini-market.

'Beef. In a sauce. With onions.'

'Delicious,' Becky said. 'I can't wait.'

Eleni nodded her head and finally disappeared into the property. Still all eyes were on them and Becky smiled at the locals in the hope they would find something more interesting to focus on very soon or it was going to make for an awkward evening. None of them looked much like they were the types to fill them in on information about one of their own.

'She doesn't put any question marks at the end of her sentences, does she?' Petra remarked, rubbing her leg with her hand before straightening back up.

'I'm sure the food is going to be very nice,' Becky answered. 'Traditional home-cooked beef in a sauce.'

'It's a bit odd that they don't have a menu,' Petra remarked. 'In Asia the only places that didn't have menus were the street vendors, or the restaurants you really didn't ought to be eating in.'

'Well, I don't think it's like that in Greece,' Becky replied, relieved that at least some of the other patrons were now going back to their games and conversations. 'I read in my guidebook that at some tavernas they only sell one or two dishes that the grandmother has cooked that day. It's like sitting down to dinner with the family. And it saves waste obviously.' She drew in a breath, gazing out over the little square with its wooden benches, fat-trunked olive tree and spiralling floral displays from the surrounding balconies. She liked it here. It was old-fashioned and slow-paced, like time had completely bypassed it. It was a little like how the UK used to be before everyone got glued to their iPhones and there were news alerts about whatever senior members of the royal family were up to.

'I think we're going to have to look further afield if we want to find some action of the male variety,' Petra whispered. 'All the men here are over fifty. *All of them.*'

'That's not true,' Becky said. 'There was that group of boys we passed on the way here, on bicycles.'

'They were *boys*. About ten years old. Not men. No,' Petra said. 'We are going to have to have a few nights out in Kassiopi, I think. Check out the under-thirties of the island.'

'How long are you planning to be away from home for?' Becky asked. 'It sounds like you've been to so many exciting places already.'

Petra shrugged. 'I'm not really counting the days or anything. She's coming with the wine. It looks a bit of a funny colour.'

'Well,' Becky said. 'Don't say anything about that. We need to keep her on side otherwise she might tell Ms O'Neill that I have someone staying with me or that we had a bear-thing and cats and a flamingo in the house.' *If she hadn't told her already.* Although Becky suspected that if Ms O'Neill *did* know about it, she would have contacted her already.

'It's dark brown,' Petra said, wrinkling her nose.

Becky swallowed to almost brace her palate.

'Wine,' Eleni said, banging a very large jug of haven't-had-a-pee-all-day-coloured liquid into the centre of the table.

'Ooo, that's an unusual shade,' Petra remarked, despite Becky's raised eyes the second she had opened her mouth. 'What type of wine is it?'

'*My* wine,' Eleni snapped her reply. 'It is a recipe handed down from my grandmother's grandmother.'

'That sounds… perfect,' Becky said quickly. 'Traditional.'

'The *stifado* is coming. You will have bread.'

Petra opened her lips to reply.

'It wasn't a question,' Becky mouthed across the table.

As Eleni left them again, Petra put her nose to the large carafe, sniffing. 'Jesus, it smells like it's come out of someone's grandmother's grandmother. If we drink this we're probably going to die.'

Becky nodded. 'But, on the other hand, if we don't drink it, she'll probably kill us anyway. How would you rather go?'

'Pass me a glass,' Petra ordered.

Thirty-Seven

'Shit, I'm pissed,' Petra hiccupped and leaned so far back on the tiny chair that she almost toppled it over backwards. Only grabbing the table with her fingertips prevented her spilling onto the floor. 'What is in that wine?'

'Do you really want to ask?' Becky was feeling a little on the blurry side too and it was nothing like any of the on-the-way-to-drunk feelings she had had before in the UK. This was on a whole new level. She mustn't drink any more. And she mustn't let herself be in charge of anything – things with wheels, credit cards, her phone.

The *stifado* had been wonderful though. The hunks of beef tasted like they had been quietly, oh-so-slowly stewed for at least a whole day and the rich, red sauce had a gravy consistency that tasted of paprika, cumin, nutmeg and cinnamon. As good as it was though, Becky couldn't help but think there was something missing. She couldn't quite yet put her finger on what it was though.

'We need to ask someone,' Petra loud whispered.

'Ask someone what?'

'Ask someone about Elias,' Petra said. 'You know, our mission for being here was to find out more about him, not to get as fat as a big, fat Greek *meze* or as drunk as... as drunk as... as drunk as we are already.' Petra hiccupped again then sneezed.

'You speak about Elias?'

It was Eleni. Where had she come from? Becky sat up a little taller and straightaway felt under the deepest scrutiny.

'Elias Mordos,' Petra spoke, her words very slurry. 'Do you know him? Six-foot, short dark hair, quite hot for a man in his thirties, fit body...'

'It's Ma*r*das,' Becky interrupted. 'Not M*o*rdos.'

'Is it?' Petra asked, toying with her plaits.

'I know him,' Eleni answered. 'Wears the expensive suits. Has money.'

'He has money, does he?' Petra asked, showing a little too much enthusiasm in Becky's opinion.

'You want his money?' Eleni snapped, almost baring teeth.

'No,' Becky said. 'We met him... on a plane and...'

'Three planes actually,' Petra reminded.

'He does not fly a plane that is private anymore?' Eleni said. 'He cannot have as much money as we think.'

'That's an excellent point,' Petra mused, a finger in the air, eyes a little glassy. Becky hoped *she* didn't look quite that intoxicated.

'But,' Petra began again, 'rich people these days, they are absolutely paranoid about their carbon footprint, aren't they? And flying with other people is eco-friendlier and better for the environment. Well, not *better* per se but, you know, slightly less harsh on the ozone.'

'He has good shoes, doesn't he?' Eleni carried on. 'A well-styled carbon footprint.'

'So, you know him well?' Becky asked her. 'Elias.'

'We are very close, if you know what I mean.' Eleni touched the side of her nose with a finger. 'We have been as close as two people can be.'

'Ugh! No! Seriously?!' Petra exclaimed in horror. 'That's like Dick Van Dyke… but in reverse. Loved him in *Murder 101* on Hallmark but… no.'

'Petra!' Becky didn't know exactly how old Dick Van Dyke was – or if he was even still alive – but there was no way Eleni was in her – nineties? – or… dead.

'You think a woman like me could not be attractive to a younger man?' Eleni asked, her face suddenly very in the middle of their space. She smelled of the *stifado*. What *was* it that was missing from that dish? Something to just add a little extra zing… Becky shook her head and re-engaged.

'I don't think Petra meant that. At all.' But the reality was, Eleni seemed to be telling them that she knew Elias intimately and that made her even more suspicious about who he actually was. Could the man who had held her in his arms so tenderly have a penchant for the older woman? But who was she to judge? And she guessed everyone had a past.

'I can't believe I've half-kissed someone who would be "as close as two people can be" with someone like—'

'Petra,' Becky said warningly. Had Petra said 'half-kissed'. What did that mean? There had been no half measures of a kiss from where she had been standing in Kefalonia. She was starting to get a headache and she looked at the dark white wine and wondered whether more of it might be the best cure.

'You kiss Elias?' Eleni blurted out suddenly. It was a horrified sound like Petra could have infected him with something she might have picked up in the darkest corners of Bali.

'I… not really… it was just the most fleeting of touches,' Petra backtracked. 'You're not still together, are you?' Becky watched her shrink a little.

'You like men?' Eleni continued, picking up their used cutlery and brandishing it as she prepared to clear the table.

'I don't know what the right answer is,' Petra said, her usual bluster diminished.

'You do not kiss a man one moment and then a woman the next?' Eleni continued.

'You really can't ask questions like that in 2020,' Petra responded, a little confidence coming back. 'And you certainly cannot make a judgement on it. I believe very strongly that love is love.'

'I think,' Becky began, 'that…'

'I think that you are not for Elias,' Eleni concluded. 'You are too… English.'

'Oh my God!' Petra gasped. 'You can't say that either!'

Becky wanted the whole conversation to stop. How had it developed into this in the first place?

'I can say what I like,' Eleni responded. 'This is *my cafeneon*.'

'And you should be accepting of everyone if you want people to spend their money here,' Petra told her.

'Could we have some more wine?' Becky asked.

Eleni glared at her. 'You have not finished the first jug.'

'I know,' Becky replied. 'But we will. Look, I'm having the last glass now.' She poured the remaining wine into her glass and held it in the air as proof... and a passing mosquito dive-bombed right into it.

'Eleni!' The voice came from inside the building and the woman turned her head to see who was calling her. Then she grabbed the plates from in front of the women, turned and headed back inside.

'Shit!' Petra announced, grabbing Becky's glass of wine and downing it in one.

'Petra, there was a mosquito in there. I was going to fish it out.'

Petra wasn't listening. Petra looked to be in shock. 'Can you believe it. Elias and *that* woman? I mean, it doesn't make any sense, does it? A guy like that and... *her*.' Petra chewed on the end of one of her plaits. 'But, then again, you know, maybe it *does* make sense. Maybe that's exactly why he wasn't into our kiss.'

Elias hadn't been into the kiss with Petra? Becky couldn't help but sit further forward, bumping her small chair in slightly. 'Elias wasn't into your kiss?' Repeating that sentence seemed to set off a chain reaction of events inside her. She was feeling Elias's fingers on her skin, the warmth of his hand in hers, the movement of their dancing... This wine was definitely potent and she needed to remember that the more she found out about him the less she seemed to know.

'No,' Petra admitted with a sigh. 'It was alright, you know, obviously because he's hot, but I could just tell he wasn't really in the moment with me.'

'Oh,' Becky said. Would *she* know if Elias hadn't been in the moment with *her*? She didn't have a great track record on that score. She hadn't known that Mr Eighteen Months hadn't been in many moments with her. 'That's... upsetting.'

'Not really,' Petra said with a sniff. 'You win some, you lose some. And I said before, he's *way* too old for me. Practically Dick Van Dyke.'

Becky shook her head. Petra seemed to think that anyone over twenty was halfway to the grave. And how old could Elias be? Thirty, perhaps?

'Now, those guys over there, they're much more my thing,' Petra announced. 'Definitely under thirty and hot with it. And here! In the Village of Retired People! I'd better go and introduce myself before they get snapped up by someone else who's bored of looking at grey matter.' And just like that, Petra was up off her seat and rushing from the terrace of the *cafeneon* and across the road to the restaurant named 'Panos's Taverna'. Becky could see there were a group of three men in their twenties, arriving at the entrance. They very much looked like they wanted a meal and not to be jumped on by a very full-on Brit under the influence of local wine.

'Dark Dating!'

Becky jumped in her seat as Eleni banged down a day-glow orange flyer on the table, the salt and pepper pots rattling against each other. There were letters and words she could not comprehend. Greek words in the Greek alphabet. There was a number seven and that was about all Becky could get from it.

'What is this?' she asked, picking the paper up and pretending to look interested. What she really wanted to do was pay for the meal and get back to the house for a late-night swim to cool off from the humidity. Another jug of wine came crashing down. No swimming if she had to drink the wine she shouldn't really have ordered more of.

'This is something you will come to on Saturday.'

'Oh, well… I don't know what Petra's plans are and…'

'You tell me she only stay at the villa for a couple of nights.'

Bugger. Eleni remembered everything. 'I…'

'Dark Dating,' Eleni said, snatching the paper out of Becky's hands and translating it for her. 'I see this on TV. I make this in Corfu. But with the twist.'

'The twist?' Becky queried.

'You cannot see *and* you do not speak.'

'I don't understand.' How could you date in the dark and not speak to your date either? How could you get to know anything about anyone? By touch alone? Becky shuddered. She really didn't want to think about the connotations of that!

'You will come,' Eleni ordered. 'You and the rude girl. I find you nice Greek men who are not Elias.'

'Oh… well, I'm not looking for any men,' Becky said, a blush covering her entire face and rapidly spreading to her neck. All she could see in her mind's eye was the cover of *How to Find the Love of Your Life or Die Trying.*

'You look for women?' Eleni asked, raising an eyebrow.

'No, but—'

'Good. You come. It is ten euros. There is food. I add to your bill.'

'Well, I need to—'

'Drink the wine,' Eleni ordered, pointing at the new carafe. 'No one leaves my *cafeneon* until they have finished.'

'*Efharisto,*' Becky said, reaching for the jug. '*Yammas.*' Resistance was apparently futile.

Thirty-Eight

Villa Selino, Kerasia

Elias sat in his hire car outside the property watching the light of the moon reflecting off the roof tiles. He had the window of the car down, the temperature cooling only slightly, the burr of the bugs from the trees and the occasional hooting of an owl were the only sounds.

Earlier, he had spoken to Chad on FaceTime and told him that Kristina was currently not in Corfu as first thought. Elias had been honest and said that although his initial plan had been to speak with her personally, to put the offer they had devised to *her* rather than through her own solicitor, that perhaps her absence was fortuitous. He had asked Chad to provide him with an inventory of what should be in the villa and Chad was going to put this together overnight. What Elias *hadn't* told Chad was that when he had looked through the window of the property that morning, there was an obvious absence of artwork on the walls. Bare space and tell-tale fading of the paintwork told a story. Perhaps Kristina had simply got bored of what was there. But, equally, perhaps they had been expensive pieces she had sold already, or was planning to sell without Chad's knowledge. And that was the dilemma. Elias had Chad's authority to go into the house and assess the situation and now he had his mother's set of keys to give him access to the villa. But all he could think of was the underhandedness of it all. He shouldn't be acting like some sort of private investigator. If he needed to creep around in the dark to get results then there was something very wrong with his life. And then there was Becky. Becky who he should stay away from, thrown back into his orbit by complete coincidence. Or perhaps, fate. What was he going to do about it all?

The one thing he was certain of was that drinking *ouzo* in the middle of the day with his father was not going to help either of them solve anything. But the male-bonding had helped him discover that whatever was wrong with his parents' relationship it hopefully wasn't terminal. Spiros had talked of Eleni's boredom and dreams and his father had said it all in such a way that Elias could understand completely why his mother might have got frustrated with him. Spiros was a simple man at heart. He thought that dreams were for other people. His mother however had always been far more ready to experiment with life. Yes, she was big on certain traditions, but she also broke boundaries, albeit in a small way. She was never afraid to be vocal to the mayor about refuse collection or broken streetlights. She organised events to bring the community together. She encouraged the widows of the village to wear colour again and reembrace life. Yes, it was true she might be a little – or a lot – bullish about things, but deep in her heart it was because she cared about everyone.

'I am walking in a straight line! It's you who isn't!'

Elias froze. It was Petra's voice and he hunkered down into his seat like he was a cop on a stakeout trying not to be discovered. He had assumed they were inside the house. It was well past midnight. He didn't even know why he had driven up here on his way back to Liakada. Except that half an hour ago he felt looking at the property might make him come to a decision about going in and making an inventory tomorrow. But he knew, if going in was what he decided, he was going to have to be upfront with Becky. He wasn't sure he had it in him to go behind her back and let himself in when she was staying there. It would be wrong. Her things would be there. Her pad and pen maybe. Drawings of animals with holes in them...

'You told me you drank *tsipouro* with those guys. I only drank wine.'

It was Becky's voice now and Elias lifted his head a little, daring to look out of the open window to see her. The women were walking, slowly, at varying degrees of wobbly, heading towards the gate of the property.

'The wine!' Petra exclaimed, throwing her hands in the air. 'It looked like it had come from a ninety-year-old with a bad urine infection.'

'How do you know?' Becky responded. 'How many pots of pee belonging to ninety-year-olds with urine infections have you been witness to?'

'You really don't have a clue what goes on in Bangkok, do you?'

'I don't seem to have a clue what was missing from that *stifado*, either.' Becky stopped walking and let out a sigh. 'And that means I'm losing my touch. And if I'm losing my touch then that means I really am just someone who butters bread for a living.'

'Bread is important though,' Petra replied. 'Like, you can eat it and you can spend it. You can never have enough of it.'

'You are definitely more drunk than I am.'

'Not too drunk to do sailing tomorrow though.'

'What?' Becky exclaimed.

Elias watched them. Both still stood outside the gate of the villa, underneath the full moon illuminating them like a spotlight. Swaying a little...

Petra laughed. 'The guys – the ones I met in the restaurant. They're meeting us at Avlaki beach tomorrow and we're going to do sailing.'

'Oh, Petra, no. I'm not really very good at things like that,' Becky protested.

'Things like what?'

'Anything that involves any sort of coordination.'

'Like putting one foot in front of the other right now?' Petra asked, pushing the gate open.

'Well, if I'm going to be forced to go sailing then you're definitely going to have to do Dark Dating,' Becky told her. 'In fact, I've already had to pay for our entry so...'

'Dark Dating? What the hell is that? Do you have to have dinner with vampires?'

'You can't see, and you're not allowed to speak either,' Becky explained.

'What kind of dating is that?'

'Very quiet dating I'm guessing.'

Petra let out a burp. 'It's that *stifado*,' she announced. 'It's given me all the indigestion.'

'Nothing to do with the shots with those guys then?' Becky asked.

'I think that Eleni put something extra in my meal. She doesn't like me.'

'There was definitely something missing from the recipe, I wish I could figure out what it was.'

'We should have swapped bowls. I probably had what was missing in mine. You could have shared the burping with me.' Petra held her breath for a few seconds and then spoke again. 'Now, let me tell you about Atlantis because I think you and he could definitely be a match made in...'

'Atlantis?'

'I was going to say "heaven" but—'

'Atlantis can't be his real name!' Becky exclaimed.

'I met someone called Golem in Ho Chi Minh City.'

'No!'

'I swear! Now, Atlantis is tall, but not too tall. Dark hair and lean, but not too lean and he doesn't smoke. Well, he didn't smoke at any point during the six or so shots we did and he would have done, wouldn't he? If he was a smoker. I'm guessing you wouldn't be into a smoker.'

'Well... I might not hold it against a guy if he was, but I do prefer—'

'Ha!' Petra laughed. 'You mean you *might* hold it against the guy. Hold it against him. Get it? Hold *it* against him, as in your vag—'

'I get it, Petra,' Becky answered.

Elias watched the two women open up the gate then, after a few attempts, successfully close and lock it. They had been to Liakada. They had met his mother. Of course they had met his mother. His mother had most likely been here at the villa when they arrived. How crazy was this? His own mother cleaning the very house that belonged to his client from the UK! Except that streak of coincidence was not what was bothering him the most. What *was* concerning him was the fact Becky might already know he had lied about his occupation. *And* that she was going sailing tomorrow with someone called Atlantis.

He waited a few moments until a light went on inside the property and then he started up the car and drove away.

Thirty-Nine

Avlaki Beach

'It's a great view, isn't it?'

Becky, wearing a pair of sea shoes she had found in the utility room that were at least a whole size too big, crunched the soles down into the stones. It was another beautiful beach. White stones and small patches of sand in between, leading down to a shore where the waves seemed to be increasing in intensity the more she eyed them up. The sky was still a perfect blue, but it was windy. Petra had claimed it perfect sailing weather and she had bounced around the patio earlier, holding up miniscule swimwear in an effort to get Becky to help her choose an outfit for the expedition. No hangover was evident in the demeanour of the twenty-year-old. Becky, on the other hand, had already downed five super-strong Greek coffees and didn't feel vaguely normal at all. But the scenery was helping. This beautiful aquamarine bay with the rise and fall of the mountain behind it and again, with the peaks across the water in Albania.

'The waves are starting to look fierce,' Becky commented.

She was wearing a life-vest and that had worried her from the very outset.

'I didn't mean *that* view!' Petra remarked. 'I meant Atlantis and Troy.' She made some strange feral-cat-style noise. 'I like a bit of a wetsuit look.'

Except the men weren't wearing wetsuits. They were wearing nothing on their torsos and some sort of tight-fitting bottoms that stopped mid-thigh. It was all a little bit *Aquaman*.

'You have to admit they're both fit,' Petra said, continuing to admire the men who were now in the water and taking ownership of two rather flimsy-looking craft. The sail was tall like a yacht and billowing with the force of the wind, but the hull of it was small. It barely looked able to contain a whole person, a bit like the chairs in Eleni's *cafeneon*.

'Becks! Are you listening to me?'

'No,' Becky answered. 'I'm concentrating on looking at those boats that are bumping up and down on the waves like they're made of paper.' And not a nice, plush thick kind you might make a glossy leaflet out of. No, the really thin printer paper that usually got stuck in the roller.

'Come on,' Petra said, swinging an arm around her shoulders and pulling her forward. 'Once you're on the water you'll love it. And you can stop worrying about someone nicking the Aston Martin because you'll be at sea and not able to do anything about it.'

'Petra!' Becky hissed. 'I'm worrying about it again!'

'We parked it behind a bush!' Petra reminded. 'With the cover over it. Which I think makes it look well-dodgier but…'

'At least it doesn't quite shout "Hello, I'm worth seven million pounds".'

'The latest estimate is nine million,' Petra told her,

walking to the sea's edge. 'The value seems to be going up every time I look. Oh,' she said turning to look at Becky. 'I found something else out this morning too.'

'The flamingo isn't back, is it?' Becky asked. 'Because I thought I saw it this morning in the garden.' But it could have easily been a mirage due to her hangover. She'd been seeing two coffee machines for the first hour...

'No, but I know that Elias isn't an estate agent,' Petra told her with a knowing nod. 'You were spot on there.'

'He's not,' Becky said. She didn't know whether to feel pleased that her suspicions about him had been correct or to be disappointed that he *had* been lying to her since they first met.

'I Googled him this morning. The right spelling of his name this time.' Petra waved at the men and urged Becky forward again. She was glad she was wearing the sea shoes. She couldn't imagine how Petra was gliding over the pebbles so at ease with being barefoot.

'Well,' Becky said. 'What does he do for a living? Who is he?'

'He's—'

'The boats are ready! Come on!'

It was Troy calling. Atlantis, Becky had discovered over the one coffee they had shared at the taverna before they came on down to the beach, didn't smoke but didn't seem to talk much either. It had been hard work trying to build on pleasantries when someone didn't appear willing to get on board with the conversation concept. At first Becky thought it might be because he was Greek and didn't know much English, but he'd managed to say quite fluently that he hated tea and he hated rain and he hated the colour white because it wasn't really a colour at all. White was, according to Atlantis, an 'irrelevant body'. Becky had wanted to say that made no sense at all, but frankly she couldn't be bothered. Who hated a colour so passionately that they had made up a stupid little phrase to accompany the hatred?

'Are they getting on the boats with us?' Becky asked, sea shoes meeting the foaming water breaking on the shore. As much as she was apprehensive about the whole sailing thing, she also didn't want to be too up close and personal with the man named after a fictional island.

'No, don't be silly,' Petra answered. 'They're one-person boats.'

'I'm going to sail it on my own?' Perhaps sidling up to Atlantis mightn't be so bad.

'Yes. But you'll be fine. We'll get a little instruction before we sail off and the four of us are heading out together so you won't really be on your own. And it's only around the bay. It's not like we're going to end up in Albania.'

'But, Petra, I've seriously never done anything like this before,' Becky told her. She realised she was shivering and in the intense heat of the day, the water around her shins not even tepid, that couldn't be a good thing.

'I know,' Petra said, grinning. 'And that's why this is so great. Think of it...' She looped her arm around Becky's shoulder again. 'After this holiday you can add so much more to your CV. Cave-explorer, Greek dancer, sailor, cat-wrangler...'

'Petra, what does Elias do for a job?' Becky asked.

'What do *you* think he does for a job?'

Not this again. This man had definitely had far too much time spent with people trying to guess his occupation.

'Just tell me,' Becky demanded.

Petra smiled. 'The first thought I had when I found

out was "wow, how boring is that" but then I visited his website, and then I read this four-page article in *All Life* magazine and my tongue seriously hung out of my mouth for the photos and I thought "wow, maybe I should have kissed him harder even though he's twenty-nine". I worked out his age from the article.'

'Petra! What does he do?!' Becky's heart was racing. She had no idea what her housemate was going to say. Perhaps he *was* a model or an international playboy or an heir to a cobalt mine…

'He's a big-shot lawyer,' Petra announced, confidently wading into the sea like she was half-mermaid. 'Has his own company. Making shitloads of money and having to turn down clients because of his popularity among the elite. The article called him "Mr Divorce". He only deals in matrimonial cases… oh, and the article also accused him of hating women because he *allegedly* only takes on men as clients.' Petra had made quote marks in the air when she had said the word 'allegedly'.

Elias was a divorce lawyer? He only took on men because he hated women… Becky shook her head. It didn't sound like the person she thought she had been getting to know a little. This news proved all the things that Hazel and Shelley had warned her about. And she *had* heeded their warnings, but she had also thought she knew better, had let herself feel an attraction…

'Come on, Becks!' Petra called, beckoning her.

Shaking her head to dismiss this new news, Becky stepped into the sea. She had a date with a dinghy to conquer before she did anything else.

Forty

Elias looked at his laptop, re-reading the email for perhaps the fourth or fifth time. He had lost count and now the words were swimming in front of his eyes as he attempted to concentrate. *Swimming.* That's what perhaps he should be doing. Calling a day on this case – for a week or so – taking some time for himself? He couldn't remember the last time he had taken time for himself. Slowing down meant switching off a little and switching off a little meant there was more time to think. Thinking involved re-evaluating, re-evaluating meant considering things other than work. He didn't have anything much apart from work. And he had made it that way.

He raised his head from the words on screen and took in the view from the taverna on Avlaki beach. Ordinarily calm, the waves were rolling hard and fast, white fizzing foam hitting the stones with force. Most of the holidaymakers were content on loungers under the scorching sun, none of them attempting to cool off in the water just yet. Why was he here? Why this beach? This taverna? Seeing the sails of four small boats rippling into the wind a little way along the beach he knew exactly why he was here. That overheard conversation last night. Petra and Becky going sailing. *Becky*. Why was this woman dominating his thoughts? He had barely learned the name of any woman since Hestia…

And there she was. Even from this distance he could clearly make out Becky's outline. Her caramel hair was loose, flying out and around in the breeze and she was wearing a bright blue lifejacket over a swimsuit. She wasn't like Petra, all lean limbs and tight torso. Becky had curves, a softness, altogether womanlier. He vividly remembered the arc of her waist as they'd danced in Kefalonia. He let out a breath and looked back to the email. Was he going to send it or not?

'Come on, Becks! It's not that hard!' Petra yelled across the water.

It was easy for Petra to say it wasn't hard. Petra had already got into the tiny hull of the boat like she was simply slipping into a bath. For Becky, the boat rocking back and forth untethered, her gripping on, it felt like mounting a moving camel. Not that she had mounted a camel before, but she had seen lots of camel footage on *You've Been Framed*.

Maybe, if she was pathetic enough for long enough, Petra, Troy and Atlantis would get bored, sail off and she could tear off the lifejacket and settle on a sun lounger. Or grab a frappe from the taverna. It looked like a nice taverna here. All of the sea view and none of the waves trying to mash her into the pebbles…

'Becks! Get in the boat! Come on!' Petra yelled.

Petra seemed to be actually steering her vessel already, somehow turning the mast so the sail reacted to the wind direction. She looked completely in control.

'It is the white colour of her boat!' This shout came from Atlantis. He was the closest to Becky but didn't seem in any way keen to help. 'I tell you, white is unlucky.'

Becky took a breath. The sooner she got in the boat, the sooner she could angle it away from Atlantis and head off somewhere he couldn't be heard. Although she wasn't sure even Albania was going to be far enough...

As soon as the next wave had passed, Becky jumped, landing flat out on the boat like a marooned cuttlefish. Sprawling, the sea still claiming half her legs, she wiggled and writhed, hauling herself up onto the constantly rising and falling almost-ship. This was completely undignified. She could already feel her swimming costume had ridden up into parts of her even a gynaecologist would have a hard time finding.

'That's it, Becks!' she heard Petra shout. 'Now get your leg over!'

Becky closed her eyes, knowing the entire shoreline would have heard her friend's words of encouragement. Where *was* the hole that was meant to house her? She crawled, backwards, commando-style, immediately thinking about Megan and her assault-course triumph to win the army catering contract, up the length of the boat until she found the niche she was supposed to be sitting in. There was no chance of turning around to face the correct way, she just had to somehow wind her legs underneath her and slot her body where it was supposed to be. When they had explained how the vessel operated, they hadn't said it was going to take quite so much effort to get onboard. With one final effort, the waves cresting over the front of the boat, Becky pushed herself back and she somehow found the spot, dropping into the oblong opening with a thump. Her half-exposed bum took a hit and she actually wanted to cry. What was she doing here? She wasn't a seasoned adventurer like Petra. She should simply be sunbathing or learning a few words of Greek while admiring the scenery. Not pretending she was Ben Fogle.

Now, what was it she had to do with the ropes and the rods? Water was slopping into the area she was perched on and the constant rolling motion was not letting up at all. It was like being on an airport walkway that was malfunctioning – taking you nearer to the gate then changing its mind – and repeat, at max speed.

The sail was making a noise now. A thumping then a thwacking like it was angry. It probably wasn't used to being manhandled by a complete novice. Becky took control of the thin rope and then... she was off! With a scream, she was thrown back against the rear of the carved-out section, lifejacket cutting into her ribs, zipping across the ocean like the yacht had been given an engine. Sea salt and spray flashed into Becky's eyes and coated her lips and she hurriedly wiped at her face in order to maintain some sort of visual on where she was going. It was all too fast now, and rocky and... should they really be out in the water in these flimsy things when the sea seemed to be on the verge of ferocious?

'Becks! Slow down!' It was Petra's voice, only a whisper on the wind. Did Petra really think she *wanted* to be sailing at this rate of knots? She didn't want to be sailing at all! She had only really come along because she didn't think Petra should be on her own with two random men. Playing the mum/big sister and acting older than twenty-five again…

Becky pulled the rod and leaned back a bit, attempting to change her direction. There might not be a lot of sea traffic in this cove at the moment, but there were orange buoys to avoid and there were three other dinghies like hers… and she seemed to be somehow on a direct line to Atlantis.

'Oh God. Oh God.'

What would happen if she couldn't slow it down? What would a crash do? Kill them both? Smash the boats to pieces? How much would it cost to replace a boat like this? Hopefully nowhere near as much as it would cost to replace an Aston Martin…

'Becks! Go another way! Becks!'

It was all very well Petra screaming at her, but some practical advice as to how to achieve 'another way' might be nice. No amount of pushing or pulling or shifting her body out of the oblong and leaning to the right or the left seemed to be having any effect whatsoever. She couldn't crash. Could she? Surely Atlantis would move seeing as he had all the experience.

The sail seemed to be trying to escape from the boat completely now, billowing and rippling, straining tight then arching to capture all the wind. What if it actually came off? What then? Would she stop dead? It should kill her speed, shouldn't it? Could you detach a sail? No one had given her any instruction about that!

Water lashed at her face as the boat banged over another wave, still heading directly for the other dinghies who seemed to be finding it really hard to change their course and move away from her. Petra had her hands clamped to the side of her mouth, standing up inside her rectangular section. Becky couldn't hear a word she was saying. Was that the word 'right' or 'tight'? She was already holding on tight. So tight her knuckles were hurting.

Then, above the rushing of the wind and the slapping of the water spraying up onto the body of the yacht, came another sound. The sound of a much larger boat than the one Becky was aboard. Definitely one with an engine. She didn't need more boats on the water, she needed less of them. None, in fact, would be great.

But the sound of the engine was getting louder and the roar sounded like it was coming closer and Petra was closer too, as was Atlantis. It looked like Troy had been able to sail away, his craft now heading for the other side of the cove. Becky didn't know where to look, neither it seemed, did Atlantis and any second now she would almost be able to see the whites of his eyes...

As a speedboat arrived at her side, its powerful spray delivering more wet salt to both the dinghy and her face, it was all Becky could do to hold on at all. The rope was wet between her hands and she still had no idea what the pole could achieve. It actually looked like something that could slip inside the canvas of a tent, not something that had the potential to steer a yacht.

Becky screamed and let go of the rope completely as something landed on top of the boat. The vessel began to sway and lean and veer up on one side. She ducked down slightly, closing her eyes, terrified it was an octopus. Petra had informed her octopuses could jump out of the water just last night and forced her to watch a terrifying video where the eight tentacled fiend took a crab hostage and sucked out its insides. Crashing was inevitable now. She was going to be thrown into the sea and meet a watery end, probably on top of Atlantis...

'Becky!'

Forty-One

Becky opened one eye. It was a voice she knew, but it didn't belong here. Perhaps she was even imagining it. She opened her other eye and realised it wasn't her imagination. It was Elias, wearing nothing but very small swimming trunks and grappling for the rope and the pole she had discarded as useless.

'Becky, you have to be ready to jump off the boat if I can't turn us away in time.'

'I… don't know what to do,' she answered. She had never felt so stupid. It had been madness to agree to captain a craft when she was obviously completely incapable.

'If I say "jump" you must jump!' he told her. He was standing, every muscle in that tight torso straining and working, giving Becky a show worthy of a night at *Magic Mike Live*. And there was that tattoo. Finally fully on display. But with the wind and the sea spray and the fact they were in jeopardy, Becky couldn't focus enough to see what it was. Just like the last time he'd had his shirt off in

Kefalonia when she'd had to keep her attention on a half-drowned Petra.

'Becky! If I say "jump" you jump,' Elias repeated.

You jump I jump. Jack and Rose. That famous doomed vessel. Argh!

'I can help,' she insisted, trying to stand like Elias was.

'Don't come to this side,' he shouted. 'You'll tip us.'

'Then what can I do?' she called back. Petra and Atlantis's boats were so close now and Becky's dinghy showed no signs of slowing down.

'I am trying to turn it away from the wind,' Elias told her.

'I've been trying to do that,' she insisted. 'The wind is everywhere!'

Becky watched as Elias leaned back with the rope, desperately trying to manoeuvre the sail and change the direction of the yacht. He definitely had a gym body. A defined six-pack and muscular pecs but not in that overdone body-builder way, more in a way that said toned but not obsessed. And she needed to stop staring at him and concentrate on not dying.

The waves were still cresting and Petra started to scream as Becky's boat began to come within inches of hers. Becky held on tight, almost knowing the call to jump was coming. How could it not be?

But then, with one almighty groan from Elias, suddenly the boat stopped its full-on assault of the ocean and the wind dropped out of the sail, turning slightly to the right and in just enough time for it to skirt past Petra and Atlantis.

Elias fell down onto the boat, breathing hard, perspiring, eyes now closed as the yacht continued to drift – but lightly – out around the cove.

'You did it!' Becky exclaimed excitedly. 'No one died! And the boat isn't wrecked!' She clambered on all fours, from the sunken section, to the part where Elias was laid out.

'I feel like I have died,' he admitted, eyes still screwed up tight. 'It is too long since I have sailed one of these things.'

Becky sat down, crossed her legs and took a moment to admire his physique again. The tattoo had branches, an olive tree, spiralling around a letter. H?

Elias eyes flicked open and Becky averted her gaze. 'I haven't sailed one of these things my whole life.' She smiled. 'What are you doing here? I mean, how come you were here when I got in trouble?'

'I was at the taverna,' he told her. 'I saw you getting the boats and then I saw what was happening, so I called the lifeboat.'

'I feel so embarrassed,' she admitted. 'All of that because I can't sail a boat around a cove.'

'It is not always that easy if you have never done it before.'

'Petra doesn't seem to be struggling.' Petra was now looking like an expert in all things nautical, the breeze blowing through her plaits, Troy coming back into her orbit to admire her prowess.

'Do you want to learn?' Elias asked her.

'I'm not entirely sure.'

'I can teach you,' he offered, sitting up.

'Oh, I don't want to put you out or…'

'I'm already in my swimsuit, on board… it's going to take the same amount of time to shower and clean up no matter when I do it.'

The alternative seemed to be calling back the lifeboat and being taken back to shore, humiliated. She was already going to have to brush it off as nothing with Petra later.

'Well,' Becky began. 'If you think you can teach the unteachable then I guess I'll give it a go.'

'OK,' Elias replied. He stood up again, balancing carefully as he made his way to the captain's position. 'But before we get started with the lesson, there's something I need to tell you.'

Becky swallowed. Was he ready to be honest with her yet? What did it matter? He was a passing crush…

'You're a lawyer,' she told him.

He let out a heavy sigh. 'You know already.'

'Petra and I asked around at the village and then she Googled you.'

'OK,' he answered, nodding. 'OK.'

'I don't know why you wouldn't want anyone to know that,' Becky started. She could see that her knowing his real occupation had affected him. Gone was any self-assurance he had possessed in all their earlier interaction. Now he looked a little like he wished he had had to jump off the boat. And what was she expecting him to say next?

'It is difficult,' he answered. 'Even more difficult now we are in Corfu.'

'I don't understand.'

Elias motioned for her to get back in the driving seat of the boat. 'The first rule of sailing is to know that there is only ever one boss.'

'Me, the captain,' Becky answered. 'That was the whole reason for the failure of sailing so far.'

'No,' Elias told her. 'You are never in charge. The only thing in charge is the sea. Always respect the sea. Always.'

'O-K.'

'OK, relax. Hold the rope in this hand, like this and remember that it is your steering wheel. You drive, right?'

'Currently a ride James Bond would approve of.'

'Now, the boat needs the wind to power it, but equally, you need to control how much.'

'Yes,' Becky said. 'I got that. Not a clue how to achieve it though.'

Elias put his hand over hers and helped her with the rope. 'Learn to feel how the boat is moving. Understand by the reaction it has on the water, with the wind, what you need to do.'

Becky let out a squeal as the boat suddenly gathered momentum again.

'You feel that?' Elias asked her.

'Yes!' she exclaimed. 'I feel it!'

It wasn't all she was feeling either. Elias's hand in hers felt a lot more powerful than the signals the rope was giving off. It was firm and tender all at once and he was guiding her fingers with his.

'One of the reasons I could not tell you what I did once we got to Corfu was...' He took a breath. 'My client, the one I have come here for, needs me to go into his house to create an inventory of what's in there.'

'An inventory?' Becky queried, not understanding.

Elias nodded and shifted his position, coming up close behind her, squeezing into the small space and helping her gain more traction on the rope. That fine torso was pressing into hers, solid, muscular, the heat from his body transferring.

'I needed to know if the person that has been living at the house – not my client – is attempting to hide assets they have bought during the marriage and with joint funds.'

Then, all at once, it completely clicked for Becky. 'Villa Selino. That's why you were there. Not to put it on the market.'

She felt Elias take a breath in, then slowly exhale, nodding. 'Yes.'

Becky shook her head. 'Of all the villas and the people, you are connected to the one I'm staying in.' She paused before finishing. 'The man I sat next to on a plane from London.'

'I know,' he breathed. 'And I had no idea, not when we talked in-flight, or in Athens or Kefalonia, or even when we arrived at the airport here.' He slipped his fingers around hers, helping her to manipulate the rope to steer the dinghy. 'And I hate it.'

'You're the person Ms O'Neill doesn't want me to let in,' Becky stated. 'She's not worried about security because of thieves, she's worried because of you. She somehow knows you're coming here.'

'Yes,' Elias replied. 'I think so.'

'And she's using me to keep you out. Away from whatever she's hiding away along with the…' She stopped herself. She had been going to mention the expensive cars.

'Along with the?'

'Along with the… luxury expensive face creams that Petra's dying to dip in to.'

'Pull the rope a little to the right now,' Elias encouraged, his forearms touching her sides. 'Look to the horizon. See, what progress we are making.'

'What are you going to do?' Becky asked him. 'You know I can't let you in. It would be compromising my staying there and I've—'

'I wouldn't ask you to do that.'

'No?' Becky said. 'Because when you turned up the other day you pretended you were selling the property and wanted to take measurements.'

Elias had no answer to that. She was absolutely correct, of course. Even after he had realised exactly who was staying at Villa Selino, he had continued regardless. Lying to Becky and Petra, doing his upmost to keep his business on track.

'I know,' he replied.

'So, what's changed?' Becky wanted to know. 'Why now are you telling me the truth?'

'I don't know,' he admitted. 'Except that none of it feels quite right anymore.'

It was this damned island and being back with his mum and dad. It was Panos's Taverna and the stray dogs and Areti with her piles of washing. It was a world away from what he had changed his life into. It was all seeping under his toughened shell, more of the moist centre exposed, like a snail losing its outer cover. And, more disconcerting than all of that, he had a feeling it was also down to Becky…

'Captain Rebecca,' he sighed.

'No promotion to a general yet.'

He ignored her joke. 'I have a key to Villa Selino now,' Elias admitted. 'I have full permission from my client to go into the property.'

'I see.'

'But I'm not going to do it.'

'I don't know what you expect me to say.'

'I don't expect you to say anything,' Elias replied. The

boat had good, even speed now and was sailing around the cove, the glistening blue water licking the sides of its hull. 'But, I hope, maybe, that you can forgive me for not being honest with you from the beginning.'

'Isn't it what people do when they're seated next to one another on a plane?' He watched her sigh, a little more relaxed now, looking across the water, the sunlight on her face. 'Not give their real name. Make up a story about what they do for a job. I did that, remember? Captain Rebecca.'

'But when we started to get to know each other a little…' He took a breath. 'In Kefalonia. I thought—'

'I'm not like Petra,' Becky blurted out, taking her hands from his. Elias immediately felt the absence. His fingers cooled against the rope, his heart dropping.

'I know you are not like Petra,' he whispered.

'I don't have great hair you can wind into any imaginable style. I don't have her incredibly tight body that looks like the most perfect mannequin of health. I carry around a book called *How to Find the Love of Your Life or Die Trying*.'

She tried to shift a little away from him, but the boat rocked and he put a hand on her shoulder to steady her.

'I don't want you to die trying,' Elias told her sincerely.

'I'm not sure I even want to try,' Becky said, a little sadly.

'I understand that too,' Elias said. 'More than you know.' He needed to follow that sentence up quickly, because something *had* shifted. 'But life is full of coincidences, is it not? And those simple coincidences can change things.'

'I still don't know what you're trying to say,' Becky responded.

No, he didn't really know what he was trying to say either. He should say that he felt something for her. He should say that he did not know what it was, but that it was something. And it had been so long since he had felt *anything*. He should say that it was new and exciting, but also terrifying and confronting.

'I am saying… you do have… great hair.' He closed his eyes, glad that she was unable to see his face right now. He was an idiot. The silence seemed to elongate, the sound of the sea, rushing under them, the spray spitting and hissing. He didn't trust himself to open his mouth and say anything better, so he kept his mouth closed.

'The last boyfriend I had… he didn't think I had… great hair.'

Was she going to open up to him now? He wasn't sure he deserved it. In fact, he *knew* he didn't deserve it. But he wanted it. He wanted to know so much more about Captain Rebecca Rose.

'He pretended to like… my hair. He actually pretended to like my hair for quite some considerable time. Over a year. Eighteen months. Eighteen months of telling me… that my hair was all he had ever wanted and…'

Elias wanted to touch her hair now, even though he knew the conversation wasn't really about that. He wanted to run his fingers over the caramel-coloured waves, the sunlight picking out notes of red and gold as it danced over the strands.

'And then I realised that the hair he really liked, the hair he really wanted to spend all his time with was… my sister's hair.'

'What?' Elias had gasped.

⋆

Yes, what. What exactly was she doing telling Elias any of this sad pathetic story she should have long since recovered from? Dean. The man her sister was forming a life with, would probably marry and have babies with, had been *her* boyfriend for eighteen months and three days.

'It's OK,' Becky said. 'I mean, it wasn't, at first. At first it was really awkward and uncomfortable and he only left it four weeks before he moved on with Megan but, to be fair on her, she did keep asking me if it was OK. And I said yes. Even though it wasn't OK. It was painful and I didn't really understand it and...'

'This man is with you for eighteen months...'

'And three days.' Becky put her hands back to the rope and steered the vessel a little, as if suddenly, under Elias tuition, she had got the knack.

'Then after four weeks he dates your sister?'

It sounded even worse when it was someone else speaking the timeline of events out loud. She had fallen hard for Dean. He had been sweet and funny and indulged her love of crazy when it came to experimenting with pizza toppings like she experimented with sandwich-fillings...

'He is... the worst kind,' Elias spat.

It sounded like he was forcing the words out through gritted teeth. It sounded like he was furious. She could imagine the look on his face, the raised eyebrow, the pursed lips, a little like the expression he'd worn when he'd had to rescue Petra from the cave lake.

'He's been loyal to my sister so far. They seem completely devoted. We don't go out as a three now. After a rather awkward meal at a restaurant Dean and I used to go to when the waiter thought *we* were still together it seemed better to not encounter that scenario again. And, if I think realistically about it, they are much better suited than Dean and I ever were. I should have realised that at the time and—'

'I hate him,' Elias hissed, his body shifting. 'I do not know him and I hate him.'

'I hated him too. For a while. Until I saw how happy he was making my sister.' She sighed, looking at the beautiful view around the bay, the perfect picture postcard blue sky and warming sunshine making the water sparkle like it was laced with jewels. 'And that's one of the reasons I decided to come to Greece. Because staying in Wiltshire all the time is making me stagnate. As much as I love where I live and my job, I'm not going to find what it is I really like, or who I want to spend time with, unless I try other places, other things, other people...'

For a second she had forgotten exactly how close Elias was sitting to her. As she said the word 'people' it became completely obvious they were tightly melded into the space really meant for one. It was disconcerting as well as seriously sexy. And why was she telling him this? Just because it was time she got it off her chest? It had been on her chest and inside of her for so long, no one knowing except Megan and Dean. How much more awkward would it have been if Hazel and Shelley knew Dean had started off with her? There would be the looks and comments and misunderstanding. It was far better for Hazel and Shelley to think she had only ever had casual drinks with people like Angus from the sausage shop, not a real-life eighteen months and three days with a conservatory salesman they knew all too well.

'Being here is my time-out from everything I know. It's going to give me and Megan some much-needed space.

It's going to be time for me to work out if my destiny lies with making sandwiches for my sister's business and give her time to find out whether she needs me to keep her firm successful. Maybe she *will* need me. Maybe she won't. Maybe I will decide to start something of my own.'

Was starting something of her own what she wanted to do one day? All the 'one days' that had gone before had been usurped by the death of her dad and Megan needing someone to drive her out of the grief she was ignoring. Becky had always been the sister who made sacrifices.

'We are drifting a little close to the rocks,' Elias said all of a sudden. He put his hands over hers again, helping her to manoeuvre the boat away from the coastline.

'Yes,' Becky answered, reticent. 'It's rather a constant theme with me. Although I always do it in a very quiet way so no one notices.'

'We always think that it is sometimes safer to hide. To not show that things hurt. To cover up how we really feel,' Elias whispered so close to her ear.

'Yes,' Becky breathed. 'Exactly.'

He squeezed her hands in his, firm, soft, all the hotness...

'We make things all about the other people. Do not make other people feel bad. Do not make a scene. Do not stand up for what matters to you.'

'Yes,' Becky stated, smiling. 'You understand.'

'Of course,' Elias replied. 'I am... the same as you.'

She could feel the warmth of his breath against the side of her neck, the heat of his fingers on hers, hands clasped over the rope in the sunlight, sailing together across the now much less choppy sea...

Slap!

Becky screamed and reared back into Elias as something landed right in front of her on the boat.

'Get it off! Get it off! Arrggh!' Becky was trying to flip her body out of the sunken niche in a bid to get further away from their sea-life visitor.

Elias began to laugh and she could feel it, rumbling through him from inside that taut stomach that was nestling into her back, then up through his chest until release into the sea air. It was a warm sound, a genuine sound and Becky always liked hearing it.

'It is only an octopus,' Elias said, still laughing, taking control of the boat as Becky had dropped the rope in her panic.

'You wouldn't be saying that if you had seen the monster in a video Petra showed me last night.' She shuddered and Elias leaned his body into her again.

'It is a fine specimen,' he continued. 'I expect it would be delicious.'

'I can't… I couldn't eat it… not now I've seen it, alive and… wriggling. Argh!' Becky exclaimed as the octopus shuffled along the deck, closer to her. 'Make it stop.'

Elias slipped his body away from hers and attempted to stand up on the boat. His motion made the yacht sway a little and Becky screamed again.

'*Yassas*,' Elias said and he took hold of the creature and tossed it back into the ocean.

'Is it OK?' Becky asked as Elias turned to face her, expertly keeping his balance. She admired the physique of him in those tight trunks – not dissimilar to something David Gandy could model.

'You are enquiring after the health of something you were terrified of?' Elias asked her, a wry smile on his face.

'I just didn't want it to be like coral or something else from the sea that dies if you touch it.'

'Let us hope it does not try to find the love of its life or it might be the trying that kills it.'

'Ha ha,' Becky replied. 'Very amusing.'

'Come on, Captain Rebecca. Let us see if you can sail this dinghy without any help from me.'

Forty-Two

In the past four days Becky had seen the flowers of Villa Selino really come into their own. She had watered them thoroughly morning and evening, but she had done something else too, something she did to the herbs and plants in the garden of It's A Wrap. She had spent time talking to them. Now, with Petra lying in the pool, inside a bright pink flamingo ring that Becky was concerned might attract the *real* flamingo to mate with, she was holding the hosepipe over the blooming urns of lilac anemone and bright yellow marigolds whispering to their petals.

'It's been four days,' Becky said, watching the water tumble into the soil. 'Four days and I haven't heard anything from Elias. And I shouldn't be thinking about him because, he was a stranger on a plane and he told me he was an estate agent and... countless other reasons. But...' She paused, as if waiting for the marigold to give an answer. 'He was the first person I told about Dean and that means that I obviously liked him enough to tell him that and that... well, that's important.'

She moved the hosepipe from one urn to the next. 'But he knows where I am, and he hasn't been here, and he could be here. He's meant to be here for his job. Except he doesn't want to come in while we're here and he's... thinking more deeply about the morality of this case. I think.' She let out a sigh of frustration.

Despite not having seen Elias since they had sailed around Avlaki Bay together, Becky had relaxed into Greek life and had managed to avoid any suggestion from Petra that they 'hit a club' or 'book a booze cruise'. They had attempted to cook a barbecue – huge pork chops and village sausages – that had ended up with the reappearance of the bear-thing and half the neighbourhood cats. They had tasted at least four different village wines in one night in a bid to find the most superior kind of the ones that were less than three euros and came in a plastic bottle. And Becky had told Petra about It's A Wrap, her fight with her sister and her magical sandwiches, while Petra again told her absolutely nothing apart from travel stories. Becky still didn't know about the rest of Petra's family or exactly where in Kent she came from and the girl seemed to push every conversation away from real life and towards debates about the best Bridget Jones movie.

'I need to think about someone else, don't I?' Becky asked the red bougainvillea. 'Or no one else at all. Or everyone else if Petra has her way.'

'Are you talking to the flowers again?'

Petra's shout had Becky freezing, the water from the

hosepipe trickling away from the urn and going all over her feet and the pleather espadrilles.

'Bugger!' Becky exclaimed, lifting the hose up again and shaking one sodden foot. Could Petra really hear what she was saying? She wasn't sure she wanted her plant therapy sessions to be eavesdropped on.

Petra laughed then and Becky looked up over the small natural stone wall at her friend in the water. She was wearing giant sunglasses, the smallest of bikinis in an electric blue colour and was now riding the flamingo ring like it was a rodeo bull. 'You've spent more time with those plants than you have with me!'

That wasn't true. They had both spent the most time with the sparkling sea only a few steps away from the villa. Kerasia Beach was serene and perfect and absolutely what Becky had been expecting of this Greek trip. Swimming in the water, letting the refreshing saltwater run off her shoulders, soak her hair, hold her up in a starfish float Petra had taught her, was one of the best things she had ever experienced. She was starting to find perspective in the Greek water. Whatever happened next for her she needed to make *her* choices, not choices she made for the sake of others.

'But tonight's the night, right?' Petra called back, breaking Becky's train of thought as she gave the next pot a soaking.

'Tonight?'

'It's Saturday! Come on, Becks, you booked us into it!'

Oh God. Now she remembered. It was Dark Dating. Tonight in Liakada. Did they really have to go? It was only ten euros each. She could forfeit twenty euros to not go. Except Petra sounded way too enthusiastic.

'Dark Dating!' Petra called out. 'I know I thought

it sounded like a pile of shite when you first told me but... I'm quite excited about it. I mean the dark bit of it must mean that you can't see people, right? Well, that's really mysterious, isn't it? You could be holding a conversation with literally anyone.'

'But there's no talking either,' Becky reminded, coming out from behind the wall and walking over towards the pool, mainly so Petra didn't have to keep disturbing the peace with her shouting.

'No talking? Are you sure?'

'That was what I was led to believe.'

'By the old woman who's shagged Elias?'

And there was that. Despite *really* liking Elias there was the issue of him having had relations with the woman from the *cafeneon*. It seemed unlikely, didn't it? But the idea of it made Becky feel a little bit uncomfortable. She felt that he had been honest with her, cooped up in that tiny boat space, helping her learn how to sail. She had felt as if she was finally finding out at least some of the real him. But she also suspected there was much more to Elias Mardas and perhaps she had still only just scratched the surface. Was it a surface she wanted to continue to scratch at though?

'The thought of that!' Petra exclaimed. 'She has hairs on her chin. Did you see? I was scared one or all of them might end up in that stiffy she gave us.'

Becky had to concentrate really hard to work out what Petra was referring to. The beef *stifado*. She still hadn't figured out what was missing from that meal. Something sweet, but not more cinnamon. Something spicy, but not extra paprika or the twang of ginger. She might have to eat it again to really nail it down. Or, perhaps, forget about it.

She didn't have to be the girl who came up with crazy food concoctions here in Greece. Suddenly, thinking about It's A Wrap, Becky realised she hadn't heard from Shelley or Hazel for a couple of days. It was Saturday today though. Unless there was a wedding booked in – which there hadn't been when she'd checked the diary before her break – they wouldn't be at the unit until Monday.

Her mobile buzzed in her pocket, then gave out a chime she recognised straightaway. It was a tone she had set to alert her when she received something from Ms O'Neill. Elias story about a divorce had rung alarm bells and she was a little on edge as to what she had waltzed into the middle of. She didn't know her homeowner or anything about her. The cars worth millions in the garage had not been mentioned and you would have thought that if you had put someone in charge of goods *that* valuable, there might have been some mention of them...

'Is that the divorcee who's hiding the Crown Jewels and a Van Gogh original somewhere?'

'Petra, you haven't been trying any more sets of keys to open that cupboard in your room, have you?'

'Aren't you a little bit curious about what's in there? I mean, it might not even be a cupboard. I might open the door and there might be a foldaway staircase that leads to an underground drug laboratory.' Petra wriggled a little on the flamingo. 'Maybe that's it!' She waved a finger in the air. 'Maybe it's not about jewels or paintings. Maybe it's all about the pill production!'

Becky shook her head and looked at the screen of her phone. It was a text message.

Someone is coming to the villa on Monday at 5 p.m.
His name is Lazarus. He will have a key so no need to
be there. He will be removing a few boxes to take for a
local charity

'Ms O'Neill says someone's coming to the house,' Becky announced.

'A drug lord! I told you!'

'He's called Lazarus.'

'Yeah, right. That sounds *totally* legit.'

'He's going to be removing some boxes from the villa.' Becky sighed. She felt really uneasy about this now Elias had told her about the imminent divorce. She didn't know any of the details, but this *did* sound like Ms O'Neill might possibly be removing things that were half her husband's. *Grr*, why did she care? It was none of her business what went on between them. She was simply here to house sit not get embroiled in matrimonial disputes.

'I bet he is!' Petra said. 'Boxes of laundered money or… cannabis plants!'

What was Becky going to do?

Forty-Three

Panos's Taverna, Liakada

'What are you doing in here?'

Elias looked up from his laptop to see his mother standing over him, an apron tied around her middle, what looked like batter in her curly black hair. He picked up his coffee cup and raised it slightly as if that told her enough.

'I have coffee in the *cafeneon*,' Eleni reminded him, folding her arms across her chest.

'Mama, I wanted a cup of Panos's coffee,' Elias replied.

'Here we are, Elia,' Panos announced as he appeared holding a plate full of sausage, bacon, eggs, hash browns, black pudding, fried bread, tomatoes and baked beans. He placed it down on the table and stood back to admire his own presentation.

'What is *that*?' Eleni wanted to know. 'That is... the breakfast of the English.'

Elias nodded, already having grabbed a fork and put baked beans into his mouth. 'It's good.'

'The tourists love it,' Panos announced. 'I start doing this

this season and I have the best reviews on TripAdvisor.'

Eleni tutted as if both of them were committing a crime against Greek cuisine. 'You will die of heart failure. This is what I tell your father. This is one of *many* things I tell your father.'

This breakfast *was* good. As good as anything he had tasted in the UK. 'This is so good, Panos,' Elias told him through another mouthful of food.

'Good enough for the five stars?' Panos asked, lowering his glasses a little.

Elias nodded, smiling. 'I will do a review.'

'Oh, thank you, Elia. Thank you.' Panos then retreated away from the table and Elias was left with his still-glaring mother.

'What time do you come home last night?'

Elias shrugged, still enjoying the food. 'I do not know.'

'I know it was after one in the morning,' Eleni said, tone accusing.

'Then, if you know, why do you ask?'

'Were you with your father?'

'I thought you did not care what my father does any longer.'

'I do not.'

'I do not believe you.' Elias looked at her directly then. 'And I am still unhappy that he is living in a shed and that you did not tell me he was sick.'

'He was not sick. He had a heart attack because of the eating the breakfast of English people and the smoking.'

'So, you throw him out of his home?'

'I do not throw him out. He walked. Badly. Like a man twice his age with no springs in his step.'

'Ah,' Elias stated. 'Now we are getting somewhere closer to the truth.'

'Like you hiding the truth from me that you are a man in charge of divorces, determined to make women pay for their mistakes of believing everything a husband tells them?'

Elias shook his head, but the fried bread he had just attempted to swallow was catching in his throat. He focused on the fluffy stray dog that had just poked its head onto the stone of Panos's terrace. It might be hard being a stray, but it was infinitely simpler than his position right now. 'It isn't quite like that.'

'Your job?' Eleni asked. 'Or the lying to me about it?'

'Mama…' He stopped eating now, longing to down the deep, dark coffee and order another.

'No,' Eleni said. 'You might be clever with your words of divorce, but you do not know about things with me and your father.'

'I disagree,' Elias dared to say. 'I think I know exactly what is happening with you and my father.'

'I do not have to listen to this,' Eleni began, and she turned as if she was going to walk away.

'No, you do not,' Elias interrupted. 'But you should.'

Eleni stopped walking then and turned back to face him. The stray dog let out a whine as if sensing the unrest.

'Mama, I know you have dreams. I know you want to travel. And I think you should. I think you should take some time away from the village and the *cafeneon* and you should go wherever you want to and see whatever you want to see. Italy, perhaps? You and Papa in a gondola sailing along the canals of Venice.'

He saw his mother's expression change. Her eyes lighten,

a glow to her cheeks, her appearance uplifting, all framed by the trailing grapevines hanging from the beams of the taverna's terrace roof. His mother suddenly looked ten years younger. It was a snapshot of a youthful Eleni who perhaps had not seen her whole life being played out on the island of Corfu.

'One thing I have learned from my business is... men and women, they are definitely not the same.' Elias took a breath. 'They have different ways of looking at things and one way is not the *only* way. But you do have to accept that there are vast differences to the thinking. And embrace those differences. Because if we were all the same, it would make for a very boring existence.'

Eleni shook her head as if to dismiss him, but there were tears in her eyes and Elias could tell that she was taking on board what he was telling her.

'There is nothing wrong with you wanting something else, Mama. But you need to talk to Papa. You need to tell him what it is you long for.' Elias paused before continuing. 'Because I do not think you want Constantine or any of the other men from the village. I think you still want Papa, but you want Papa to understand that Corfu is not enough for you. You need a break from the *cafeneon*. You need a holiday.'

'He doesn't want anything else,' Eleni stated firmly. 'He wants only to drink *ouzo* and smoke cigarettes and play backgammon with his friends.'

'I don't really believe that,' Elias replied. 'I believe he wants to make you happy too. You just need to explain to him what is wrong and be open to letting him try.'

Eleni shook her head. 'And if he does not listen?'

'Mama, you are scared of exposing yourself,' Elias stated.

'But if you do not expose who you are, completely, you can never live your fullest life.' The content of this conversation was sailing very close to being about him. Or, rather, about Hestia. Perhaps it was about them both now. Hestia must have held her true self in for so long before she came clean about her love for Thalia. And now Elias was hiding behind the past and using it to govern his future. 'And then, nothing will change.'

'This place!' Eleni exclaimed, arms in the air like she was calling things down from the heavens. 'I love this place. But sometimes I also hate it.'

'I know,' Elias replied, reaching for his coffee and taking a sip.

'I do not want to *live* anywhere else. I would not know what to do living anywhere else. But…' Eleni began.

'Italy,' Elias whispered to her. 'Eating delicious pasta by a fountain, gazing out over the Amalfi coast, seeing the famous coliseum.' He smiled at his mother. 'Dancing with my father across a *piazza*.'

Eleni made a noise and flapped a hand in the air. 'Your father dancing? I tell you already, he can barely walk in a straight line these days and if you add in the *ouzo* drinking then…' She sniffed. 'You have now broken the fantasy.'

'Talk to him, Mama. Tell him,' Elias said softly.

'Before I talk to him, I need to talk with you.' Eleni pulled an orange piece of paper from her apron pocket and slapped it down onto the table next to Elias's plate of breakfast.

'What is this?' Elias asked, picking up the flyer and starting to read.

'Dark Dating. At the *cafeneon*. You will come. It is tonight. I will find you someone who is not like Hestia.

Someone who likes men would be a good start.'

'Mama,' Elias began to protest. He now wanted to only immerse himself in the fried breakfast. Except, he had heard about this 'Dark Dating' before. But what he hadn't realised was his mother was the host.

'You will see,' Eleni continued. 'There are some good women in Liakada. And this way... it is fun!'

It appeared there was nothing more to be said. Elias speared a sausage with his fork and bit off its end.

Forty-Four

Liakada Village

'I had no idea what to wear to Dark Dating, did you?'

Becky looked up from her phone as she and Petra ambled along the road towards the village of Liakada. She was worried. She had texted Shelley and Hazel earlier and they had both responded with a very short message and no real reply to any of her questions. Hazel's text had said 'Nothing to worry about here, dear' and Shelley's had said 'All good. Enjoy' with emojis of wineglasses. It was unusual. For two people so animated about her trip it seemed odd they weren't more forthcoming. Becky really hoped nothing was wrong.

'I mean,' Petra continued, 'if no one can see you it shouldn't matter what you're wearing. Ah! I've just realised. This is like *The Masked Singer*. It isn't just that you can't see anything and it's kind of creepy and kind of funny, it's so you don't judge people on how they look or who they are. Maybe that Greek mama isn't quite as simple as she appears.'

'Petra! That isn't judgemental at all, is it?'

And it wasn't really like *The Masked Singer*. Because you apparently weren't allowed to use your vocal cords either and no one had been told to dress up like a unicorn or a queen bee. Becky wondered just how much information you were supposed to get from potential dates if there was zero interaction. Sense of smell? Touch? Taste? Bleurgh!

'I see you went for something a little brighter than usual,' Petra remarked, pulling lightly at Becky's pink sundress with a tiny little forget-me-not flower-print all across it.

'Well,' Becky said. 'If it's dark, there may be a chance I won't get walked into with this outfit on.'

'I wonder if Atlantis and Troy will be there.'

Becky really hoped not. Atlantis had spent the whole time glaring at Elias when they had had coffee together after the boating at Avlaki. Becky hadn't been able to help herself, getting the word 'white' into as many conversations as she could. *White coffee for me, please. The white caps on the waves were so extreme, weren't they?*

'You didn't *really* like Troy, did you?' Becky asked her.

Petra shrugged. 'He was less than fifty and not quite as old as Elias.'

'Petra, don't you want to meet someone that means something to you?'

Becky slipped her phone back into her handbag and focused on the beauty of the walk. Gardens with allotments, giant squashes poking out from underneath fat green leaves, orange lilies, their trumpets trailing down over fences, cats licking themselves clean at the side of the road… What did she know about people meaning something? She thought she had meant something to Dean.

'No, I don't,' Petra replied brusquely. 'Well, that's a little white lie. They need to be compelling. Just for one night... or maybe two at a push.'

'Is that all?'

'There are a lot of people to get to know in the world,' Petra remarked, kicking a stray olive, still green and unripe, fallen too early from the tree. 'If you spend too long with some of them then you'll never get time to meet the rest.'

Becky looked at her friend, brushing the soles of her high shoes against the rough road. Looking younger and more vulnerable than ever.

'Besides,' Petra continued. 'The deeper you care about people, the worse the hurt is when they leave you.'

That comment dug crampons into Becky's heart and she thought not of Dean, but of her dad. Even after the stroke, when he was so completely changed, she still had him with her. It had simply been a case of getting as comfortable as they both could be with the practicalities of how life was now. She had to be the one in charge, guiding, supporting, like *he* had her whole life until that fateful day. Had she taken over? Had she shut Megan out at that time? She hadn't meant to. She'd only thought she was better placed to navigate everything with her organisational skills that was all. Maybe this argument they had had over Becky leaving to come to Greece had been about so much more. But neither of them had yet admitted to that...

'It doesn't mention anything like that in that shitty book of yours, does it?' Petra said.

'What?'

'*How to Find the Love of Your Life or Die Trying*. If that's not a crappy title then I don't know what is!'

'Petra, have you been in my bedroom?'

'Keep your tits on. It isn't *your* bedroom. It's the master suite for the Great Pandora Bracelet Thief or whatever she's got in those cupboards we can't get into.'

Becky could already feel her cheeks blushing and it wasn't because of the humidity or the insect repellent. She hated Petra knowing she was reading a self-help book for relationships.

'Anyway, I'm surprised you have time to read. Shouldn't you be finishing writing "roll out the barrel" and "spam" a hundred times on that quote for the old people's party.'

'The quote is done,' Becky answered, flapping a rather large and noisy hornet away from her face.

'How much is it for a load of sandwiches and ration cake then?'

'I don't know.'

'But isn't that what a quote is?' Petra wanted to know. 'Telling people what you're going to do for them and how much it's all going to cost?'

Yes, it was. That's exactly what it was. And Becky had the costings all worked out and totted up and the whole afternoon planned. Individual Lord Woolton pies – a recipe of swede, potatoes, turnips and carrots, with rolled oats to thicken the filling and hide the absence of meat (to remind them of rationing days) – served with a dripping coulis and mash. Corned beef hash inside Winston-Churchill-style pastry hats with Spam and onion fries. Next, the delicacies brought over by the Americans – including those tinned peaches everyone raved about – and ending in eggless ration mini-fruitcakes with Union Jacks iced on top. She had decided to go for comfort food most of the residents would be familiar with, but served in what she hoped would be a stand-out way. A way that would do It's A Wrap proud. Except she was too scared to email the proposed menu and price. Had she missed something vital? Would she end up costing the company money if she had? Should she add it all up for the millionth time? Or just bin the entire idea altogether?

'Once upon a time in Qatar, me and this guy I met crashed this wedding reception and the food...'

'Was it good?' Becky asked with a sigh as they came in sight of Liakada's square. Here was where Petra regaled her with a story about fantastic Persian cuisine and all Becky's flags on the tinned peach tarts dropped to half-mast.

'Oh God no. It was awful. Walnut stew! Shouldn't be allowed. And the falafel was so dry I think they rolled it in the desert. And everything that *wasn't* the stew had yoghurt with it, or on it, or in it.'

Becky smiled. That was a good story. She felt slightly encouraged now.

'Speaking of food. What was included in our ten-euro entrance fee? You did say food, so what food? A proper meal or bread and dips or some of that deep-fried feta with honey and sesame?'

'I'm not sure,' Becky admitted.

'Oh, there she is,' Petra remarked, stepping closer to Becky and whispering in her ear as they neared the *cafeneon*. 'What *has* she got in her hair?'

Becky focused her vision on Eleni. She was standing outside her establishment with a clipboard in her hands, dressed in a long yellow patterned dress that skirted the floor. Her hair had been made into a beehive style and it looked like it was currently housing two birds.

'Are they birds?' Petra questioned. 'Real birds? Nesting in her hair?'

'No, they can't be,' Becky replied, trying to look closer but still be inconspicuous. 'No, they're hair clips. I think.'

'Who buys hair clips with giant birds on the end of them?' Petra wanted to know. 'I know those bands with flowers on were popular in Claire's Accessories for a while but... birds?'

'*Kalosirthate*! Welcome! This way!' Eleni called, beckoning them towards her.

It was pitch black. It was darker than parts of the cave had been in Kefalonia. Elias was sitting in a part of his parent's *cafeneon* he had never known existed. He had been led – by his mother – into this dark tent structure that smelled of humidity, *ouzo* and other people. He was sitting at a table – he knew that much – and he had drunk a shot of *tsipouro* that had been handed to him. He wanted to speak, find out who else was in the room with him, but he had been warned – very forcefully – that if he *did* speak he would be in the deepest kind of trouble with his mother. And that was never a good place to be.

'Welcome everybody to... Dark Dating, the only place on Corfu where the views are not the main attraction.' It was his mother's voice. It was echoey like this room was a lot larger than he had imagined.

There was a ripple of laughter, but it didn't last long...

'Silence!' Eleni boomed. 'From this moment you will only respond to the questions that I will ask you to answer.'

Elias felt the urge to laugh. This was, without a doubt, the craziest thing his mother had done. How many people were actually here? He admired his mother's ingenuity though. Ten euros per person, and if the laughter was his only way to estimate there could be what? Thirty perhaps?

'In just one moment you will be joined at your table by your guest. They cannot see you. They will not speak to you. And you will not speak to them. This event is all about listening. And I mean *listening* not *hearing*. Listening is very important in a relationship. If you do not listen to your partner the end will be very quick and sharp... like a knife stabbing into an apple!'

Something made the noise of a guillotine. Perhaps an actual guillotine and there were gasps from the room. My God, his mother and father really did need to talk to one another.

'Silence!' Eleni called again. 'Your first dates are coming.'

'I can't see a fucking thing!' Petra hissed, bumping into Becky.

'Sshh!'

'Was that *you* saying "sshh", Becky?' Petra asked. 'Or was that the person who has hold of my arm? Is this our first date? A guy leading us into the dark... that doesn't sound dodgy or anything.'

'No talking,' a voice ordered.

'Mmm, so you are a man,' Petra continued. 'Are you under thirty?'

Becky was trying to tune in to her other senses. The floor underneath her feet was changing from a hard concrete tile to something softer. Grass maybe? Were they outside?

She sniffed, but all she got was heat that almost took the nose hairs off the lining.

'You sit here,' a man's voice told Becky. She put her hands out, felt the back of a chair and her guide helped her down into it. How could *he* see? She couldn't see even a flicker of light. It was like someone had wrapped the room in those wartime blackout curtains!

'Where do I sit?' Becky heard Petra ask. 'Don't take me far away from my friend. I've seen all the bad films where they separate people!'

'Silence!' Eleni ordered. 'When everyone is seated, we will begin.'

Petra was nearby. Elias couldn't help hearing her voice, such as it was. Was Becky close too? His stomach was currently tying itself into all the types of knots you could use to secure a boat to a mooring. He had thought about her a lot over the past four days. She had opened up to him on the water in Avlaki and he knew that hadn't been easy for her. It had led to him thinking that perhaps he should... ask her on a date. Tiptoe back in to being open about the future. Her being here at this mad dating night of his mother's had to mean she was open to the possibility. Maybe. Or perhaps it was already too late. Could she already be considering something with someone called Atlantis?

'*Endaksi*, your first partner is now opposite you,' Eleni informed. 'Take a long, slow deep breath and let their aura soak into you.'

What? Breathe in someone's smell? This was unorthodox but, Elias supposed, it would be an aroma you could be getting used to if you began dating… He closed his eyes, even though he could see nothing, and inhaled long and slow. Flowers. Definitely flowers. One thing he did know was he wasn't sat opposite Becky…

'Next, I will ask you a question and you must respond so your date can hear the answer. But you will not answer with words. You will answer with… a sound.'

Elias shook his head. Where was his mother getting this all from?

'So, let your date know your favourite animal. Go!'

Elias was momentarily dumbfounded. Favourite animal? Suddenly the room was filled with a cacophony of different noises and it was hard to differentiate one from the other. Until…

'Rooooaaarr! Rooooaaarr!'

The person seated opposite him let out a noise Elias couldn't distinguish between dragon or wolf protecting its young. And while he tried to decipher it, like it really mattered, he was still wondering what *his* favourite animal was. An octopus came to mind. No, they didn't make a noise, did they?

'Rooooaaarr! Rooooaaarr!' The roaring was getting fiercer now, definitely dragon not wolf, but he was getting interference of chicken, cat and… pig? Was that a pig sound he could hear coming from across the room?

Now Elias really tuned into the pig sound. It was a gentle snort. Not the right at the back of the throat hocking up a large male hog might do. This was more of a quiet, considered, mere reference to a pig. And he knew exactly who was making it. He stood up and almost fell into the table.

Forty-Five

However strange Becky had thought Dark Dating sounded, nothing she had envisaged conjured up this. She was sat in a black room, sniffing her date's aroma of figs and fish guts and making the sound of a piglet while her date pretended to be... well, she hadn't quite worked out if he was a donkey or a camel. How long did they have to continue making this sound for? And what exactly was it supposed to tell you about a person?

Becky gave one more snort and decided to give up. She sat back in her seat and willed it all to be over. It didn't seem like her date was going to give up braying or, whatever that sound was, any time soon and she already knew she wouldn't be having any dates with anyone who could make that kind of noise, for fun or whatever else...

Except then the growling stopped, abruptly and Becky sat forward wondering what had happened? The rest of the room was still involved in the farmyard activity. Had he choked himself on his saliva? Had a heart attack? Then there was a whisper.

'Captain Rebecca.'

'Elias?' God, had it been Elias making the camel noises? She might look at him in a different light now. It wasn't the most attractive attribute…

'I have come to rescue you. The only man in the village who makes a donkey noise like that is Manilos when he is herding his into their pen.'

It hadn't been Elias making that row. This was good. Except…

'What have you done with him?'

'Don't worry,' Elias replied. 'He is going to be enjoying the company of someone whose favourite animal is a dragon… or a wolf… I am not quite sure.'

She laughed, feeling a little more comfortable in this situation all of a sudden. Why did being with him do that to her? She shifted in her seat a little.

'My mother has come up with some out-there ideas before… dinners dressed in nightwear, bring your *yiayia* to cake and coffee and leave with someone's else's, but…'

'Your mother,' Becky breathed, another laugh escaping. 'Eleni is your mother.'

'Yes,' Elias answered. 'Sorry, you did not realise? She has not said anything to you?'

'No, I… we… that is, Petra mentioned you and Eleni gave us the impression…' This was not going to sound right whichever way she put it. 'Or rather, we got the impression she was your… lover.'

'I feel sick,' Elias announced. 'Really sick. I might have to make the noise of a donkey.' He began to cough and Becky really *really* wanted to see the expression on his face.

'Are you OK?' she whispered, leaning a little nearer the table. She could reach out. How big were these tables? Could she connect their hands?

'No,' Elias answered. 'I need another drink.' He cleared his throat before carrying on. 'You really thought that we were... I cannot even say the word.'

'Well,' Becky said, 'I still don't know much about you.'

There was a silence between them and then the animal noises all stopped as Eleni spoke again.

'Silence! Remember the animal noise that your date made. For the next round the men will be moving tables.'

'Oh no,' Becky said aloud. She didn't want that. She was quite happy sitting here with Elias sharing this crazy mad experience together, if he was still going to be talking to her after what she had said about Eleni.

'Becky,' Elias whispered. His fingers found hers across the table and she held on. 'I am not going to move from this table.'

'OK,' she answered.

'And, believe me when I say this, you know more about me than anyone in this village... even my mother.'

Elias put a fork full of his mother's *stifado* into his mouth and mused a little as the flavours coated his taste buds. They still could not see but finally they were allowed to talk. So far, through noises alone, he had learned that Becky was a morning person rather than a night owl – she had been very creative with hooting followed by the noise of a gunshot – and that her favourite music was a little bit Katy Perry, mixed with Sia and sometimes Bon Jovi. He hoped he had managed to get across that he was a morning person too and that he liked all kinds of music – it wasn't often he had to attempt to make sounds of drums, electric guitar and saxophone…

'Cinnamon,' Becky told him. 'A little too much. There was less cinnamon in the one I ate last time we were here.'

'Do not tell my mother that. This is her grand recipe. The one she is well-known for all over the north of Corfu.'

'There's still something missing from it though,' Becky continued. 'I thought that last time, but I couldn't put my finger on what it was. I still can't.'

'You sound disappointed about that.'

'I am,' Becky told him. 'I told you on the boat. It's what I do. Find the perfect food combinations, the correct balance.'

'And I told you that that is a real skill.'

'I don't know anymore,' she answered with a sigh.

Elias could imagine her expression. Her eyes would be lowered, her shoulders a little hunched, her hair a little over her face. He wished they could end this sideshow of Dark Dating and just spend the rest of the evening talking face to face, or rather, eye to eye. 'Why do you not know anymore? What has changed?'

'Because it doesn't matter, does it? If people get the perfect sandwich. It doesn't exactly change the world, does it? It's lunch. It's not… saving the rainforests or… building schools in deprived countries or…'

'Helping men screw over their wives in divorce cases.' He really wanted to see her expression now. Now he had admitted that was exactly what he had been doing. Yes, it had been about getting the best for his clients, but it had also been about trying to punish Hestia in the only way he could think of. It sounded so juvenile. And that was what his life had come to. Rage and childishness.

'People, they've always needed me,' Becky continued.

It sounded like she was eating again. Elias took another mouthful of his meal as he listened.

'My mum and dad, they always turned to me if they needed advice on some modern-day technicality they didn't understand, like online shopping or the Sky remote. Then, when Dad got sick, I naturally filled that role of visiting the nursing home the most and then Megan, with starting the business...'

'It sounds to me that what you do is every bit as important as saving the rainforests to the people that care about you.'

'You don't understand,' Becky answered with a sigh. 'I don't want to be needed.'

'You don't?'

'No.' She sighed again, this time far more heavily. 'I want to be wanted. And although Megan needs me, she doesn't want me. And... there's no one else left.'

'Becky...' Elias began. He reached out to find her hand but connected with something else, something hard. Whatever it was fell to the table.

'It's OK. It's been kind of nice being here in Greece and not being needed. Apart from with Petra, because she really does need someone and I haven't quite got to the bottom of why yet, but, in between eating meat together and watching romantic comedy DVDs, I really think she's starting to open up a little to me.'

'You're a caring person,' Elias told her. Where were her hands? He was trailing fingers over the table, trying to distinguish what things were. Salt and pepper pots, the edge of the cloth, olive oil and vinegar… why had his mother put so much on the tables?

'And my caring nature means I'm easy to take advantage of. That's why I'm still working at It's A Wrap, in the town I grew up in. Helping my sister not lose her business while watching her make a life with my ex-boyfriend.'

'OK,' Elias said. 'I have had enough of this.' He didn't care about leaving before they had finished the meal. They could eat somewhere else. Somewhere they weren't going to be watched or matched.

'What?' Becky asked.

'We are getting out of here.' He stood up, still disorientated by the dark but now no longer caring. 'Mama! Put on the lights!'

'Elias, she is not going to be happy if you do that,' Becky gasped.

'I do not care. I cannot sit here a moment longer talking with you but not being able to see you. This whole thing is ridiculous. Why should you like someone more if they make the sound of a stray dog or think the *stifado* is spicy yet sweet?'

Becky couldn't help but laugh.

'Mama! Put the lights on now or I will wander around the room, knocking into everything and everyone until I find the switch!' He took a step to the left and banged into a table. '*Signomi.*'

'Elia! What are you doing? Sit down!' Eleni ordered him.

'Mama, Becky and I are leaving now. Please show us where the door is.'

'You cannot leave with the English girl.'

'What?' Elias baulked.

'She is not your match,' Eleni responded. 'She make the sound of a pig.'

'It was a cute-sounding pig,' Elias said.

'Your match should be Maria. I tell her to make the sound of the hoopoe bird.'

'Mama!'

'You liked to watch the birds when you were a boy.'

And now his mother was obviously intent on embarrassing him. He reached into the pocket of his trousers for his mobile phone. Swiping up and trying to remember the location of the 'torch' function he held his breath and hoped.

'What are you doing?' Eleni asked him.

Music started to play. The last thing he had listened to. It was Camila Cabello. He had pressed the wrong icon and now 'Senorita' was filtering out into the dark. He made a stab at the screen and finally a beam of light came from the top of the phone. He staggered back, confused by what he was seeing. His mother was wearing something over her face. Was that... were they...?

'Mama! Are you wearing... night vision goggles?'

Eleni threw her hands up the air in frustration. 'How else am I supposed to see anything?'

'Becky,' Elias said, turning to her and reaching out a hand. 'Let's go.'

'Elias... Miss English... there are still two other rounds to go.'

He felt Becky's hand meet his and he realised there was no way he was going to stop.

Forty-Six

Tavernaki Taverna, Kassiopi

This harbour was so beautiful. Becky was sat at a table outside a gorgeous cream-coloured old stone restaurant, overlooking speedboats, tourist cruisers and, across the gently swaying water, larger yachts – their masts tall, sails wrapped up for the night. Lights from the bars and tavernas reflected on the sea, trails of gold softly rippling with the movement of the ocean. It was one of the most idyllic settings she had ever seen. Sipping at a cold glass of white wine, she sat back against her seat and let the realisation of being here settle on her. She was here with Elias, about to eat food she wouldn't have to describe the texture of, a car ride away from Liakada and Villa Selino. And they weren't here together because they had been thrown together through a missed connection or stormy weather, they were here together because they wanted to be. It was a date... and it was something Becky definitely wasn't going to consult *How to Win the Love of Your Life or Die Trying* about.

'I am so sorry that call took so long.' Elias eased himself

back into his seat opposite her. 'Nikos's father answered and then he had to find Nikos and then Nikos wasn't where he was meant to be and, well, I had to listen to father and son have an argument about why Nikos wasn't where he should have been before I could even get to speak to him.'

'He's going to give Petra a lift back to the villa though?' Becky asked, slipping her phone out of her bag. 'And he's trustworthy. He isn't going to try it on or anything.' She looked at him. 'Is he under thirty?'

'You are worried about *Nikos* trying something with Petra?' Elias asked. 'I am more concerned for Nikos.'

'Elias, I know she comes across as this strong, take-on-the-world type but she's really not... I don't think.'

'You can trust Nikos,' Elias told her. 'I promise.'

'OK,' Becky answered. 'I'll text her.'

'And then you will stop worrying?' Elias asked. 'So we can enjoy the fantastic food coming our way?' He swallowed. 'And, so I can tell you everything else my mother doesn't know about me.'

'Yes,' Becky promised, tapping out a quick message.

Elias was going to do it. He was going to be completely honest with Becky about what had happened with Hestia and how he had built his business on the back of that betrayal. He was both apprehensive and a little bit high on the anticipation. No matter what Becky thought or felt, even if nothing ended up happening between them, it would be a step forward for him. To admit to what happened. To tell someone how desperate he had felt, how cursed somehow. It was important.

'Tell me,' Elias said when Becky had put away her phone again. 'Have you finished the plan of the party you were creating on the plane?'

'Oh… yes, I have.' She blushed a little and reached for her wineglass.

'You are happy with it?'

'I… think so.'

'You do not know?'

'I don't know if I know,' she answered softly, her eyes dropping to the table just as a waiter brought thick slices of bread together with garlic butter and a beetroot dip.

'Why do you not have confidence in this?' Elias asked once the waiter had gone. He offered Becky the wooden bread box and she took a slice, immediately tearing a piece off and dropping it to her plate.

'Because I've never done it before. I've never pitched for a catering job.'

'But,' Elias began, smearing some beetroot spread onto his bread, 'you tell me that you create all these unique recipes for customers sandwiches.'

'I do.'

'Then…' He paused, watching her expression before he took a bite of the food.

'It isn't the same. What I do with people's sandwiches is on such a small scale and it's all about the individual. This has to be right for the whole group and if I don't get it right and we don't get the job then Megan will say "I told you so".' She pushed a piece of bread in her mouth and chewed. 'But, then again, if we *do* get the job, she doesn't want the job so… I'm pretty much screwed all round.'

'You are not going to submit the plan at all, are you?' Elias guessed.

He watched Becky shrug. 'I don't know.'

'Captain Rebecca.' He sighed. 'Because you are worried about what your sister will say?'

'I care too much about people. You said so yourself.'

'What worries you the most about your sister? Because I think I know you are not someone who cannot handle a little "I told you so".'

Becky looked across the water then, as if gazing at the view might help her answer his question. He took a sip of his wine and gave her time.

'I worry that she will realise I've been holding her up since our dad died. I know that sounds silly because, in some ways, actually most days, I want her to know that I *am* more than someone who butters bread for her business. But, in other ways, her realising that will probably mean this distance between us will get wider and wider until maybe it won't ever be able to be bridged.' She sighed. 'Don't get me wrong, I don't want an MBE for services to Megan or anything, I think I just want her to take charge. That's why I left on this housesitting break, to force her to take control, to back off a little and let her manage It's A Wrap. I think maybe I've been doing too much handholding and maybe I've made her the way she is.'

'Your sister needs to stand on her own feet and you need to discover where yours want to discover.'

'Yes,' Becky agreed, looking happier now. 'I mean, if I send the party plan to the nursing home and we got the job I would feel compelled to follow it through and perhaps, after this break, I might want to do something else. Maybe I'll be like Petra and travel some more.'

'Really?' Elias asked. His insides were quirking just a little. Knowing her base was in the UK, like his, had always felt like fate, but she wanted to explore and who could blame her?

'I mean, I don't really know. I don't think I want to visit all the hotspots where they give out crap T-shirts and tattoo the wrong name on your arm but...'

Elias laughed then and brought a napkin to his lips.

'How about you?' Becky asked him. 'When do you go back to the UK?'

'I... am not sure.'

He wasn't. He was still holding Chad at bay, leaving it twenty-four hours before responding to his emails, ignoring calls and blaming the time difference. Half of him was hoping Kristina was going to come back and he could have a frank and honest conversation with her about everything. The other half knew, as much as he had wanted to get in and take an inventory of the house, that wasn't playing fair at all and any approach he made should be via her solicitor. But would he be the lawyer everyone wanted if he changed tack? His brand had been built on being cut-throat and taking risks... except it didn't feel so good any longer.

'My parents are... not together anymore.'

'Oh!' Becky exclaimed. 'I didn't think about Eleni being married.'

'Because you thought she was my cougar.'

'Well... Petra did more than me really.'

Elias sighed. 'They are two very stupid people who choose not to communicate once there has been a breakdown in marital harmony. Instead they pretend not to care about each other, gossip about one another to their friends, then cry at night because they are not together.'

'I… don't know what to say.'

'I know what to say,' Elias replied, topping up Becky's wineglass and swatting at a mosquito at the same time. 'And I have said it to them both. But, as well as stupid, they are both proud and very stubborn. It will take a while for my words to sink into their incredibly thick skins. So, I think I will be here, until that has happened.'

'You think it will work? That what you have said to them will make them get back together?'

Elias nodded. He was convinced. 'Oh, yes, there is no doubt about that. It is simply a matter of when.'

'And that is your professional opinion? As a divorce expert?'

'It is my professional opinion as their son,' Elias replied, taking another slice of bread. 'And, as someone who has been through a marriage that never had any chance of working from the very beginning.' He looked directly at Becky then, wanting to see the reaction in her eyes.

Elias had been married. Did that shock Becky? Not really. She had assumed the letter inked on his chest would stand for something or someone close to his heart. Although Becky had half-hoped it was a sister…even know he'd told her he was an only child. But what was more interesting was that he was telling her about his marriage now. Telling her because he wanted her to know… that he was single? Or that he was still married? Her pulse was beating in her neck as she tried to quell her feelings.

'I am divorced, Becky,' he told her. 'Two years now.'

'Oh.' What did she say? The word 'sorry' wasn't appropriate, was it?

'I have not been back to Liakada since my wife left me because… it was the scandal of the village, the talk of the municipality of Thinali.' He drank a large mouthful of wine.

'What happened?' Becky asked him.

'What happened,' Elias repeated, his eyes in the mid-distance.

'You don't have to tell me, if you don't want to. I mean, if it's—'

'No,' Elias interrupted. 'I *do* have to tell you. I have to tell you because I have never actually told anyone else. That is, anyone else, who wasn't involved in the divorce proceedings.' He took a breath. 'Becky, I have never felt able to sit down and tell anyone about it before because I've been too embarrassed and too stupid and too wrapped up in other people's opinions and… life is too short to keep doing that anymore.' He sniffed. 'Otherwise, one day, I might be on a plane, in heavy turbulence and get diverted straight into the Alps and never get the chance to… start again.'

She reached for his hand, seeing all kinds of emotions written in his expression. She entwined her fingers in his and held on tight.

'I'm listening,' she answered.

Forty-Seven

Kassiopi Castle

Elias felt taller somehow and lighter, definitely so much lighter. Except for his stomach. His stomach was so full and heavy, if the rest of him hadn't felt quite so elated he might be too weighted down to lead the way from the edge of the harbour up this steep and winding path to the ruins of the fort.

As he had opened up to Becky about Hestia and Thalia and that night in the village when his marriage had ended, all the hurt and anger and sadness came rushing out. In a flood of emotion Elias was trying hard to keep in check, amid the grandmother's lamb and *spaghettada*, he had told Becky everything. And all the way through, between mouthfuls of the delicious cuisine, she had held his hand, whispering reassurance, telling him that everything was going to be OK. Somehow, the way she had said it, the way she had looked at him when she had said it, he truly believed her. *Was* it all going to be OK? Could it really be so?

He squeezed her hand now, slowing their pace a little

as the humidity kicked in. It filled his lungs with warm air as the incline hampered any chance of normal, balanced breathing. 'You are OK?'

'Gosh, this is like the walk we did in Athens,' Becky remarked, her sandals slipping a little on the shiny well-worn stones.

'It is a little like that,' Elias agreed. 'Houses on the edge of the pathway, passing almost through people's back gardens, a small track leading up to the top.'

'I would never have found this on my own,' Becky told him.

'This is one of the most notable ruins on the Ionian islands. It is from the Byzantine period, built to help defend Corfu,' Elias explained. 'When we reach the top, you will see the views they had to enable them to see potential invaders.'

'We are safe now though?' Becky asked, finally able to stand next to him, a little out of breath.

'Well,' Elias said, 'you will be pleased to know this stretch of water is patrolled by the Greek navy and there is a modern look-out tower not far from here.'

'Gosh, really? I was only joking. I presumed the only water traffic would be cruise liners. Actually, if Hazel was on board, Corfu ought to be a little afraid. Particularly the men of a certain age.'

'There's nothing to be afraid of up here. Only the wildlife. Maybe a few tortoises if we are lucky, or a pine marten in the trees.'

'I have no idea what that is.'

'It looks like a fox and a squirrel have mated and then the head of a small bear has been added.'

'Oh, God, I know exactly what you mean now. Petra and I had one in the house. We called it "bear-thing".'

Elias laughed. 'It was *in* the house?'

'With cats... and owls... and a flamingo.'

'Do I need to mention this to my client?'

'I haven't mentioned it to Ms O'Neill.'

'We will keep it a secret in that case.' He squeezed her hand again. 'Come. I want to show you the view.'

Becky smiled and let him lead on, his strong hand so warm in hers, so right somehow. She had seen the real Elias tonight. There had been no bravado, no cool or aloof, just a gorgeous man baring his soul to her so bravely, so genuinely. She hadn't just wanted to squeeze his hand and tell him it was OK, she had wanted to put her arms around him and lift some of that hurt from his shoulders. But, she knew, like with her grief over the loss of her father, there was a process. Pain didn't disappear like magic, it needed time and it needed its own space to build and build, until one day it started to recede and you could own the opportunity to change. And that's what Elias was doing now and, somehow, she seemed to be becoming a big part of that.

'The trees are so beautiful here,' Becky said. 'They're so twisted and gnarly and arched, like they're a natural tunnel almost.'

'The wind must take the blame for some of that. On Corfu we can have the most terrific winds.'

'Wow,' Becky said, stopping still.

A large ancient stone doorway stood ahead of her, steps leading up to it and over where there was another identical doorway in the brickwork. It was like going back in time. She followed him up the steps to stand in the gap.

'This is mostly what is left of the castle. The main gateway building. There has been restoration. It is better than it ever was but…'

'But to have anything left at all is… wonderful.' She put her hand out to touch the stonework, enjoying the coolness on her skin.

'You are right, Captain Rebecca,' Elias said. 'In connection with Kassiopi Castle and with life. To have anything left at all *is* wonderful.'

She felt him tighten his grip on her hand then and pull her a little closer towards him. It sounded so clichéd that there had been something between them from their very first meeting in Row 18, but somehow there had. Despite all the telling him she was in the army and him saying he sold houses, there had always been a spark of something. And despite everything that had happened in such a short space of time, those moments had led them here.

'Becky,' he whispered and her name on his lips sent a shiver running down the length of her spine where the feeling began spiralling like a firework around her coccyx. Should she say something? What did she want to say to him? That she was definitely considering binning *How to Find the Love of Your Life or Die Trying*? Not that he was the love of her life because, well, she hadn't exactly *had* a life yet…

No, Becky didn't want to say anything. She only wanted to look. Gaze at him, this spectacularly gorgeous Greek vision she only felt more drawn to now he had opened up to her. She wanted nothing more than to inch herself forward a little, beneath this dark blanket of sky perforated only by the constellations of a thousand twinkling stars and the moon. She thought back to Petra's story about the moon being made up of the souls of people who had passed. Was her father watching her now? Proud that she was standing on Greek soil, having an adventure of a lifetime? She looked at Elias again, wanting to bring back those memories of him holding her close on the makeshift dancefloor in Kefalonia but something was stopping her...

'Wait,' she said, putting a hand to his shoulder as he leaned towards her. Instantly he shifted back and she swallowed, internally cursing herself for breaking the moment.

'Did I do something wrong?' Elias asked, eyelashes blinking over those azure eyes.

'Not now,' Becky breathed, still touching his shoulder. She could feel the heat of his skin beneath his shirt and she left her fingers there, tracing the outline of the tattoo she knew lay underneath. 'But in Kefalonia.'

She saw his body visibly sag. Was she being stupid? Too cautious?

'It's Petra, isn't it?' Elias stated with a sigh.

'I thought... when *we* danced that *we*... connected somehow but then...'

'We *did* connect, Becky,' he said immediately. He reached out, touching her hair.

Another fizzy moment ensued, like champagne was running through her veins. With every gentle motion of his fingers her heart came alive a little bit more.

'But it scared me,' Elias continued. 'It scared me how much I felt when you were in my arms and I... didn't want to get it wrong. I know we had not known each other long but I did not want to mess it up or to... hurt you. I particularly did not want to hurt you.'

'I'm not that fragile,' Becky whispered, leaning into his hand a little, listening to the faint sea sounds from below them. 'I've survived many things now… turbulence and… narrow caves and… octopuses coming at me from the water.'

Elias smiled for a second and then the look faded. 'Petra… she landed on me and for the briefest of moments I did kiss her back.' He sighed again. 'But the truth is… my eyes were closed and in my mind… and in my heart I… was still on that dancefloor with you. And I know how that makes me sound but… as soon as I really realised what was happening, as soon as I knew how very stupid I was being…' He placed his hand on hers, still firm against his shoulder. 'There are no words, I know. I deserve to be thrown aside for being so weak and running away from you and…'

Becky reached up, fingers shaking, and palmed his face, holding that strong jawline in her hand, just the merest hint of stubble on his skin.

He breathed out, long and slow, as if in response to her touch. 'I feel for you, Captain Rebecca. I feel only for you.'

She let his statement settle on her subconscious. She wanted to believe him. She really wanted to *allow* herself to believe him. Because the way she was feeling now wasn't commonplace in her life. This wasn't a date with Angus from the sausage shop. This wasn't appreciating the visual appeal of Kelvin Fletcher on *Strictly*. This was real. And this was close. And this was happening if she wanted it to…

Becky moved her hand, pressing it to Elias's chest until she felt the thrum of his heartbeat pulsing against it. She wasn't waiting the required number of seconds that Hazel's book had suggested. She wasn't going to wait any longer at all. With the olive trees surrounding them, those ancient walls the only barrier to the harbour, the water and the twinkling lights of Albania beyond, Becky drew Elias towards her, connecting their lips with a passion she had forgotten she owned.

And it was heavenly. She was in sole charge of this moment and she knew exactly what she wanted. Him. Elias. Doing unspeakable things to her for days.

He tasted of life's sunniest moments, of lemon and bread and somehow seaside, and as his tongue danced with hers, slow then fast then teasing, Becky found herself tight to his body, enjoying every inch of that taut physique up close and very personal.

'Becky,' he breathed, separating them for a second.

'You're not going to run away again, are you?' she asked, looking up at him, eyes moist with anticipation of hopefully more kisses to come.

'No, not at all,' he answered. 'I just... want you to be sure this is what you want.'

'I am sure,' Becky answered positively. 'This is what I want. Even if it means I die from the trying at some point.' She smiled. 'I mean...what a way to go.'

Elias smiled too and, with the history of more than a thousand nights around them, a very full moon the only illumination, Becky pulled him back to her and connected their lips again.

Forty-Eight

Kerasia Beach

'Tell me more about your father,' Elias said. 'He sounds like someone who has shaped your life so much.' He wrapped his arms around Becky, drawing her back into his body.

They were sitting on the white stones of Kerasia Beach, having walked through the garden of Villa Selino to the shore. It was still warm, possibly somewhere in the twenties, with definitely no need for a jacket or a wrap. The beach was deserted, the water gently shushing onto the pebbles. Becky felt content here. Sitting close to the sea, in the arms of this intriguing man she was finally getting to know more completely. It was like the best experimental sandwich she'd ever concocted.

After their visit to Kassiopi, Elias had driven them back here and neither of them had wanted the evening to end. It was edging towards 1 a.m. now and before she and Elias had made their way down to the ocean, Becky had popped her head around Petra's bedroom door. Thankfully Petra was home *and* alone. Still clothed, one leg out of the light cover, hair still immaculately pinned up, the young woman was clutching hold of a well-worn teddy bear. On first glance she might have been ten years old...

'My dad was inspirational to me,' Becky replied without hesitation. 'But in the quietest of ways. That's who he was. Unassuming, shy almost, and very softly spoken.' She paused, remembering. 'He never said anything unless it was worth saying. Everything he put into words... it meant something.' She turned her head a little, looking up at Elias. 'Does that sound weird?'

'No,' he answered. 'Communication is everything, I truly believe that. But that does not mean that you should talk for the sake of filling spaces. Sometimes a silence can say as much as a hundred words.'

He was so right. She sat quietly now and listened. The cicadas were chirruping from the eucalyptus trees at the edge of the beach, the fenders of boats nudged at the wooden dock, squeaking slightly, the ocean lapped and splashed.

'I did not mean for us to stop talking,' Elias told her. A light rumble of a laugh moved from inside him then hit the night air. Becky laughed too as he tightened his hug around her.

'My sister and I stopped talking productively a long time ago. Before what happened with Dean and after our dad died and our mum moved away.' Becky sighed. 'I guess that's as much my fault as it is hers. I think, when Mum decided to move, it hurt Megan. Whereas I saw it simply as my mum making a new start and wanting something different, you know, getting over having to look after someone who needed a lot of care. Megan, I think, saw it as a kind of abandonment. Not that she would say. And I did try. I always tried. But when it's only one person trying it gets exhausting.'

'Sometimes,' Elias began, 'it is too hard to talk.' She felt him take a breath. 'And sometimes, everyone tries to do the talking for you and… you are simply not ready.'

'Is that how you've felt?' Becky asked. 'About Hestia?'

'We were talking about your father,' Elias reminded.

He may have made this huge step tonight by telling Becky about what had happened with his ex-wife, but it still felt incredibly raw.

'Have you seen Hestia at all since you divorced?'

'No,' he said quickly.

'Do her parents live in Liakada too?'

'No,' he answered. 'But they do not live far away. In Episkepsi. It is a village not far from here.'

He couldn't imagine seeing Hestia's parents now any more than he could have imagined seeing them two years ago. What was there to say? What purpose would it serve? But he would like to think, if he saw them in passing, that he would say *kalimera*. And if he saw Hestia again? Would he say something? And, if so, what?

'Hestia… she emailed me, after the divorce was finalised.' He took a deep breath wriggling a little on the stones but not letting go of Becky.

'What did she say?'

'I did not read it. Not at first. Back then I saw her name and all kinds of feelings came out of me, and none of them were good. But, a few months after, when I was clearing my inbox, I saw that email again and, for some reason, I clicked on it.'

He remembered how it had felt to read the words. It had been Hestia reaching out, the Hestia he had met and fallen for, but more honest and a lot braver.

'She apologised to me, more times than anyone really deserved to be apologised to, given the circumstances. And, in parts, she was saying sorry for being true to herself because, if you break everything down, that was the only thing she did. She was putting an end to a life she had never wanted and starting something she should always have followed. Yes, she hurt me, but she had also hurt herself every single day by pretending to be someone she was not.'

His anger about the situation had lessened after that email. He still hurt. He was still the owner of a business championing men in divorce proceedings, but the note had gone some way to helping him come to the realisation that there was absolutely nothing he could have done in that situation to stop the spontaneous combustion of his marriage.

'Did you reply?' Becky asked.

He took hold of one of her hands then. 'No,' he answered. 'But I should have. Perhaps it is not too late.' He toyed with her fingers. 'I don't know.'

'I should speak to Megan,' Becky said. 'I know that. Because I also know that she isn't going to make the first move. Megan, she sits on things. She festers. She would rather time went by and she was forced to act by circumstances. It's…'

'Exhausting,' Elias filled in.

'Exactly.'

'Perhaps she will surprise you,' Elias suggested, intertwining their hands again.

'What do you mean?'

'Well,' he started, 'you will have been away. She will have had to manage her business without you. You will have been missed... no matter what she tells you.'

'I don't know,' Becky said. 'I've trained Hazel and Shelley well. She might not even notice I'm not there.'

'How could anyone not notice your absence?' Elias asked.

Becky sat bolt upright, leaning away from Elias's embrace. 'Did you hear that?'

'What?' he asked.

'It was whistling.' She turned her head, looking over both their shoulders at the trees and the road. 'I'm sure of it.'

'Perhaps it is the flamingo,' Elias suggested. 'Come to ask for the keys to get back in.'

'There it is again,' Becky said, this time moving out of his arms and getting to her feet. 'Can't you hear that? It sounds like someone's coming and they're calling for something.'

Elias stood up too, trying to somehow hone in on the darkness. He stilled, focusing. Then he heard it. It was a whistle and then a name being called... Maverick?

'It's Petra,' Becky said, rushing up the beach. 'It's definitely Petra.'

'Becky, wait,' Elias said, racing after her.

Forty-Nine

Villa Selino

'You're fussing like a nana,' Petra said, shrugging off the blanket Becky was attempting to put on her shoulders. 'It's not Scotland. OK, the mozzy bites are on a par here but it's still warm, so no blanket required.'

The women were in the vast kitchen of the villa and Becky was making a cup of tea. After all, when in doubt about how to solve a problem, tea was always the answer. With one eye on the boiling water and the other on the young girl sat at the kitchen island, her mind was on the rather inadequate kiss goodbye she had given Elias. After a few spins around the garden they had finally managed to get a sleepwalking Petra back into the house, onto the sofa and settled, until she promptly woke straight up. It had felt a little 'three's-a-crowd' after that and Elias had suggested he leave, saying he would call her tomorrow. Their kiss had been infuriatingly brief, when what she really wanted to do was snog all the other parts of him she hadn't seen yet...

'I'm going to go back to bed now. If that's OK, Nana.'

Petra slipped down from the island seat.

'No, Petra, it's not OK,' Becky said, turning away from the kettle and facing her again. 'We need to talk.'

'About Elias?' Petra asked, grinning. 'Because don't think I didn't see that little lip contact before he left. Although it was a bit restrained. You don't want to do restrained for too long.'

'No, this isn't about Elias,' Becky said, torn between sitting down and finishing making the tea. 'I want to talk about you.'

'My favourite subject,' Petra said, grinning as she re-took her seat. 'I have so many stories. Do we have snacks to go with the tea? It's hours since I had *baklava*. I told Eleni mine had a body of a bee in it. You should have seen her face! I had to tell her I was joking in the end. I thought she might stroke out!'

Becky made the tea as quickly as possible. She wasn't going to let Petra skirt over anything this time. Bringing the cups over, she sat up at the island and pushed a cup closer to Petra.

'Where shall I start?' Petra asked. 'Did I tell you about the floating market in China? Or when I once bartered with a bartender for fifty-year-old vodka?'

'Petra,' Becky said softly. 'I want you to tell me who Maverick is.'

Suddenly it was like every colour particle had disappeared from Petra's face. But then, almost as quickly, the girl smiled and laughed. 'The guy from *Top Gun*? Mr Cruise when he wasn't ancient?'

'No,' Becky said firmly. 'I don't think so.' She held her mug in both hands. 'You were sleepwalking, out of your room, outside, down the path, to the beach, calling "Maverick" like he/she/it was someone you know.'

'Really?' Petra said, dismissive. 'How strange. I mean, I did sleepwalk one-time near Mount Midoriyama, but I put that down to altitude sickness and...'

'Petra!' Becky exclaimed, now a little annoyed. 'Mount Midoriyama isn't real. It's from *Ninja Warrior*.'

'I meant... Kilimanjaro.' She sniffed, looking into her cup. 'It's late. I'm tired. I should—'

'Tell me who Maverick is or I'll... I'll make you find somewhere else to stay. Which I should have done anyway. Days ago!'

Becky hadn't meant to sound quite so harsh, but she was worried about Petra. It seemed, as time went by, just as she thought she was getting to know her, the girl was still holding back. There was still something else going on under the surface.

'You really want me to leave?' Petra asked. Her bottom lip was quivering and Becky had never felt so heartless. She didn't want Petra to leave. Despite basically forcing herself on her from the outset, Becky couldn't imagine ending this housesitting break without Petra with her. They had shared so much together. It had been a little like her relationship with Tara before the whole astro-dating, Jonathan and couples' dinner parties situation...

'I want you to tell me more about you, Petra... and your family. Not tales from your world travels, something about where you're from. You know almost everything about me. The sandwich-making, my annoying sister, how I'm not exactly confident like you. I want to know a little bit more about *your* family. This Maverick sounded important to you.'

Becky took a breath. 'Important enough to go sleepwalking through the garden for. Was that your dad's name?'

And, at the mention of her father, just like that, it happened. Petra burst into tears. Becky jolted on her chair with the sheer ferocity of it. It was like Niagara Falls and Victoria Falls had had a baby and Petra Falls was suddenly the new sight to see. Quickly, amid the heart-rendering sobbing, Becky slipped down from her seat and headed towards the kitchen towel. She reeled off ample amounts then returned, standing next to her friend and putting a hand on a shoulder, passing her the tissue paper.

'I'm sorry, Petra, I didn't mean for you to—'

'Burst the mains drainage?' Petra said, voice thick with upset.

'Yes, I mean, I wanted you to talk but I didn't want you to cry.'

Petra blew her nose. 'Well, they kind of come together now.'

'Tell me,' Becky begged. 'I'm your friend, aren't I? Friends tell each other things they're worried about and we've shared so many moments since we met on the plane, haven't we? Platters of great meat and... that awful movie called *Lost Love at Sea* and... vintage cars and...'

'Vintage men,' Petra added with half a smile.

'Who's Maverick?' Becky asked again, pulling her seat closer to Petra's. 'Tell me.'

Petra nodded, the ball of kitchen roll now all scrunched up in her fist. 'Maverick is... *was* my cat.'

'Oh.' Becky hadn't been expecting that. 'Did he pass away too?'

She nodded then, fresh tears arriving in her eyes. 'Yep. 2018. March 22nd.'

'I know how much pets can mean. One of my customers, Milo, has a canary who likes to go in the shower with him. You must have loved him ever so much,' Becky said.

'I did,' Petra agreed. 'I loved him so so much. He was as much a part of the family as anyone else.'

'I can understand that. People do say that losing a pet is exactly the same as losing a family member.' She gave Petra's shoulder another heartening rub of reassurance. 'And you lost your dad too. Was that around the same time?'

'It was,' Petra said, taking a big breath. 'I… lost my dad, Maverick and my mum at the very same time. On the very same day. In the very same accident.'

The tears began to flow again and this time Becky was there to catch her. Sobbing hard, Petra fell into her arms and Becky held on tight. 'Sshh, it's OK, Petra. It's going to be OK.'

'I'm sorry,' Petra wailed. 'I shouldn't be talking about it. Talking about it makes me panic again and I don't want to panic again.'

'It's OK,' Becky reassured. 'I'm right here.'

'But you're going to be gone soon,' Petra said with another cry. 'When your holiday is finished you get to go back to your sister and your friends and I'll be moving on to a new location meeting new people I'll never tell any of this to because it's too hard to share.' Almost like she was doing it subconsciously she began to unpin her hair until it started to fall loose around her shoulders. Then she began to work her fingers around it, turning it into braids. 'I want to pretend,' Petra stated. 'That's what I spend my time doing while I'm travelling. I pretend.'

'It's OK,' Becky whispered, the girl's grief pulling at her

heart. 'We're all guilty of doing a bit of that every now and then to protect ourselves.'

'Who am I on my own, Becks?' Petra asked Becky, eyes wide and startled.

'Oh, Petra, you don't lose who your loved ones were to you when they pass away,' Becky assured her. 'They might not be here in person, but I believe they are here in spirit. I mean… if it wasn't for your dad you wouldn't have known what kind of cars we had sitting in the garage here.' She rubbed the girl's shoulder. 'His knowledge has helped you and, you said yourself, about the moon.'

'I don't know what to do next,' Petra admitted, leaning on Becky for support. 'What do I do next?'

Becky put a hand to Petra's head and drew her closer. 'We're both going to take it one step at a time,' Becky told her. 'You just keep breathing.'

Fifty

Liakada Village

Elias shook the frying pan in his mother's kitchen and looked pleased at the contents. He had bacon griddling to perfection on one ring, sausages under the grill, and now he was making fried eggs to sit upon the toast when that was ready. The baked beans were gently warming in a pan.

'What are you doing in my kitchen? It is six o'clock in the morning.'

He had wondered how long it was going to be before his mother sensed there was someone working in her domain and came to investigate.

'I am sorry, Mama. I was trying to be quiet, but I woke up Areti's rooster and then it woke up Areti and I made her coffee. She is sitting in the *cafeneon* folding laundry.'

Eleni put her hands in her hair and screeched a little like a rooster herself. 'I do not know how many times I have told that woman not to bring laundry into my *cafeneon*. It is not a good look, Elias.'

He turned away from the hob for a moment and

observed his mother, still in her dressing gown. 'If we do not want anyone to see, perhaps we could pull down all the blinds and get out night vision goggles for us. Give service like last night.'

'You are mocking me. I do not like it. And I am unhappy with your behaviour at Dark Dating. You left with the English girl. That meant a change to my Circle of Couples later on. I had to try to pair Panos with someone more age-appropriate than Maria from the supermarket. The English girl was supposed to be with Spiros Boatyard.'

'Spiros Boatyard!' Elias exclaimed. 'He is forty-five.'

'He looks young for his age.'

'You sat her with Manilos. He is even older, and his sound of the donkey was a little obvious, don't you think?'

His mother was now just looking at him, an all-knowing expression on her face. *The eggs!* He had forgotten the eggs. He turned back to the hob, fish slice in hand, delicately trying to lift them off the bottom of the pan without disturbing the yokes.

'I see what is going on,' Eleni told him.

'Yes,' Elias agreed. 'If you keep talking to me and do not go to see Areti she will be arranging to bring over her washing machines.'

'You and the English girl. This is not the first time you have met. They ask about you. The *one* and the not the one.' Eleni sniffed as if she was using her nose to find out secrets.

'The English girl has a name,' Elias said.

'And you know it,' Eleni continued. 'You have known it for a while. That is why you are back here.'

'No, Mama,' Elias insisted. 'I am here for work.'

'What is going on at Villa Selino? I know someone has had my keys. I am guessing that is you,' Eleni continued.

Yes, Elias had felt bad about taking them without asking. It had been a mad few hours of deliberating with himself about the legality of it all, but he had made the right choice. And he was now more confident of that than ever. The keys had gone straight back and he was doing what he told Becky he was doing. The right thing. No more underhand or under the carpet, everything strictly by the book.

'The owners of Villa Selino are getting a divorce,' he admitted. 'But you cannot tell anyone about that. And I mean anyone. Not even Areti.' He lowered his voice. 'Especially not Areti.'

'Are they selling the villa? Will they not want me to clean? Is the English girl a relative?'

'I cannot tell you any more than that,' Elias said to her, lifting the pan from the ring, turning the gas off then setting it down again. 'Except the English girl… she is called Becky.'

'What sort of a name is "Becky"? It is not good. Not like "Maria" or "Pelagia" or—'

'Hestia?' Elias offered.

'No,' Eleni said quickly. 'That is not a good name. You know it means "by the fire". A warning we should have taken notice of before it was too late.'

'Mama,' Elias began. 'I do not want my life to be about what Hestia did anymore.' He took a breath. 'It has been too long.'

'You are forgiving her?' Eleni asked, eyes on stalks like it was an impossibility.

'I am… moving on. I am making what comes next be

about what I want, not about what someone else did.' He took a breath. 'I want you to have the house back.'

'What?'

'The house you gave us as a wedding gift. I want you to have it back. You can... rent it out or you can sell it for air miles. It should not be left empty as a statuesque reminder of something that died long ago.' He swallowed. He couldn't even bear to go and look at the house.

'Elia...'

'No, Mama, I mean it. It is time for... fresh starts and second chances.'

'You have gone soft,' Eleni immediately responded. 'You do not sound Greek.'

'Because forgiveness isn't in our nature? Mama, that is exactly where you and Papa are going wrong.'

'Very clever, Elia the Lawyer. Making this now about me and not you.' Eleni clapped her hands together. 'Bravo!'

Elias turned off the rings on the hob then, letting the eggs and bacon stay warm from the heat of the pans alone. He put his hands on his mother's shoulders and looked directly at her. 'Please go and sit at the table I have prepared for you. If Areti has put washing on top of the placemats and knocked over the flower arrangement I will be disappointed.'

A confused expression arrived on Eleni's face. 'What are you talking about? I have work to do. I have to prepare for the post and clean the bar and find all the things my guests left behind in the dark last night. I—'

'You are having breakfast with your husband,' Elias told her, strengthening his grip on her so she was unable to run away.

'Your father is coming here!' she gasped. 'You have

invited him here! For the breakfast of the English? Are you trying to kill him? Because it was the food high in bad fats that gave him the heart attack!'

'Mama,' Elias said softly. 'Relax. I am making him soft boiled eggs with *horta*.' In a throwback to his childhood spent in Liakada, he had seen the wild greens flourishing at the edge of the olive grove he had run through earlier when sleep had decided he only needed three hours of it. Pan-fried in a little olive oil and mixed with garlic, lemon and a little black pepper, it was keeping warm in the oven.

'You picked ingredients for *horta* this morning?' Eleni exclaimed.

'I did,' Elias replied.

Her eyes glistened a little then as she looked back at him, seeming briefly at a loss as to what to say next. 'Well...' Eleni began.

'Well?'

'You will have to hide the pot of salt or your father will be putting too much over those eggs.' She sniffed, fingers preening her hair as she used the stainless-steel splashback over the hob as a mirror.

'Mama, promise me you will listen to him.'

'I always listen to him,' Eleni insisted. 'It is simply he never says anything that I want to hear.'

'Give him a chance,' Elias begged. 'Please.'

'I will listen,' Eleni promised.

'And not argue?'

'You ask a great deal, Elia.'

'Mama,' he said, smiling. 'I have picked *horta* for you and made you an English breakfast that will change your mind about the delicious nature of it.' He rubbed her shoulder again. 'Maybe you will change your mind about my father too.'

Eleni made a tut that seemed to indicate this was unlikely, but she was still checking out her appearance in the metal, tweaking at her hair. 'Your father's nature is not delicious,' she said. 'His nature is old and wrinkled like toes that have been in the bath water for too long.' She turned to Elias then. 'But, if I make promises to you about sharing a breakfast, then you must make a promise to me.'

He hadn't bargained on that being a clause to this situation. Knowing his mother as he did, he maybe should have been ready for it.

'Come for the *panegyri* this year.'

The annual village festival. The one night everyone came together to celebrate. There were lambs on spits, *loukoumades* (doughnut balls usually drizzled with honey but, in Elias's opinion, much better with chocolate sauce), homemade wine, beer and dancing to the musicians in the village square. It was very much like a Greek wedding. And that's why joining in and celebrating with the villagers who had been there for the doughnuts and the music of his marriage to Hestia would be challenging for him. But, if moving on was what he had set his heart on and his mind to, there was only one answer he could give.

'Yes,' he told his mother. 'I will come for the *panegyri*.'

Eleni made a whooping noise he had never heard from her before and suddenly he was caught up in her rough embrace, her cheek pressed tight against his. 'I did not think you would say yes. I thought you would say you were too busy, or you could not face it or...'

'Moving on, Mama,' Elias reminded her. 'Embracing

change. Listening. Speaking from the heart. Tell Papa you want to visit the canals of Venice.'

'If I am to do that,' Eleni began. 'I will want at least three sausages and very, *very* strong coffee.'

'Coming right up,' Elias replied with a smile.

Fifty-One

Villa Selino

Everything about Petra's family had come pouring out last night over several cups of tea and an almost-incident with the TV that popped out of the breakfast bar unexpectedly.

Petra was alone in the world, apart from, in her words, one 'crusty great-aunt I met once when my mum had to bail her out of jail for crimes against pop socks in the Edinburgh Woollen Mill'. Becky hadn't quite got to the bottom of *that* story, but what she *had* got to the bottom of was Petra's parents and her beloved Maverick had all perished in a fire that had ripped through the lodge they were staying in while Petra, missing the holiday, attended a music festival with her friends. She had gone from having it all to having nothing at all. Well, nothing except the small fortune in property and share portfolios her family had left behind for her. Financially Petra was set for life. Emotionally she was hanging on by a thread. She had no compass and that was why she was swinging up and down and all around the equator every chance she got. She was spending that fortune like it was a bottomless reservoir because she didn't know what to do and she had no one to do it with. Petra might act like the proverbial free spirit but, in truth, she was lonelier than the last dodo.

And now, despite Becky slipping a shot of *ouzo* into her morning coffee, Petra had clammed up all over again. She was lying on one of the luxury padded daybeds, ear buds in, sunglasses on, unspeaking. It was another beautiful day, the sky cloudless, the sun already hot. And now the truth had come out, Becky was worried about her travel companion. What *did* happen to Petra when Becky's time in Corfu was over? Was Becky going to be able to say goodbye and not worry that the young woman was most probably going to carry on her rootless existence full of deep sadness? She wasn't sure she could wave Petra goodbye at the airport knowing the likelihood was the girl would be hotfooting it to the next Greek island with no reservations made or plan to look after herself.

With Becky's finger hovering over the 'send' button on the email to the nursing home with the party pitch attached, she was distracted by Petra's plight and decided to test if she was listening.

'Petra, would you like to borrow my book?' From her position, on a daybed a few loungers down, Becky waved her copy of *How to Find the Love of Your Life or Die Trying*.

No answer. Maybe she *was* enveloped in music, listening to the latest from Ellie Golding or someone...

'Would you like some water? Or another coffee?' Becky tried again.

Usually, offering to wait on Petra got a response, even if her whole head was ensconced in a towel after the shower.

'I don't want another coffee if you're going to put more *ouzo* in it.'

Yes! Petra might be snapping back but she was listening and engaging.

'Oh, you noticed.' Becky got up, still holding the book.

'What was the plan with that?' Petra asked, head still facing the pool and the view beyond. 'Get the orphan girl softly pissed so she doesn't cry anymore?'

'No. Petra, no, of course not.'

Petra moved then, swinging her legs over the side of the daybed and standing up. She was a lot taller than Becky in those wedged sliders she had on.

'And as for your book. I wouldn't wipe my arse with it.' Petra grabbed the tome out of Becky's hands and glared at it like she might want to psych it into having an arm-wrestle with her. 'I mean who *is* Camilla Forth anyway? Because she sounds like a stuck-up bitch to me. Writing books about love and life like she's an authority on it. I bet she hasn't had as much experience as me.'

'I... don't expect she has. Although there is a paragraph at the back about her degree in—'

'And there we are! That's it exactly!' Petra flapped her arms in the air, agitated.

'What's it exactly?' Becky asked.

'It's all about degrees and certificates and letters after your name, isn't it? If you don't have a magic piece of paper or a knighthood you can only get a crappy job like... like... carrying people's bags or something.'

'You want a job?' Becky asked. She was astounded. She had almost choked on the sentence. Serial holiday-er Petra wanted to join a workforce?

'No… well… maybe… I don't know.' She sighed. 'Because my parents left me and I bombed my A-levels because they left me and then I thought "travel", see some of the things they had seen and all the things they never got to see and, you know, I've worked a bar and I've picked fruit but I don't want to do that for the rest of my life. But what *do* I do for the rest of my life?'

The tears were coming back and the aggression about her situation was subsiding. Petra's shoulders slumped and Becky stepped forward, wrapping her arms around her friend.

'Petra, you do know you're the most interesting person I've ever met,' Becky told her.

'You said you live in a Wiltshire backwater where the big news of the week is how much lead has been stolen from the church roof.'

'You're still the most interesting person I've ever met *and* the most resourceful. I mean, you are not scared of jumping headfirst into anything and I am so, so jealous of those skills.'

'Anyone and everyone can be reckless though,' Petra said, sniffing back tears.

'Oh really?' Becky answered. 'Because you've seen me being totally reckless the whole time we've known each other.'

'You were reckless in your own way by even *coming* to Greece and housesitting for some antiquities hoarder,' Petra replied. 'You stood up to your sister and told her you were having this break whether she fired you or not.'

Becky had forgotten she had told Petra all that. And she still didn't know if she had been fired because there had been zero communication from Megan. She had had a couple of really odd texts from Hazel and Shelley too. They'd both said 'Elsa is coming' and Becky had no idea who Elsa was. Her first thought was someone from the nursing home, but the manageress was definitely called Stephanie. Oh, what was going to happen when she came home? Would Megan have changed the locks? Was sending that pitch to the care home going to add fuel to the fire? Or perhaps, if she had been given the boot, she had no authority to make the pitch on behalf of It's A Wrap anymore…

'You make connections with people,' Petra carried on. 'Proper, meaningful connections.' She sighed. 'When people talk you really listen and you engage… you know, sensibly, with words… not your tongue… with the promise of other body parts later if people give you a little attention.'

'Oh, Petra.'

'I'm too scared to stay in one place and get to know people, because I lost all the people I knew the best and… I can't go through that again. So, I do lots of different places and lots of different people and lots of everything, so I don't have time to think about it or know anyone well enough to talk about it.' She nodded firmly, as if that plan was still somehow working for her. 'Except with you. I told you.'

'You did,' Becky said softly. 'And that's a huge step.' She took a breath. 'I understand how you feel, Petra, I really do. But if there's one thing I've learned from losing my dad, it's that you can do all the remarkable things there are to do – the Great Wall of China, the Great Barrier Reef—'

'A Roger I had in Switzerland was pretty great.'

'Petra!'

'Sorry.'

'Remarkable things like those wonders of the world are only remarkable because someone else has said they are. What's really remarkable about life *is* the little things.' Becky put an arm around Petra and drew her closer, moving them both so they were facing the lush vegetation that surrounded the villa, the ocean lying out in front of them, the bright pebbles of the beach accepting the constantly moving carpet of waves. 'It's about moments, sometimes quiet and insignificant moments. Like listening to the sound of the sea or… listening to people make animals noises in a ridiculous dating game in a Greek village or…'

'Sitting on cushions drinking beer in the Plaka District of Athens… with… friends.'

'Yes!' Becky exclaimed. 'It's exactly that. It's laughter and sunshine and…'

'Getting pissed at the TV that keeps popping out of the breakfast bar.'

'And being scared of bear-things.'

'And finding a flamingo in the bath.'

'Or drooling over Greyston Holt… He's my favourite Hallmark actor by the way.'

Petra was looking much brighter now and Becky was warmed by her enthusiasm. Telling Petra her mantra about simplicity was helping her to realise exactly what she had been hoping to find in Greece. Initially she had thought it would be adventure and sightseeing, just like Petra, but really the most fun, the times that had touched her soul were all the details. It was eating the most succulent meats, learning a few words of Greek, nearly dying trying to sail a tiny dinghy, kissing Elias inside an ancient castle… especially kissing Elias.

'I don't know what I want to do next,' Petra admitted. 'I've never known what I want to do next.'

'No one really knows what they want to do next,' Becky told her. 'Honestly, even those who think they have it all together usually don't.' Like her? Wondering whether sandwich-making was really her future, or the future she'd chosen because it meant she could help her sister and release her mum for a new life in Blackpool.

'I've never given myself time and space to think about it,' Petra admitted, looking wistful now.

'Well, why don't you do that?' Becky suggested. 'While you're here in Corfu, take time to think about what you want to do next. You don't have to tour the Greek islands and tick off all the great sunsets…'

'Although that does sound kind of fantastic.'

'Maybe you want to study some more? Or learn to be a… deep-sea diver.'

'Did you see me in the cave?' Petra asked. 'I nearly killed myself showing off. If it hadn't been for Elias…'

Elias. Her Elias. Was he? Could he be? The very thought of it warmed her more than the Corfiot sun. That would be an unexpected little thing that was actually quite a big thing. A man in her life. Someone who in such a short space of time had become so important to her.

'Oh snap,' Petra said in a thick American accent. 'You're in love.'

'No… no… don't be silly.' It couldn't be love. Love at first sight, or after a few romantic interludes, only happened in those Hallmark movies she and Petra loved. Usually there was plaid involved… and an all-seeing, all-knowing grandmother figure…

'You're in love with Elias. The second I mentioned his name your face went all melty on me... like someone with dodgy fillers standing too close to a fire.' Petra made the shape of a love heart with her hands, curling her fingers then moving the heart shape towards Becky.

'I did not go melty! I don't even know how to go melty!' Had she? Was it love? Whatever it was, it was something. And *he* had said it was something too.

'I think you two could work. As much as I know about relationships working, because you know my hooking-up lifespan is generally shorter than Warwick Davis.' Petra pointed a finger. 'And there's the issue with him liking the much older woman. I mean, I know you're late twenties but...'

'About that,' Becky said. 'Eleni... she's Elias's mother.'

'What?' Petra asked.

'Yes.'

'Well, I'm pleased he wasn't boning her, obviously, but a potential mother-in-law who wears night vision goggles... I'm not sure *I'd* go there.'

Becky's phone bleeped then and she looked to the day bed it was resting on. Was it finally a sensible text from Hazel or Shelley? Before she could even think about going to get it, Petra made a dash, plucking the phone from the mattress and observing the text.

'Petra! Don't you read that!' Becky rushed after her.

'It's from Elias!' Petra looked up from the screen. 'Look! Look at you already glowing. What *did* you two get up to last night?'

Becky snatched the phone out of Petra's grasp and read the message.

If you are free I would very much like to take you out today, Captain Rebecca. Dress code is swimwear. 11 a.m.? Elias x

'It's very formal for a text,' Petra remarked.

'You read it already?'

'I'm a fast reader.' Petra smiled then. 'I could put that on my C.V.'

'I wonder where he's going to take me?'

'Oh, Becks, the opportunities here on an island!' Petra said. 'Have you ever done it on top of a cliff? Or underwater? Or there was this one time in Tunisia I actually did it in a tuk-tuk… and he was driving!'

Fifty-Two

Kouloura

His mother and father had both laughed. He had heard it loud and rich and warm while he was helping get Areti's washing in order at one of the tables inside the *cafeneon*. As well-meaning as the Greek woman was, he also knew she had only lingered to see what would develop between his parents. And things *were* developing, he could see that. In fact, such was their engagement with each other, he had had to remind them to eat their breakfasts before the food went cold. Finally, when Becky had responded to his text about meeting up, he had left them both dealing with customers like old times. Except he hoped that this time they would be more honest with each other about what they wanted from their life together. Maybe a breakfast could not fix everything, but he hoped his intervention had given them a springboard to whatever came next.

'I like this boat a lot more than I liked the small one.'

Elias smiled at Becky and passed her a glass of champagne.

She was sitting on the bow of the cruiser dressed in a rather nice black one-piece swimsuit that had slightly see-through mesh in certain sections of it. It was very her. Slightly sultry, classy, definitely hot…

'I like *you* on this boat more than the small one,' he replied, moving to join her on the padded sunbathing area. 'There is currently less screaming and—'

'No octopus.'

'That is something I cannot guarantee for the whole of the day.'

'Please say you mean we're going to be eating them.' She smiled and took a sip of her champagne. 'As much as I'm not giving up my meat addiction, I'm enjoying trying different things.'

'Is that so?'

They had sailed from Kerasia where he had picked Becky up and were now anchored just outside the bay of Kouloura. There were several yachts and small tourist boats in the harbour, but nothing too close. It was very private and secluded. It was peaceful and, he hoped, romantic.

'This is not my boat,' Elias told her, gazing out over the water.

'Oh,' Becky answered. 'Here I was, expecting you to tell me that you're really a Greek prince in another twist to our tale.'

Elias smiled at her then. 'I like that.'

'That I suggested you might be a prince?' she asked as he sat a little closer to her.

'No,' he replied immediately. 'That you said "our" tale.' Just repeating her words give him a little kick of joy deep inside.

'Well,' Becky said. 'We can't deny that we do have a tale together. It started at Heathrow and...'

'It moved to Greece,' he said, his fingers coupling with hers. 'Unexpectedly to Kefalonia and even to the very same part of Corfu.'

'Like it was meant to be,' Becky breathed.

'Yes.' Elias's heart was galloping now, like a racehorse who was sprinting through the final furlong to hopeful victory.

'But, it's too fast, isn't it?' Becky asked, leaning back a little and taking back her hand.

She was backing off and being sensible. She was evaluating the probability of this being nothing more than a holiday flirtation. It was what he had done himself, thinking firstly about Chad's case and then simply the complications of getting involved with someone again.

'Who or what is it too fast for?' Elias asked her. Because he was certain now. He wanted to see how this panned out. Not just here in Corfu, but when they got back to the UK. Surely they were not too far away to be able to maintain a connection? Although she did say she might want to keep travelling. How would things work between them then?

'I don't know,' Becky admitted. 'It just... seems crazy to think of how we met and how this happened and...'

'It will make the best of stories to tell at dinner parties,' Elias told her.

'You seem so sure,' Becky whispered, looking directly at him.

'Because I am sure,' he told her. 'To begin with, when confronted by my feelings for you, I tried to tell myself it was not happening, that maybe I had been struck by some temporary insanity that had descended like a flu virus...'

'I'm feeling exceedingly flattered to be compared to a contagion,' Becky answered with a wry grin.

'But,' Elias continued, 'I wanted to be infected. That was at the heart of it. Denying that truth was like denying I am Greek or denying that I work too much.' He trailed his fingers down her arm, feeling every nuance of the softness of her sun-kissed skin. 'I am completely sure that you are the only woman who has even turned my head since... in years,' he carried on. 'And I am also sure that you are the most kind and caring, the most funny and engaging... the most beautiful person I have *ever* met.'

'Elias...'

He could see she was blushing now. She had dropped her eyes from his and was now looking out at the sea as it swayed around the boat.

'What?' Elias asked her. 'It is all true. But you should know you are terrible at taking a compliment.'

'I don't... get them every often.' He saw her look increasingly uncomfortable. 'Not like that.'

'What can I do to make you believe me?' he asked.

'Oh, Elias. You are...'

He shifted closer to her, until their bare thighs were touching and there was a tightening in his Speedos. 'I am what?'

'All the sexy,' Becky breathed, finally meeting his eyes. 'All the hot... and all the compelling.'

'Compelling,' he said, one eyebrow raising.

'Yes. Compelling.'

He brought his mouth to the soft, delicate skin of her neck and dropped a kiss on her throat, feeling her shiver.

★

Becky wanted to feel this way until the end of time. She was on the brink of something here, something that could be the most special time of her entire life. But she was as much filled with excitement and anticipation as she was filled with nervousness and tension. She closed her eyes, letting the heat and motion of Elias's mouth be her only anchor. Gradually, as his lips swept over her, she lowered herself down onto the soft, leatherette pads of the boat and revelled in the uncharacteristic naughtiness of this.

Her fingers reached up to the straps of her swimsuit and she lowered them off her shoulders.

'Captain Rebecca,' Elias whispered.

She kept her eyes closed and managed a small high-pitched noise of reply, wriggling with want. She was so deliciously warm, her skin from the Greek sun, her insides from the Greek man... except Elias had stopped kissing her. Why had he stopped kissing her?

She opened her eyes then and he was still half-sitting, half-lying next to her but there was indecision written in his expression.

'What's the matter?' Becky whispered, edging upwards a little. 'Did I do something wrong?'

'No,' Elias said immediately. 'My God, no.'

'Then please, kiss me again,' Becky begged, reaching to palm the light stubble on his jawline. 'Take off my swimming costume and kiss me all over. And then...' She stopped, the words almost catching in her throat.

'And then?' he queried, putting his hand on hers.

'Then... make love to me,' Becky said, her voice thick with desire. 'Make love to me on this boat... and all the days after today... until we... until we die from the trying.'

It seemed that Elias needed no further encouragement and his mouth was instantly on hers, hot and filled with passion, his chest aligning with hers, his hips close. Becky reached up, encircling her arms around his neck. She didn't want to wait any longer. She pulled him down on top of her.

Fifty-Three

'Open your mouth.'

'Again?'

'You are crazy,' Elias breathed. 'I meant for the octopus.'

'Oh... really?'

'You sound disappointed.'

'There's always dessert, isn't there?'

Who was this wanton individual who suddenly knew more flirtatious banter than all the *Take Me Out* contestants put together? Perhaps it was down to the fact she had spent the past hour exploring every square inch of Elias's body – and there were a lot of inches in the very best of ways – and also feeling confident enough to display herself exactly as she was for the first time in a long time. There was no hiding on the sunbathing deck when you were completely naked. And there was also a unique thrill when she recalled that, at any moment, another boat could arrive alongside their vessel and see literally everything. Although Becky wasn't sure she would have noticed if anyone had arrived. The only coming she had been aware of was her own. Four times.

Then Elias's, in a jumble of holding tight, wanting to be even tighter, gasped breaths and a squeal from her not dissimilar to the noise she had made when pretending to be a pig...

And then they had swum. She, Becky Rose, had jumped into the air off the front of the boat uncaring about which sea critter might want to nibble her first. She was high on life, celebrating the gorgeous Greek sunshine and the cooling, aquamarine ocean and realising just how lucky she was to be experiencing all this.

Becky smiled at Elias then and opened her mouth, ready for whatever he was going to put in there. Although she suspected it really was going to be food this time...

A delicate piece of something hit her tongue and she let out another noise she didn't usually own. 'Oh, Elias, what is this?'

'You cannot tell?' Elias asked. 'I thought you were the woman with the most refined palate who can tell almost anything.'

'OK,' Becky said, eyes still closed, sitting forward a little and concentrating on the flavours in her mouth. 'Give me a second...' She could smell the sea air and even the sunshine and it was distracting her from the task in hand. She honed in on the subtleties currently resting on her taste buds. 'It's lobster,' she said, breathing quietly through her nose and pushing the food gently over her tongue so as to absorb all the flavours. 'With... fennel... definitely fennel.' She concentrated harder. 'Lemon... and... onion and maybe white wine and... dill. A little dill.'

'Wow,' Elias replied.

Becky opened her eyes then, finally swallowing the delicious food. 'What?'

'Your skills *are* impressive,' he told her.

'I think you also said that earlier,' Becky answered. 'Except earlier you said I was "amazing" and—'

'Incomparable,' he finished.

'That was really, really sexy,' Becky told him, leaning forward and pressing her lips to his.

'You are really, *really* sexy,' he answered, kissing her back.

'Can we do it in a tuk-tuk one day?' Becky whispered.

'What?'

'Never mind.' She laughed and looked for her glass of champagne. She had had three glasses of champagne and was thoroughly glad she wasn't driving the Aston Martin... or the Ferrari... or actually even a bicycle. 'Where did my glass go?' she asked Elias. 'I didn't knock it overboard, did I?'

'We are done with champagne,' Elias told her.

'Oh.'

'Do not sound so disappointed. I have something else I would like you to try.'

'Another position?' Gosh, the alcohol was loosening her tongue... or maybe she had sunstroke. She put a hand to her head to feel if it was too hot.

'Captain Rebecca...'

'Field Marshal,' Becky said, connecting their lips again. 'Call me Field Marshal.'

Elias quickly ducked down a little, producing a fat-bottomed glass from the hamper he had been picking delicacies from and began to pour a golden-brown liquid into it. It smelled divine and Becky immediately felt a spark of familiarity somehow.

'What is it?'

'Oh no,' Elias said. 'You have to taste it first. I want to

know what you sense from it.'

'I'm not a circus act, you know,' Becky teased. 'I don't read food and then tell fortunes like Zoltar.'

'Take a sip,' Elias encouraged, offering out the glass.

Becky took it, cradling its bottom with her palm and swirling it a little. 'It's a brandy.' She put her nose over the rim and inhaled. 'Or is it? I'm not quite sure. It's rich but also light.'

'Taste it,' Elias encouraged.

Becky put the glass to her lips and took the tiniest of sips at first. Then, she took in more, letting the amber-coloured liquid coat her tongue. 'Wow… it's sweet and warm… *so* warm and… there's fruit notes and maybe… toffee?'

'My God,' Elias said. 'You really *are* a tasting genius.'

'What is it?' Becky asked, enjoying the spread of heat to her throat as the drink slipped down.

'It is Metaxa,' he replied. 'This one a seven-star. And you just told me the exact taste sensation it should provide as written on their website.'

'What can I say?' Becky asked with a smile. 'Except… yes!'

'Yes?' Elias asked, watching her animation.

'Yes! This is it!' Becky exclaimed, bouncing a little on her seat. 'This is what is missing from your mother's *stifado*.'

'Metaxa?' Elias queried.

'I've been trying to think what it was that would bring all of her flavours together and increase the richness. I was thinking of a cognac my dad used to drink that Megan and I were only allowed the tiniest bit of at Christmas, but it wasn't quite right. But *this*. This is it.'

Elias shook his head, smiling at her as he took a sip of his own glass of Metaxa.

'What?' Becky asked. 'What's funny?'

'Not funny,' he told her. 'Incomparable, like I said before.' He took hold of her hand. 'You are so enthusiastic about tastes I cannot believe this is not something you have wanted to do your whole life.'

Becky sighed. 'My whole life has been taken up reacting to other people's situations. I haven't had a chance to own anything. Not even my own future.' How did that happen? How had Becky allowed that to happen? She knew with regard to It's A Wrap it had been about protecting Megan. Megan had steamrollered into the business venture like she blustered into everything in her life – 200 per cent committed with all of the passion and none of the thinking about practicalities. Megan hadn't asked outright for her help – that had never been Megan's style – but Becky instinctively thought she knew it was what her sister wanted. And Becky also knew that having the two of them engaged on a joint project – albeit with Megan's name alone on all the paperwork – their mum could relax into life in Lancashire. But what came next?

'And now?' Elias asked her.

'And now I feel different… stronger,' she admitted. 'Coming here, it's been so good for me. It's shown me there's so many sides to myself. Sides I didn't even know I had.' She took a breath. 'When I get back to the UK I'm not going to be the same slightly-terrified-of-everything person who sat down next to you in Row 18.'

'I am not going to be the same either,' Elias breathed.

He had made another one of his pro/con lists early this morning. The pluses for keeping his business exactly how it was and the minuses. He had come to only one conclusion.

'I am changing my business model,' he told her. 'I have acted appallingly in a number of my cases, if not all of them, and the satisfaction that I have a 100 per cent record of winning does not sit well with me anymore.' He took another breath, stilling in the moment. 'I made other people suffer to try to ease my *own* suffering and all it did was make me feel even hollower than I felt in the beginning. That isn't the way to run a business. I may have success but... it is not a nice success.' He squeezed her hand. 'I want to do what I do and feel happy about it. Yes, I will still want the right results for my client but... at any cost?' He shook his head. 'No.'

Becky threw her arms around him then, pressing her body against his. She was still damp from their swim and she smelled of the saltwater coupled with the sun lotion he had massaged into her shoulders. Then, there was another scent he recognised. His scent, the aftershave he wore, lingering on her skin because of the closeness they had shared. He held her tighter.

'I wanted you to say that,' Becky said. 'Because now I feel I can tell you something I'm most definitely not supposed to. But I'm coming to the end of my stay now and I'm pretty convinced something underhand *is* going on so...'

'I have no idea what you are going to say,' Elias said as Becky sat back from him.

'Ms O'Neill has someone coming to Villa Selino tomorrow night at 5 p.m.,' Becky told him. 'I think you're right. I think there are valuables in the villa that she is hiding from her husband... your client.'

Did he want to hear this? He had told himself everything

by the book from now on. Whatever the rights and wrongs of this case he wasn't the police.

'I think this person... this dodgy-sounding Lazarus... I think he's going to come and take the valuables for her, or sell them for her, or do something so her husband can't have his share of the money in the divorce.'

Elias groaned then, dropping his head to his hands. 'This case! This fucking case! I wish I had never taken it on!'

He felt Becky put a hand on his shoulder then, palpitating the skin. What was he going to do? He raked his hands through his hair and then sat up, looking at her. 'There are missing paintings, aren't there?'

'There's a large walk-in wardrobe we can't find keys for in one of the bedrooms,' Becky informed. 'Petra thinks it's going to be an Aladdin's cave or, you know, where they keep the cash for *Who Wants To Be A Millionaire?*'

'OK,' Elias said, his brain trying desperately to regroup.

'And I guess you still don't know about the cars,' Becky carried on.

'What cars?'

'O-K,' Becky said, patting his shoulder again. 'You might need to pour a bit more of that Metaxa.'

Fifty-Four

Villa Selino

'You can't come in?' Becky asked Elias. She was coiling herself around him in the garden of the villa. He had anchored up the boat and walked her up the beach, and into the villa grounds like the gentleman he was... when he wasn't doing all the ungentlemanly things she had requested. But she didn't want him to go. They had had such a perfect day together and she was reluctant for it to end.

'I would like nothing more than to stay, you know that,' he breathed, kissing her lips. 'But we agreed. I need to speak to Chad. I need to speak to Kristina's lawyer. I need to do this right.'

'I know,' Becky said. 'But... can't you do it right after you've... done all the bad things to me?'

'The bad things?' Elias queried.

Becky could smell the olive tree sap in the air and the fragrance of clematis, hear the insistent song of the cicadas... 'I meant all the things that are so bad they're so good.' She kissed him then, hoping to make it last so long that he was completely powerless to resist her invitation to stay... It seemed she *had* that power with Elias.

'What the hell is going on here?! Who are you and what are you doing? Put her down!'

Becky literally fell out of Elias's embrace, her bum hitting the paving of the patio before she could completely come to as to what was going on.

'For God's sake! Why weren't you picking up your phone?!' Petra called, rushing into the scene. 'I tried to warn you! I tried at least a zillion times to ring and I sent text messages that were basically longer than... than... all the Harry Potter books... including the ones about beasts and Quidditch.'

It seemed Petra had to stop and take a breath now, which was bad, because without her incessant rambling it gave Becky all the time to focus on the fact that her sister was standing in front of her. *Megan was here.*

'Are you OK?' Elias asked, taking Becky's hand and helping her up from the floor.

'No... I... yes.' Words were failing her and the weight of Megan's stare was searing her skin like she was pressed between the hot plates of It's A Wrap's toasted sandwich maker.

'Didn't you hear me, Becky?' Megan continued, louder and sounding angrier than ever as she took steps towards her.

Wearing patent nude-coloured heels and a matching jumpsuit Megan usually only wore to pitches, suddenly Becky's barely-there sundress over her swimming costume felt completely inappropriate. What was her sister doing here? How had she got on a flight to Corfu – maybe even via Athens – without Hazel or Shelley having a chance to warn her of the incoming sister missile? Becky suddenly felt unsteady on her feet again. 'Elsa is coming'. They *had* warned her and she hadn't got the code. Shelley had once named Megan after the ice queen when she'd taken the triplets to see *Frozen 2*. Whatever had happened at home was bad if her friends had been scared into communicating with code…

'What are you doing?' Megan repeated. 'And who *are* these people?'

Becky watched her sister look Elias and Petra up and down like they were species from another planet who had no place on Earth.

'I told you my name when you barged through the door. Very rude by the way,' Petra snapped. 'I'm Petra.'

'And I am Elias Mardas,' Elias interjected, offering Megan his hand. 'It is so wonderful to meet you. Becky has told me so much about you.'

'Has she indeed?' Megan said, folding her arms across her chest.

Suddenly and quickly, Becky got cross. Her sister *was* being rude, just as Petra had said, and as shocking as Megan's arrival was, she wasn't going to let her strut in here and start calling the shots… was she? She swallowed. She had to be strong. She had to make Megan see that she was not going to back down just like that anymore. She had her own life and her own opinions and she wasn't going to be forced to sing the same tune as Megan any longer. It was time her sister had a dose of the truth.

'Megan,' Becky began. 'This is Petra, my housemate and this is Elias. He's my—'

'We need to talk,' Megan abruptly interrupted. She

sleeked her hand down her blonde bob as if she was about to start filming for something. And she was still in charge of this conversation apparently.

'OK, well, I'll make us some drinks and we can—'

'You can listen,' Elias said firmly.

Becky looked to him and Megan was positively glowering at him.

'You can both *listen* to each other,' Elias continued, somehow manoeuvring deftly in between them. 'Because, if there is one thing I have learned through my career, it is that the listening counts far more than the talking.'

There was silence for a beat. Becky didn't know how to follow what Elias had said and she couldn't believe he had come in and tried to exude authority over her sister when he was wearing nothing but a completely open white shirt over those tight trunks...

'Sorry,' Megan said, seeming to lean in a little and sniff Elias. '*Who* did you say you were?'

'Elias is my—'

'I am Becky's lawyer,' Elias broke in with a determined nod.

'Well,' Megan replied. 'I've never seen a lawyer dressed in Speedos before.'

'In Greece this is the uniform of all the best lawyers,' he answered, seeming unfazed.

She had been going to be really honest and brave and all the things she needed to be with Megan. She hadn't been going to say the word 'lawyer', she had been going to say the word 'boyfriend'. Because that was what Elias was to her now? Wasn't it? *Ugh!* Why was Megan's arrival here making her doubt everything?

'Right!' Petra exclaimed. 'I'm done with this *Fighting*

With My Family vibe. I'm going back inside to try again to break into that mystery cupboard.' She about-turned and headed for the bi-fold doors.

'And I also should go,' Elias said. He looked at Becky as if to remind her that he had been going before Megan had suddenly appeared. But also his look said that one word from her and he would stay. No, she was going to handle this on her own. She didn't need Elias to sit them both down around the infinity pool and mediate. It was time to remember all the things she had learned here. She had grown. She had found out what independence truly meant. And although at first it was difficult and a little bit terrifying, now she rather liked it.

'Perhaps you *should* stay,' Megan suggested haughtily, picking some lint from her jumpsuit and letting it drift away in the slight breeze. 'If you really *are* a lawyer.'

Becky shook her head. 'Megan, I've thought about this a lot since I've been here.' She stood tall, rolling her shoulders back, inching her chest out a little. 'There have been many *many* occasions when I've taken a lot less than what I've been due for holiday. And there have been times – a lot of times – where I have worked many *many* more hours per week than is legally acceptable for someone to work. So, if there's anyone who needs a lawyer then it's you.'

Eek! She hadn't meant to sound quite so confrontational. She did want to keep her job… at least until she had time to properly think through any alternatives. No one with half a brain put themselves out of employment without anywhere else to go. And maybe she didn't *want* to go. She did love making the sandwiches… Why was Megan here now? When there were only a few days until she returned? Perhaps something else was wrong. Maybe it was Mum…

'Is that so?' Megan asked, a smirk appearing on her lips.

Oh God. It was the self-satisfied smile her sister always owned when she knew absolutely she was going to win an argument over pricing with the prawn man. Or perhaps it was simply bluff and bravado. Megan was quite good at that too. Becky would like to think that if it was something to do with their mum then Megan would have got to the point by now. So, it was a case of fold, or raise the stakes?

'Yes,' Becky found herself saying, stepping slightly closer to Megan, her pleather espadrille-covered feet making squelching noises from the sea water trapped in the hessian. 'That is so.' She took a breath. 'I don't need a lawyer to tell me I've more than given enough to It's A Wrap over the years and you have absolutely no grounds to fire me.'

Megan linked her fingers together and almost triumphantly flexed them out. The sound of her sister's knuckles cracking made Becky flinch.

'Well,' Megan stated as brusque as anyone could sound. 'How about if I told you that Martin from the florist's had an allergic reaction to the latest "creation" It's A Wrap made him?'

'What?' Becky could hardly breathe now. Martin from the florist's had an allergic reaction to something? Something *she* had made? Martin was usually a brie and bacon man. Had he opted for something else? Something from the range Megan knew nothing about? She was shaking, from head to foot, the Corfu sun doing nothing to raise her temperature from Alpine conditions…

'He's still alive. But it was touch and go for a while and—'

'Oh my God!' Becky exclaimed. 'The reaction was *that* bad?!' *Poor Martin. Poor, poor Martin.*

'Yes!' Megan shouted. 'The reaction was *that* bad! And the very worst thing was… there was no label on the packaging! Nothing to tell anyone exactly what ingredients were in there!'

Becky couldn't catch her breath. She had to phone Hazel and Shelley. She had to find out what they had given to Martin. Surely they wouldn't have been stupid enough to give him a lunch meant for someone else… 'I have to call Shelley… and Hazel.' She was looking around for her bag. Where was it? Had she taken it off the boat?

'Becky, take a second,' Elias ordered, reaching for her hand.

'I can't take a second. I need to find… where's my bag?' She looked up into his face, those gorgeously bright eyes, those full lips… all the while she had been stepping outside of her comfort zone and *finding herself*, one of her customers had been nearly dying because of a sandwich. She couldn't focus. Her eyes began to swim, her vision blurring.

'I think… I think I need to sit down,' Becky managed to say before she fainted on the floor.

Fifty-Five

Becky was quite sure *ouzo* wasn't the best thing for someone who had fainted but, right now, it was the only thing hitting the spot in terms of her revival. Despite his protests, she had made Elias leave as soon as the olive trees stopped looking like they were tripling in number in her vision. Now on her second glass of the Greek spirit, with ice and a little water, she was making the most of the brief moments she had before she knew Megan would want to engage in battle again. And she didn't blame her one bit. This was huge. This was terrible. Someone could have died because she had hidden part of the business from her sister. It didn't get any worse than that.

'You're not pregnant, are you?' Megan wanted to know.

Becky looked up out of the *ouzo* glass and observed her. She was tightly wound, like a dog who had been cooped up for days without a walk or, someone who hadn't been able to leave the house between Christmas and New Year. Her drawn-on eyebrows looked tenser than the rest of her and the jumpsuit couldn't possibly be perspiration-friendly.

Surely even Megan would perspire in the Greek heat.

'No,' Becky replied. 'Of course not.'

'Good,' Megan answered. 'Because I don't want anything stopping me from tearing strips off you for this, Becky.'

There was pure venom in her sister's voice now. And Becky knew this went far deeper than Martin from the florist's.

'I'll resign,' Becky said immediately. 'I'll take all the blame and I will resign. Straightaway. Right now.'

'You will not!'

'I should!'

'Yes!' Megan agreed. 'Yes, you should. Because I know *everything*, Becky.'

Becky had a vision of Hazel and Shelley being strung up in the cold room like the carcasses in the Maroon 5 video for 'Animals' – Megan a psychotic Adam Levine with a cleaver. It wouldn't have taken much for either of them to start talking and Becky would never want nor expect them to suffer any duress keeping her secrets.

'I know,' Megan continued, actual, real perspiration beading on her lip, 'that this crazy undercover enterprise of yours has been going on for over a year! That you have been selling all types of God-knows-what to *my* customers for over twelve months!'

It was eighteen months or more, and they were *her* customers too. But Becky wasn't going to bring that up right now. 'I have,' she admitted, running a finger around the rim of her *ouzo* glass. 'But I never, ever thought anything like this was going to happen.'

'How could you not think that?! Are you an imbecile?! Have you not read or heard the news about labelling on food products? *Pret A Manger*, Becky! *Pret A Manger!*'

'So,' Becky began nervously. 'This is just about the fact my products didn't have detailed labels on them?'

'Do we think that Martin from the florist's would be in hospital right now if they *had*?' Megan yelled. She was flailing her arms around now, mosquitos would be taking cover and so they should.

'Well… you haven't told me the circumstances of Martin's allergy,' Becky reminded. She was probably clutching at straws. Megan wouldn't have flown to Corfu if she wasn't absolutely sure this was all Becky's fault. But what *was* Martin's allergy? She was keen to know exactly what he had ingested that had landed him in hospital.

'What circumstances do you need to know about?' Megan hissed. 'Do you want to know the part where his face went red? Or about when his lips swelled up? Or perhaps the bit where his boyfriend had to put him in a wheelbarrow to get him to the doctors because no one was answering at the surgery?'

'Poor Martin,' Becky said with a sigh. She felt nothing but pure white-hot guilt.

'Yes! Poor Martin and stupid, *stupid* you!'

Perhaps this was for the best. She would be sacked from It's A Wrap and Megan would hate her and she would never have the chance to inform Megan that her sister's whole life was based around the fact that she had never grieved properly for their dad and she was planning a life with Becky's ex-boyfriend. Maybe Megan didn't need to hear how Becky's concoctions had kept It's A Wrap afloat for so long, or that she had often told people Megan was the genius behind the flavours…

But that wouldn't be being true to the new her. The her that wanted Megan to know that she was more than a simple bread-butterer. The her that had been the glue holding Megan together since they lost both their parents from their everyday lives. She wanted her sister to realise that *she* had feelings and needs and apparently a new penchant for a Greek aperitif and a Greek guy...

'Just tell me what wrap he ate?' Becky asked, watching Megan sip at her water glass.

'God! Is that all you're interested in? What it was that sent him spiralling towards unconsciousness?'

'Well,' Becky said in matter-of-fact tones, 'it would be nice to find out what he was allergic to, because in all the time I've known him he hasn't mentioned any allergies and I'm very careful about asking that.'

'Really? Are you? Because you hand out ingredients without labelling and completely hide this from your boss!'

'And why do you think I did that?' There was no shying away now. If Becky was going to be dismissed in disgrace, then it may as well be all out in the open. She raised a glance to the olive tree providing them with some much-needed shade and internally she whispered an apology to it. All these years standing in this garden, all the conversations it had overheard and now it was about to be witness to a Rose Family smackdown.

'I have no idea! No idea at all! And Dean has no idea either. He actually suggested you had early-onset dementia.'

Becky closed her eyes and simply tried to keep breathing. Dean had never known her at all. But now was not the time for stopping...

'I hid it from you because I knew you wouldn't approve.'

'Damn right I don't approve! I mean who in their right mind would?!'

'Someone who realised that their sandwich flavours weren't inspiring enough. Someone who could see that other local businesses offering cous-cous and healthy grains were going to swallow us up if we didn't do something different.'

'Rubbish!'

'It's true, Megan. Don't you think I did the research? I ate at every one of the nearest sandwich places like ours and I tried to think what it was we could offer that they weren't offering. And yes, it was a little out-there and quirky, but it worked! I made the herb garden – I told you about that—'

'You think I'm so dumb I wouldn't have seen a load of plants in the garden?' Megan shook her head. 'Dean thought it might be weed.'

Again, Dean wasn't the sharpest tool in the box. But Becky wasn't going to let Megan cut through this conversation like she did all the time.

'I experimented for weeks in my kitchen at home. What flavours went together. Things people wouldn't expect. I researched what was the best for overall health and energy and what additions could help with certain conditions like… lack of iron or arthritis or indigestion. I made suggestions to customers, I went out with sample trays, I…'

'Took over the spare phoneline with an answerphone you hid from me.'

'I had to Megan. I couldn't tell you the business was going to go bust if we didn't try something a bit out there. I didn't want to upset you. I wanted to take on that responsibility and help out.'

'Like you always do!' Megan spat. She stood up then, fanning her jumpsuit, sweaty patches appearing under her boob line. Megan was actually sweating.

'Yes!' Becky countered. 'Like I always do! Like I always have! Like I've been doing for so long without any thanks for it!' She got to her feet too.

'Oh, so you want thanks now, do you?' Megan snapped, her face a picture of fury. 'Thanks for always taking over… when it came to Dad being ill… when Mum was moving… being first with the man I'm planning to marry… now having taken over *my* business!'

'I… didn't *completely* take over when Dad was ill or when Mum was moving.' Except a creeping sensation was travelling over her shoulders now. She hadn't *entirely* taken over, had she? She had needed to step up quickly, make arrangements, ensure their dad got a place at the best nursing home and make sure their mum was completely sure about the area of Blackpool she was moving to. All Becky remembered was Megan's disinterest. But… what if she had translated that wrong? Maybe disinterest was simply distance because of fear. Had her sister just been so scared about what was happening to their family that the only way to cope was to emotionally run away?

'The business is all I have!' Megan was truly raging now and tears were spilling from her eyes like someone had opened the release on a dam.

'That isn't true,' Becky said. 'You have Dean.'

'And Dean loved you first!'

'Megan, he absolutely did not love me.'

Megan let out a sob, the anger seeming to diminish just a touch and Becky moved towards her, feet still squelching.

She tentatively reached out and put a hand on her sister's shoulder. 'Dean adores *you*! Anyone can see that. We merely... shared a few pizzas together and a few awful films and...'

'Sex.'

'That was pretty awful too if I'm really honest.' Becky swallowed, a flashback of her and Elias on the boat earlier coming to mind. *That* had been nothing like what she and Dean have ever shared. With Elias it had been almost otherworldly. Then she caught herself. She had said *out loud* that the sex with Dean had been terrible. Her sister was planning to marry him... She spoke quickly. 'Awful because... we never matched. Not like you and Dean match.'

Megan sniffed, lifting her head and looking at Becky. Her eyes were black with half-washed away eyeliner, shadow and mascara. It looked like she had been making up in a coal-yard. 'I don't know if we match,' she said sadly. 'I just agreed to go out with him because I knew you would hate it.' She snivelled. 'And how sad does that make me?'

'Oh, Megan!' Becky exclaimed. She was shocked. That couldn't be true, could it? Megan loved Dean. They were a gloriously perfect power couple on the networking scene – Megan the sandwich entrepreneur and Dean in charge of bringing the outside in with the conservatory business.

'You think that I don't care what happened to Dad. But you're wrong.' Megan sniffed hard. 'I cried for him. I just didn't do it in front of you or Mum.' More tears were falling now. Megan continued, 'I know you're better at me with the sandwiches. You're better than me at everything. You always were! And although I should be grateful to have someone so talented running the kitchen, I'm not. I'm jealous and I hate it. I really hate it!'

Becky didn't know what to say. Perhaps it was best not to say anything at all. She could feel the emotion building up in herself now. She bit her lip, trying not to cry.

'You not telling me about these *other* sandwiches tells me that you don't think I'm capable of anything at all.'

'I don't think that,' Becky insisted. 'You're *so* capable. Much more capable than me. I mean, if you put me in a room with businesspeople talking about "propositions" and "bottom lines" I would want to hide in the nearest cupboard until it all stopped. *You*, you revel in all that. And no one else would have been able to get the contract with the army.'

Megan shrugged, her face softening a little. 'You think I don't care about It's A Wrap. You think it could be any sort of business… a nail bar or… a coffee shop… you think the only reason I wanted a business was because I couldn't get a job working for someone else. You don't even know why I chose sandwiches, do you?'

There was a *reason* her sister had wanted to go into the catering market? Becky had assumed it was because it was relatively simple to set up and that it was profitable if they could tackle the competition. Great reasons but Megan was somehow now talking like filling rolls had been a life-long ambition. 'No,' Becky replied.

More tears dropped onto Megan's cheeks then, flowing slowly down her face. 'Sandwiches, rolls and wraps were what I shared with Dad. Every time you and Mum went to the library or to Old Mrs Mason's house or to whatever *joining* activity you were involved in at school, Dad and I had a tea party.' Megan sniffed. 'We made all kinds of buns and fingers of sandwiches and pretended we were having tea at the Ritz.' She smiled. 'Dad would make the fillings and I was the bread-butterer then. And I always made the tea too. Not too strong, not too weak, with proper tea leaves. The sandwiches were *our* thing and that's why I wanted to create It's A Wrap, to remember him by. For Dad.'

Becky felt the pain in her heart as if it had just been pierced by one of Elsa's sharp icicles. How had she not ever known? Why had Megan never told her? Why had their dad never said anything? *Because it was their thing. Just like her gardening and herb-planting and fixing things in the shed with their father*. It seemed she had completely misjudged her sister in so many ways and she felt like the worst sibling in the world right now.

'But,' Megan carried on, taking a breath and turning a little to face the sea scene, 'none of that is going to matter anymore. After this incident I could lose the business and—'

'No,' Becky said firmly. 'You're not going to lose the business. I will take full responsibility, obviously. It *is* all my fault. I should have told you what I was doing. I knew that and I did it anyway because I thought that was the right thing to do and...'

'And I made you feel you *couldn't* tell me,' Megan said, looking back to Becky. 'Because I always accuse you of taking over.'

'Which I do... because otherwise we wouldn't be in this situation.'

'Beck-Beck,' Megan breathed, eyes still watery. 'I know that – even though it's super annoying and despite what I just shouted at you – I know that everything you do is to try to make my life easier.'

Becky couldn't remember how long it had been since her sister had called her 'Beck-Beck'. There was a total softening in Megan's tone now.

'I tried,' Becky said. 'I wanted to be there for you because, well, Dad had gone and Mum's—'

'Spending her money on arcade versions of *Tipping Point*.' Megan smiled then, a whisper of it meeting her eyes.

'I wanted to let you know that I wasn't going anywhere. That I was here for you…'

'I know that. I've always known that. And you forget sometimes that *I'm* the older sister. And maybe I'm not the most organised, or the most practical, but I *can* do life without you holding my hand.'

Megan was right. Megan was absolutely right. Sometimes, if you held somebody's hand too long they forgot how to function without the support. She had said the same to Elias earlier.

'I didn't mean to say your sandwich fillings weren't exciting enough.' Becky was imagining Megan and their dad spending time together in the kitchen, laughing as they prepared delicate rolls and enjoying afternoon tea.

'I did mean that you always take over,' Megan replied.

Becky laughed then. She couldn't help it. Amid the sadness and the crossness, their bond was reaching out, trying to find a way through.

Megan fanned the neckline of her jumpsuit. 'It's so hot here! Is it like this all the time in Greece?'

'I don't know,' Becky admitted. 'I haven't spent all the time here yet.'

'Oh, Beck-Beck, what are we going to do?' Megan exclaimed, putting her hands into her hair and giving it a plump. 'If Martin decides to sue over this then I really could lose everything.' She swallowed. '*We* could lose everything.'

'I'll sort it out,' Becky said, flinging her arms around her sister and holding her tight. 'Let me interfere just this once more and I'll try to make everything right again.'

Fifty-Six

Liakada

'Is there something to need to tell me, Elia?' Eleni asked him as she joined him at the bar of the *cafeneon*, hair wild, a spot of sauce on her left cheek.

Elias turned from his view of Becky, Petra and Megan. The three women had arrived half an hour ago all in much better humour than they had been at Villa Selino. Becky's sister had even let Becky introduce him properly and given him half a smile. Her eyes might have shot a look that he had interpreted as he was under deep scrutiny, but she hadn't voiced that opinion. They were now seated at a table outside about to tuck into plates of *souvlaki*. It was night. The sky was an inky blue, the air still humid and there was a buzz around the village. Panos's Taverna opposite was alive with diners which might warrant the old man to serenade them with his violin later. Elias was waiting on a call from Chad.

'I don't think so,' he answered his mother.

'You and the English women. First two and now three? Do they follow you here from London? Is this how things work in England?'

He smiled and shook his head. 'No, Mama.'

'What is wrong with a nice Greek girl? I can make arrangements. Babis's daughter from the hardware store is still available although, Areti says she has been seen at Fuego Bar with the son of the owner of the horse-riding centre.'

'Mama, it isn't that I am opposed to Greek girls,' Elias answered, taking a sip from his bottle of Alfa beer.

'It is not?!' Eleni's hand went to her heart then. 'Well, I feel like I have been re-born.'

'Nationality is not important,' he continued, his eyes on Becky. He was watching her chatting to Megan and Petra, more animated than he had seen her before. The tension of earlier between the sisters seemed to have dispersed significantly. He looked to his mother then. 'When you meet someone. When you connect with someone. You just know that it is right.'

Eleni seemed to hold her breath for a moment and Elias wondered how she was going to react. Would she see his moving on as a good thing? Or would she be disappointed that he was moving on with someone not from Liakada?

'It is the one with hair like toffee,' Eleni said with a sigh. 'The one who tells me there is something missing from my *stifado* recipe.'

Elias smiled at his mother. 'Yes,' he answered. 'And her name is Becky, Mama.'

'I know what her name is. I do listen!'

'Good,' Elias said. 'Because there is more great news.' He put an arm around his mother's shoulders. 'Becky has worked out what should be added to the *stifado*.'

'What do you mean what should be added to my *stifado*?! There is nothing to be added. Nothing at all.'

Eleni's arms went up in the air like a protestor marching outside parliament. 'That recipe was my grandmother's and her grandmother's before her and—'

'And it has really stayed *exactly* the same?' Elias asked. 'No one made any alterations in all these years?'

'No.' Eleni folded her arms across her chest.

'How would you know?' Elias queried. 'If you were not alive at the time.'

'I just know! It is tradition! Traditions are things that are passed down from years before.'

'I know what tradition is, Mama. But even traditions can be improved and changed.'

'I do not like change.'

Elias shook his head. 'Is this the same woman who wants to travel around Europe?'

'That is different,' Eleni told him. 'I am not going to put all my possessions into a backpack and never come back. It is a holiday and we need to make sure your father is fit to fly.'

Elias felt his heart lift. They *had* talked about his mother's adventure. She was planning a trip. They were planning a trip together. He squeezed his mother's shoulder, unable to easily find words.

'Stop looking like that,' Eleni ordered him. 'Your father is on probation. We are going to take things slowly. He is going to stay in the shed until I am ready for him to come back.' She sniffed. 'He is going to take me out. Like he used to. We are going to start dancing again. There is a place in Corfu Town.'

Her eyes were sparkling as she spoke and Elias caught that moment before she shut it down again.

'Nothing is decided,' Eleni said quickly.

'OK,' Elias replied, still smiling.

'Stop looking like that,' his mother ordered. 'We might not require your legal services yet, but anything could happen.' She sighed. 'I will not, and never will be, making him the breakfast of the English.'

'OK,' Elias said again, watching his mother start to toy with the strings of her apron.

'And he needs to… start wearing aftershave again and… learn how to iron his own clothes.'

'OK.'

'And… and… I will stop taking him for granted,' Eleni said, her voice choking up. 'Because as irritating as he is for all of the time, I could not imagine my life without him.' A tear escaped her eyes. 'I don't want to explore Europe on my own. Always the dream was to have him by my side.'

Elias drew his mother into a hug then. 'I know,' he whispered. 'I know.'

'And now you have made me cry!' Eleni exclaimed in horror. She wrenched herself from Elias's embrace and dashed away her tears with a fist. 'I do not have time for tears. I have a party of walkers coming in in half an hour so…' She waved her hands around as if she was waiting for Elias to complete the sentence.

'So?'

'What is this mystery ingredient the English girl is suggesting will improve the taste of my *stifado*?'

Elias smiled again then. He knew his mother would really want to know.

'You will have to ask her,' he replied. 'And, Mama… her name is Becky.'

Fifty-Seven

'So, asking for a friend... not really, I'm asking for me... how does it feel to know you almost killed someone?' Petra asked with a grin.

With a mouthful of succulent chicken and red pepper, Becky couldn't immediately respond. She desperately tried to chew so she could make comment, but it wasn't happening. She knew that Megan wouldn't hold back and Megan didn't know how fragile Petra really was...

'You really have no filter, do you?' Megan retorted. 'It's very concerning.'

'More concerning than nearly killing someone?' Petra carried on, sucking on an olive.

'Petra,' Becky said, finally being able to speak. She took a sip of water to clear her palate. 'We don't know all the facts yet.'

They still didn't. Megan had called Hazel earlier and Hazel said she thought Martin had grabbed the chickpea, chilli and cauliflower flatbread usually destined for Ambrose at the petrol station but someone had come into the florist's to order for a funeral and Martin had got distracted and had flung a note at her and said 'keep the change'. The allergic reaction had apparently been witnessed by Clare from the Co-op who was buying retirement party flowers and it was her who had alerted Martin's boyfriend and Dennis the local builder who had provided the wheelbarrow to get Martin to the surgery… These details were great, but it didn't help in terms of getting to the bottom of things. The three ingredients in that flatbread were not high-allergy risks. But Martin might not have known he was allergic, and if the flatbread wasn't labelled… it was likely It's A Wrap was going to be culpable.

'Maybe,' Petra began. 'It's all a con. You hear about it, don't you? Like those people who claim they've had whiplash when they've been in a car accident that isn't their fault.' She slugged down the rest of her wine. 'Maybe this Martin and his boyfriend are feigning this whole thing to sue you.'

'I don't think you can fake anaphylaxis,' Megan responded.

'No?' Petra asked.

And suddenly Petra seemed to go rigid in her seat. Her face was turning chilli red, eyes bulging and she was gripping at her neck, mouth gaping like she couldn't inhale.

'Becky, where did you find her again? She's quite mad,' Megan said.

'Petra, stop it,' Becky ordered, flapping her napkin in the young girl's face. 'You'll burst a blood vessel.'

Petra laughed out loud then and finally stopped herself from reddening, relaxing back into the chair. 'See! Dead easy to fake.'

'He went to the hospital,' Megan told her. 'I don't think he could fake it in front of the doctors.'

Petra sniffed. 'Well, these doctors work such long hours, don't they? He'd only have to convince a really *really* tired one or a really *really* crap one and then job done.'

'I'm sure it isn't that,' Becky said, popping a square of feta cheese into her mouth. Eleni's food *was* excellent. This was simple fayre but delicious.

'Martin has been a customer for a long time,' Megan agreed.

'There's no loyalty these days though. It's everyone for themselves. You've only got to look at these places that offer special deals for new customers only. Still,' Petra said, 'you're going to get that party at the nursing home before your business goes under. Becky's menu looks amazing. Even *I* wanted to eat it and I don't remember any of the wars.'

Becky froze, the succulent tomato piece in her mouth suddenly tasting like the sourest gooseberry. *The nursing home party pitch*. The pitch Megan had told her to drop. Was this going to break them apart again now that Martin's drama had strangely started to bring them together?

'You did a menu for the nursing home? For their summer party?' Megan asked.

'Megan, I can explain. I—'

'You didn't listen to me,' Megan interrupted. 'You ignored everything I said to you.'

'Well,' Becky began. 'I—'

'Thought you knew best?'

'Maybe.'

What else could she say? Everything her sister was saying to her was true.

'Do I need to get another carafe of wine?' Petra asked. 'For the next bout?'

'Not this wine,' Megan and Becky said together. The speaking in unison might have been funny if they weren't in the middle of another spat.

'The food is very nice,' Megan remarked. 'But the wine is terrible. Why did you have it?'

'Ha!' Petra said. 'Let's see how you get on saying no to Eleni.'

'Megan,' Becky started. 'I'm sorry—'

'No, you're not.'

'Well—'

'You're not sorry, are you?' Megan said, fanning her napkin in front of her face. 'Let's be honest here.'

Becky swallowed. Yes, honesty was always the best policy. 'I'm not sorry.'

'Good,' Megan said. 'Now we're getting somewhere.' She picked up her *souvlaki* skewer and bit a piece of perfectly chargrilled chicken off it.

'You're not angry?' Becky asked.

'I knew you were going to do it anyway.' Megan shrugged. 'Because I know you and although I said I didn't want you to do it… I don't know… I sort of *did* want you to do it.' She took another breath. 'I was just frightened for It's A Wrap to try and do it.' She paused for a beat. 'Because, where you saw it as an opportunity to honour Dad, I saw it as something I was worried we wouldn't get. And if we didn't get it, I knew we would *both* be disappointed. Or, if we *did* get the job, I would be worried we wouldn't be able to do it real justice.'

'Oh, Megan,' Becky said. 'Really? That was all it was?'

'It was enough,' Megan said, about to take a sip of wine then seeming to think better of it. 'Enough to send me into a frenzy and—'

'Send me off to Greece.'

'Quite.'

'And I'm so glad you had this massive catfight over sandwiches otherwise I wouldn't have met Becks,' Petra added. She poured more wine into her own glass. 'If I hadn't have met Becks, I might have been in Piraeus with Marathon right now. Or in Kefalonia with Agelos. Or stroking Plato *and* Panos.'

Megan stared at Petra with no understanding whatsoever.

'Don't ask,' Becky suggested.

'And Becky might still be reading that book I threw into the sea earlier.'

'What book?' Megan asked.

'It's nothing!' Becky said quickly. She shot Petra a warning look then followed it up with a second one, then a third…

'*How to Find the Love of Your Life or Die Trying.*'

Becky was cringing now. She really didn't want her sister to know she had given the slightest bit of interest to a self-help book of that nature. She hadn't… well, only a bit. And only because it was there. Forced on to her by Hazel.

'It's Hazel's book,' Becky said out loud. 'She forced it on me and I used it to… send me off to sleep when the sound of the air-conditioning was keeping me awake.'

'It did help you snare Elias though, didn't it?' Petra said, her words flowing even more smoothly than the wine. 'Was it the chapter on body language? *When a smile is really give my number a dial*?'

'It sounds like you've read more of the book than me,' Becky insisted. 'A lot more.' She turned her attention to the fluffy white dog who had stuck his head through the railings next to her. She petted its head and wondered if they could trade places...

'Hazel loaned me a book once,' Megan informed. 'It was called *Groomed: Care Down There*. It was then I was convinced she had been looking at my online shopping order. One purchase of Nair and you have a problem apparently.'

Becky didn't know whether to laugh or cry. Instead she did neither and took a drink of wine, pretending it was something nicer and sweeter and not like she imagined the piss of the bear-thing to taste like.

'Is it a holiday romance?' Megan asked.

'Petra and Marathon?' Becky replied innocently. 'Plato's a cat by the way.'

'This thing with Ell-he-has.'

Petra burst out laughing, slamming the table with her hand. 'What did you call him? Ell-he-has? Well, Becks, answer that one. Is it "Hell He Has" or "Hell He Hasn't"? Personally, I think it's "Hell She Definitely Wants To If She Hasn't Already".'

'Ignore Petra please,' Becky said to Megan. 'She gets even crazier on this horrible wine.'

'It's one of the benefits,' Petra responded. 'The only benefit actually.'

Becky looked to Elias then. He was sitting at the bar inside, his fingers coiled around his mobile phone that was next to his ear. Immediately the butterflies began inside her. He was so sexy and caring and intelligent and humorous and all the things a partner should be. Yes, they hadn't known each other very long but the connection they had was real and it was strong enough to want to see where it led. Becky was certain of that.

'I like him more than I've ever liked anyone in my life,' she admitted.

'More than Dean?' Megan asked.

'More than anyone,' Becky reaffirmed. 'I meant what I said about Dean. Yes, at the beginning I was hurt he had spent so much time with me when it was really you he was interested in. And I realised that after you got together. All those times he'd smiled when you walked into a room and laughed more at your jokes – even when they were truly terrible.'

'Hang on,' Petra said, leaning across the table, her plaits falling into a bowl of *tzatziki*. 'You two dated the same guy?!'

'So, to answer your question,' Becky said, fixing her gaze on her sister. 'No, I don't think it's a holiday romance.' She took a breath, watching Elias end his call and get off the stool. 'I think, and I hope, it's going to be much more than that.'

Before Megan could make any reply, a large bottle of amber-coloured alcohol was slammed down in the middle of their table. Becky flinched and looked up. *Eleni*. It was then Becky read the label of the bottle. *Metaxa*.

'So, Miss Becky from England, you think this is what is missing from my *stifado*.'

'I...'

'Elia says for me to "ask you, ask you" and then, finally, he tells me and I laugh. I laugh in his face because I know what this tastes like. This is Greek. I know all of Greek. And this will *ruin* my *stifado*.'

'Well, how do you know?' Petra piped up. Becky really wished she hadn't.

'How do I know?' Eleni asked.

'How do you know it will ruin your stiffy if you don't try it.'

'Petra,' Becky said warningly.

'Petra is right,' Elias stated, arriving next to the table and looking straight at Becky. 'You need to try it, Mama, exactly like I said. Because Becky is an expert at flavours.'

She looked up at Elias then and saw the adoration in his eyes. He really believed that. He believed in her madly skilled taste buds like he believed... octopuses could jump out of the ocean or... a missed connection and turbulence could lead to a love affair...

'I agree,' Megan said, breaking into the conversation. 'You should try it before you make a judgement.' Megan looked at Becky. 'My sister is the most talented person I know.'

Becky felt like her heart was going to burst with utter joy. Here she was in gorgeous Greece with a new wonderful man entering her life, reconciling with her sister, mainly still rolling her eyes at Petra, being told she was special...

'Technically,' Petra began. 'She might have almost killed someone with a sandwich but... we don't know all the facts.'

Elias plucked the bottle from the middle of the table. 'Well, let us give it a try.' He looked to Eleni. 'You are not afraid of being wrong, are you, Mama?'

'I am afraid I will kill the group of walkers I have coming in for dinner.'

'Take a chance,' Elias suggested. 'Things can change and it will be OK, remember?'

Eleni seemed to absorb his words and Becky watched her

expression change from fierce to not-quite-so-fierce. And then the Greek woman full-on faced her.

'Finish your *souvlaki*. Then you will find out what it is like working in a Greek kitchen.'

Fifty-Eight

Villa Selino

Becky's cheeks were flushed now, not from the humid night as she sat in the garden of Villa Selino, but from the furious temperatures in Eleni's kitchen. Despite living and working in one of the hottest places in July, Eleni had no air-conditioning in her traditional kitchen. With the outside temperatures in the late twenties – even at night – the heat while cooking had to be racing into the forties.

'I did think she was going to boil your head if I'm honest,' Petra commented. She was off the wine and onto the *ouzo* now. It wouldn't be long before she suggested a late-night swim and Becky would feel compelled to watch her every stroke in case she got into difficulty.

'Do you think she'll sulk forever?' Megan asked. 'Because she was definitely sulking when the walking group asked to see the chef and said they had never tasted anything like it before.'

'She will definitely sulk forever,' Elias concurred.

Becky smiled, staying quiet. Having them all together like

this was still something special and she was simply taking time to appreciate it. Elias had offered to walk them home and she had invited him to stay for a drink. Secretly she was hoping he would stay for more than a drink...

'I'm glad I'm staying here,' Megan announced. 'If this is my last trip abroad before the business goes into liquidation because of Martin's impending lawsuit then... it's very nice.'

'Where *were* you staying?' Elias asked.

'Megan didn't know quite how far the airport was from Kerasia so she booked a hotel in Corfu Town,' Becky filled in.

'It was lucky I ticked that free cancellation box,' Megan told them.

'Listen, I can help if you need someone to deal with any litigation,' Elias said. 'I have a guy I can recommend.'

Yes, as special as this moment was, Becky had to remember that things could turn really bad the minute they touched down in England. Someone had been made seriously unwell, because of Becky's inventive treats.

'Thank you,' Megan answered. 'But it might be better if we find someone a little closer to home. Someone in England.'

'I am from England,' Elias explained. 'I live in London.'

'Oh,' Megan remarked. 'Becky didn't tell me that.'

'Well,' Becky started, 'I haven't had much of a chance to tell you anything. It's all been a bit of a whirlwind since you arrived. Allergic reactions and... family politics and...'

'Next we have a nut job arriving tomorrow evening to nick all the antiques.'

'What?' Megan queried.

'And did Becks tell you about all the animals we found when we first arrived here? It was like a scene out of *The*

Durrells. There was even a flamingo in the bath!' Petra carried on.

'Becky?' Megan asked, as if looking for clarification.

'It's all true,' Becky admitted with a nod.

'Anyone for a swim?' Petra suggested.

It was late now, Megan and Petra had long since gone to bed, and Elias knew he should be walking back to the village. He had a lot to organise for tomorrow. His hope, now he had made contact with Kristina's solicitor, was for her lawyer to talk some sense into her over the 'secret' valuable joint assets at the house. The solicitor was supposed to tell her that the game was up, that deliberating deceiving the other party was going to be frowned upon by the court and it was likely already, that this deception was going to cost her part of her settlement from Chad. But, if this Lazarus did turn up here at the villa, Elias was going to be there, along with the local police.

'What are you thinking about?' Becky whispered across the table. 'I can almost see the cogs whirring around.'

Beautiful Captain Rebecca. Her sun-kissed complexion, bright eyes and the soft waves of brown hair framing her face...

'I am worried,' Elias began, 'that if I have another glass of wine with you, I will not want to leave.'

'Do you have to leave?' Becky replied.

Her intense look was enough to send his heart into meltdown and he remembered everything from their day on the boat.

'No,' he whispered. 'I do not.' He wet his lips. 'But...' He couldn't finish the sentence. His fingertips grazed the wood of the table between them.

'But…' Becky asked.

'Captain Rebecca, you should know something before I stay.' He took a deep breath. 'I know I have said this before but… I need you to know, for certain, that I am in this with you… not for a holiday romance… not for a rebound or a quick fix.' He took another breath. 'For as long as you can put up with someone who has made many many mistakes along the way.'

He could feel his heart swelling, still a little anxious for her response. But then she was reaching for his hands and holding them so tightly in hers, her delicate fingers wrapping themselves around his.

'I am in this with you,' Becky whispered. 'For as long as you can put up with someone who isn't keen on enclosed spaces… who will probably unintentionally verbally pick apart anything you ever cook trying to decipher the ingredients… who might be about to be sued and lose everything she doesn't really even have…'

'Stop talking now,' Elias ordered her. He stood up from his seat, making his way around the table to be next to her.

'OK,' Becky replied.

She got up too, meeting him – eye to eye, body to body – mere inches between them, both standing so still under the gently swaying branches of the olive tree, the sound of the sea in the distance…

The time for more words wasn't now. He needed to taste her and touch her and show her exactly how much she had already grown to mean to him. He kissed her then, his lips meeting hers in a passion so strong it rocked him on his feet.

He tried to steady himself but feeling her deep response he was struggling to stay still.

'Elia,' she whispered, momentarily dragging her lips from his, her fingers touching his chest.

'Yes,' he answered, looking at her and trying to read the emotion in her eyes.

'*How to Find the Love of Your Life or Die Trying* was completely wrong.'

'That book!' Elias exclaimed. 'I should never have given you back that book at Heathrow. I should have thrown it in the nearest bin.'

'It told me you should always pause and consider the implications before you do literally anything.'

'I see,' he said.

She was still looking at him but saying nothing. It was just her eyes meeting his and the silence coupling with the intent lying in her expression was torpedoing him into sensual waters.

'I've done way too much pausing in my life up to now,' Becky announced then. 'It's time to press "play".'

'I'm so glad you said that,' Elias answered, closing the slight gap between them.

'Take me to bed, Elia,' Becky ordered.

He didn't need any more of a green light than that and in one quick motion, he scooped her up into his arms and began marching across the patio towards the bi-fold doors.

Fifty-Nine

'Elia,' Becky whispered, running fingers across his bare shoulder and down his arm.

Every inch of her skin was zinging like it had been treated to the very best exfoliating technique. In truth it was glowing with the increased blood flood to every tiny area and a lot from Elias's slight stubble. Becky shivered, remembering the hours that had gone before. With the light of the moon coming in through the balcony doors, the humid air wrapping around them, they had moved together slowly and deeply, then more quickly and urgent, then slowly again until Becky thought her body was actually going to soar off the bed and hit the ceiling fan she had opted for putting on instead of the air-conditioning. Elias really was the perfect lover, strong and masculine yet also patient and subtle, asking her if she was OK, saying he wanted to hold her forever, kiss her forever. She had drowned as much in the sensual lull of his words as she had in the firm, muscular lines of his body. Last night had been different from the time on the boat. It had been softer, deeper, taking their time, knowing time was theirs to take now…

'Elia,' she said again, this time running her fingers down his waist and over his hip. He was unmoving, lying on his side, his back to her, the up and down movement of his body suggesting he might still be asleep. 'Elia.'

'Becky,' he whispered. 'We cannot do it again right now. After last night, a man needs a little time to recover.'

'How much time?' Becky asked. She got up on her knees then and crawled over the bed until she was at the bottom. Then, like a leopard stalking its quarry, she slowly crawled her way up the mattress until she was straddling Elias. He turned, almost sending her off balance, looking up at her naked body in the same appreciative way he had the night before. It made her feel both sexy and yet a little bashful. She shook her head and leaned forward a little.

'I know what you're doing,' he said, reaching up and pushing her hair back behind her shoulders. 'Don't.'

'What?' she asked, laughing.

'You were trying to cover your breasts with your hair.'

'No,' Becky said, dropping her eyes to his rather Pierce from *Neighbours* bod.

'It is too late,' Elias told her, reaching up and cupping one of her breasts in his hand. 'I know every inch of them. Every inch of all of you.'

Becky leaned into him then, dropping down onto his body and finding his mouth for a long, slow kiss. He tasted of her, she knew she tasted of him, and the memories of last night made her tremble all over again. When she sat up, looking down on him again, she traced a finger over the letter 'H' on his chest, swirling over the lines.

'Another mistake I made,' Elias said, sighing. 'Becky, I want you to know that I am not the kind of man to have names tattooed on my body. It is just... I was getting married and...'

'You don't have to explain and you shouldn't feel embarrassed about it,' Becky reassured him. 'It's a really nice design around the letter. I like the olive tree.' She traced its boughs and the delicate ink drawing of the leaves. 'And, we all have history. Granted, I don't have my ex's name tattooed on me – that would be weird as he's now dating my sister – but Petra has a man's name on her wrist that she's never even dated so...'

Elias smiled then. 'This is a fact.'

'And Hestia was part of your life. You'll always have those memories of your time together. A bit like old photographs you put into a box.' She spiralled over his pectoral again. 'Sometimes it's good to get them back out again and look through them. You can remember the happy times, remember the less happy times and then... box them back up again.'

'I could get a new tattoo,' Elias suggested. 'I am sure they could make an "H" into... I do not know... a pig with Bic stab wounds... to remind me of when we first met.' He laughed out loud then and Becky reached for a pillow, thwacking him with it.

She stopped the assault when the doorbell sounded. Gasping, she got off Elias and began scrabbling for any item of clothing that could cover her nakedness. 'Oh my God. Who is that? What time is it?' Pulling her sundress over her head she looked at her watch. 'It's only 8 a.m. Who calls round at 8 a.m.?'

'Wait there,' Elias said, rushing out of bed. 'I will go.' She watched him begin to locate his clothes.

'You think this is something to do with the divorce? Is it your client? Or Ms O'Neill?' Becky shook her head. 'No, they would both have keys, but they might think it polite to ring if they know someone is staying here.' She gasped again, slipping her feet into her espadrilles. 'And I'm the only one meant to be staying here! No couples she said. No other people! I've got you and Petra and my sister! She's going to sue me! I'm going to be sued by two people over two different things! I've never even dropped litter before!'

The doorbell rang again. This time more insistently.

'Becky, relax, I will answer it.' He kissed her lips before leaving the room.

'I'll be two minutes. I just… need the loo.' She had a sudden thought. 'If it's Ms O'Neill, say you're… helping me water the flowers. Please.'

Smoothing down his shirt, then running his fingers through his hair, Elias opened the front door. A man was standing there, finger about to jab at the doorbell again. Contrary to the already warm early morning, this man was wearing a three-quarter-length leather coat, black trousers and a black T-shirt, a gold chain around his neck just visible. His hair was slicked back from his face and was tied in a thin ponytail. He was perhaps fifty years old, maybe a little older.

'*Kalimera*,' Elias greeted.

'Oh,' the man replied, looking a little unsettled. 'Do you speak English? I was told an English woman would be here. Miss Rose?'

'Yes, I speak English,' Elias answered.

'And Miss Rose?'

'Who are you?' Elias wanted to know. Although, from the looks of this shady character, he was in little doubt as to who this man was. He was a good few hours early. Half a day early in fact.

'My name is Lazarus. I'm just here to pick up some boxes on behalf of the owner.'

'Is that so?' Elias stated. 'Under whose instruction?'

'Sorry,' Lazarus said. 'I didn't catch *your* name.'

'There are two owners of this property,' Elias told him. 'And… I am the other one.' He stuck his hand out then. 'My name is Chad.'

'Who is he and why are we making him coffee?' Petra hissed as Becky took her time putting different pods into the machine she didn't really know how to work properly.

'Sshh,' Becky said. 'He'll hear you.'

'Are you sure?' Petra asked. 'With your sister telling him about everything *Dean* has ever bought her? By the way, this Dean sounds like a right dickhead. You've definitely traded up with Elias.'

'Chad!' Becky reminded. 'Elias has told him his name is Chad.'

'Shit,' Petra said suddenly. 'Chad is the husband, isn't he? The one who doesn't know about the uber-expensive cars and the shit load of stuff in the cupboard we still can't get into.' Petra gasped then, a little too loudly. 'Shit, is this that dodgy Lazarus?'

Becky pressed a button and the coffee machine set to

work. 'Yes. We just need to keep him talking and get him to stay here long enough so Elias can get an injunction or the police or something. He's on the phone right now in the garden.' She didn't really know what the actual plan was. She wasn't sure she wanted to know. She felt uncomfortable about the whole thing.

'We could drug his coffee,' Petra stage-whispered, eyes roving over to the table where Megan was still talking at a rapid rate.

'What with?' Becky didn't know why she had said that. She should have said 'are you mad?'.

'Well,' Petra began, 'I picked up quite the pharmacy from this stall in the backstreets of Mumbai. I'll go and get my backpack.'

Before she could try to leave, Becky grabbed her arm. 'No! Don't be ridiculous!' She lowered her voice again. 'We can't drug him. *I* certainly can't drug him. I'm already under scrutiny for food collaborations that have caused injury.'

'I'm quite happy to do it,' Petra insisted. 'It might even help me get into a forensic psychology course I was looking at. You know, add a bit of spice to my CV... if I don't overdose him... and kill him... and end up in prison.' She sniffed. 'What are the Greek prisons like do you think? On a scale of one to Guatemala.'

'You're looking at further education! That's great!' Somehow that news was the most vital part of Petra's sentence.

'Yeah, well, I decided that you might be right. That I need a goal and something to focus on that doesn't involve jumping on a plane. I'm actually surprised my mum hasn't come back to haunt me because of all the money I've spent on food that's full of E numbers. One of the last things she said to me before I went to the music festival was I had to start eating more spinach...'

Becky threw her arms around Petra and squeezed her tight. She had grown to really *really* care about her. Yes, she was all kinds of flippant and fickle and annoying, but she also had a good heart and a soft soul.

'You're squeezing my boobs!' Petra said, trying to wriggle herself free. 'And I don't have much in that department as it is! And I really *really* want to be Rebel Wilson when I grow up!'

Becky let go of Petra just as Lazarus appeared in their side of the kitchen. Megan was in hot pursuit, waving her hands in the air and looking concerned.

'I think I'll pass on the coffee,' Lazarus stated. He looked at his watch.

'Oh,' Becky said. 'But it's almost done. It's going to spit and gurgle and be sip-perfect any second now.'

'I think I ought to get what I've come for and leave.' He stood a little taller... if that was possible. 'My client said I am to take the cars in the garage too – I have a trailer waiting on the road – plus the contents of her bedroom cupboard.'

Petra stepped forward. 'Well, you might have a problem there. Because there's no key for that cupboard.'

Lazarus patted the left breast of his leather coat. 'I have the key.'

Becky didn't know what to say. She looked to the window, Elias was still pacing around the terrace, his phone glued to his ear. How was she going to stop this man from taking everything? Should she just let him? It wasn't her fight, after all. But it *was* Elias's. And Elias was planning to change his business, be less ruthless and win fairly. This wasn't fair, this man under Ms O'Neill's instruction taking assets that were jointly owned...

'Shall you show me the way? Or shall I find it myself?' Lazarus asked.

Becky ran then, to the door of the kitchen that led back into the hallway and the bedrooms. She slammed the door and leaned against it. 'I can't let you do that.'

Lazarus was moving towards her now, a determined expression on his life-worn face. Whoever this man was, he certainly looked like he was involved in all kinds of shady. 'Ms O'Neill will be very disappointed to hear that. She did tell you I was coming here, did she not?'

'Well, yes. But—'

'But she said five o'clock,' Petra jumped in. 'Not eight in the morning when some of us haven't even had a chance to cleanse, tone and moisturise yet.'

'I am not leaving without what I have come here for.' He reached forward and Becky held her breath and squinted her eyes closed. Was he going to manhandle her? She held her back to the door and waited for the inevitable...

Suddenly there was a thud and Becky opened her eyes and leapt out of the way as the towering bulk of Lazarus dropped to the floor. Becky looked from the man to Petra and then to Megan. Her sister was holding her new handbag in a combative way...

'As nice as this bag feels, it's way too heavy,' Megan announced, putting it back on her shoulder. 'Especially when it's full of duty-free perfume bottles.' She stepped over one of Lazarus's legs. 'And *no one* threatens my sister.'

'I like you!' Petra announced all grins and excitement. 'I wasn't sure when you first got here but... I like you.'

Sixty

'I still can't believe it! Three days in and I still can't get my head around it!' Petra exclaimed. 'Even after seeing it all with my own eyes – and I did try to cuddle most of it until the policewoman dragged me away – Ms O'Neill had a Banksy *and* a sword that used to belong to Napoleon.'

'Don't forget the vases from the Ming dynasty,' Megan added.

'Honestly,' Petra said, spreading a thick layer of olive tapenade on the fresh bread then dunking it in the pool of olive oil she had poured on her plate. 'If I was going to spend my husband's cash on valuables, I would have at least cashed in on something I could use. The cars I totally get – the Aston Martin was a dream to drive – but I would have bought up all the Hermes and Louis Vuitton before I wasted it on a sword that didn't even win the Battle of Waterloo.'

'Oh, I hear you,' Megan agreed, taking a bite of *saganaki*.

'I'm sort of glad you didn't have a Louis Vuitton when you decided to hit Lazarus over the head with a handbag,'

Becky said, sipping a glass of Panos's much-better-than-Eleni's wine.

'I agree,' Megan answered. 'I wouldn't have wanted to damage it. I probably wouldn't have even wanted to use it for handbag purposes.'

'Just slip it out of its dust cover every so often – wearing gloves obvs – and cuddle it,' Petra said with a sigh.

Becky gasped, almost spilling her wine. 'I've just realised you said you drove the Aston Martin! When? *When* did you do that?!'

'Er… ha ha… moving on… someone, anyone… say something before Becky goes loco on me,' Petra begged.

'I'd like to say something,' Megan said, addressing all three of them. She put her hands down on the table, fingers smoothing over the cloth like it was made by Louis Vuitton. 'I'd like to say that I am so glad I came to Corfu. Yes, I booked the flight when I was full of rage and I entirely intended to sack you, Becky, after I had made you clear out your bank account to settle whatever lawsuit came It's A Wrap's way…' She took a breath. 'But somewhere in between the sweating from the humidity and the gorgeous views over that infinity pool and listening, *really* listening to my sister and—' she directed her gaze at Becky now '—sharing feelings I should have shared so much longer ago… no matter what happens next with Martin or… with Dean or… with life… I think the Rose sisters have got this.'

Becky felt her throat tighten as a knot of warm emotion lodged itself there and her eyes filled with tears. They were leaving tomorrow. Even Petra, who was heading to Switzerland to meet up with her crusty old aunt before she settled on selecting a college course. At the moment she was looking at two colleges, one in Hampshire and one in Lincolnshire. Becky was hoping she would plump for Hampshire because, for selfish reasons, it was much closer to Wiltshire and she really did want to keep in close contact with the girl she had grown so fond of. So, in just a few hours Becky's Greek adventure was going to end. But wow, what an adventure it had been. And she hoped there was going to be much more Greek in her life from now on…

'And,' Megan carried on, 'there's something else I have to tell you too.'

Becky closed her eyes, fearing the worst. Why did she always fear the worst? She snapped herself out of it and opened her eyes, ready to face whatever news this was.

'I'm pleased to say… that It's A Wrap got the job of catering the nursing home summer party,' Megan finished with a smile.

Becky's mouth dropped open. 'But… how? I don't understand. I… didn't pitch it. I didn't think, given everything that…'

'*I* pitched it,' Megan informed. 'After you showed me the menu, the absolutely *brilliant* menu by the way, I thought what sort of businesswoman am I aspiring to be if I'm just going to fall down and give up on It's A Wrap after one incident? A possibly near-fatal incident, granted, but only *one* in all our time trading.'

'I am really *really* sorry about that and I will get to the bottom of it and I will make sure that no ingredient is left unturned in the search for the truth.'

'We will work it all out together,' Megan said, putting a hand over Becky's. 'Plus, I need you to bring this old people's party together. They were ecstatic in their reply.'

Becky was glowing now. It was the best piece of news they could have received before they travelled home.

'*And* I would like you to carry on creating your unique brand of flavours... if you want to that is,' Megan said. 'I mean, I don't know what plans you have now you have a man in your life. Maybe you're going to move to London and set up your own catering firm and take over the world. Which you probably should and definitely could. Or maybe you don't want to do sandwiches at all anymore. Dad always said you could achieve *anything* and he was absolutely right.'

'Megan,' Becky said, hearing her sister catch her words. She squeezed her hand. 'The way I remember it, Dad always said *we* could achieve anything. I'm not going to move to London. I'm not moving anywhere.'

She might have had her eyes opened to exploring a new country, but home was where her heart was. Leaving It's A Wrap would be cutting her nose off to spite her face. She loved what she did and now she and Megan had a brand-new understanding, Becky was sure things could only get better.

'Phew!' Megan said, flapping her hand in front of her face. 'Because as competent as Hazel and Shelley are, they're not... you.'

'In that case,' Becky said, 'as I'm so highly thought of now, I do have a few conditions.'

'I think we should discuss a pay rise *after* we've dealt with the Martin situation,' Megan jumped in.

'It's not money,' Becky said.

'Shit, she's offered you a pay rise. Take the money!' Petra ordered.

'I will want to visit London. As much as possible.' Her heart was bursting with love for the man she had met in Row 18. The man she was spending the night with after this meal with Petra and her sister. They had plans for the kind of dessert that burned calories instead of putting them on and it made both her sets of cheeks flush at the thought of it. 'I'll obviously take my holiday days as usual, but I'm thinking… as many long weekends as I can. Working around events obviously.'

Megan smiled. 'I'm sure we can accommodate that, but you must promise me one thing from now on.'

'What?'

'No more secrecy, Beck-Beck. Everything above board and labelled.'

Becky nodded. 'Absolutely. I promise.'

'Oh, about time!' Petra said as Panos arrived at their table with his little notebook. 'Now, I know it's a bit out there for an evening meal but I've heard you do a cracking English breakfast. Can I have that?'

'One breakfast of the English,' Panos said writing it down.

'But can I have it with a side of *spanakopita*?' Petra grinned. 'More spinach like my mum wanted.'

'Could I have the *kleftiko* please,' Becky said. 'But could I have some of your honey with it, Panos?'

'You want honey?' Panos asked. 'On the side?'

'Well,' Becky said, 'I'd really like it spread all over the lamb knuckle, but I can do that myself.'

'Honey on the lamb?' Panos checked.

Becky nodded, smiling. 'It goes really well together, trust me.'

'Yes,' Megan chipped in. 'Do trust her. She completely knows what she's talking about. I'll have the swordfish, please.'

'You want honey on this?' Panos inquired, bushy eye-brows raising.

'Definitely not.'

Becky looked out over the village square of Liakada and marvelled at its simplicity and homage to bygone times. A simple square of concrete earth, a few benches where men sat passing the time of day with each other as the sun went down, the grand olive tree watching over it all. The cream-coloured stray dog was sitting outside Eleni's *cafeneon*, head through the railings, eyes hungry, waiting for a titbit of anything... and then Elias's mother came onto the terrace heading towards the animal. Was she going to shoo it away? Becky watched. Eleni bent down towards the dog and threw down pieces of meat onto the street. It sucked its head through the rails and bent down, gnawing excitedly. Becky smiled to herself. Eleni's bark was definitely worse than her bite. She had a good heart, exactly like her son.

Suddenly her phone started to ring, vibrating on the table, a FaceTime call clearly visible. It was Hazel's number.

'What time is it in the UK?' Megan asked, looking at the phone display. 'Shouldn't she be making fillings for tomorrow morning?'

'It's seven o'clock in the UK,' Becky informed. She took the call, holding the phone in front of her and Megan. 'Hi, Hazel.'

'Hello, dear!' Hazel shouted as if because they were in Greece she needed to yell to reach over the distance.

'Hazel, there's no need to shout,' Megan said.

'There is if you want to hear me over the sound of Shelley and her boys playing pole vault in the garden... and yes, I am inside the unit and yes, I have the door closed and yes I did say "pole vault".'

'Is everything OK?' Becky asked.

'Yes,' Megan chipped in. 'And please, please tell Shelley that if she or the triplets get hurt on It's A Wrap property doing anything other than making rolls, *she* is personally liable and not the business. I've got one potential suing on my hands, I really don't want to start collecting them.'

'That's why I'm ringing,' Hazel said, the camera moving as if the woman was struggling to hold it in front of her face. There was now more view of the countertop than there was her.

'What d'you mean?' Megan asked, eyes widening in alarm. 'She's hurt herself already? Or is it one of the kids?'

'No,' Hazel interjected. 'I mean, I'm ringing about the suing, dear.'

'Oh, God,' Becky said, her heart on her chest. She wasn't ready to hear bad news now. Yes, there was facing up to things and handling whatever was thrown your way, but this was their last night. She wanted sweet Greek dreams and nothing to spoil her goodbyes.

'I went into the florist's today. To check up on Martin really, but I made up an excellent story about needing some oasis for a WI event.'

'Oh, God,' Becky said again. This wasn't sounding very good.

'Is he alright?' Megan asked.

'Has he had a relapse?' Petra shouted. 'I hear that can happen sometimes.'

'Who was that?' Hazel asked. 'Are you not alone? Should I call another time?'

'No,' Becky said. 'Don't call another time! Just tell us!'

'Well,' Hazel continued, 'Martin is fine and you'll never guess what.'

'No, we won't!' Megan exclaimed as if completely exasperated at her employee's inability to get to the point. 'We won't be guessing as you are hopefully going to tell us *right now*!'

'Well,' Hazel began again, 'his allergic reaction… it was nothing to do with the wrap he ate.'

'What?' Megan said, turning her head to Becky then back to Hazel, then back to Becky again.

'It was a spider bite!' Hazel continued. 'Apparently, a couple of days before he was taken ill this *beast* that looked like one of those false widows, leapt out of a bunch of his Dusty Millers. Martin brushed it off and didn't think anything of it, *but* it had bitten him on the wrist. Then, forty-eight hours later, infection started to take hold just as he decided to sink his teeth into his lunch hence why everyone thought it was food-related.'

'And that we were to blame,' Megan responded.

'*I*,' Becky said. 'That I was to blame.'

'Beck-Beck, there is no "I" in "team", you know that.'

'Anyway,' Hazel went on. 'His wrist is the size of a baby elephant's leg and the colour of a saveloy now, but he's on antibiotics to sort him out so, all's well.'

'I can't believe it,' Becky breathed. 'I can't believe it's all going to be OK.'

'I can,' Megan said confidently. 'I definitely can. I… just need to work out how I really feel about Dean and then things are going to be absolutely perfect.'

'One more thing, as you're there, Megan,' Hazel said,

moving the camera into a better position again.

'Only good news,' Becky begged, not wanting the bubble to be burst.

'Dean's here!' Hazel announced. The camera swung around the kitchen and there was Megan's boyfriend looking a little like nothing in the long-distance connection had been lost in translation.

Sixty-One

'Close your eyes,' Elias whispered into Becky's ear.

'This feels like Dark Dating,' she replied, taking tentative steps forward.

He guided her gently along the path towards their destination, the fragrance of jasmine heavy in the air. It was a perfect night, the sky speckled with stars like someone had liberally thrown shiny confetti over the dark.

'I don't have to make animal noises, do I?' Becky asked him.

'Animal noises are optional.'

'Is it far?' she asked.

'No, not far,' he told her.

'How far? Because I'm so full of dinner I might need to lie down soon.'

'Lying down is definitely a requirement for tonight.'

'Sexy,' Becky said with a giggle.

'I hope so,' he whispered in her ear again.

He was buzzing tonight after a successful online meeting

with Chad, Kristina and Kristina's lawyer. They had all talked openly, frankly and honestly and made a great deal of headway towards a finalisation of the divorce agreement. Once the police had arrived at Villa Selino three days ago and Elias had explained the situation with the valuable goods – and attempted to explain the situation of Lazarus's facial bruising – the bedroom cupboard was finally opened revealing a wealth of extravagant spending Kristina had been doing in secret. Paintings, sculptures, relics from far-flung lands and all manner of collectibles were stored high and wide, plus the two vehicles in the garage and apparently a third in storage at the port... Everything was out in the open, both parties had agreed to be completely transparent and Elias had suggested to Chad that this settlement must now not be about the 'winning' but about the fair resolution of this chapter in his life. That was what he wanted for his business now. *Honest. Just. Honourable.* The him he had been before a broken heart had altered his axis.

'No confined spaces though?' Becky asked, her voice catching a little.

'You are concerned about being in a confined space when I am here?' he asked. 'It might be fun... a tight space, our two bodies very close together, sharing each other's air...'

'As much as I love you, Elia, you're making it sound like a double coffin and that really *really* isn't sensual.'

He stopped walking then and gazed at her, his heart in his throat, his mouth dry. 'You... love me.'

Becky's eyes were still closed and he watched the rise and fall of her chest, her lightly bronzed skin moving against the neckline of her cream-coloured sundress. She wasn't saying anything yet, perhaps it had simply been a figure of speech...

'I do,' she whispered. Then quieter still. 'Is that too soon? Do you think I'm rushing things and—'

Elias answered her with a kiss, a delicate, but definite, touching of his lips on hers to ensure there was no misunderstanding. She kissed him back, one hand smoothing over the back of his neck, her fingers tickling his hairline. He wanted to hold her forever... and wasn't that what love was?

'Can I open my eyes now?' Becky asked him, ending the kiss.

'No,' he replied. 'Not yet.'

'But I want to look at you.'

He was enjoying looking at her, her gentle, sweet, beautiful, soft perfection shining from the inside to the out. He really had never met anyone like her before. And, more than that, she had helped him to find himself again. He put his hands on her shoulders and guided her forward once more, along the path, past his father's newly dug allotment, along by the chickens and the goats, to the final part of his father's land, a bamboo-ringed clearing. He smiled to himself as he looked at the tepee he had constructed with his father earlier. Made from some old sheets he had managed to obtain from Areti, over long sturdy bamboo canes tied together at the top with strong wire, it was like the fortress he had made when he was young. Except back then the tent had been filled with dinosaur toys and card games. Tonight it was filled with blankets and pillows and surrounded with strings of fairy lights.

'Open your eyes,' Elias breathed, turning Becky so she was facing the tepee.

Becky's heart was thudding in her chest, wondering what she was about to look at *and* thinking that although Elias had kissed her when she admitted she loved him, he hadn't actually acknowledged it with words of his own. She was telling herself it didn't matter. It didn't. This relationship was very new and they were both a little damaged from relationships past. She was overthinking things.

'Becky,' Elias said. 'You can open your eyes.'

Overthinking and keeping her eyes shut. Mad. And likely to spoil the evening if she didn't shake herself out of it.

She opened her eyes and gave a gasp. 'Wow... Elia... wow! It's so... beautiful.'

Stepping quickly over the grassy ground she approached this triangular wigwam, the warm glow from inside making it look like the cosiest resting place. 'This is amazing.' She stopped at the entrance, two sheets pegged into place to create the opening. 'Did you make this?'

'I did,' he said, standing beside her. 'With quite a lot of help from my father. Please, do not tell my mother he was standing on two very unstable boxes to reach the top. I offered to do this, of course, but he said I would not do it right.' He shrugged. 'What can I say? He is Greek. No care for health and safety and as stubborn as a goat.'

'Elia, it's so... perfect,' Becky said stepping inside. It really was a little haven just for them. The floor was covered in thick matting and there seemed to be dozens of cushions and pillows and rugs and blankets. There was also a small table holding a bottle of wine in a cooler and two glasses.

'It isn't your mother's wine, is it?' Becky asked, the tang of it somehow arriving in the back of her throat.

'Is there something wrong with my mother's wine?' Elias asked. He couldn't seem to hide the knowing grin.

'Does she not know it's awful?' Becky said. 'Is everyone too scared to tell her?'

'Yes, everyone is too scared to tell her,' Elias said with a laugh.

Becky sat down, leaning back on the cushions and gazing out into the night. 'Oh, wow, the view from here is amazing.'

She could see the sea, the twinkling lights of the villages below and the sound of the night-time bugs was all around.

'It is even better in the daytime but, in the daytime there is also the view of the neighbour, Areti's laundry.'

Becky laughed as Elias sat down beside her, then lay back too. Tomorrow all this would be far away. It wouldn't be fairy-lights it would be fairy-cakes, or rather, large filled baguettes to feed a battalion...

Elias took hold of her hand. 'We should make plans,' he told her. 'We should make plans tonight, before you leave.'

'What plans?' Becky asked, turning a little and looking into his eyes.

He sighed. 'I wish I was getting on that plane to London with you, but I have to stay here a little longer to finalise things with the goods from Villa Selino.' He paused before carrying on. 'And also, I want to spend a little more time with my parents, make sure my mother plans the holiday she so badly needs and I need to do something about my empty house. Do you understand?'

'Of course I understand,' Becky said, squeezing his hand

in hers. 'And, I might not be a seasoned traveller just yet, but I have experience in managing almost perfectly well on air travel even when the most extraordinary circumstances are thrown my way.'

'You certainly do,' Elias agreed.

'And I'm going to be busy,' Becky told him. 'Preparing to cater for the nursing home's special summer party next month.'

She watched Elias's face light up. That was why she loved him. Because he truly cared about things that were important to her.

'You pitched for the contract,' he said excitedly. 'You pitched and you won.'

'Actually,' Becky said, '*Megan* pitched my menu and yes, we got the job.' It still gave her a thrill saying the words. It was going to mean so much to their family as well as the business. 'And I won't need any lawyer services with regard to the suspected unintentional poisoning.'

'No?' Elias asked.

'No,' Becky said with a breath of deep relief. 'It wasn't my food that made Martin have a reaction. It was a spider bite would you believe.'

'Wow,' Elias remarked. 'In England?'

'Maybe a false widow… no one seems to know. But he's on the mend and I'm off the hook. And Megan wants to keep my ideas with the tasting platters and tailored ingredients but everything labelled and above board, which is how things should have been in the first place, if only we could have actually, really talked to one another.'

'I am so happy for you,' Elias told her.

'I am happy for me too,' she admitted. 'Deliciously happy.

In fact, I don't think there is anything that could make me happier right now.'

'Nothing?' Elias asked, turning onto his side and studying her face with those aquamarine-emerald eyes.

'*Maybe* nothing,' she said, her heart performing its own dance.

She watched him seem to still then, his pupils widening, his eyebrows arching, his lips softening. She wanted to reach up and palm his olive skin, feel the warmth of it in her hand.

'I love you, Captain Rebecca,' he breathed. 'With every piece of my heart.'

Elias's words brought tears to her eyes and she didn't hesitate to move into his arms and seal their feelings with another kiss... and then another and then...

'Two weeks,' he told her, the heat of his breath against her skin. 'I will be back in the UK in two weeks.'

'Do you realise that's the length of time we've known each other.'

'Well then,' Elias said. 'What can happen in two short weeks?' He stroked her hair back from her face.

Listening to the still of the night, underneath the moonlight, Becky let herself drink in the ambience of one last Greek island evening. The hoot of an owl, the spitting of a bear-thing, a distant honk of a flamingo...

'Everything,' she whispered to him. 'Everything can happen.'

Epilogue

Liakada Village

Late September

Becky fastened the pleather espadrilles onto the branch of the olive tree in the square. It was about time they went. They had never been the most stable. Above there were a pair of sturdy boots with holes in, weighing down the limb, and a pair of sparkly slippers adjacent, some of the sequins missing. It was evening and the annual festival had just begun. There were musicians (bouzouki and mandolin) and a singer encouraging residents to join in with the dancing being performed by the local school children. The sizzle of lamb *souvlaki* from the rack of spits slowly revolving was providing stomach-pleasing sound and scent, as was the popping of wine and beer bottles as the villagers celebrated.

'Why exactly are we tying shoes to a tree?'

It was Megan asking the question as she climbed up onto a chair to try and attach shoes that looked way too expensive to be getting rid of.

'It's a Liakada tradition,' Becky said to her sister. 'Eleni told me. In fact she told me that if I came to the festival and *didn't* tie a shoe to the tree that I would have bad luck for the rest of my life.'

'Wow,' Megan remarked. 'Your future mother-in-law does love you. Are you sure you want to run her business for the next two weeks?'

Becky smiled, looking across the square to Elias who was drinking a beer with his father. It looked very much like Spiros was trying to get Elias to join the dancing. Despite living a couple of hours away from each other, Becky and Elias had got together every chance they had since leaving Corfu. Becky had even taken Elias to visit Blackpool and her mum had adored him – even more so when he had managed to win a Forky from *Toy Story 4* from one of the claw machines. She had also spent weekends in London, meeting some of Elias's friends from the leisure club – that had involved all the hot and steamy in the sauna *and* the jacuzzi and a lot of amazing cuisine she had taken so much pleasure in unravelling over her taste buds. And now they were here in Liakada for a little over two weeks, taking care of the *cafeneon* while Eleni and Spiros had an Italian holiday. Becky was going to be doing the cooking and Elias had promised to handle all matters postal in between remotely running his law business.

'Do I want to be in Corfu for two weeks enjoying autumn sunshine and sea views instead of buttering bread for the soldiers and hearing about the latest broken bone of Shelley's triplets? Hmm, let me think about that...'

Megan poked her with the heel of the shoe she was trying to get onto the tree. 'You love working for me.'

'Sorry, what?' Becky said, holding a hand to her ear.

'You love working *with* me,' Megan re-phrased.

There had been a recent restructuring with the shareholders of It's A Wrap and Becky was now an equal partner. Megan had paid back what she had borrowed from Becky and Becky had re-invested that and a little more of her inheritance from their dad into the firm. It felt right, to be continuing with Megan in a business she loved, using skills she knew were a little be out-there but also, apparently, brilliant.

'Megan, are you sure you want to leave those shoes in the tree? They look expensive.'

'Oh, they are,' Megan answered, trying to balance the heel on a branch without it tumbling off again. 'Dean bought them for me.'

'Oh,' Becky said.

'Yes,' Megan replied. '*Oh*. And an *ex*, like the song.' She sighed. 'I think he did love me. And I think I loved *that*. I... needed the attention and he was there for me.' She gave a sad smile. 'And I liked the dinner parties and the networking. And I was mad at you and sad about Dad and Mum had left and... God, all that sounds so childish but...'

'But we're moving on from all that. Sisters running the world, remember?' Becky smiled. Their relationship was in the happiest of places now.

'Running the world,' Megan said, straining on tiptoes to reach a higher branch. 'And, lobbing shoes into a tree!' With that said, Megan threw her heel up into the arms of the olive tree and jumped back down onto the ground, ducking for cover.

'Eleni didn't tell me how much bad luck you might have

if a shoe falls down and hits someone,' Becky told her as they headed towards the wine stand.

'I think local law enforcement would probably have the last say on that,' Megan answered, linking her arm with Becky's.

'Becks!'

Becky's heart contracted at the sound of a familiar voice and then there was Petra running towards her. Familiar giant backpack on her back, hair completely loose, wearing a T-shirt that stated 'Gimme The Stud in Study', over tiny denim shorts. She flew into Becky's arms nearly toppling her over.

'You look older,' Petra breathed into her hair. 'Good, but definitely older.'

'Thanks, Petra,' Becky replied. 'Did you hook up on the plane?'

'Well,' Petra said, stepping back from Becky's embrace and adjusting the straps of her rucksack. 'There was this cabin crew member called JJ who had all the Jesse Metcalfe cute, but he seemed more interested in the guy in Row 12. Who was pretty hot but, you know, not *quite* as hot as me.'

'Please tell me she isn't here to help you cook,' Megan said, nodding a greeting at Petra.

'You've never seen me cook!' Petra exclaimed, looking affronted.

'Exactly!' Megan replied. 'You didn't even lift a peach at the nursing home party and you were supposed to be working for It's A Wrap.'

'I *was* working,' Petra said, grinning. 'My skill set is entertainment. I spoke to everyone at the party. I even made one lady called Gladys's eyes water when I told her about my time in Spain when I ate an entire bull's—'

'O-K,' Becky said, ending the conversation. 'Let's get you a drink.'

'Italy is going to be expensive,' Spiros said sipping at his glass of *ouzo* and water.

'Papa,' Elias replied, watching the dancers spinning around the square, traditional costumes swirling, footwork perfect. 'What is the money from the sale of my house meant to be spent on if not you and my mother enjoying yourselves?' He smiled. 'Italy is going to save your marriage.'

'What?!' Spiros exclaimed. 'I thought I had already saved my marriage. I have done the ballroom dancing. I can even use an iron. Now you say there is more work to be done?'

'I would say there is work to be done just about every day, Papa,' Elias said with a smile. And then his expression changed just a little. A nervousness caught in his chest, like moths were mating or perhaps fighting each other…

Across the square, arriving at the festival, hand in hand, was Hestia and Thalia. He swallowed, looking and seeing his ex-wife for the first time since she had left him.

'Oh, Elia,' Spiros said, his eyes focused in the same direction. 'This should not be happening. I don't know how she can come back here again.'

'I do,' Elias answered, putting his drink down on the makeshift outside bar. 'She is coming back because I asked her to.' He looked at his father and smiled. 'Excuse me.'

As he walked towards Hestia and Thalia a pinball of emotions pinged around his body. He smiled a greeting and raised a hand, the crowd quietening as if sensing something was about to occur they should take notice of. Elias had no care for anyone else. He only cared about making this right.

'Hestia,' he said, reaching her. 'I... wasn't sure you would come.'

'Elias,' Hestia answered, smiling. 'After your email, how could I not?'

He was emotional in her presence and he bit back tears that were trying to escape. He had finally replied to Hestia's previous reaching out like he should have done so much earlier. Except, responding now, later, when he now had the clarity he did not have before was perhaps better. Standing in front of her, at first glance, Hestia hadn't altered at all. She still wore her curly hair long and loose, with minimal make-up, wearing a flowing boho dress down to her ankles and flat sandals on her feet. But there was a difference to her, and the difference was she was glowing with happiness. Complete and total relaxed confidence in who she was and who she was standing next to, hands entwined.

'Come here,' Hestia ordered. She let go of Thalia's hand and threw her arms around Elias.

He closed his eyes and held her close, feeling none of the emotions he had felt for her when they were in a relationship. What he felt was something even better. It was as if he was finally finding out who the real Hestia was for the first time and it was all wrapped up in this one hug. It was only when she released him from the embrace that he realised the music of the festival had completely ceased and the only sound was the spits still turning the skewers of lamb *souvlaki*. It was time he had his say in Liakada.

'This is Hestia, everybody!' Elias called to the crowd. 'Remember she grew up here among you just like I did!

And yes, we were married! And yes, we have divorced! And yes…' He paused briefly. 'We have both moved on. Exactly like… when you, Georgios stopped dating Maria and started dating Rhea.' Elias looked around the gathering of villagers all a captive audience, but an audience that wasn't any longer looking *quite* like a disgruntled group ready to shun. 'Or when you, Theo, had to admit that your goat Iris was never going to be able to breed and so you bought Gaia.'

Theo burst into tears and passed his bottle of beer to his brother before leaving the group.

'Sorry, Theo,' Elias called. He gathered his thoughts again. 'I'm simply saying that tonight is a time for the village to celebrate. *All* the village. And Hestia… and her partner, Thalia, they should both be part of that celebration.'

No one cheered. But also no one said anything at all. That was progress for Liakada. And then Eleni bustled into the centre of the square, still wearing her apron over a dress, but with sparkling shoes on her feet. She raised her arms in the air. 'What are you all staring at?! Why have you stopped playing the music? This is a festival not a funeral!' She met Elias's gaze. 'And everyone is welcome!'

He had never loved his mother more than right now. She gave him a nod of approval and then accepted the hand of his father who drew her close and into a dance as the band finally recommenced.

'Elias,' Hestia said, tears rolling down her face. 'You didn't need to do that.'

'Oh, Hestia, I really did. And…'

He looked to Thalia. She was smiling too.

'And I really wanted to,' Elias finished.

Hestia caught Thalia's hand in hers again. 'Elias, you haven't met properly. Elias, this is Thalia.' She paused, emotion evident. 'My love.'

Elias put out his hand. 'It is so nice to meet you, Thalia.'

Hestia was beautiful. Thalia was beautiful too. They made the perfect pair and, watching them talk to Elias, Becky couldn't have been prouder about what her boyfriend had done by asking them to come to the festival. It was the closure that everyone needed to move towards a new future and she felt so excited about that future.

'Becky,' Elias called. He had turned towards her now, beckoning wildly.

She moved towards them, ducking around the ever-growing throng of dancers to get there. She had been practising Greek dancing a little but she definitely needed to work on her stamina. Elias said he had plans for upping her cardio and Becky didn't think he meant the gym at the health club… and she was more than glad about that!

'Becky,' Elias said, putting an arm around her shoulders and pulling her close. 'This is Hestia and Thalia.'

Becky smiled, holding her hand out to them both in turn. 'It's so nice to meet you both. And thank you for coming tonight. I know it can't have been easy. I am getting to know what Liakada can be like.'

Hestia laughed then. 'Most of it is still following rules made in medieval times.'

'Only most?' Becky asked.

'She is right,' Thalia agreed.

'Wait,' Elias said. 'I have not introduced you properly.'

He hugged Becky even closer. 'Hestia, Thalia, this is Becky Rose.' He gazed at only her, love shining so brightly. 'My everything.'

Becky's heart swelled and that feeling spread over and through her, warming her every part as the man she loved so deeply drew her nearer still. She was sure *How to Find the Love of Your Life or Die Trying* would have some theorised explanation for how she was feeling right now, *and* what she should do about it. But she absolutely, definitely, 100 per cent, did not care. From now on there was no second guessing, she was completely going to wing it... with a man she met on a plane.

Acknowledgements

As always, a huge thank you goes out to this fabulous team of people who support me through each and every book and keep me grounded in so many ways: -

My agent, Tanera Simons and all the crew at Darley Anderson. You really are a team of amazing professionals!

Hannah Smith, Vicky Joss, Rhea Kurien, Nikky Ward, Laura Palmer and everyone at Aria Fiction and Head of Zeus. I cannot tell you how special it is to work with such a proactive, forward-thinking team.

My best writing buddies – Sue Fortin, Zara Stoneley, Rachel Lyndhurst. Where would we be every day without iMessage and Messenger…

My street team – The Bagg Ladies. My most trusted supporters who advise me on all sorts of writing malarkey and are the first to get to social media with my news! Thank you for being there for me!

My Mandy Baggot Book Club members – we have such fun in the Facebook group, especially on a Friday! Keep sharing the reading love!

My friends in Corfu – every moment I spend on this beautiful Greek island sharing amazing times with you is a gift. Particular thanks in this book goes to the team at Tavernaki, Kassiopi, who have provided me with the most amazing food for the past few years and are always fantastic supporters of my novels. I hope my characters Elias and Becky dining at your taverna in My Greek Island Summer, brings you even more customers this season and beyond!

And, as always, a big shout out to my husband, Mr Big and my girls, Amber and Ruby. Another book for me to go on about to you! I love you so much and I'm looking forward to all the Greek research we are going to do this summer ready for 2021!

Finally, wow, my 20th novel! It doesn't seem real. It especially doesn't seem real when it's actually 20 books in 12 years! THANK YOU to everyone who has bought, read and reviewed my books over the past 12 years. I appreciate every turn of the page and I hope to bring you many, many more!

Dear lovely reader,

That's it! You've finished my 20th book! How does it feel? Are you bereft? Left wanting more?

I hope you really enjoyed Becky and Elias's story in Corfu and loved the bonus of exploring Athens and a little of Kefalonia in this book too!

Who was your favourite character? Did you resonate with Becky – someone who was quite comfortable with her life but had an itch to explore? What did you feel about Megan? Was she mean to Becky or were her actions justified because she'd always felt a little like a bystander in the family dynamic? How about Petra? Was she deeply annoying, or simply grief-stricken? Did you enjoy her travel stories and flirtatious banter?

And what about Elias? Did the hero for my 20th book live up to expectations? Would you like to get seated on a plane next to him?!

Whoever you enjoyed the most, I hope you relaxed into Greek life at my fictional village of Liakada and the real-life beaches at Kerasia and Avlaki. In my mind, Liakada is made up of a little of many Corfiot villages I have visited on the island and I hope it gave you an insight into life and customs in Greece.

If you did enjoy the book, please consider leaving a review on Amazon. Reviews do mean so much and they help other readers find books they might like to read on their holidays or staycations.

Now, as it's my 20th novel (have I mentioned that at all?!) there are going to be lots of things to join in with over the summer. Stay tuned on social media for competitions and much more… and keep an eye out for #MandyBaggot20 on Twitter, Facebook and Instagram!

Follow Mandy on Twitter: @mandybaggot

Follow Mandy on Instagram: @mandybaggot

Like Mandy Baggot Author on Facebook:
Mandy Baggot Author

Join the Mandy Baggot Book Club on Facebook

Visit Mandy's website and sign up to her monthly
newsletter: www.mandybaggot.com

About the Author

MANDY BAGGOT is an international bestselling and award-winning romance writer. The winner of the Innovation in Romantic Fiction award at the UK's Festival of Romance, her romantic comedy novel, *One Wish in Manhattan*, was also shortlisted for the Romantic Novelists' Association Romantic Comedy Novel of the Year award in 2016. Mandy's books have so far been translated into German, Italian, Czech and Hungarian. Mandy loves the Greek island of Corfu, white wine, country music and handbags. Also a singer, she has taken part in ITV1's *Who Dares Sings* and *The X-Factor*. Mandy is a member of the Romantic Novelists' Association and the Society of Authors and lives near Salisbury, Wiltshire, UK with her husband and two daughters.

Hello from Aria

We hope you enjoyed this book! If you did let us know, we'd love to hear from you.

We are Aria, a dynamic digital-first fiction imprint from award-winning independent publishers Head of Zeus. At heart, we're committed to publishing fantastic commercial fiction – from romance and sagas to crime, thrillers and historical fiction. Visit us online and discover a community of like-minded fiction fans!

We're also on the look out for tomorrow's superstar authors. So, if you're a budding writer looking for a publisher, we'd love to hear from you.
You can submit your book online at ariafiction.com/ we-want-read-your-book

You can find us at:
Email: aria@headofzeus.com
Website: www.ariafiction.com
Submissions: www.ariafiction.com/ we-want-read-your-book

🖪 @ariafiction
🐦 @Aria_Fiction
📷 @ariafiction